MYSTERIES OF THE DIOGENES CLUB

KIM NEWMAN

Mysteries of the Diogenes Club

Copyright © 2010 Kim Newman

Cover illustration and design © 2010 Lee Moyer

Logo Design by Tom Orzechowski

A MonkeyBrain Books Publication
www.monkeybrainbooks.com

The stories first appeared in the following venues:

"Sorcerer Conjurer Wizard Witch"
in *The Book of Wizards* (2008).

"Kentish Glory: The Secrets of Drearcliff Grange School"
is original to this collection.

"Moon Moon Moon"
in *Subterranean Press Online* (2009) and first appears in print here.

"Organ Donors"
in *Darklands 2* (1992)

"Seven Stars"
in *Dark Detectives* (1999)

MonkeyBrain Books
11204 Crossland Drive
Austin, TX 78726
info@monkeybrainbooks.com

ISBN: 1-932265-30-9
ISBN: 978-1-932265-30-9

Printed in the United States of America
10 9 8 7 6 5 4 3 2 1

for Christopher Fowler

Thanks to editors Marvin Kaye, William Schafer, Chris Roberson, Nicholas Royle and Stephen Jones. And to artist Lee Moyer.

CONTENTS

Sorcerer Conjurer

Wizard Witch

I: **'pools of poison, my dear fellow'**

Brownish-grey clouds boiled low, threatening drizzle. Two keepers loomed out of the bracken, casually directing shotguns at the Bentley. Despite the overcast day, they wore heavy dark glasses. Charles shuddered, recalling the *eyes* behind those goggles. The keepers' plus-fours, Norfolk jackets and flat caps were midnight black. No brown check tweeds need apply. Spent-match stick-figures against red undergrowth, they turned in unison as the big car passed.

Charles Beauregard of the Diogenes Club was come a-calling on a long-standing rival agency. The Bentley bumped along wheel-ruts carved over centuries. The carriages, carts and armoured cars that had passed this way were equipped with iron or silver bars to restrain passengers who wouldn't be making a return journey. Huntstanton, his driver, took the speaking tube to apologise for the rough ride.

'It's like the Somme, Mr B.'

'With fewer infernal devices, we trust,' said Charles.

'I'd not lay a bet on it, sir. My phantom foot's twinging. Usually means land-mines.'

Charles scanned the landscape. The 'men in black crepe' probably had littered Egdon Heath with mines and man-traps, though the unrelieved redness was more than enough to deter most hikers and cyclists. Trust the Undertaking to inhabit countryside more like Mars than England.

A lifetime in the most secret service honed a suspicious mind. Could the well-worded summons, tactfully conveyed through intermediaries, be a stratagem to lure him here for a malign purpose? He had no wish to become an 'item' among the Egdon Heath Collection. Edwin Winthrop, the Most Valued Member, advised against Charles paying this call in person. But a Name was invoked, and only the current Chairman of the Ruling Cabal would do.

These were serious times. Another War was coming. In fact, two. Winston was quite right about that little Herr Hitler, just as he had been quite wrong about that little Mr Gandhi. The new Chancellor of Germany had revived the Thule Society, but was capable of doing more than enough damage without adding dark magic to his love of Teutonic pageantry. Eventually, his Third Reich would move against encircling European nations. The Empire would have to stand against Greater Germany. Charles, heart heavy, knew mechanised mass slaughter would resume. War was unavoidable, and must be won convincingly this time. If not in 1935, then 1940, 1950.

However, that would not be Charles Beauregard's Next War. Another global conflict was in the offing, and the Club was on the front lines. Like the Second World War, it already had names: The Witch War, the Weird War, the Wizard War. If won, it would be written of only in secret histories. If lost, there would be no histories, secret or public.

The Mausoleum—by tradition, 'Mouse-o-lay-um' not 'Maws-o-lee-um'—was invisible from the track. Surrounded by a thousand acres of knee-deep bracken, it had no proud towers and flew no flags. The greater part of the keep was below ground. It had been erected—excavated?—in 1588, by Royal Decree. With Queen Elizabeth as first patron, the Undertaking claimed nearly three centuries' start on the Diogenes Club, but had broken with the Crown upon the Stuart Succession. A few maintained the 'undertakers in smoked glasses' had never truly returned to the fold. The Undertaking often acted as a supra-national body, indifferent to the wishes of sovereign, parliament or people. The Club's lot would on occasion have been easier if they were accorded such a free hand, but Charles had spent a long career resisting the temptation to take liberties. When his juniors ran the show, would they continue to be as fastidious? Winthrop, the Undertaking's fiercest critic, had a certain contradictory admiration, not unhinged by envy, for their methods.

Before the War, the inter-service rivalry must be settled. The Diogenes Club must find a way to work with the Undertaking. Both operated under Royal Charter, notionally constituted as arms of British Intelligence. But Charles had seen behind the spectacles. Could any public servant truly have common cause with those who saw the world through such *different* eyes?

Mausoleum Hollow was a meteor crater, ringed by weathered standing stones. Archaeologists reckoned them the Neolithic equivalent of the 'Danger—Keep Out' signs put up at the site of a bad fire or a subsidence in the road. Something once fell from the sky and smote the land. The stones, ingeniously hauled from a quarry in far-off Wales, told folk to be wary of lingering dreadfulness. The long-ago meteorite merely seeded the earth with iron enough to redden bracken until the end of time. The undoubted dreadfulness was of more recent vintage.

It took a *significant* invocation to bring Charles here. The War was closer.

Signs had been there to read for a generation. Five years ago, a Bureau of the American federal government (the so-called 'Unnameables') conducted raids in the coastal town of Innsmouth, Massachusetts. Officially, they were after violators of the Volstead Act, but the actual target was a peculiar, un-Christian sect, the Esoteric Order of Dagon. In the end, dynamiting certain offshore structures forestalled an invasion from the Deep. Charles had lent Captain Geoffrey Jeperson, a Valued Member, to the Yanks, though a transatlantic alliance in these matters was resisted on both shores. The American tendency to address problems with high explosives and machine guns was admittedly worrying. When the Club had to act against the likes of the Esoteric Order, there was rarely necessity for a cover story. Gentlemanly discretion meant avoiding loud bangs.

In 1903, an ab-human entity came close to committing the most colossal crime ever contemplated—the murder of space and time. Charles, then Most Valued Member, assisted Mycroft Holmes, the Club's founder and original Chairman, in a procedure which saved that day. No fewer than fifteen of the world's premier magicians, occult detectives, psychic adventurers, criminal geniuses and visionary scientists set aside profound differences and worked under Mycroft's direction to avert the rending-asunder of the universe. Yet the only allusion to the affair in the public record was an aside by the biographer of Mycroft's more famous, frankly less perspicacious brother, concerning the 'duellist and journalist' Isidore Persano, who was found 'stark staring mad with a match box in front of him which contained a remarkable worm said to be unknown to science.'

That unique annelid wriggled still, with a silver pin stuck through it, within the Mausoleum. The contents were referred to as 'the Egdon Heath Collection', as if it were a museum of ancient curios or a menagerie of uncatalogued fauna. It was both, but, as envisioned by Good Queen Bess, primarily a prison. The 'worm unknown to science' was designated a permanent detainee at His Majesty's Pleasure. So, come to that, was Isidore Persano. Along with others too dangerous to be let loose, too valuable to be thrown away or too singular to be stifled and interred in the adjacent cemetery.

Huntstanton steered between two stones, under a heavy arch-piece. Within the circle, protected by the inward slope, the wind dropped and watches stopped. Charles wondered whether the cylinders would seize, but the superbly made Bentley was proof against magics whipped up to coddle the Mausoleum. The car purred to a dignified halt outside the squat, greystone block. It had started raining.

Mr Eye, the Warden, stood by the front door, top hat doffed. An attendant shielded his hairless skull with a black umbrella. When Charles came with Mycroft to hand over the wretched worm, he had waited in the carriage while the Chairman went into the Mausoleum. Now, the keep was open to him.

He had a momentary stab of pain. Huntstanton had to get out of the car, limping, to open the door. Charles hoped Mr Eye would assume protocol was being followed, but his arthritis was bad at the moment. He *could* open the door from the inside, but only by fumbling the handle. Showing even tiny weakness to the Undertaking would be a mistake. Ignoring cramps in his legs, he unbent to step out. He put all his weight on his sword-cane. Blooded too often for his taste, it was now more for support than defence.

'Beauregard, good day,' said Mr Eye, thin lips parting to show entirely black teeth. 'I trust you have had a pleasant journey, yes?'

'Quite, quite,' Charles responded. Catching himself sounding irritable, he opted to play the game. 'You've a bracing climate here,' he said, genially. 'Excellent for the circulation.'

'Indeed. Care for a pick-me-up?'

The umbrella-wallah offered a flask.

'Not at the moment, thank you very much. If we could proceed to the *lady*, I would appreciate it. I've had a long drive down, and it's as long going back.'

The black smile curved. Mr Eye's teeth weren't rotten, just ebony. Was his whole skeleton like that?

'Ah, the *lady*,' said the Warden. 'An unusual item. We're not much on the distaff side, you might say. We've the Angel Down Changeling, but that's an it, not a she. Most of the time, it looks like little lost Rose Farrar, but it's not her.'

Mr Eye was referring to one of Winthrop's finds. The Most Valued Member hotly resented the Undertaking's assumption of authority in the matter. Years earlier, Charles had allowed something similar to retreat rather than become an 'item'. The slight had not been forgotten. He trusted the 'Rose' did not suffer on his account, though the Changeling constituted a significant threat. It would not have lost its venom sacs in captivity.

'But the *lady* is a lady,' continued Mr Eye. 'Whatever else she might be, she is that. I needn't tell you to be wary, Mr Beauregard. Watch your throat and don't look into her blue, blue eyes. Pools of poison, my dear fellow. She's bitten three we know of, lately. One fatality. Be wary around all our, ah, items, come to that. You have been briefed, yes?'

Mycroft had been privy to the inventory and left memoranda in the files Charles inherited when he took the Chair. Now, the Diogenes Club was routinely apprised of Egdon Heath acquisitions.

Don Felipe Molina and Sir Timothy ffolliott, the original items, were still here, bodies strapped to racks. Their tongueless heads were kept separately, in leather buckets. As Charles understood it, the sorcerous nobles—who might have changed the course of history—still whispered inside keepers' skulls. If beheading had been the end of them, Elizabeth wouldn't have needed the Mausoleum.

Mr Eye ushered Charles into the hallway. A nine-foot *mi-go*, or 'Abominable Snowman', dominated the vestibule, stuffed but snarling. According to a plaque, it had been shot by a Jesuit in 1802. Its claws still looked sharp.

'You'll have to leave the pig-sticker with Mr Arrh,' said Mr Eye, indicating the sword-stick. 'And your loaded revolver, yes. The fossil in your hip-pocket, hmmn. The note-book with the backward writing, I fear. The scarab amulet on your watch chain, a-hah. The watch itself—with those intricate little crystal workings—*most especially*. And the silver scalpel in your note-case. Have I missed anything?'

Mr Arrh, whose glasses were a visor-like attachment to a bowler hat, stood ready to take custody of the weaponry. Instead, Charles handed everything over to Huntstanton, who had a valise ready. Mr Eye tutted as the watch was in view. How the Undertaking would like to tinker with that particular timepiece!

'So much distrust,' Mr Eye lamented, satirically.

'I understand the need for precautions,' said Charles.

Mr Arrh patted Charles's pockets deftly and gave Mr Eye the nod.

'Let us proceed,' said the Undertaker.

Huntstanton and Mr Arrh remained in the vestibule, regarding each other with suspicion. If it came to blows, Charles would lay bets on his driver. In tight spots, he made wicked use of his tin foot.

Mr Eye led Charles to a cabinet, which opened to reveal a spiral staircase. A rope banister provided support. Charles was not too proud to avail himself of this. A nagging concern was that he would find coming up a deal more difficult than going down.

'The *lady* turned up in Weymouth, of all places,' said Mr Eye. 'It was your classic story. Bites in the night. A pick-pocket and a drunkard. Then, a corpse drained of blood, stuffed into a bathing machine. Traditional holes in the throat. A footpad, according to the local plods. They nearly let the case slide, thinking he'd got what he deserved. Our bad lad had burked more than one holidaymaker, it seems. We owe this catch to the coroner. The item wasn't hard to track to her lair. I say lair, it was more of a boarding house. I suppose *nosferatu* take seaside holidays too. More fool they. Harder to get rid of the empties outside a city. Still, she could have done a *little* more to hide among the teeming crowds. She might as well have dripped splotches of blood along the sea-front and pinned a black bat to the door of her room.'

Charles knew most of this story. It sounded even less credible from Mr Eye.

'Vampires aren't supposed to exist anymore,' said Mr Eye. 'Van Helsing claimed he hunted them to extinction.'

Charles paused to catch his breath. 'There've been unsubstantiated, out-of-the-way reports in the last few years. The Club was never entirely convinced by the little Dutchman.'

'Didn't you black-ball him?'

'Not me personally. I wasn't on the Ruling Cabal then.'

Membership of the Diogenes Club was by invitation only, and invitation was rarely extended to foreign nationals. Charles understood Abraham Van Helsing had dropped a brace of freshly severed heads on a table in the Strangers Room and had the temerity to *make an application*. The specialist's achievements were noteworthy, but the Club wasn't comfortable with his tendency to issue type-written press releases and pose for victory snaps like some Great White Hunter in front of burning crypts or piles of fresh ashes.

'I doubt Van Helsing's stalwart little band bothered to comb Weymouth for the blood-drinking undead,' said Mr Eye. 'Their quarry preferred the Northern resort towns. No, the *lady* came as quite a surprise. If vampires are officially extinct, we'll have to class her as a living fossil. Like the cedar wood wasp, the tuatara and the Lake LaMetrie elasmosaur.'

They were—at last!—at the bottom of the staircase, in a chilly passage with a flagstone floor and brick walls. Water ran nearby. A string of electric lamps lit the area, poorly. A woman Undertaker sat at her post, in black skirt and riding boots, veil over her dark glasses. She was perusing a fan magazine with Jean Harlow on the cover. When Mr Eye stepped in view, she swiftly slid her reading matter under a blotter and stood.

'This is Miss Jeye,' said Mr Eye. 'She participated in apprehending the item.'

'The *lady* came quietly?'

'Yes. That's unusual too. We approached with the usual caution. Wafers and crosses and sharp sticks, yes? Inky string and sticky rice, which works wonders in the Far East. She showed her wrists for the silver cuffs. She more or less said "it's a fair cop, guv". Miss Jeye was disappointed. You'd boned up on slaying skills, hadn't you, dear?'

'Tumbling and Japanese wrestling,' explained the woman, adopting a stance, then shrugging.

'We barely got a flash of teeth and a hiss out of her,' said Mr Eye. 'Bit of a let-down, you might say.

'When did she invoke the Name?'

'Not until she was here, in her new quarters. That's a puzzle, too. If she had the Name, why not use it earlier? Save herself a bother.'

Charles wondered if the Warden wasn't talking theory, rather than practice. The Undertaking was capable of pretending not to hear, especially if the Club was involved.

Miss Jeye pulled open a drawer and took out a calling card. She handed it to Mr Eye, who glanced at it, and presented it to Charles.

'She was thoroughly searched, of course, but this got through. Mr Arrh was most displeased. She got to her quarters, sat on her, ah, sleeping contraption... and conjured it seemingly out of the air. As you see, it's not *her* card.'

Charles looked at the white oblong. Heavy, gilt-edged, expensive, more like an invitation than a *carte de visite*. On one side, over a sigil few would recognise, was stamped 'Mycroft Holmes, the Diogenes Club, Pall Mall.' On the other, written in a hand he remembered well, was his own name.

He felt a touch of ice between his shoulders and in the small of his back.

'You have been *named*, Mr Charles Beauregard,' said Mr Eye, reappropriating the card before Charles could slip it into his pocket. 'You and your, ah, distinguished predecessor. Two Chairs for the price of one.'

'Let's see her,' he said. 'And fathom this.'

Miss Jeye took a ring of keys from her belt and unlocked a stout, silver-bound door. The room beyond was also lit by electric bulbs, burning behind grilles. Charles expected bare dungeon walls, but the room was papered (cream with violets) and carpeted. Against one wall was a long wooden box, like a packing-crate for a grandfather clock.

The lady sat at a writing-desk, playing patience. As her visitors stepped in, she swept the cards together and performed a lightning-fast shuffle, then tapped the deck. Kings in succession levitated from among their fellows. The fourth king turned out to be a jack. She frowned and shuffled again.

'Whenever you're in prison, learn something new,' she said, in a pleasant, clear voice. Sharp little teeth showed in her small, pretty mouth. 'Another month and I'll have this down pat. Stage magicians have an unfair advantage. They're all men. With big hands. I have to make do with dainty little digits.'

The kings rose again, all four this time.

'Eh, *voila!*' She smiled, showing her sharpest teeth.

Mr Eye laid Mycroft's card down on the desk in front of her. Charles put one of his own beside it.

'I know who you are, Mr Charles Beauregard,' she said, dropping a black ace on the cards as if taking a trick.

He knew her too. He had seen her twice. In the year of Queen Victoria's Diamond Jubilee, he had noticed her one afternoon in the British Museum's Hall of Egyptian Antiquities. A pale girl wearing blue glasses. Twenty years later, no older, she had been in Kingstead Cemetery at Mycroft's funeral. Both times, Charles had been preoccupied. He had not spoken with her, but her face—among so many seen on the street or at the theatre—stuck in his mind. He knew she was part of the great story of the Diogenes Club. It did not surprise him that she was what she was, though he had not considered the possibility. There were other ways of not ageing, none of which he had availed himself of.

Even before his second sighting, he had thought of her, often. Somehow, she was among the women of his life—his wife Pamela, dead twice as long as she had been alive... Pamela's cousin Penelope Churchward, who'd once set her cap at him... Kate Reed, his loving companion of decades, now a busy, elderly gadfly for constitutional reform in the Irish Free State.

'You have the advantage of me,' he said.

'I'm Geneviève,' she said. 'Geneviève Dieudonné. Geneviève Sandrine Ysolde Dieudonné. I'll be in Mr Mycroft's precious files under that, though I've more often used "Jennifer Dee" lately.'

'We have her as "Geneva Deodati",' put in Mr Eye. 'She is named as such in a writ of excommunication, dated 1638, on record with the Roman Inquisition.'

Geneviève poked her tongue out at the Warden, and seemed for an instant younger even than her face.

'They tried Galileo around then,' she said. 'It was God's work to make him recant. Do you know why it's put about that vampires shrink at the sight of the cross? Because we have long memories. Holy Inquisitions, crusades, Borgia popes, wars of religion, burnings of heretics, sale of indulgences. Live more than a century or two and you lose respect for anybody's church. I'm not afraid of the crucifix. It's afraid of me.'

She made a fangface at Mr Eye, then winked at Charles. Cooped up here, she had grown bored. Tweaking her gaolers was too much of a temptation.

She was light blonde, with unfashionably long hair. He would still have taken her for eighteen or twenty. She wore a white cotton summer dress with navy trim. He imagined a straw hat went with it. Without her tinted spectacles, he saw the blue, blue eyes the Warden had warned him of. Threaded with the tiniest veins of scarlet. Aside from sharp teeth, she showed little outward trace of her condition. No talons, no pointed ears, no rat-nose, no wings.

'Might we have privacy?' he asked Mr Eye. 'Miss Dieudonné and I have confidential matters to discuss.'

The Warden had known this was coming. He began to babble about the danger of leaving visitors alone with the item.

Geneviève held up her hands. Her wrists were shackled with leather-padded silver handcuffs. Her ankles were similarly restrained. Additionally, she was chained to the wall.

'Quite clever,' she said. 'The leather means I don't burn, but the silver means I can't break the cuffs.'

She dabbed a forefinger against an unpadded link. There was a tiny hiss. She withdrew quickly and showed the small, fast-healing weal where flesh had touched metal.

'Has anybody worked out why that happens? It's always puzzled me. Like the thing with mirrors. And garlic. The rest of it's nonsense, though. Or I'd be a pool of mist seeping out under the door and flowing upstairs.'

Mr Eye grunted irritation and left the small room.

'Now, now, Mr Beauregard,' said the vampire, raising an eyebrow, 'we're unchaperoned. What will become of my reputation, tralala?'

Charles looked around. There would be an eavesdropping hole somewhere, probably with a wire-recorder at the end of it. He was here because the item hadn't been forthcoming. She might open up if they called her bluff and presented the Named individual.

'I'd offer you a chair, but there's only one and, as you see, I'm chained to it. Would you like to drag over the crate? Don't worry. I've not slept in it. That's nonsense, too. I've always preferred soft beds. Not that I need to kip more than once a month. An afternoon nap and I'm set for weeks. Honestly. I told Mr Face-Ache I needed my native soil and tried to get them to send to Burgundy for it, but they saw I was joshing. I've never had a coffin or a

grave. Most *nosferatu* die and come back, but I just *turned*. You must think
I'm a chatterbox. I've had no visitors and the black hats aren't much for chit-
chat. Except Miss Jeye. She is quite enthusiastic about Mr Clark Gable.'

Charles was irritated at himself: Without his stick and after all those
stairs, he really would like to sit down. He was worried that if he plonked
himself on the crate, he'd be unable to stand up again unassisted. So he
leaned against a wall. He mustn't let his pains distract him.

'Mr Charles Beauregard,' she said, savouring his name, 'I know
something you don't. Two things, in fact.'

'I shouldn't be surprised. The older I get, the less I seem to know.'

'Now *that's* being overly modest. As a former Most Valued Member and
current Chair of the Ruling Cabal, I daresay you know a great many things
the rest of the world doesn't. Part of your duty is to keep most people in the
dark. Mr Mycroft's motto was "don't panic the populace". The first thing I
know that you don't, you must have a tickle of suspicion about.'

She held up Mycroft's card.

'Yes,' she said, 'I am a member of your Club. A unique auxiliary, off the
books, inducted even before you were. The young Mycroft—sleeker, not
quite the corpulence he became—saw a need for me. It was the beginnings
of the Great Game. In the 1860s, I was not in one of my more personable
phases. I blame the gin. Everyone was soaked in it. Little children as
young as... though, of course, I never took my sustenance in that manner.
That strangler in Weymouth was only my third killing-by-feeding in five
centuries, you know. And the other two were worse than him. I may be a
creature of the night, but I avoid murder. Mr Mycroft's primary talent was
to know everything and everyone. He found us—you, as well as me—and
cultivated us to serve. I've seen you six times, Charles, and let you see me
twice. But we're cousins in service. I am your shadow. You are not a public
figure, but you are acknowledged. You'd have a knighthood if you hadn't
quietly refused the honour. Twice. You—and the Valued Members you've
brought along—are known about in circles, called on in circumstances. In
many ways, you are a policeman. Better-spoken, of course. A Harley Street
specialist among policemen. Me, I can't be a policeman, woman, matron,
whatever. I am the other thing Mr Mycroft made. I am a *secret* agent.'

She pulled the Queen of Spades out of thin air.

'I'm tired, Charles,' she said. 'I've been in the cold for sixty years. All
the things I avoided for centuries—and you know who and what I mean—I
have had to associate with. Mr Mycroft needed me to be a monster. To be
in the society of monsters. To gain their trust. To learn their plans. When he
died, I was set free of an obligation but had no way back. And nothing to
come back to. That's the joke of it. In sixty years, I was no use. As a rule,
monsters are dull, petty folk. I learned few plans and those fizzled. While
you and Mr Mycroft and Carnacki and Dr Nikola and the rest were saving
the universe from Persano's Wriggling Horror, I was posing as a Limehouse

opium addict to infiltrate the Tong of Weng-Chiang. They were wiped out in a turf war with the Si-Fan before their High Priest posed a danger to anyone but his tailor. Oh, I knew Dracula was coming, for what it's worth. Terrible gossips, *nosferatu*, as you must be noticing. Some lesser leeches had inflated expectations of their self-declared King. They said he'd elevate them to their proper position, and you warm fellows would be naught but cattle. "Naught but cattle". That's the sort of thing they always said. No wonder they're all gone now. Mr Mycroft categorised the Count as a minor nuisance and left him to that Dutch madman. So that's another report I needn't have bothered with. But I stuck with it. At the funeral, I was given an envelope by Mr Mycroft's adjutant, Dravot. The card was in it, with your name on the back. Before we proceed to the second thing I know that you don't, the really frightening thing, I don't suppose...'

He took out the card Mycroft had left, clipped in an empty file. It had the single name 'Geneviève' written on the reverse.

'Snap,' she said. 'I don't suppose it would have hurt to tell you who I was and what I was about, but it would have broken the habit of a lifetime. Mr Mycroft didn't mention he had a brother until the fellow became famous. He liked to keep us all in our holes until we were needed.'

A tiny glint showed in her eye. A red tear. She wiped it away.

'Mustn't get emotional,' she said. 'It offends the English.'

'I miss him too,' he said. 'I sit in his chair...'

'Lots of room, then.'

He laughed. 'It is rather wide for my behind. That's my situation entirely. I sit in his chair, but can't hope to fill it.'

'Too modest, the English, too. Which is alarmingly attractive.'

It occurred to Charles that this creature was flirting with him. Age difference ought to have made that absurd, but he found it rather warming. He remembered to be cautious. She was still what she was. With Mycroft's imprimatur, however, he trusted her. In a tight corner, he'd choose her over an Undertaker.

'When he was alive, Mr Mycroft sent me little notes. Never anything as obvious as an order. Hints, as it were. News clippings, sometimes. Puzzles and acrostics. He loved them. He indicated avenues I might pursue. There was also a retainer, deposited annually at Coutt's. Most of it's still there. I have few expenses. Three weeks after the funeral, when I called at the bank, I was given a post-dated note, in his hand. Another direction to pursue. I've heard voices from the grave, and this startled me more. Since then, there have been seven more notes. I've destroyed them all. I assume you're not responsible for sending them?'

Charles spread his hands.

'Mechanisms set in motion,' she said. 'Even without the prime mover, the clockwork ticks. I'd look to Dravot.'

'Retired.'

'No one retires from the Diogenes Club.'

'And dead.'

'That wouldn't stop Dravot. Mr Mycroft saw the great patterns of history, the secret patterns. The Witch War, the Weird War, the Wizard War.'

Charles felt a chill. He had never spoken those words, only thought them.

Geneviève smiled. She tapped her temple, rattling her shackles.

'He's still in our minds, Charles. He shaped us, how we think, how we act. He wanted us together.'

'Was this in one of your notes?'

'No, those were the usual clues. I was directed into an abyss. An underworld. I have lived among our enemies. Otherwise, I wouldn't have killed to get your attention. It's too easy to give in to the red thirst. The last note came as I was on the point of changing. It was a reminder—not a clue or a name, but a wake-up call. To stay myself. For a second time, Mr Mycroft saved me. A third, if you count the time he saved everyone. I know how the War is supposed to start. By now, you know who you'll be facing. This era's Great Enchanter. Colonel Zenf.'

Charles was familiar with the name.

'All indications tend to suggest him.'

'I can confirm it. I've looked into the eyes of that Austro-Hungarian nobody. I've seen them before, in other times, other faces. The eyes of a Great Enchanter are always the same. Beside him, Dracula and Napoleon and the Beetle are petty thieves. The plan is that London should fall, smashed entirely. Not just the physical city, but its shadow, its *idea*. Then they'll all come up from the depths and the outer darkness and it'll be on. The Weird War. But it can be stopped. The great danger comes from a traitor in our ranks. Not just an ordinary rat, but a King Rat. Someone you rely on, Charles. Someone who can hand a city to the enemy. Find this traitor and the black tide can be broken. This is what Mr Mycroft made us for, Charles. He knew he wouldn't fight this battle himself. He left us this trust. We don't have much time before the Thames starts boiling with lepers' blood and a rain of screaming severed heads stops play at Lord's. That's speculation, by the way, but *informed* speculation.'

Charles looked into her blue, blue eyes and saw fire. The chill returned, all over his body. But his other twinges fell away. He felt as he had in 1881. A hollow youth back from India, knotted into an agony of grief for Pamela and their son, he had been drawn into the Diogenes Club by Mycroft Holmes. His first case had been the Purley Horror. Then, as now, he had been terrified, but alive. Strengthened by the confidence an extraordinary man had in him. Determined not to disappoint.

'I know what to do,' he said.

Geneviève rattled her chains, as if applauding.

II: 'the realm of Ravens and Rats'

Late in the afternoon, Edwin Winthrop returned to the Bloomsbury rooms
he shared with Catriona Kaye. The flat was above an artists' supplies
shop. With his clientele too busy arguing about cubism to buy brushes, the
proprietor had avoided bankruptcy by turning half the shop into a café and
selling watery coffee and hard biscuits. Most of the artists looked as if they
subsisted solely on this fare.

As Edwin climbed the hallway stairs, he didn't hear the clack of
Catriona's typewriter. She was working on a book provisionally entitled
Howling Hags, about the Mexican *llorona*, the Irish *banshee* and the Welsh
gwrach-y-rhibyn. He hoped she had written her pages for the day, since he
wanted to apply her sharp mind to the problem the Old Man had shared
with him. Half in and half out of the shadow-world of the Diogenes Club,
Catriona brought a valuable, commonsense perspective to affairs which
would drive most people to the bottle or Bedlam.

She met him at the doormat and kissed him on the cheek. 'Hot Voodoo'
came from their big-belled Victrola. She shimmied back into the flat, shaker
in her hands.

'Cocktails before sunset,' he observed. 'This is a decadent turn of
events.'

'Judge not till you know all the facts,' she said, with a twinkle. 'Pick up
a glass.'

Edwin followed orders, taking a cocktail glass—a funnel-shape with an
octagonal base—from the cabinet. Catriona made a final shake, placed a tea-
strainer to catch the ice and decanted. He raised the glass to his lips.

'Hold on a moment,' she said. From a bowl, she took a cherry—which
she dropped into his drink. 'The final touch,' she said.

Edwin wondered what the occasion might be. They were no great
drinkers, or concocters, of cocktails. Otherwise, they would undoubtedly
own a purpose-made ice-strainer and Catriona wouldn't have to cadge vital
equipment from the tea-service.

'Go on,' she said, eagerly. 'Take your medicine.'

He took a sip. It was a Manhattan. 'Very nice.'

'What do you taste?'

He took another sip. Then a gulp.

'Two parts Irish whiskey to one part vermouth. Two dashes of Angostura
bitters. A cherry. And a twist of lemon. Perfect, Catty-Kit. The bartender at
the Algonquin couldn't do better.'

'You don't taste anything else?'

He took another gulp.

'Ice shards?'

She smiled. 'No hint of... burnt almond?'

He swilled the liquid around his tongue. 'No, not a trace. I assume
you're *not* trying to poison me? There's no cyanide in this?'

'No, but there *is* burnt almond. I burned it myself in a crucible.'

He finished the Manhattan and still couldn't taste any added ingredient.

'What's this about?'

'Glad you asked, Ed,' she said. 'I'm demonstrating that Olivia Gibberne, Countess of Chelm, *could* have made away with her husband last season at Monte.'

'Didn't the Earl of Chelm fall from a hotel balcony? After staggeringly ruinous losses at the table?'

'Dead before he went over the rail, if I'm any judge. Would you believe it, there was no proper post-mortem! Methinks, the slyboots widow spread some of her inheritance around. I understand a coroner is cruising those famously winding roads in a new Hispano-Suiza.'

One of Catriona's hobbies was finding out folk who think they've got away with it. She would worry away until the Countess answered for her crime, if not in court then in an appropriate alternative manner. Some people were more upset if left off guest lists than sent to the gallows.

'Is there any more poison?' he asked. 'I'm about to bring you something more momentous than the third-dullest society murder of 1932.'

Catriona refilled his glass, and poured the last of the mix for herself. She popped in the cherries.

They settled on the divan that dominated their reception room. Catriona lifted the needle from the gramophone record and took up her pad and pencil. Note-taking was a habit with her. She also kicked off her shoes and slipped her feet into his lap. He stroked her tendons.

'We're in the realm of Ravens and Rats,' he said. 'We have to bone up on four eminent personages. One of them's no good and it's up to us to spot the ringer. The King Rat. A high degree of diplomacy will be called for. The fate of—well, everything, as usual—is in play.'

'Thrilling,' she said, satirically.

'*Mountebank, Mesmerist, Warlock, Mage,*
Sorcerer, Conjurer, Wizard, Witch...'

'What's that?' she asked, dotting and dashing shorthand.

'A mnemonic for our *dramatis personae*. Sorcerer, Conjurer, Wizard, Witch. Easier to remember than the names.'

'Which are...?'

'Rennes, Stone, Drake, Device.'

'Spelled Da*vis* or Da*vies?*'

'Spelled, and spelling is important in this case, De*vice*. As in "infernal device". But pronounced "Davis".'

'How obstreperous of him.'

'Her. She's "Witch". Margery Device, the Hag of Harrod's.'

'The society hostess?'

'The very same. Squiffy Oates-Haldane got tossed out of one of her

shindigs for tipping a bowl of punch over Lady Londonderry. Witch—
so they say—turned him into a toad. Actually, Squiff came down with a
tropical disease, hitherto unknown in Kensington, which causes a toadlike
skin condition.'

Catriona chewed the end of her pencil. Edwin considered telling her
she was adorable, but decided to raise the matter later. There were facts to
be set out.

'Who are your other mnemonised individuals?' she asked.

He ticked them off on his fingers.

'"Sorcerer". Marcus Rennes. Not as in Wren, the bird or the architect.
R. E. Two Ns. E. S. Deputy Astrologer Royal.'

'Astronomer, but never mind. I know who he is and how to spell his
name. I half-followed a lecture he gave last year, refuting the late Professor
Moriarty's book about the dynamics of an asteroid. Rennes says the planet
isn't doomed to be knocked out of orbit like a billiard ball. Which is a relief.
Though, if you say we're in peril again, possibly not true. That flags him up
as a suspect, does it not?'

He tweaked her little toe. 'We suspect everyone. And no one. Remember
how it works?'

'Indeed. Proceed.'

'"Conjurer". You'll know him too. Robert Edmond Stone. He really is a
conjurer, in the sense of prestidigitator, as well as... ah, raising demons and
that sort of palaver. The Great Edmondo. Twice nightly at the Astoria.'

'So he's real pretending to be fake pretending to be real?'

'Such are the circles we move in, Catty. And "Wizard" is what you'd
expect. White beard. Pointy hat with astronomical symbols on.'

'Astrological?'

'Both. Connaught Drake. Bet you've never heard of him. He doesn't go
on the halls or give lectures or throw parties.'

'In this field, I assume *lack* of notoriety implies a degree of achievement
in excess of his fellow magical practitioners?'

He slid along the divan, under her legs, put an arm around her waist and
kissed her on the nose. She was appreciative, if a little impatient.

'So who is Mr Drake?'

'Officially, Keeper of Ravens at the Tower of London. They're supposed
to stay put because if they ever flap away, the kingdom will fall.'

'Don't the Yeomen Warders clip their wings to make sure it never comes
to that?'

'A calumny, a rumour and a lie. The clauses of the legend are quite
specific.'

'A legend has *clauses?*'

'Afraid so. The Old Man has a copy in the files. The "ravens" aren't just
the birds. They're the mystic guardians of the city. Sorcerer, Conjurer and
Company. When the legend says "kingdom", by the way, it means London.

It's possible that, say, Birmingham might stand after whatever deluge affects the capital.'

'Is this all to do with the Tower?'

'So far as we can tell. I went there once with a school party.'

'So did I. Some years *after* you.'

He passed over the tiny dig. Catriona was a Century Baby, a 1900 birth—but he'd been around for most of the last decade of the 1800s. She sometimes twitted him for supposed Victorian attitudes.

'Like most people who live in London, I've not been back since,' she said. 'Have you?'

'Once, my love. With some Crown Jewel or other in my pocket. You know how often they go missing and have to be retrieved.'

'I do, most people don't.'

'Then the anecdote will spice up my memoirs when I persuade you to write them.'

She smiled at that. 'They'll never let you publish. You'd have to deposit the book in the Secret Files with the Mycroft Memoranda and Charles's Worm War Diaries.'

Edwin had an idea she was far ahead of him. Had the Old Man laid this out to her before talking with him? She had split a pot of Lyons Corner house tea with Beauregard before he set off for Egdon Heath.

'According to Mr Baedeker's estimable guide,' he began, 'the building now known as the Tower of London was begun in 1078. The White Tower was erected on the orders of...?'

'*Guillaume le Salaud.*'

'Too easy. Yes, Illegitimate Billy, William the Conqueror, the last person to whom the city fell. Since him, the ravens have been in residence, and London has survived plague, fire, stench and motorised omnibus. Neither Napoleon nor the Kaiser dared so much as set foot on the beach at Hastings. Charles the Second once got fed up with ravens leaving "presents" on the lenses of his telescope and decreed they be removed. Reminded what happened to his father, he changed his mind. Since then, the birds have relieved themselves where they want. They are important, their Keeper moreso. He's also a Raven.'

'Capital R.'

'Double-underlined Capital R. The Four Ravens are constituted in accord with the legend. William of Normandy's court wizard made castings from the top of the White Tower. He established wards and protections which, mercifully, are still in force. William's Wizard was the first of a line, and his descendant is...'

'Connaught Drake?'

'No, surprisingly. It's Marcus Rennes. I wonder if that causes friction among the Ravens. Does our "Sorcerer" resent the fact that "Wizard" has his *grand-grand-pére*'s old job? Could this festering resentment lead to dark places? Worth thinking on?'

Catriona made a shorthand hieroglyph.

'What do our Ravens *do*, exactly?' she asked. 'Stand at the top of the tower, scanning the horizon for fires?'

'In a manner of speaking. That's "Sorcerer"'s job, mostly. He spends his days inside a large clockwork model in Greenwich. It represents our universe and its environs. Imagine a chicken-farmer who has a hundred miles of ribbon strung around every inch of his property, hung with bells. Rennes has to listen for the tell-tale tinkle of foxes. Foxes with tentacles, as it happens. Or horns. Lots of the blighters have horns. And more eyes than we find reasonable. You know what I mean. The Deep Old Dirty Ones.'

Catriona shuddered. 'Pray continue. What about "Witch"? I've met Miss Device. All I got from her were impossible-to-confirm tid-bits about the private lives of an overrated poet, a very *active* bar-maid in the Spaniards and the current King of the Cats.'

'Margery Device knows all, tells all,' he explained. 'A city isn't just stone. It's people. And *doings*. Whether we like it or not, we all want to know the other fellow's business. Witch tattles the tales. Don't mistake her for the Queen of Trivial Things, though. Think of her as a safety valve. A city can have only so many secrets before it explodes, like a stoppered kettle. She lets the steam out as *gossip*.'

Catriona whistled. 'Fair enough. Now, why do we need a "Conjurer"? Does London, perhaps, have a shortage of rabbits?'

'Stone is our artilleryman. An attack magician.'

'Don't like the sound of that.'

'Frankly, me neither. He's supposed to terrify the other lot. One way to stay safe is to have a bigger sword. Remember, the Ravens were constituted by someone who liked to be known as "the Conqueror". Stone's the youngest Raven, a recent recruit. "Wizard" has been looking for someone with his Talent for thirty years. We lost the last "Conjurer" in the Worm War. Janus Stark, formerly "the India-Rubber Boy". Trust me as someone who's *read* the Beauregard Diaries, we needed an attack magician then and need one now. Stone blunts scissors. Stone tears paper. Stone smashes other stone. If he's our King Rat, we'll be in hot water indeed.'

'So noted.' Catriona made a mark. 'We don't want it to be him.'

'But if it is him, we'll need to know. Just don't expect anyone to be happy.'

'What about the Keeper himself? Connaught Drake? "Wizard"?'

Edwin sighed. There was no easy answer. 'That'd be calamity too. If anyone can wrap Stone, it's Drake. He holds London's shadow. That's something all cities have. It's supported by the specialties of the other three— spiritual barriers, the doings of men and beasts, trickery—but it's a world entire and to itself. You know all the stories of London... Dick Whittington's Cat and the Temple of Mithras, Jack Shepherd's buried fortune and the black swine in the sewers of Hampstead, the curse on Mitre Square and the ghost of the Little Match Girl, the Invisible Theatre where Shakespeare put on the Secret History plays. Those are all wrapped up in the city's shadow. Drake can pass between here and there and keeps everything in shape. He has to polish the London Stone every few months. Some shadows can exist without their cities. Troy is still pretty much with us, for instance, though the physical place is long gone. But without a shadow, no city can stand. Terrified yet?'

'Since I met you, my love, I have dwelled in a state of perpetual fright. I dyed the first white streak out of my hair on my sixteenth birthday. When the horrors go away, I miss them.'

'If you'd seen the Old Man's expression when he brought me into this, you wouldn't joke. I know we're always in some peril or other. This is the King Peril we've been building up to.'

She saluted, fingers crossed. Edwin had an inkling he'd be grateful for her levity before this thing was over. He held her more tightly, feeling warmth through her dress. At bottom, Catriona Kaye was a Very Serious Person. It was why she didn't let the terror take over. To her, there were more important things to worry about.

'If one of our Ravens has gone over to the Enemy,' she said, 'then my next question will be... who or what exactly *is* the Enemy?'

'Our best intelligence is that we're facing a retired Austro-Hungarian soldier.'

'*Him?* Isn't that too obvious? I've been boring everyone stiff for five years about Herr Hitler.'

'Ah, not him. Not yet. The Old Man says he's the war after next.'

Catriona went limp in his arms and hung her head in mock despair.

'This fellow is Colonel Zenf,' he told her. 'No first name listed. Which is sinister in itself, I think you'll agree. Some call him "the Great Enchanter"...'

'The perhaps-imaginary arch-enemy of Don Quixote?'

'Perhaps not-imaginary. Other aliases include "the most dangerous man in Europe", if you'll pardon the expression—"His Satanic Bastardy", "the Big Eater" and "the Crack of Doom". He's either the Devil in the flesh or the Devil's Best Chum. "Sorcerer" says he registers on his model of the universe as a white nothing. The worst people you can think of are either his friends or more afraid of him than we are. Disciples, past and present, include Declan Mountmain, Oliver Haddo, Adrian Marcato, Hamish Corbie, Anselm Oakes, Hjalmar Poelzig and Pius Mocata.'

'I know who most of those people are. Quite a few met nasty, well-deserved fates. Usually in fires or the madhouse. Being friends with the Devil hardly helped them.'

'They did a great deal of damage first.'

'I'm supposed to be impressed?'

He did kiss her nose.

'No, you're supposed to be cowering under the sofa. The fact that you aren't is why we're elected to find out who's cosying up to Zenf. Here's another name you know, Julian Karswell.'

Catriona twisted in his arms. She had written a book on Karswell, *The Biter Bit*.

'*Him*,' she said, with disgust. 'The greatest modern-day exponent of rune-casting, which—as he must have realised in the last few seconds of his life—is quite the stupidest, most dangerous method of magical assassination on the books.'

'Colonel Zenf is a great admirer of Mr Karswell. The unsigned review of *The Biter Bit* in the *Neue Wiener Tagblatt* was almost certainly by him.'

'And you haven't had him killed for that? You are slipping, my love.'

'Sadly, though there are plenty of other reasons for having the Colonel killed, the Old Man hasn't yet authorised that measure. It's one of the things that makes our side better than theirs, remember?'

'Still... "poorly researched"... "childish inability to grasp profound truths"... "overuse of ellipses"! The man's a beast.'

'Can you quote from all your *positive* notices?'

'No, they tend to blur together. It's only the bad ones anyone remembers.'

Catriona settled in his lap. She had covered several pages with hieroglyphs. They might be Karswell's runes for all he knew.

'My last question... at least for this session... is, of course, how do we *know* we have a Rat among our Ravens?'

'We've a whisperer in their ranks, dear,' he said. 'It's how *espionage* works. The Great Game. You might say a little bat told us.'

III: 'a courtesy call'

Rooms open to Ordinary Members—those tiresome, dusty fellows who maintained the pretence that the Diogenes Club was merely a haven for the unsociable—enforced strict silence. Fifty years after the Club's heyday, only two or three OMs were present at any time. They sat in deep armchairs, radiating disapproval, trying not to doze for fear their fellows might expel them for snoring (such things had happened), determinedly ignoring the comings and goings of the Valued Members. Charles wondered whether he should take the effort to recruit a new generation of crotchety (preferably deaf) buffers or abandon entirely the fiction that the Club was not an arm of British Intelligence.

In most gentlemen's clubs, a Quiet Room was where noise was discouraged; in the Diogenes Club, mere *quiet* meant unavoidable talk was at least tolerated. The Quiet Room was dominated by a Hallward portrait of Mycroft Holmes. The painting was fully four-fifths voluminous waistcoat, buttons shining like extra eyes. Charles was always conscious of his late mentor gazing down at him—though he felt that the artist had not, in this case, truly caught his subject's soul. In Mycroft's lifetime, the picture was relegated to the Club's store-house in Clerkenwell, but after his passing the Ruling Cabal felt it should hang on the premises, in honour of the first great (in every sense of the word) Chairman. Charles had abstained from the vote. He worried future holders of his office might also feel dwarfed by this unavoidable reminder of the colossal position he—or, in more enlightened future times, she—was expected to fill. Now Charles looked up and wondered—as he had often during his tenure as Most Valued Member— whether he was anything more than an especially shiny cog in a mechanism confidently set in motion by Mycroft Holmes.

Geneviève had told him she was 'off the books'. Even in Mycroft's most confidential, triple-ciphered files, there was no trace of her association with the Club. Charles expected as much but still made the effort to go through the paperwork.

How many other 'secret agents' were out there, in the cold? Or had lived whole lives without being able to show their true colours?

Yesterday, he had briefed Edwin Winthrop. By now, the Most Valued Member would have told Catriona Kaye.

Already—assuming the Undertakers had eavesdropped on his tête-a-tête with the pale lady—too many people were in the know. Investigating the Ravens was a tricky proposition. If one was indeed a King Rat, it was vital to determine which and take immediate action. But the Guardians of the City were a sensitive, powerful group. If they thought they were individually under suspicion, there was no telling how they would react. Charles could count on Edwin and Catriona to snoop with a high degree of tact, but they were still carrying flaming torches into the powder magazine. A traitor among the Ravens was a calamity waiting to happen, but unless the matter was handled with finesse, the whole flock could easily take flight. Then, the Kingdom would fall.

The Inner Chamber, where the Ruling Cabal convened, was dimly lit to emphasise the secrecy of the business conducted there. Charles's routine involved a great deal of reading, and the Quiet Room had large windows of extra-thick glass, so he made it his office. Sunlight poured in as Huntstanton brought him Bill Owen's Long Box, a daily miscellany of newspaper clippings with scribbled annotations. The Club retained Owen to pore through the press, tearing out items which might fall within their purview. Getting on in years when Mycroft put him up for membership in '97, Owen was nearing his full century and could not be relied on much longer. Another pillar in need of shoring up or replacing.

Charles broke the seal and opened the Box. The papers were musty, as if stewed in tea. For decades, Owen had sat in a corner café, ripping up newspapers, tying and untying complicated knots. Most who saw him took him for a harmless lunatic. It was possible that, undoubted genius aside, Owen *was* a lunatic, though at one time not harmless. His *life* was an allowance from the Diogenes Club. Mycroft could have seen Owen hanged for a murder no one else, including Mycroft's brother, had suspected. Now only Charles knew the secret. Every time he looked over a Long Box, it nagged him. It had often been Mycroft's way to make use of criminals rather than see justice done. Charles hoped to be different.

The first clipping was a tiny notice about an inquest on the Weymouth exsanguination. After what Charles intuited must have been undue influence from Egdon Heath, a coroner's court had brought in a verdict of natural death. If Charles followed his instincts and trusted Geneviève, he was making use of a murderer too.

Next came humorous items from yesterday's evening dailies. Pranksters had stolen wax figures from Madame Tussaud's Chamber of Horrors and treated them to a night on the town. Photographs showed effigies of Charlie Peace, Mrs Manning and William Corder stiff among blurred crowds in Piccadilly Circus, jammed into seats on a Number 1 omnibus to Canada Water, or convivial around a table in an upstairs room at the Newman Arms. Charles would have assumed a circulation stunt, but the items were in rival papers.

Normally, Charles would have had a Valued Member call on the waxworks. With Edwin occupied and Captain Jeperson in New York, he didn't have anyone first-rank to spare. Oh well, there was no shortage of titled busybodies eager to poke noses into any mystery that afforded an opportunity to make the police look foolish. Let one of their lordships tackle the Perambulating Horrors.

Otherwise, Owen had turned up a report of the doings of the Thule Society. They had been involved in the construction of a vast electrical device either to predict the future or to manufacture gold from sea-water, which had thus far resulted only in the electrocution of several acolytes. Then came shudder pulp business about a ring of mad surgeons abducting Philadelphia debutantes for unholy purposes. Charles bundled these away. At the moment, he was concentrating on matters closer to home.

If London falls...

A discreet cough brought him out of a reverie which was threatening to become an afternoon nap.

Huntstanton brought in a familiarly dressed visitor.

'I am the new Mr Hay,' announced the young man in mourning clothes. He doffed his top hat.

Charles stood up to receive the Undertaker.

It was as rare for the first of the alphabet men to pay a call upon the Diogenes Club as for the Chairman of the Ruling Cabal to visit the Mausoleum.

Huntstanton eyed the Undertaker with suspicion, but withdrew.

Charles understood there had recently been a succession, but was not sure how the Undertaking went about cultivating new recruits. Talk was that they were grown from seed, mulched with the remains of their predecessors. Mr Hay still had a shiny freshness to his pallor, and red scratches across one cheek and his forehead.

The Undertaker's entire body swivelled and his head angled up at Mycroft's picture. Then he paid full attention to Charles, who saw himself reflected twice in dark glasses. As always when he caught sight of himself in a mirror, his reflex was to wonder who that strange old person was.

'You may be proceeding under a false assumption,' Mr Hay told him, flatly. 'An item has gone missing from the Collection. We have cause to doubt her—its—provenance. I fear you've been the victim of an elaborate deception.'

The words slid into Charles's chest like a jack-knife.

'How...?'

'We hoped you might be able to shed light on the matter. A day after your interview, the *lady* went missing. Shackles neatly fastened but empty. Door firmly locked. Guards undisturbed and unmolested. But the cupboard bare. She was under constant surveillance, of course. In a matter of seconds, she was not where she was supposed to be. The expression that comes to mind is "spirited away".'

'You think she had outside aid?'

'As a matter of fact, our first suspicion was that you were responsible. Upon reflection, it is too deft a trick for the Diogenes Club. Quite beyond your capabilities. Beyond ours too, which is not an admission we make often.'

The 'how' was beside the point. The 'why' troubled Charles. Why would Geneviève escape? If escape she had—there was always a possibility of abduction, or assassination. He didn't doubt Mr Hay was telling the truth, but he hadn't doubted Mycroft's 'secret agent' either.

'We shall, of course, take steps to reacquire the item. You may leave the matter to us. But, and I cannot stress this enough, you should weigh most carefully any action you take upon information passed from this source. The Undertaking believes it tainted. We presume the vampire Geneva Deodati to be a creature of Colonel Zenf.'

Charles had not thought the Undertaking aware of that name.

'Her sole purpose in letting herself be apprehended was to talk with you, Mr Beauregard. To gull you into setting on a course which leads to the disaster we hope to avert.'

Charles fought hard to keep his hands from trembling.

'This has been a courtesy call. We shall keep you informed of our progress. That is all.'

Mr Hay put on his hat and left.

Now, Charles had trouble breathing. Huntstanton rushed in and fixed a medicinal brandy and soda. Charles took the drink.

His breathing difficulty passed.

But his troubles were compounded.

IV: '*everyone* is invited'

Catriona wore a breathtaking gown—mid-length, clinging and silver-white; matching cape, pumps and a cap which fit perfectly over her bobbed hair; blood-red rose pinned to one shoulder. Like every other man in the room, Edwin had to make do with white tie and tails.

Harry Roy's Band, on loan from the May Fair Hotel, played 'We're in the Money'—which, in this company, was hardly front-page news. Lord Kilpartinger, the railway magnate, shot back his cuffs to show off ruby links prised from the eye-sockets of a little yellow idol purchased at auction last month. He must feel protected. Edwin held up an alchemist's eyeglass which passed as a green-tinted monocle and confirmed his suspicions. A purple-black aura throbbed around Kilpartinger. Wisp-things battered themselves to pieces against it.

He passed the glass to Catriona, who peered at His Lordship.

'Those wards won't hold forever,' she commented. 'I'd rather receive one of Karswell's *billets douces* than wear blood-cursed stones.'

'Everyone's luck runs out, Catty-Kit.'

'Except ours.'

'We don't have luck, dear. We have *caution*.'

'Then remind me why we're here.'

'"Witch" is the easiest of our Ravens to get close to. She's usually in public, on display. Think of her as a figurehead.'

Margery Device held court in a corner of the ballroom. This season—after experiments with dirigibles, barges and trains to Scotland—her party was held in a conventional mansion fronting Hyde Park.

'Good grief, what *is* she wearing?' said Catriona.

Tonight, their hostess was bright green, with real vines threading through a diaphanous gown with an eight-foot train that had taken root. Her red-dyed hair was sculpted into a thicket of shrub, blooming with corpse-flowers. A bodice of bark was bound tight around her torso. Miss Device had to be the most outrageously dressed woman at her party, and some of her guests set the bar high.

A thin woman in a cream dress approached Edwin and Catriona. She wore eggshells as earrings.

'Darling Cat,' she shrieked, kissing the air six inches away from Catriona's cheek, 'what delight to run into *you* here! That dress... very thrifty. Admirable in these hard times. We all must watch the pennies.'

Catriona smiled sweetly and said, 'Hello, Ollie. What odd earrings.'

'Do you like them? Dodo eggs.'

Ollie primped the fragile ovoids. They were more distinguished by scarcity than appearance.

'So sorry to hear about the Earl,' Catriona sympathised.

Ollie adopted a tragic face. 'It's been trying, but people have been *so* kind. Only those beastly newspapers have thrown dead cats.'

'If there's anything I can do...'

'I'll give you a tinkle. You're still in that dear little slum in Bloomsbury?'

'Yes, and you still own Norfolk?'

'As far as I know, darling. It's hard to keep track of one's *portfolio*. That's my word for the day.'

'That's funny. Mine's *apnoea*.'

'What does that mean?'

'Look it up, Ollie. Or you'll never learn.'

There was a glint in the woman's smile. 'I'll do just that. Now, must dash, Cat. Have to circulate. Wouldn't want to monopolise you. Toodle-oo.'

'See you in court, dearie,' said Catriona, after Ollie was gone.

Edwin had an inkling what that had all been about. 'That was...'

'Ollie. Olivia Gibberne, the Countess of Chelm. I was just talking about her the other day.'

'So you were. The cocktail-mixing minx. *Apnoea* is the primary symptom of death by cyanide poisoning, isn't it?'

'Literal loss of breath. Does a Countess rate the silk when she's hanged? Or is that only peers of the realm?'

'Not my field of expertise, love. The Old Man would know.'

'No matter. So long as justice is done.'

Across the room, Olivia Gibberne waved a long ivory holder with an unlit cigarette stuffed into it. Three smart young fellows produced flames. She smiled back at Catriona, who waved cheerfully.

'I had no idea you knew the Countess,' said Edwin.

'Didn't I mention it? We were at school together.'

'Gal pals, eh?'

'Not exactly.'

Edwin scanned the room and clocked fourteen murderers that he knew of. He thought it best not to mention them to Catriona. Then he glimpsed a pasty face, lurking beyond Noel Coward and Ivor Novello.

'Hey up,' he said to himself. 'Fifteen.'

Catriona snagged unpoisoned cocktails from a passing tray-bearer—a gilded youth in a loin-cloth and turban.

'Don't stare,' he said, 'but you see the famous folks over there?'

She looked at him askance.

'The *very* famous folks. West End.'

'Oh, *them*. Stay between me and Novello. He always pretends he wants to fetch me away to some little chalet. It's not very flattering. He thinks I look like a chorus boy from Cardiff.'

'Look without looking at the fellow just behind them. Round-faced cove with thinning hair. Listening to the Earl of Emsworth's pig stories.'

Catriona did a little twirl.

'Got him,' she said. 'That can't be right.'

She looked again, blatantly this time. The Earl's auditor didn't notice. His eyes were glassy anyway. He was a little man with a drooping moustache and Teddy Roosevelt spectacles.

'Speaking of hangings,' she said. 'He was.'

'You agree with me, then?'

'Hawley Harvey Crippen.'

'Let's drift over,' he said, putting his empty glass and hers on a passing tray. 'I know Miss Device boasts everyone who is anyone comes to her party, but even for her this is out of the ordinary.'

'Don't let him give you a drink.'

'Ha Ha.'

'I'll see your "Ha Ha" and raise you a "Tee Hee".'

'I'll take your "Tee Hee" and trump it with a "Chortle".'

As they passed, Novello opened his mouth to speak to Catriona. Noel Coward tossed the olive from his cocktail into it. The matinee idol swallowed like a trained seal.

By the time they got to Emsworth, Crippen had moved on.

'B----y queer little b-----n' c--t,' grunted the Earl. 'Shows no f----n' interest at f----n' all in pigs. Probably b-----s goats in his spare time, the s--t-headed weasel-f-----r! What a f----n' stupid f--k-faced b-----d!'

It occurred to Edwin that Plum Wodehouse considerably worked over the Earl's country language when writing about him.

Their quarry had plunged, alone, onto the dance-floor, jostling packed couples.

Harry Roy was leading a lively 'Puttin' on the Ritz'. Crippen got buffeted.

'He's heading for the punch-bowl,' said Catriona, urgently.

Edwin took her in his arms and danced her in the murderer's wake, whisking between less-coordinated folks.

At the edge of the dance-floor, they bumped against two implacable bodies. Above immaculate evening dress, they had beefy, brutal faces— swollen noses, open pores, tufty side-whiskers, worked-in dirt, glittering eyes. They were Burke and Hare, Old Edinburgh's most notorious suppliers of fresh cadavers for anatomy lectures. Their heads didn't fit their suits.

Crippen took something like Catriona's cocktail shaker out from his shirt-front. It must have been in his chest cavity. He poured into a cauldron-sized bowl.

The brutes blocking Edwin's way wouldn't let him pass.

Catriona slipped out of his hold and, with a skirl of silver, got round the long-dead miscreants. She laid a hand on Crippen's shoulder and pulled his arm off. At this, people took notice.

'B----r me!' exclaimed the Earl of Emsworth.

A dowager raised a just-filled glass to quaff away astonishment. Catriona used the severed arm to bat the drink from her lips. Liquid fizzed on the floor and ate into the varnish. Other would-be poisonees poured their glasses back into the bowl.

Edwin adopted a pugilist's stance.

Burke and Hare came for him. In the popular imagination, the pair were remembered as resurrection men—but they hadn't the stomach for the honest work of exhumation, and took to suffocating folks then pretending they'd been found dead or dug up. Few things were lower than a bogus body-snatcher,.

He landed a solid right on Burke's chin and the head flew off. A mannequin body fell to pieces. Then he rounded on Hare—the slimiest of the pair, who peached on his brother-in-law to escape the gallows. The bounder pulled a dagger from his trousers, but Edwin knocked it away. He punched Hare square on the nose. His wax face cracked across and fell away, showing a pair of glass eyes (one milk-white) and a set of false teeth on a wooden frame.

Panic and commotion spread through the crowd.

'Look to "Witch",' Edwin shouted.

Catriona nodded and let a couple of young bloods pull Crippen apart. Once the heads came off, the murderers were incapacitated.

Edwin knew where he had seen the malefactors before. In the Chamber of Horrors at Madame Tussaud's Wax Works.

Catriona slid through the crowds towards their hostess, who had realised this was more than the usual fun and games. Determined wax guests were taking the same route. Louis Bauer, the Pimlico poisoner. George Joseph Smith, the 'Brides-in-the-Bath' murderer. Rodger Baskerville, the damnable dog-trainer. Amelia Dyer, the baby farmer of the 1890s. Sir Francis Varney, the vampyre.

Edwin had a loaded revolver in a special pocket inside his tail-coat. Too many people were blundering about for him to make use of it.

Smith got to Miss Device first. She plucked a thorn from her hair-piece and darted it into his face, which melted and froze into a shapeless mass with eyes. Then she took a length of vine from her train and used it as a switch, whipping Bauer and Dyer to segments.

Many of her guests applauded.

'It's another turn,' commented Noel Coward. 'One is humiliatingly upstaged again.'

Some foolish fellows, a little the worse for drink, set about Ivor Novello and began pummelling him. He swore at them in his original Welsh accent.

'It's bloody Jack the Ripper,' said a rugby prop forward. 'I'd know that face anywhere. Saw it in the flickers. Twice.'

'He only *played* Jack the Ripper, you utter idiot,' said Coward. 'In *The*

Lodger.'

'Silent and talkie,' grunted Novello. 'And I was innocent both times, boyo.'

'He's right, you know,' said the rugger player, calling off his team-mates. 'I remember now. This is the fellow who was *mistaken* for the Ripper. Fearfully sorry, old son. It must happen to you all the time.'

'Funnily enough, no,' said Novello, straightening his coat. His collar was exploded and he'd have to cake powder over black eyes if he went on stage in the next week. He kneed the prop forward between the legs, doubling him over. 'I must apologise,' he said. 'Sheer reflex. It must happen to you all the time.'

'Steady on, old chap,' said the forward's least-intoxicated friend. 'Play the game and all that.'

Catriona was by Miss Device, standing in a pile of broken dummies. She had her little pearl-handled automatic out of its inner-thigh holster.

The crowds stood still to applaud and Edwin made his way to the dais. Harry Roy struck up 'Don't Bring Lulu', and many revellers joined in the refrain.

Edwin wasn't sure all the wax murderers were weeded out.

'This is a pretty pass, Mr Winthrop,' commented Miss Device, flexing her willow-switch. 'I thought the Diogenes Club was in the business of nipping these bothersome trifles in the bud.'

Catriona sorted through the pile of mannequin parts. She found something inside a coat pocket. A card. She passed it to Edwin.

'It seems they were invited,' he said, giving it to the hostess.

'*Everyone* is invited,' she said, airily. 'There's a list.'

The card had a name and address in copperplate. Rodger Baskerville, c/o Beryl Stapleton, Merripit House, Dartmoor.

The party swallowed the excitement and got on with revelry. There were always unadvertised occurrences. Most guests would think an attack by waxwork horrors was part of a sparkling array of entertainment.

'You, Mr Winthrop, Miss Kaye, have cocktails. Consider it an order.'

Miss Device snapped her fingers. An attendant stepped out of a plume of red smoke with a tray. Edwin took a glass for Catriona and one for himself.

'Now,' said their hostess, 'what is all this nonsense?'

The cocktail was sweet yet tart. For a moment, Edwin feared he had been slipped waters of truth at precisely the moment he most needed to be evasive.

'We have worries, ma'am. About the Ravens.'

'Well, *don't*. It's our business to have worries about you. As you see, we're not in danger. That's your lot. We keep *you* safe.'

Under her penetrating gaze, Edwin couldn't doubt it.

'Still, *quis custodiet ipsos custodes*, Miss Device?' put in Catriona.

'*Quis* indeed?'

'*Nos*,' said Edwin. 'Sorry about it, but there you are. Someone has to.'

Attendants discreetly took bits and pieces of the Chamber of Horrors escapees out of the room.

'Robbie Stone said this sort of thing was happening all over town,' said Mrs Device. 'He's supposed to be here, but cried off. Rather pull artificial flowers out of real rabbits for the one-and-nines.'

Was that suspicious? Neither of the other Ravens was here. Except under extra-extraordinary circumstances, the four were never in one place at the same time. It was a precautionary measure. Still, one or two of the others would be admissible.

'Might we have a talk with you, ma'am?' asked Edwin. 'In private.'

'You sound like a policeman, Mr Winthrop. Am I to help you with your enquiries?'

She might almost be flirting. Then again, her calling involved flirting. And diplomacy.

'That's a stunning gown, my dear,' she told Catriona. 'How did you pull your little gun out of it?'

Catriona smiled slyly. 'There's a slit, but you can't see it. Hooks and eyes.'

'Very ingenious. You must give me the name of your dress-maker. By the way, did you see Ollie Gibberne earlier? Cream's not a good colour for her. I understand she has an appointment with the silk rope.'

Margery Device, of course, knew everyone's secrets. And none were safe. She doled out gossip the way other hostesses dispensed drinks.

'Look at Wallis Simpson, by the way,' she said. 'Now *there's* a threat to the kingdom. Trust me, that horse-faced American gold-digger will crack the throne.'

'If you say so, ma'am.'

'But you're not here about that crisis a-brewing, are you? I've heard *whispers*. A veritable stormcloud of little birdies have been chirruping in Mama Device's shell-likes. I've had word from your Mr Beauregard on the subject. The Great Old Ones. Writhing Chaos in the Outer Darkness. All God's Chillun Got Horns.'

She tugged a rope and a curtain parted. Beyond was a small reception room, with comfortable chairs and a low table. A silver service was laid out.

'Now, join me in a pot of tea and tell me your troubles.'

'Miss Device,' he said, 'you really are the perfect hostess.'

'Did you doubt it? How disappointing. I must be slipping.'

V: 'silver shot will fit any Webley'

Traditionally, three office-holders constituted the Ruling Cabal: two Chairs and a Chairman. The Cabal convened in the Inner Chamber and sat at the High Table. The Inner Chamber, a windowless room, did not feature on the registered building plans. Behind oak-panelling was armour plate. The High Table was exalted in significance rather than stature—in point of fact, it was no higher than an ordinary dining table. Up to seven Chairs had crowded around the Table, and—in certain unlikely-to-be-repeated circumstances—the Cabal had consisted solely of a Chairman (Mycroft, of course). Charles had taken a Chair when he stepped down as Most Valued Member and become Chairman upon Mycroft's death. He had served two non-consecutive terms.

The Inner Chamber was threaded with cigarette smoke. Charles was tired and his temples throbbed.

The other Chairs were the voluminous Sir Henry Merrivale and the rake-thin General Lord Hector Tarr. H.M. had succeeded Charles as Chairman but resigned in 1928, outvoted on the question of admitting lady members. The diehard was still not reconciled to women having the vote, let alone joining the Diogenes Club. Tarr was a veteran of Military Intelligence under Mansfield Smith-Cumming and the Royal Society for Psychical Research under Sir Michael Calme. A canny, practical man, he was all for 'modernisation', an adherent of 'the scientific approach' and the sort of person who habitually drew up detailed contingency plans.

Charles had apprised the Chairs of recent developments. Sir Henry responded by telegram, claiming to be too caught up with a knotty locked-room mystery (he was a noted amateur sleuth, i.e.: pompous busybody) to attend the emergency meeting but wishing to be kept informed.

So, Charles was closeted with Tarr and his adjutant, Captain Giles Gallant. The junior officer stood at hand with a thick buff folder of papers. Tarr puffed methodically, as if under orders to transform a certain number of cigarettes into smoke and ash before dawn.

Sir Henry's absence was strategic. H.M. was letting Charles have enough rope, trusting Tarr to hang him. Two Ruling Members formed a quorum, and could make decisions for which the third could not be held accountable. In differences of opinion, the Chairman's vote decided. Charles would have to answer alone for any ensuing disasters. Sir Henry planned graciously to resume Chairmanship, sweeping away all that nonsense about letting in women. If it were up to H.M., electric wires would be stripped out of the building and gas-lamps put back in to get things back to the way they were 'in Mycroft's day'. He didn't take Tarr and his typewritten, triplicate reports and memoranda seriously. It didn't even occur to him that Tarr would make a play for Chairman. Charles assumed there was an 'eyes-only' memo in Gallant's folder, outlining post-Beauregard stratagems for the Diogenes Club. In this utopia, General Lord Hector Tarr ran the Ruling Cabal, with every report rubber-stamped and acted on. There wouldn't be much room for windy old H.M. in such an efficient organisation.

'I've framed a plan of action, Beauregard,' announced Tarr, as if he were doing the Chairman a favour. Gallant gave him a sheet of paper. 'We must track this vampire down, put it to the question, and have its head off. Your man Winthrop is chasing his tail round the Ravens. He's too compromised for the mission. These are my suggestions for suitable operatives. Good men, all of 'em.'

Charles looked over the list. He knew the names.

Dennis Rattray. Hugh Drummond. Dr Jonathan Chambers. Michael Bellamy.

'Four Just Men,' he observed. 'You've a whole Black Hand Gang here.'

'If that's what it takes, Beauregard. We can find the bloodsucker before it does any more damage. Get answers.'

'Isn't Captain Rattray *hors de combat?*'

'His medical condition is in check. He is highly motivated, needs to make a name for himself again. "Blackfist" always got results.'

Of Tarr's list, only Jonathan Chambers—better known as 'Dr Shade'— was even an Associate Member. Charles had worked with him on several cases, and they had a guarded mutual respect. Dr Shade kept well-appointed lairs around London, including an apartment inside the Clock Tower of the Houses of Parliament. Mostly, he flapped about the night on a near-silent autogiro, terrorising 'evil-doers' with 'shadow gas' and 'dark matter'. The doctor's style—his usual get-up consisted of black slouch hat, ingenious night-sight goggles and flaring black coat—was closer to the Undertaking than the Diogenes Club, though he was more of a scientific than a mystic bent. For Charles's taste, he tended to leave too many corpses lying about.

Dennis Rattray, formerly of The Splendid Six, had once been black-balled by the Ruling Cabal. Also, Catriona had pinned an ordinary murder on his band of heroes. Rattray was at least out of the ordinary. He possessed the Fang of Night, a gem which endowed great strength upon anyone who held it in a closed fist. However, overusing the jewel gave rise to an embarrassing medical complication which was the frequent subject of indecent jokes. During a messy divorce action, Rattray had been hauled over the coals in court and the press. Tarr's other nominees were little more than posh thugs. Bellamy liked dressing up as Robin Hood and calling himself 'the Green Archer'. Drummond was a loose cannon with a penchant for thumping tradesmen and blaming the Jews.

If Charles wanted anyone dead, he might have called on any of these volunteer public servants. He rarely did, however. That sort of thinking led to the other camp.

Charles slid the list of head-breakers back across the table.

Tarr's tactic was to get him to discuss *which* of his proposed 'operatives' should be turned loose in pursuit of Geneviève, not *whether...*

'I don't think we need to let slip the bulldogs of Britain yet.'

'We can't afford that sort of woolly thinking, man,' said Tarr, pluming smoke from his nostrils. 'If you're wrong, we could lose the Ravens. And then...'

'You don't need to tell me, Hector.'

'At least, call off Winthrop and Kaye,' insisted Tarr. 'Who knows what damage they'll do in Mayfair!'

'They have proved their discretion in the past.'

Catriona Kaye was the first of the Lady Members who so incensed Sir Henry. A generation ago, Charles had offered to sponsor Kate Reed, but she'd refused the 'honour', responding with choice words on the subject of the Club's occasional anti-Fenian activities. And Geneviève Dieudonné had been a Member all along. Charles would have given ten shillings to see H.M.'s face when he had learned that the sainted Mycroft Holmes covertly extended membership to Geneviève—a woman, a vampire and French.

'We should have people around all the Ravens at all times,' said Tarr, tapping his list. 'Trained men. Skilled operatives.'

'I don't disagree. However, we require tact and discretion, not a show of force.'

During the Worm War, Mycroft Holmes had dipped into a desk drawer and withdrawn a sealed envelope. Inside was a plan, drawn up years earlier: It did not precisely fit the situation, but was a starting-point for an ultimately successful course of action. There were other envelopes in the drawer, for other potential crises. These contingencies, framed after consultation and speculation, were Mycroft's legacy to the Ruling Cabal. There was even an envelope, in another desk drawer, in the event of the Cabal being suborned by hostile elements. Mycroft had commissioned this plan from his brother, whom he could trust to be suitably devious. As Chairman, Charles had only once had recourse to one of the contingencies. In 1926, opening the sealed envelope marked 'in the event of a General Strike', he'd found a single sheet of paper inscribed with Mycroft's copperplate handwriting, advising the Club to stay out of it as much as possible. That, he conceded, was a good idea.

There was no envelope marked 'Rat Among the Ravens', though there were contingencies for an occupation of Great Britain by a foreign (i.e.: German) army, an aggressive visitation by beings from another world, the marriage of the sovereign to an evil consort with supernatural powers, and the rising from the sea of a malign lost continent. He had shuffled through the private files, in the hope Mycroft had considered a situation even slightly similar to the present crisis.

If the Diogenes Club—and the kingdom—weathered this storm, Charles would commission fresh plans. He would gather the most imaginative pessimists in the land and have them consider every possible, or even impossible, disaster. Then, he would have experts plot courses of action for each dire circumstance. He would not find himself in a room with Tarr and Gallant, or even H.M.—and having to make up strategy on the hoof.

'What about the *thing?*' queried Tarr.

'The thing has a name,' Charles reminded him. 'Geneviève

Dieudonné.'

Tarr did not respond. He had signed up to exterminate creatures of the night, not get on first-name terms with them.

'From what we can gather about her bloodline,' said Giles Gallant, 'she should be susceptible to these.'

The adjutant put a box of cartridges on the table.

'Silver shot,' he said. 'Will fit any Webley.'

Charles looked at the wall. Geneviève's face floated in his memory. He instinctively put his trust in her (and, even more, in Mycroft), but weight of evidence was piling up. Whether she stood with the Club or (the thought chilled him) Zenf, she was out of her cage. He had thought to get her free of the Mausoleum. Perhaps he should have demanded the Undertaking turn her over? Now, she was running loose.

He picked a shell out of the paper box and rolled it between his fingers.

'I thought these were for werewolves,' he said.

'According to field tests,' said Gallant, 'they'll bring down vampires, zombies, your common shapeshifters, ghouls, sundry revenants, and some of the more physical species of ghost. People, come to that. Bloody nasty thing to be shot with. Silver is a soft metal. Fragments on impact.'

Charles came to a decision, and held the silver bullet like Blackfist gripping the Fang of Night.

'We let our money ride on Geneviève,' he said. 'Edwin and Catriona stay on the Ravens. *I* can be fooled by a pretty face and a sharp mind. Mycroft Holmes could not. He made our choice.'

Tarr smoked. He was saving his shots.

'Business is settled,' concluded Charles.

VI: 'no bump of discretion'

Before Edwin had finished his first cup of tea, Margery Device explained in credible detail exactly how Wallis Simpson had ensnared the Prince of Wales ('good luck to her,' he thought). She also dropped footnotes about Haile Selassie, Simon Templar, Peggy Hopkins Joyce, Pandora Reynolds, Roderick Spode and Gracie Fields, most of whom ought to be ashamed of themselves.

'Anthony Zenith... Zenith the Albino? Dyes his hair, my dears. Naturally, he'd be yellow as old newspapers.'

Witch had inside information about the deaths of prominent folk, which varied considerably from the newspaper accounts. Arnold Bennett, who drank the water in Paris to prove it safe, was poisoned by a jealous rival... Roger Ackroyd was murdered, but not by the fellow who owned up to it... Geli Raubel was shot in the head on the orders of her devoted Uncle Adolf... Rebecca DeWinter committed spiteful suicide by nagging her husband to murder her... and John Thomson, the goalkeeper whose neck was broken during a Celtic–Rangers match at Ibrox Park, was victim of a Papist plot of

Machiavellian intricacy.

Disappointingly, Miss Device drew a blank on the escapees from the Chamber of Horrors.

'I'm in the dark, *mes amis*,' she said.

She lifted the lid of her teapot and stirred a Sargasso of leaves with a long spoon.

'Nope,' she concluded. 'No augurs as yet. Of course, tea-leaves are gypsy piffle. But signs and omens are everywhere for those who can see.'

'Wax murderers *en masse* are fairly significant,' said Edwin.

'And ominous,' added Catriona.

'As you know, you can't pull the wool over my eyes any day with a "d" in it,' continued Miss Device. 'You represent yourselves as protectors, but come here looking for suspects, not witnesses.'

Edwin tried to waffle the insight away, but was skewered.

'Don't bother to deny it. Charles Beauregard was always too transparent for this business. And the situation has changed since the little leech gave the funereal fellows the slip...'

Edwin sensed another shift in the playing field.

'Either one of the Ravens is your King Rat or we're all being painted black to undermine the defence of the realm. It's down to you to determine, eh? If I were you, I'd suspect me. I'm so open and considerate and helpful. People like that always turn out to be the murderer, don't they? Ask Lord Peter Wimsey or that appalling American upstart Vance. Of course, I haven't got a motive, but you'll ferret one out. I did seem to be the intended victim of tonight's little business, though.'

'You expertly warded off the attack,' Catriona observed.

Miss Device gave her one of her penetrating witchy looks.

'Indeed. I was merely being tested. Serious stabbing will come later. More tea?'

'Yes, thank you,' said Catriona.

Miss Device did the honours. 'If I'm out of the running, which of the others do you suspect? Mark Rennes seethes inside his mathematical construct, you know. On the wall, eternally vigilant. Must be tiresome, waiting for a war? And Robbie Stone's a common theatrical until the spelling starts. It's the eternal dilemma of the weather man. Make ready for the deluge and eventually you can't help wishing the clouds would open so you can show how clever you are. When it's dry, you're so unappreciated you start thinking. Do you have more in common with your opposite numbers in the dark than the dreary, trivial happy folks you're supposed to fight for? Rennes and Stone might well feel mothballed.'

'What about Drake?' Edwin prompted.

'Keeper of the Ravens? I don't know how Conny can have common cause with *anyone*. But if resentments, temptations or imps of perversity tug at his starry robes, I don't know about them. And I know about *everything*.'

'Isn't that, in itself, suspicious?' asked Catriona.

Miss Device looked at her again, almost showing doubt.

'Yes,' she said, candidly, 'I suppose it is. Then again, he *is* a Wizard. I'm only a Witch. Long ago, before Prince Albert had his uncomfortable alteration, Conny and I were... well, I'm not here to gossip about *myself*, fascinating as I'm sure it would be. Safe to say, I know Connaught Drake better than anyone and I know next to nothing about him. Robbie Stone has this invisibility trick—he's there in front of you, but you don't see him. It's not that you can see through him, it's that he makes you look the other way. Conny doesn't need to bother with that. He's nobody. Seven eighths of him is always out of sight. Do you have any idea of the lifelong commitment that takes? A man who can do that could do anything. The reason I don't believe he's in league with all the Devils of all the Hells is that I think he'd have to lower himself to deal with a mere Prince of Darkness. Give him my regards, by the way.'

As they left the party, while Edwin was settling her wrap on her shoulders, Catriona told him Witch wasn't a Queen Rat.

'How do you work that out?'

'The mouth on her, Ed. You said it yourself. Madame Device "knows all, *tells* all". She has no bump of discretion. If she were in the least bit ratty, she'd have squeaked on herself. She couldn't help it.'

They stepped out into the street. A red omnibus drove by. Two pale, familiar faces looked down from the upper deck. Guy Fawkes and Captain Macheath. There were still waxworks on the loose.

'You're right, as always,' said Edwin, kissing her nose.

'Did you...'

'...see the Horrors on the bus? Yes. They'll be a nuisance for weeks. This gets murkier and murkier.'

They walked towards Hyde Park Corner to pick up a taxi.

'My head is stuffed full,' said Catriona. 'The Witch stirs so much into her cauldron it's impossible to tell the tittle from the tattle.'

'I didn't like that remark about "the little leech",' said Edwin. 'Almost an aside. It was something we're supposed to know. She must have meant Charles's informant. The vampire.'

'I noticed it too,' said Catriona.

A chill wind blew down Park Lane. Cold air rippled across his face.

'Where to now?' she asked, shivering. 'Bloomsbury and bed?'

'Sadly, no. Pall Mall and an elucidation.'

VII: 'an infinity of mirrors'

A freshly deciphered report from 'Karolyi', the Budapest Affiliate, sat on Charles Beauregard's desk in the Quiet Room. Next to a pot of strong coffee Huntstanton had sent in.

Colonel Zenf had been at the Opéra two nights ago, in full view of an audience of five hundred. That evening, two men in different quarters of the city died in locked rooms, looks of stark terror plastered on their faces. One corpse was found in an apartment above a stables. Every horse in the place was dead, also a cat and—close examination showed—every mouse, rat and even fly on the premises. At the end of the opera (*The Temptation of Faust*, of course), a mystery clique insisted Zenf, who had no obvious connection with the entertainment, take a bow. Charles didn't know either of the dead men, but they had both been inconveniences to the Great Enchanter: a retired officer who wrote to the newspapers questioning Zenf's right to military rank, stating that the Regiment in which the Colonel claimed to have served had been cut down to the last man during the War; and a coachman in Zenf's employ who had lately been talkative. The Club's Man in Budapest—he had bribed the coachman, of course—was worried. 'Karolyi' no longer noticed swarthy men pretending to read newspapers while eavesdropping on his tête-a-têtes, as if someone he was less likely to spot had scared off the regular Secret Police spies.

Appended to the report were recent cables, reporting that Zenf had left for Vienna, Zurich and Brussels. The most recent wire was not from 'Karolyi' but his second, standing in while the Affiliate was indisposed. The Great Enchanter was getting near. He was the Most Dangerous Man in Europe, and maybe more than that.

Charles drank strong coffee. The fug of Tarr's cigarettes was still in his head.

There was *always* someone like Colonel Zenf. Mycroft had reckoned the financier Leo Dare the Worst Villain of the Age. Dare had fallen off the map around the time of the Boer War, then Isidore Persano popped up with a portal to another universe inside his box of Swan and Edgar. Others through the ages had earned the title of Great Enchanter. The mountebanks, charlatans and self-publicists—the Cagliostros, Rasputins and Crowleys— might be hailed the wickedest, most darkly powerful of their ages. The Great Enchanters were less obviously voluptuaries or crackpots, more likely to tear pages out of history books than inscribe their names there. Who knew, or remembered, Nicholas Goodman of Mildew Manor? Mrs Mary Braxton, who quietly slipped out of the net which hauled in Don Felipe Molina and Sir Timothy ffolliott? Cardinal Silencio, who never rose to the Papacy but cast votes which elevated five other men, then called in dreadful debts?

Charles wondered if these people didn't crawl full-grown out of filthy water, bereft of a past, suddenly gifted with great fortune and greater influence. These dark whisperers were sworn to the ruination of man's higher works. Leo Dare, it was said, invented the advertising circular. Silencio celebrated Black Mass in the heart of Vatican City.

Zenf first appeared in Vienna in 1919, around the time of the global influenza pandemic. Bill Owen argued that there was a connection. Suddenly, the Colonel was *everywhere*, if only in the shadows: buying into

Czech and German munitions firms, and patenting features of the automatic pistol; photographed shaking hands with Lindbergh at Le Bourget, though public records insisted he was at an angry stock-holders' meeting in Turin on that famous day; visiting Trotsky in Prinkipo, with a personal message from Stalin; reaping a third of Performing Rights Society royalties on comical odes to self-abuse made popular by George Formby (though Zenf's contribution, if any, to lyrics or music was hard to determine); refusing to extend bank credit to Ernst Röhm in 1925, but providing sweatshop labour (ironically, Jewish) to manufacture brown shirts for the Nazi SA; smoking a cigar in the lobby of the St Francis Hotel in San Francisco as Virginia Rappé collapsed after attending a party thrown by Roscoe 'Fatty' Arbuckle; hands stained with purple ink at the disrupted Paris premiere of *L'Âge d'Or*, pointedly not slashing surrealist paintings alongside the League of Patriots; sitting quietly in court during the trial of Nathan Leopold and Richard Loeb; allegedly fathering a child upon Magda Lupescu, mistress of the King of Romania; giving a private audience in Cicero, Illinois, to Al Capone, from which the racketeer emerged with his old scar freshly bleeding; financing the first all-talking pornographic pictures, *What the Butler Said* and *You Really Ain't Heard Nothing Yet*; facilitating the export of farm machinery to Turkey; meeting in Georgia with the Grand Imperial Wizard of the Ku Klux Klan.

The Colonel had never been charged with a crime by any government. He held high honours from most European countries, including Great Britain. H.G. Wells said Zenf was a 'samurai of science with a good, clear head'. Charles had tried to apprise the Cabinet of as much of the Zenf File as they could read without going mad. Robert Vansittart, the Permanent Under-Secretary with Responsibility for Intelligence, gave word to soft-pedal criticism of the Colonel. Officially, Zenf was a good friend to Britain. The Prime Minister cited him as 'one of the greatest agitators for peace in the world today'. If the Diogenes Club pressed the point, they risked being written off as cranks.

Charles looked up at Mycroft's portrait, wondering how much things had changed in this century. Zenf was a scientific samurai. A good friend to Britain. An agitator for peace. Yes, and James Moriarty was a humble professor of mathematics...

The door opened. Huntstanton was stationed outside.

'Anything we ought to know, Charles?' asked Catriona Kaye.

She sat down in one of the armchairs, dress shimmering. Edwin Winthrop stood like a schoolboy in the Head's study.

They both looked at him. Pointedly. It was about Geneviève.

'How the *deuce* have you heard?' Charles asked. Then the penny dropped. 'Margery Device.'

'Knows all,' said Catriona, making mesmeric gestures.

'...tells all,' said Edwin.

'Doesn't she just? Here are the facts. Our well-placed source is absent. Some argue she's playing a triple game, and your present investigation is founded upon a false premise.'

'Nice of you to let us in on it, Charlie!' drawled Catriona.

'A coded telegram awaits you at your flat, summoning you here,' said Charles. 'To be let in on it, as you say.'

'Fair enough,' said Edwin. 'Are you saying there's no King Rat?'

Charles shook his head. 'No. Others are.'

'How did the vampire fly from the Mausoleum?' asked Catriona.

Charles opened his hands.

'Aren't the Undertakers known for not letting this happen?' she continued. 'Items from the Egdon Heath Collection seldom come on the open market?'

Edwin grinned, with little humour. 'The black hats must be fuming. This is one in the eye for the Hays, Bees and Seas. I'm surprised they admit they've lost her.'

'To be frank,' said Charles, 'so am I. Something else to be suspicious about.'

'So there's a fearful bloodsucker on the loose,' said Catriona. 'Any more corpses?'

Charles shook his head.

'She couldn't have been destroyed in her cell? Turned to dust and swept away? Sunlight directed in by mirrors?'

Charles was momentarily concerned, surprisingly bereft. Not just at the notion Geneviève might be truly dead, but that he hadn't considered it.

'Disappearing acts are in the Great Edmondo's line,' said Edwin. 'We've a box at the Astoria for tomorrow night. Unless you want to call us off.'

Charles considered. 'No. Stay on it. An agent provocateur sending us on a false trail would try to be as unsuspicious as possible. Disappearing is the *most* suspicious thing Geneviève could do.'

'Unless she wants to avoid further quizzing,' put in Catriona. 'Now she's seen you in the flesh, she might doubt her ability to fool you for long.'

'Six of one,' said Edwin, 'half a dozen of the other. An infinity of mirrors.'

'Indeed, Edwin,' said Charles. 'Nothing is clear. Except that Colonel Zenf has been busy. He's in Brussels. He could be in London within hours. He's a great believer in air travel. A few of his recent endeavours could be construed as warnings aimed in our direction.'

'Is it true Karolyi's off his oats?'

Charles admitted this was so. Edwin swore.

'Good man, Karolyi. Cat and I wouldn't have got out of that business at the Café Mozart without him.'

'You've heard about the ambulatory waxworks?' said Catriona.

'Bill Owen had it before anyone else. Not that he saw where it was going. The Yard's Department of Queer Complaints are on it. They've issued descriptions of murderers thought long-hanged, and are quietly hauling them in. The cells in Holborn Central are full of broken mannequins. Sir Percival Glyde was found in Seven Dials this morning, importuning a "soiled dove" with a bottle of laudanum.'

'I should think soiled doves have changed since Sir Percy's day,' said Catriona.

'Indeed. Jenny Maple, a person well known to the police, kneed the wicked Baronet in the, ah, middle-parts, dashed his own medicine into his glass eyes and made off with his topcoat. Sadly for her, Tussaud's exhibits rarely carry cash.'

'According to Witch, other omens are indicative of a storm in the offing,' said Edwin. 'If it's any help, Margery Device thinks one of her fellows is a Rat.'

'She makes convincing cases for all of them,' added Catriona.

'Lord forbid,' said Charles.

Edwin shook his head, reassuringly. 'If things were that bad, we'd be knee-deep in burning filth already. We must have weight of numbers on our side or the Great Enchanter wouldn't have to be so infernally *sneaky*. It's got to be just one King Rat.'

Charles agreed with the Most Valued Member. Edwin's wartime background was Intelligence: He was used to thinking deviously and expecting everyone else to do likewise. Young Winthrop might well be better suited to the coming war than Charles was—though he needed Catriona, as a moral tether. Deviousness was all very well, but they all needed to be reminded that they served a just cause. Men of Edwin's generation could not believe in Crown and Country as Charles and his contemporaries had done, but women like Catriona had found other, stronger values—they would not let an injustice persist. Any injustice. He hoped Edwin would always have Catriona, as a conscience, a partner, a guide. The Club needed them both.

'One thing might be to our advantage,' Charles told them. 'This is a horribly important business. The people we're dealing with look down on us from a great height. And, in our own secret world, we're not inconsiderable.'

'We're tip-toeing around giants' feet,' observed Catriona. 'Trying to stay out from under their boot-soles.'

'Our King Rat, whichever of the Ravens he might be, is the Great Enchanter's foremost Asset. His most prized piece. Not an informant or a minion, but a near-equal. And steeped in treachery, or he wouldn't be a Rat. So Zenf can't fully trust him. The Colonel will need, especially when the situation is developing fast, to look into his Asset's ratty eyes. They have to meet.'

'You mean we should put a shadow on Zenf?'

'As you know, Edwin, that's no easy proposition. No, I mean you should *look out* for the Colonel. He displaces more water than a rabble of wax horrors. He's coming to London. For him, this is a long-nurtured scheme, about to pay off. He hopes to exceed the achievements of all the Great Enchanters before him. He knows about Isidore Persano and the Worm War. He will be mindful. Like all commanders, he will have a sense of his position, and how suddenly it can change. Anyone who can be a Raven and a Rat at the same time could contest the title of Great Enchanter.'

'You think they'll do for each other? That'd be a happy outcome.'

Charles sighed. 'Too much to ask for, Edwin. But there's no reason we can't sow dissent in their ranks, let suspicions fester. They do it to us all the time.'

'What about your vampire?' asked Catriona.

'Until firmly established otherwise, Geneviève is in our camp. She is an Asset. One of Mycroft's. I don't worry about her.'

'If you say so, chief.'

'Yes, Edwin, I do.'

Charles saw that Edwin was not convinced. Catriona was, though. Good. That balance made sense.

Where was Geneviève now? A long way from Egdon Heath, certainly.

VIII: 'uniquely unhaunted'

The Great Edmondo's act featured mannequins dressed exactly like him—in tail-coats, top hats and red-lined capes. The magician kept disappearing into his posed crowd, and a different mannequin seemed to come to life for each trick. The figure the audience took for the magician turned to show a blank where its face should be, then an apparent puppet darted up to reveal animated, moustachioed, punchinello-nosed features.

Edwin and Catriona had a box at the Astoria. Most magic acts insisted the boxes not be sold for their performances, because side-on views give away secrets. Robert Stone made a point of letting the audience close, even encouraging some to wander backstage and in the wings. He could still achieve all his marvels without anyone seeing the trick.

Conjurer repeatedly proved that his puppets had no strings by whirling a scimitar where they should be. The wax chorus danced in lock-step, moving exactly like the murderers at Margery Device's party.

'So he can make mannequins do his bidding,' Catriona whispered. 'Either he's innocent of the attack on Witch or arrogant beyond belief.'

'Arrogance beyond belief rather comes with the profession. Perhaps someone else wants us to put "Conjurer" under the grill? Everyone in this game is a trickster.'

'I'm bored with magic, Ed,' Catriona explained. 'It makes my head ache.'

The mannequins came to pieces but kept dancing to Tartini's 'Devil's Trill'. Stone swung his blade through the gaps between shoulders and arms and necks and heads, demonstrating again that no strings were involved.

'It's magnets and mirrors,' said someone, loudly, from the stalls.

'No,' responded another voice, 'it's compressed air and trained midgets.'

'Mass mesmerism.'

'Witchcraft! Warlockery! Burn him!'

The hecklers stood up, each in their own follow-spot. They were all no-face puppets.

Edwin tensed, expecting another attack.

But it was part of the act. The Great Edmondo gestured with his wand, and the hecklers vanished. In each seat was a squirming animal—a rabbit, a pig, a dove and a kitten.

There was applause. Catriona joined in.

Conjurer took a bow, with a flourish of his enormous cape. The curtains closed, then opened again—each puppet was replaced by a live, fleshy chorus girl in spangly tights and tight blonde curls. They tap-danced to 'It's the Talk of the Town'.

Edwin looked at his program. The Great Edmondo was due back on in the second half. Before then there was a patter comedian, 'Mr Memory', a dog act and a woman who tore paper into amusing shapes.

'Let's take advantage of the invitation and venture backstage,' he suggested.

'What fun,' said Catriona, dryly. 'Perhaps this time we can get to the interview without witnessing an attempted assassination?'

Edwin stepped out of the box and led Catriona along the corridor. He tugged a Victorian sconce and a small door opened, affording access to a walkway above the stage. He made an 'after you' gesture, and she squeezed through, setting ropes and pulleys rattling.

'This is where the ghost of Harry "Brass" Button, tragic clown of the 1890s, is supposed to walk, telling his famous joke to anyone he comes across. They say his victims start laughing and can't stop. There's a madhouse ward full of cackling stage-hands.'

'I know the story,' said Catriona. 'I also know Harry Button was cast out of this place in 1905 by Sandersby Scott Dignam, dramatic critic and exorcist, waving bell, book and bad review. Among London's theatres and music halls, the Astoria is uniquely unhaunted.'

On the stage below, the comedian recited a lengthy verse about a family of Yorkshire holidaymakers unwisely attending a political rally in Berlin. Edwin feared 'Little Albert' would wind up eaten by Goering.

They crossed the walkway. Edwin showed his card to a stage-hand, who helped them into a large wicker basket which lowered on ropes. The Astoria wasn't one of the larger, more labyrinthine houses, but had been built with magic in mind. One of the dogs waiting in the wings yapped as they sank through the floor, putting the comic off his patter—but allowing him to get cheer with his catch-phrase 'shoot that blessed hound oop!'

Below stage were layers of dusty machinery. Stone's mannequins were bent and crammed into the works. They hadn't yet been collected. Eyeless heads seemed to turn to follow their progress.

'That's a trick,' said Catriona. 'He knows we're coming.'

Edwin hoped she was right.

At last, the basket touched ground. Edwin lifted Catriona up and out of the wicker. She took the opportunity to nip his ear.

'Remember, we're being watched,' he whispered.

'I'm putting any spies off their guard,' she replied.

He quieted her with a long kiss. Then clambered out of the basket.

They were in a below-stage cavern, stacked with rolled canvas backdrops and left-behind props. In one corner, a collection of crushed bird skeletons was jammed into a big bin. Casualties of magic.

Edwin pulled a door open, and found himself in a tuppenny harem: a corridor packed with squealing chorus girls in states of dishabille. Artistes strategically covered themselves as he and Catriona passed through.

Catriona, rather surprisingly, met someone else she was at school with.

'All the best husbands are going to chorus girls these days,' Catriona explained. 'Lucia's adopting a policy of "if you can't beat 'em, join 'em".'

'So, is she engaged to a viscount yet?'

'No, she's "walking out" with Mr Twisty, the Contortionist. He's fifth on the bill.'

'I don't want to think about that.'

'Me neither.'

Once out of the chorus quarters, they came to a door emblazoned with a large gold star. Inside the star was a sunny face.

'The Great Edmondo, I presume,' said Edwin, opening the door.

He felt a stickiness under his shoes, and instantly recognised the coppery smell of freshly spilled blood.

Catriona crammed behind him.

Robert Edmond Stone, the Great Edmondo, lay face-up on the floor, hissing through bared teeth, blood-soaked cloak spread around him. He pressed both hands to a gouting wound in his neck. A lithe blonde woman in a green dress knelt on his chest, her own hands trying to unpick his grip as if to unstopper the flow. Her lower face and chest dripped with gore.

The woman looked at Edwin and Catriona. She had sharp, pointed eye-teeth.

'You probably think this looks suspicious,' she said.

IX: 'people of his sort don't expire in accidents'
In the foyer of the Diogenes Club, attendants politely but firmly barred entrance to Franz Beckert, the German child-murderer. He was not a member, of course. The mannequins were still a nuisance. A rash of second-

storey burglaries in the manner of Charlie Peace was bothering residents of Fitzrovia. No waxwork had successfully recreated the more appalling crimes of their originals, but that could come.

Returning from an evening constitutional which had not settled his mind, Charles was handed a report by Huntstanton. He glanced over it as he climbed the stairs.

A two-seater plane had taken off from Belgium this afternoon, and crashed in the Kent countryside two hours ago. Pilot and passenger were killed instantly, burned beyond recognition. Documents on the passenger— a large body—identified him as Colonel Zenf.

In the Quiet Room, Charles found General Lord Hector Tarr in a huddle with Mr Hay of the Undertaking. Giles Gallant was by the tickertape machine, reading off news Charles had from his own sources.

'We had nothing to do with this,' Mr Hay told Charles. 'Mrs Elle was there, but as an observer.'

'Have you heard from her?' Charles asked.

The Undertaker gave nothing away.

'You won't. And you'll have another black topper to fill.'

'Now's the time to strike, Beauregard,' said Tarr. 'While they're in disarray. Why, without the Great Enchanter...'

'"They" are not without him, Tarr. Zenf isn't dead. People of his sort don't expire in accidents.'

'Good God,' said Gallant, threading the latest report through his fingers. 'The passenger... it's a woman.'

'My condolences,' Charles said to Mr Hay.

Charles sat down. His sanctum was now a War Room.

'Colonel Zenf is in the country,' he announced. 'As of now, we have no idea what he is up to. Mr Hay, do you consent to make Common Cause?'

The words echoed. Tarr bit his lip. Tape chattered through Gallant's fingers, unread.

Common Cause was seldom invoked, and more seldom made. The Diogenes Club and the Undertaking more often acted apart than in collaboration. Charles habitually kept a wary eye on the men with smoked glasses. In 1770, Nicholas Goodman, the Great Enchanter, contrived to become Mr Zed and twisted the Undertaking's purpose. He had fetched the heads of Molina and ffolliott from the Mausoleum, intent on carrying out their long-thwarted scheme. On that occasion, only blind chance—in the shape of Eithne Orfe, Goodman's dagger-wielding fiancée—saved the crowned heads of Europe, and several of them not for long. The taint had never been entirely expunged. There was a deal of the night about the Undertaking.

One of Mycroft's contingency plans was entitled 'In the Event of the Undertaking Assuming Control Over the Government of the Day'. Charles suspected the envelope contained a stratagem for completely dismantling the organisation and breaking any power they might have. More than once, he had been tempted to break the seal and weigh up the options—it was easier to deal with the likes of the Great Enchanter or the Order of Dagon or the Lord of Strange Deaths without having to watch one's back.

However, during the Worm War, an earlier Mr Hay had taken a Chair on the Ruling Cabal, and Charles had himself worn hat and goggles as the acting Mr Bee. Stranger alliances were made in those tense weeks.

'No,' said Mr Hay. 'Not yet.'

Charles nodded. 'An exchange of liaisons, at least?'

Mr Hay ruminated. 'That is acceptable.'

'Giles, would you accompany Mr Hay to Westminster?'

Gallant was surprised to be asked. He was Tarr's man. He would have expected Charles to put forward Huntstanton. Charles saw the adjutant rapidly considering the matter—was this a tactic to separate Tarr from his most loyal supporter, or could it be to the advantage of their faction to develop ties with the Undertaking? Wheels went round in his mind as visibly as the cogs inside the glass dome of the tickertape machine.

'I'm asking you because you're in the room, man,' Charles said, letting Gallant off the hook. 'And qualified. You were in signals. Your job will be to keep open lines of communication.'

Gallant looked to Tarr, who gave him a curt nod.

'Honoured to accept,' said the adjutant.

'Who do we get in exchange?' asked Tarr.

A thin smile spread across Mr Hay's face. He snapped gloved fingers, and a homunculus detached itself from the shadow under Charles's desk.

'How the devil did he get in?' blustered Tarr.

Mr Hay's thin smile stayed even, like a healed wound.

'This is Master Wuh.'

The shadow was a child, dressed in a miniature version of Undertakers' habit: top hat, gloves, dark glasses, mourning clothes, patent-leather shoes. His face was black—not like an African but a sweep, covered with camouflage soot.

'Wuh?' said Tarr.

'It's W,' explained Charles.

Wuh grinned, showing even white teeth.

'That settled, I shall be on my way,' announced Mr Hay, standing up. 'Mr Gallant, if you will follow...'

The Undertaker led the adjutant out of the Quiet Room.

Tarr looked at Master Wuh.

'What shall we do with this little blighter?'

'Get him supper, I imagine,' said Charles, pressing the silent buzzer. 'Then turn our minds to the problem of Colonel Zenf.'

X: 'rather written in scarlet'

'"Suspicious" doesn't say the half of it, dear,' Catriona addressed the gore-spattered creature kneeling on top of the bleeding magician. 'Pardon the observation, but you take the concept of "red-handed" to a ludicrous extreme.'

Edwin knew better than to accept anything at face value.

'I know it seems rather written in scarlet,' said the vampire. Her esses susurrated through the blood bubbling in her mouth. She had a trace of accent. 'But if you'll lend a hand, I think we can stop your Conjurer from bleeding out.'

Stone bucked, as if going into seizure. His white-gloved hands flapped like landed fish. His eyes were open, but unseeing.

The blonde vampire nearly had his hands away from his neck.

'Geneviève Dieudonné, I presume,' observed Edwin.

'Call me Gené. Be careful about getting the red stuff on you. It never washes out. I ought to know.'

Edwin and Catriona knelt either side of Robert Stone, holding his arms.

'You might not have seen anything like this before,' said Geneviève. 'Please not to be alarmed. And not to make a fuss, *hein?*'

She lifted Stone's hands from his wound. The deep cut could have been done with a straight razor. Not teeth. Richly red blood welled.

'Ugh, nasty,' said Geneviève, bending over as if putting her mouth to a drinking fountain.

The vampire didn't bite or suckle. Instead, she stuck out her unusually long tongue and—with a single, cat-like slathering—licked the wound clean.

At her wet touch, Stone stopped kicking and swooned.

Geneviève wiped her mouth and swallowed a little, like a cook apologetically taking a lick of cake-mixture from a used spoon. She pulled a scarf—the first of an infinite string—from Conjurer's top-pocket and dabbed the slash in his throat, which glistened with her saliva. Edwin didn't think the procedure was recommended by any physician he knew. But, visibly, the wound knit.

'Think about it,' said Geneviève. 'You have to turn off the tap after you've had a drink. A peculiarity of vampire physiology is that our saliva glands secrete a natural coagulating agent. And a mild euphoric, too. A perk of being kissed by me.'

She used Stone's scarf to wipe herself off. As she fixed her face, her fang-teeth receded into gumsheaths and her smile closed.

Catriona nudged Edwin, jarring him out of astonishment.

'You know who I am,' said Geneviève. 'You must be friends of Charles Beauregard.'

'Edwin Winthrop,' he said, 'of the Diogenes Club. Most Valued Member.

And this is Miss Catriona Kaye.'

'The authoress? I enjoyed your monograph on Martin Hesselius.'

Catriona was taken aback. Pleasantly.

They stood. Stone seemed to be sleeping peacefully. Thanks to that mild euphoric, Edwin assumed. The dressing room was cramped for all of them at once. Behind Geneviève was a mirror, in which she cast a shadow rather than a reflection.

'If we're past introductions,' said Edwin, 'I'm obliged to ask if you have any idea how the Great Edmondo got his throat cut?'

'I bumped into a waxy-faced fellow with a razor,' said Geneviève. 'I thought London had seen the last of Sweeney Todd, but I'd swear it was him.'

'How do you come to be in the dressing rooms of the Astoria Theatre?' asked Catriona. 'Do you, perchance, have a trained bat act?'

'My standing orders are to make myself useful.'

'Standing orders?'

'Yes, Edwin. Standing orders. From the Ruling Cabal. Well, Mr Mycroft.'

'Weren't you supposed to be in the Egdon Heath Collection?'

Geneviève shrugged. 'I'd been useful there. As much as I could. Now, I'm better off out of the Mausoleum. You know what it's like being a police informant in gaol—locked up with the felons you've squealed on. Several "items" wouldn't be above bidding for the favour of the Great Enchanter by slipping a sharpened wooden spoon through my ribs. They all think Zenf will set them free to ravage and revenge, you know. Don't worry, the means by which I got out aren't available to the rest of the inmates. They're all locked up safe and snug.'

Catriona made sceptical gestures. Edwin understood her caution, but for the moment this undead woman was an Asset.

'The Old Man would like to hear from you,' he said.

'The Old Man? Charles? He's not old. I know old, and he's not, really.'

Edwin fully realised—a few minutes into their acquaintance—the implications of Geneviève being what she was.

Catriona bent over again to look at the sleeping magician. He was breathing steadily.

'Here's a funny thing,' said Catriona, unpeeling false moustaches. They brought away a bulb of nose and stretched a patch of skin. 'There's more.'

She detached a wig from the prone man's head, disclosing a mostly-bald skull.

'So, Conjurer is vain?'

'Ed, this isn't Conjurer. This is Sorcerer.'

She rubbed more make-up from the face. It was Marcus Rennes.

'Another Raven?' inquired Geneviève.

'The wrong Raven,' Edwin explained. 'Our Conjurer has made a switch.'

'It *is* part of his act,' said Catriona.

'Are you sure it was Sweeney Todd you bumped into?'

Geneviève's brow furrowed. 'His face was wax, but now I think of it he was *warm*—you know, a live person.'

Catriona exaggeratedly mouthed 'not like her' and pointed at the back of Geneviève's head.

'I might not have a proper reflection,' said Geneviève. 'But you do, Miss Kaye.'

A mirror was above the dressing room door. A smudgy column of vaguely woman-shaped smoke stood between Edwin and Catriona and the magician. Edwin would never get used to that.

'Also, it's not true. I'm undying, not undead. Death drives *nosferatu* cuckoo, by the way. It accounts for the stories you hear. Millie Karnstein, dear little thing but a total imbecile. Lord Ruthven, complete ego-maniac. Count Dracula...'

'Sorry if I was rude,' Catriona interrupted. Geneviève could be as chatty as Margery Device. 'It's been a trying few days.'

'No need to apologise. I'm used to it. After you've had six or seven mobs come for you with burning torches, you can put up with a lot.'

Catriona redirected her attention to the sleeping man. 'If Sorcerer is in Conjurer's place, where's Conjurer got to?'

'Do you think Robbie Stone is twitching like a King Rat?' Edwin asked.

Catriona shrugged. 'We've not met all the players yet.'

'I don't think Wizard would deign to come out of his tower and run about with a razor,' said Edwin. 'He'd have familiars to do that sort of thing.'

'Nothing is beneath anyone in this game, Ed.'

Catriona slapped Rennes a little, but he only snorted and turned over.

'He'll be asleep a while longer,' said Geneviève. 'Sorry.'

XI: 'some difficulty between us'

At midnight, Charles's presence was requested at Margery Device's *après-soirée*. In time of open war, he might have tendered his excuses—but no lesser crisis relieved him of the obligation.

The venue was Mekka, a vile drinking hole popular with criminals and off-duty policemen. Like other pubs which catered to trades which kept unconventional hours, it was exempt from licensing laws. Behind a deceptively small, honestly shabby frontage on the Embankment, Mekka was cavernously huge. A perpetual throng of boozers packed into a warren of underground taprooms which had once been smugglers' store-houses and still afforded secret access to the Thames through trap-doors and unofficial jetties.

The occasion was the Pick-Pockets' Ball, one of Margery's long-established annual events.

From the Bentley, Charles saw shifty characters crowded out onto the pavement. A sad-faced fellow had false arms in his sleeves, and a huge fake paunch. Light fingers could stretch from his waistcoat pockets and filch watches and coins from anyone he got close to.

'This lot'd have the gold out of your teeth and the pennies off your eyes,' said Huntstanton.

Charles emptied his pockets of anything valuable, dangerous or pertinent, then distributed worthless items about his person—gift-wrapped stones, an old wallet stuffed with strips of newspaper, a broken tin watch. A traditional courtesy at the Pick-Pockets' Ball.

He got out of the Bentley, cautiously made his way through the crowd, and eased into Mekka, keeping track of a blur at the corner of his eye. Master Wuh was his shadow. That lad had little to fear from pick-pockets. He could amuse himself by redistributing stolen items around the company, even returning them to their original owners.

Inside, the air was thick with smoke, steam and chatter, and the room filled with warm bodies. Charles negotiated a way towards the bar. Someone began to assault an upright piano. Searchlights converged on a black curtain, which whipped aside to disclose Margery Device dressed as a comedy burglar—striped jersey, battered cap, domino mask, black tights, handbag marked 'swag'.

'And the shark has pretty teeth, dear,' she sang in a thirty-cigarettes-a-day-washed-down-by-six-pints-of-gin voice, 'and he keeps them in his face... *und Macheath, der hat ein Messer*, hidden in another place...'

Margery drifted from table to table, warbling 'Mack the Knife' in a melange of cockney English and gutter German, improvising verses about notable crooks in the room. At every table, someone reached into her swag-bag and ostentatiously stole something which bit their fingers—a snapping mouse-trap, a struggling shrew, a small fizzing firework. Outrageous (but all too true) accusations raised laughter from those exposed. Betrayed confederates, unpaid mothers of wronged girls and inspectors cut out of profits by sergeants found the verses less amusing.

By dawn, everyone would know everyone else's sins—and it ought to even out. Every year, one or two knived bodies floated down-river after the Ball. As with dropped glasses or stained carpets at other parties, a certain amount of breakage was expected.

Charles felt fingers in his pockets. He slapped them away with good humour.

'H'awfully sorry, guv'nor,' said a bright-eyed, loose-limbed fellow with an enormous beaky nose. 'Force of 'abit. Didn't see it was you, sir.'

'That's quite all right, Nosey. How's your mother?'

Alfred 'Nosey' Parker looked stricken, and held a hand to his chest. 'A martyr to 'er feet, Mr Beauregard.'

'Aren't we all?'

'True, true. As Mum h'always says, "h'it comes to us h'all in the h'end". Pardon me a mo, guv'nor... H'I've just seen a cove 'oo owes me h'eight quid.'

Nosey slid away, intent on surreptitiously reclaiming the debt.

Margery concluded her turn, to vigorous applause. Post-song fights broke out and had to be stifled.

For a moment, Charles feared he would have to talk with that dreadful bore Colonel Sebastian Moran—how had he avoided the gallows all these years?—but Margery took his arm and whisked him past the gasping old reprobate.

'There's someone you should meet,' she shouted over the hubbub.

She steered him into a less-crowded backroom patronised by a better class of criminal. Or, at least, a better-*dressed* class of criminal. A duchess might look down on a dishwasher, but such mild snobbery paled beside a bogus clergyman or a Mayfair bag-snatcher turning up their noses at a safe-cracker or a strong-arm johnnie. Some villains needed to imitate perfectly their prey, assuming haughty mien, conservative attitudes and impeccable couture. When not trying to get widows to invest in non-existent diamond mines, these people had one topic of conversation—the shocking state of crime today, especially when it came to sturdy beggars and rabblesome dirty-faced urchins.

The hostess indicated a short, very fat man whose back was turned. He wore a tight coat with a forked tail and had too much pomade on thick, black, wavy hair. He waved stubby beringed fingers as he talked with Ivy Petersen, a hideously respectable old strumpet. On a famous night in 1887, she had reputedly serviced the entire Preston North End team to commemorate their record-setting 26–nil cup tie victory over Hyde United.

Margery tapped the fat man on the shoulder.

He turned, flashing a smile beneath a waxed moustache. A Napoleonic kiss-curl was slicked to his forehead. Were it not for his adder's eyes, he might have been cherubic.

'Charles Beauregard, this is Colonel Zenf.'

The Austro-Hungarian clicked his heels, striking sparks, and extended his hand.

Charles took the offered paw and shook.

Zenf's hand was soft and moist. Charles took care not to scratch himself on any of the rings.

'My good fellow,' said Zenf, who had a high-pitched voice, 'I am much pleased to make your acquaintance. We have many... associations... in common.'

Charles let Zenf's hand go. 'I did not think to find you here,' he said, weakly.

'You may think to find *everyone* here,' said Margery.

'So it seems,' said Charles.

'One or two matters intrigue me, Beauregard,' said Colonel Zenf, pin-points of fire in his eyes. 'I should like soon to have a long, private conversation with you.'

'I too would appreciate such an occasion,' Charles responded.

'Perhaps I might call on you at your Club?'

The mild suggestion set Charles's heart pounding.

'I'm not often there at present. Where are you staying in London?'

Zenf's moustache-points quivered. 'I am tending to be in different places at different times.'

Charles held Zenf's reptile gaze. 'It seems some difficulty is between us,' he said, 'in ordering our diaries.'

'Indeed,' said Zenf. 'This is... a pity.'

Margery's eyes flicked between them. She knew what was going on under the surface of chat. Surely, if she were a Queen Rat, Zenf would not be on her guest list? Unless she had a surfeit of bare-faced cheek, which—as it happens—she certainly did. Besides, this was a ball for criminals: The company would not be complete without the Great Enchanter.

Charles looked at Zenf, who seemed completely relaxed. The Colonel reached into an inside pocket and took out a cigarette case. A tiny razor-edge stuck out of the catch, smeared with blood.

'Some larcenous soul seems to have attempted to steal this keepsake,' said Zenf, carefully working a stud which made the blade recede. 'I trust he takes his regular dose of anti-venom.'

An elderly man who represented himself as the Bishop of Matabeleland fell as if his knees had been chopped out, face black and swollen, foam pouring over his chin. A young, dark-haired, violet-eyed woman dressed as a governess tried to loosen his dog-collar. She was swatted away with a rattle of unepiscopal oaths. In this company, no one liked having their clothes touched.

'A mild strain,' purred Zenf. 'Scarcely fatal.'

The bogus bishop kicked, gaiters scrabbling on the floorboards, and his entire body jack-knifed. Then he settled down and commenced snoring. The woman who had come to his aid carefully sorted through his inside pockets, making a collection. She found a gold ring, which she respectfully returned to Colonel Zenf, who screwed it onto his left little finger.

'My thanks to you, Vivian,' he said. 'I wondered where this had strayed.'

Zenf opened his cigarette case and offered it to Charles.

The cigarettes were custom-made, with symbols embossed on the paper. Charles politely declined. Burning them might have more unpleasant after-effects than smoker's cough.

Zenf selected a cigarette. Vivian, the sham governess, produced someone else's lighter and flicked a flame. Zenf lit his smoke, and exhaled plumes through his nostrils.

'Beauregard, you are familiar with the practice of "casting the runes"?'

'I read Karswell's obituaries.'

'Ah yes, Julian,' said Zenf, dreamily. 'He was... unwise.'

Zenf opened the back of his cigarette case. He peeled out some small strips of paper, neatly printed with symbols. Charles recognised one or two runes—fire and frost. Catriona Kaye, who had made a study of the Karswell case, would have known all of them.

'I took the precaution of preparing these earlier. Most potent, you understand. To each rune is bound a... how does your poet Mr Coleridge have it, "frightful fiend". By sunrise, anyone in possession of any one of these slips of paper will suffer unpleasant consequences. Would you care to take them from me?'

'Thank you, no.'

Zenf giggled. He rolled and twisted the papers into individual swirls, which he slipped into his various pockets.

'Now, as possessor of these highly dangerous shreds, I am fated to be torn apart at dawn. That would be a happy outcome for some, would it not?'

Charles regretted that he had left his sword-stick in the Bentley. He could save a lot of bother with one swift heart-thrust.

Perhaps instinctively, people in the room backed away from the Colonel, making space around him.

'I trust merciful providence to ensure my safety,' he announced. 'If even one of these charms remains upon my person a few hours from now, my number is up. Our business shall be at an end.'

Blithely, he turned and waddled out of the room, bumping into as many people as possible.

Charles opened his mouth to warn the guests, but Vivian chose the moment to faint in his arms. She locked wrists behind his neck and dragged him to the floor. His trick knee, an old wound, went out. Hot pain shot through his nerves. He bit down on an unmanly scream.

When he had disentangled himself, with the help of several guests who took the opportunity to purloin mock valuables, Zenf was out of the room. So was Vivian. Charles would remember her. Dark, pale, pretty, dangerous.

Margery helped him up. He dragged her to the door. Zenf was gone. The path he had made through the throng was closing. It was important to learn who had jostled the Colonel on his way out. Master Wuh, up on a bar with an empty glass, wiped off a milk moustache and raised both hands. Seven fingers.

Charles's head throbbed.

'What did you think of the Great Enchanter?' asked the hostess. 'Nasty little person, but he didn't seem much of a threat.'

'He's killed seven people while leaving this party, Margery.'

The hostess looked about, puzzled. The Bishop of Matabeleland snoozed peacefully, face almost normal. No one else seemed dead.

'He put runes in his pockets,' Charles explained. 'Then just walked through the crowd. At dawn, seven of these dips will get their collars felt... and not by the police.'

'Scarcely the behaviour of a gracious guest,' said Margery. 'Still, he *is* foreign.'

Charles made fists. Zenf had put him in a thorny position. He *could* go round the party, affronting the etiquette of the occasion by grilling pick-pockets about their hauls. If, by some miracle of explanation, he convinced the nimble-fingered victims of their peril, they'd likely spend the hours till dawn pressing paper dooms on other unsuspecting folks. If he browbeat the marks into parting with their runes, he would call sevenfold doom down on himself

Margery wasn't happy, either. This was too much breakage.

X: 'don't call me "doc"'

Edwin slung Marcus Rennes over his shoulder and carried him out of the Astoria. Witnesses would take him for drunk and incapable.

Catriona and Geneviève giggled conspiratorially, like schoolgirls. Had Catriona fallen victim to the vampire power of fascination? More likely, she'd taken an instant liking to the centuries-old girl. In theory, they were hailing a taxi. Several cruised by, with their lights on. One even stopped, but Geneviève threw it back into the stream like a too-small fish.

Sorcerer's deadweight was getting to be a strain.

This business was turning into a run-around. Typical 'intelligence' work—leaping through flaming hoops, tripping over gnarly branches in thick forest, too busy with the little problems to get perspective. Edwin had a nasty feeling they were all part of someone else's game, or magic trick.

Finally, an acceptable cab was secured. The driver was slightly put off by Rennes, but Catriona and Geneviève charmed him into taking the fare. Edwin gave an address in Harley Street.

'I should hardly be the one to say this,' ventured Geneviève, 'but aren't we outside regular surgery hours?'

'Dr Chambers doesn't have a regular practice,' said Edwin.

'Not *the* Dr Chambers?'

'Actually, no,' said Catriona. 'That's *Jonathan* Chambers. Dr Shade keeps night-hours, but isn't often in his office. This is his sister, Dr *Jennifer* Chambers. She's more approachable. Slightly.'

It wasn't a long ride.

Catriona paid the cabbie, while Geneviève helped Edwin with Rennes. She hefted him as if he were a papier-mâché dummy. Of course, she was stronger than she looked. Which she might have mentioned earlier—though showing off by carrying Sorcerer out of the theatre like a six-foot-six fireman would have attracted unwelcome attention.

Catriona nipped round them and pressed the door-bell.

The ring was quickly answered by a wide young man in a nurse's tunic.

'Hullo, Winthrop,' he said. 'Who's this?'

Edwin angled Rennes's face into the light, tipping up his chin to show the scarf knotted around Sorcerer's cut throat as a makeshift bandage.

Simon Pure, Dr Chambers's nurse, whistled through his teeth. 'Better come in, old son. I say, who are these pretty fillies?'

'Down, boy,' said a woman from inside the hallway. 'Miss Kaye, you know. Our other guest must be Mademoiselle Dieudonné...'

Jennifer Chambers was a tiny, fine-boned, fiftyish woman with short black hair, thick brows, sky-blue eyes and purple lips. The hem of her pristine white coat touched the floor. A stethoscope hung around her neck, business end tucked into her top pocket. Her speciality was injuries folks would be unwise to take to their general practitioner—either because of their unique nature or the unusual circumstances under which they were sustained. Her patients were drawn exclusively from the night-world which her family had been involved in for generations. Her practice extended to the Diogenes Club, the Undertaking, the Splendid Six (though not lately), most of the London-based lone wolves, and even factions on the Other Side, including the Seven Dials Sewing Circle, the New Red-Headed League and the Black Quorum.

Edwin and Geneviève heaved Sorcerer over the threshold. Dr Chambers directed them to dump Rennes on a gurney which Simon Pure wheeled into a large, well-appointed surgery. Two other patients were in the room: a shapeless lump on a cot, with a sheet over his or her face, and a little girl with an arm (too big for her body and covered in thick reddish fur) in a sling.

Dr Chambers angled a light onto Marcus Rennes's throat. She snapped on surgical gloves and delicately prodded his healing wound.

'Not a vampire bite,' she said. 'Which you know. Nice work, mademoiselle. Without your clever tongue, this man would be dead.'

Simon Pure stood by the gurney.

'Get some strong beef tea brewed,' Dr Chambers ordered, 'and pour it into him when he wakes. Take good care of him. He's one of the Ravens. If he pops, the city wobbles.'

'No worries, doc.'

'And don't call me "doc".'

Simon Pure grinned.

'You three,' said Dr Chambers, 'I want a briefing. My brother was in earlier, dropping off the Cunning Little Vixen.'

The girl with the peculiar arm looked glum.

'He was talking up a streak. Half hell is breaking loose in the city and

I'm the one who has to get out the sticking plasters. It wouldn't kill Charles Beauregard to give me an idea what to expect.'

Edwin wondered how much he was allowed to tell Jennifer Chambers. She was respected within the community of the night, but anything she knew might get passed to her brother. If Dr Shade thought one of the Ravens a Rat, his usual course of action would be to kill all four and apologise to the three innocents at the funerals. Just now, Edwin saw the appeal of such Alexandrine knot-cutting tactics, and if anyone in town was up to facing the Great Enchanter...

A telephone jangled, saving Edwin from a dilemma.

'Jenny Chambers here.' The other party spoke for a few moments. 'Charles, I thought I might hear from you,' she continued. 'Some of your strays are in my surgery... no, none of *them* is a patient. They brought in a Raven... the Astronomical one. You want me where...? Good grief, you *are* calling out the reserves... Yes, I know, I'm fed up with hearing it. "Don't bring Johnny". The way everyone carries on, you'd think he batted for the Other Side...'

Dr Chambers listened for a full minute, concentrating. Her brows touched over the bridge of her nose. She jotted notes on a pad, muttering 'anti-venom... tana leaves... penicillin'. Then she handed the receiver to Edwin.

'Your master's voice,' she announced.

'Charles?'

'Edwin. Who hurt Sorcerer?'

'Conjurer, we think. He's looking like the Rat. Your lady leech has showed up.'

'Geneviève? Good. Keep her close.'

'No problems there. She could be another of Catriona's long-lost chums. One Cat *doesn't* want to see hanged.'

'I need Jenny here. Mekka, on the Embankment. Catriona and Geneviève too. And more Ravens.'

'Sorcerer's on the sick list.'

'I've got Witch. If Conjurer's loose, that leaves Wizard. Get to the Tower and prepare him.'

'For what?'

'A scrap at dawn, probably. We're bringing him some difficult customers.'

'The Tower of London. You'll be there at sunrise, with company. Got it.'

'Edwin, watch out for Zenf. He's in a mischief-making mood. I wouldn't put it past him to show up and watch how his little joke plays out.'

'Joke?'

'You'll find out. Put Cat... no, *Geneviève*, on...'

Charles gave the telephone to the vampire.

''*Allo*,' she said, kittenish. 'Don't be angry with me.'

Geneviève turned and talked low into the phone, so Edwin couldn't hear.

Dr Chambers had put a bulky tartan car-coat over her whites, with a matching tam o'shanter. She packed a medical bag, while issuing instructions to the nurse about the three patients.

'There are silver bullets in the revolver if Johnny's pet gets frisky,' she told the nurse. Simon Pure pulled a face at the Cunning Little Vixen, who made a rude gesture with two stubby, hairy, clawed fingers.

Edwin told Catriona she was going to Mekka.

'It's the Pick-Pockets' Ball tonight, isn't it?' she said, lightly. 'That's so much tamer than it used to be. In 1915, I dressed as a boy and sneaked in, and...'

'It might not be tame this year, Cat. Zenf showed up.'

Catriona was serious and paid attention. Edwin tapped two fingers against his wristwatch and pointed them at Geneviève.

'Watch... her,' Catriona mouthed, then nodded.

Dr Chambers was ready to set out. Geneviève was off the phone.

'Charles has sent a car for us,' she announced.

'What about me?' Edwin asked.

Dr Chambers took a keyring out of her pocket, and detached a key.

'One of my brother's toys,' she said, handing it over. 'It'll get you to the Tower. If you crash it, I advise you to die instantly. There'd be no way to protect you from the wrath of Johnny.'

Edwin hoped it wasn't an autogyro.

'When's dawn?' Edwin asked.

'A little more than an hour and a half,' said Dr Chambers. 'You better get a move on. You know where the garage is. You can't miss the Night Flier.'

Edwin kissed Catriona, waved to the others, and left.

XI: 'light-fingered idiots'

Charles consulted his real watch again. In the subjective minute or so since he last looked, half an hour had sped by. Towards dawn. He didn't like the oranginess of the lamp-light along the Embankment. It wavered, as if fog were rising from the river.

Runes summoned entities who killed the unfortunate possessors of the fateful scraps of paper. Though there was debate as to what exactly the entities were, it made sense to call them demons. Seven would converge here in just over an hour. They might come out of the sky, from under the water, detach from the shadows, simply manifest...

Margery Device had winnowed the seven fated pick-pockets from her other guests, drawing them onto the street with a promise of something special. She kept the crooks entertained with rapid-fire, unverifiable gossip about famous crime-fighters.

'Sir Dennis Nayland-Smith can't keep his hands off little yellow bottoms,' she said. 'It's the real reason why he's always haring off to the Far East. Jane Marple is the most dreadful lush. Almost every murderer she exposes gets off because evidence gets lost among all the gin-bottles when she turns up blotto at the Old Bailey...'

The only dip Charles recognised was Nosey Parker, of the long-suffering mother and the h'added h'aitches. There were five men and two women. One of the men was either a police constable or wore the uniform as a disguise. One of the women looked like a bare-knuckles boxer in petticoats. The rest were middling-to-anonymous, ideally suited to their profession.

While Charles was concentrating on this, what was Zenf up to?

The Bentley reappeared and parked by Mekka. Out came three women: Jenny Chambers, Catriona, Geneviève. The vampire looked, surprisingly, as if she were enjoying herself.

Master Wuh crossed himself. Seeing the miniature Undertaker, Geneviève did a double-take.

'He's a liaison,' Charles explained.

'Pleased to meet him,' said Geneviève. 'Should he be up this late?'

A long van parked at the kerb behind the Bentley, and a top-hatted, goggled figure got out. Mr Esse, the collector. The Black Mariah could—under certain circumstances—be used as a hearse. Before calling Jenny, Charles had alerted the Undertaking. He hadn't known Geneviève would be invited to the party and run into her former gaolers.

Geneviève ignored Mr Esse and took Charles's arm, soliciting his protection. He patted her chilly fingers.

'Is that them?' asked Catriona, indicating Margery's audience. They were intent on the inside details of a titled-but-stony-broke amateur sleuth's racket—charging guilty parties fat fees to be exonerated, and innocent parties even fatter ones not to be perfectly framed.

Charles nodded.

'They don't look doomed,' Catriona observed. 'Well, no more than anyone else.'

'Undooming them isn't difficult,' he said. 'You just have to ask them to surrender the runes. Of course, whoever's holding the parcel when the music stops gets torn to the proverbial shreds.'

'Light-fingered idiots,' said Geneviève. 'No one asked them to be thieves. Why would anyone steal useless pieces of paper?'

'Professional pride, Geneviève. Traditional behaviour at the Pick-Pockets' Ball. They don't even expect valuables, just the challenge. These people have been stealing from each other all night. Some runes changed pockets several times before we extracted the current holders...'

Master Wuh tugged his sleeve, and pointed.

'Ah,' said Charles, 'even within the group, the blessed chits are in circulation.'

Master Wuh made finger gestures. Nosey had two runes now, the constable three. The other rune-holders were an effete-seeming man about town and a soberly-dressed woman with a Temperance sash and pince-nez.

'That's progress,' he said. 'Three are out of the game.'

He signalled to Margery like a racetrack tout—three fingers, individual jabs at the currently safe parties, a dismissive wave. Margery drew the four remaining pick-pockets closer, and said something which sent the others packing without offending them. As the city's presiding hostess, she was a seventh-degree master of diplomacy.

As she left, the big woman took something from the constable's pocket. Charles saw the situation getting out of hand again—but the prize was not a rune, just the constable's whistle. The anti-drink campaigner clucked near the man about town, and got his rune from him. Margery saw at once, and asked him 'be a dear' and fetch her a gin fizz.

'Now prying ears have departed,' Margery stage-whispered, 'I can reveal all. It was Sexton Blake who pushed Sherlock Holmes off the waterfall that time... being the *second*-cleverest detective in Baker Street drove him round the bend.'

'No more games,' said Charles. 'I want these three isolated, as if they were carrying a disease. We can't take chances on losing track of the runes.'

He strolled over to the little group. Geneviève sauntered with him, taking his arm. He still wanted to have a conversation with her about her disappearance from the Mausoleum.

He handed his card to the policeman, eliciting a salute.

'Constable,' he said, 'arrest these two criminals.'

'Well, H'I never...' exclaimed Nosey.

'I'll have you know I'm a respectable woman,' said the temperance lady.

The constable was taken aback. Making an arrest at the Pick-Pockets' Ball would violate agreements and truces dating back to Magna Carta. But the card of the Diogenes Club was universally recognised.

Red was in the sky, not acting like pre-dawn light. A scarlet question-mark was forming, somewhere over the river. Tower Reach.

Mr Esse and Huntstanton had the rear doors of the Black Mariah open.

'If you'll get in, Nosey,' said Charles. 'I'll explain.'

'Whatever you say, Mr Beauregard,' said Nosey, complying at once. He had good cause to trust the Diogenes Club.

'Miss...?'

'Leticia Hesketh-Stafford,' said the eminently respectable woman, bristling with practiced indignation.

'In the van, Letty,' insisted the policeman.

'I shall be writing to my Member of Parliament,' she said, clambering in beside Nosey—then cringing in horror and withdrawing her skirts, expertly sorting through several hidden pockets. If she understood what her swag meant, she wouldn't be so keen to hang onto it.

'It would be best if Constable Ottermole went with you,' said Margery.

The policeman looked suspicious but was keen not to defy authority.

'Yes,' said Charles, 'I agree. Constable, what's the time?'

Ottermole searched through his pockets and came up with three watches, all giving slightly different times.

'That's mine,' said Huntstanton, claiming one timepiece.

'Ah... evidence,' said the policeman, weakly. 'My sergeant is very particular about hanging on to evidence.'

Huntstanton gave Ottermole a shove. Mr Esse locked the doors behind the three rune-bearing miscreants.

'That won't protect them,' said Margery, meaning the van.

'Or keep them in,' commented Catriona. 'Look, Nosey's jiggling the lock already.'

'This isn't an ordinary Black Mariah,' said Mr Esse. 'The lock is trickier than usual.'

Sparks came out between the doors. Bad language was heard.

Some sober pick-pockets formed a deputation to protest. Margery had to soothe them.

'This isn't a police van,' she said. 'It's an ambulance. Nosey, Letty and P.C. Ottermole have been overcome by a mystery ailment. This woman, as you can see, is a doctor.'

Jenny undid her muffler to show her stethoscope.

'Never seen no black ambulance afore,' said a pick-pocket.

'Now you have,' cooed Margery.

Mr Esse stood beside Jenny, cracking black-gloved knuckles. His presence intimidated the deputation, who decided they'd be better employed somewhere else.

'Is that what I'm here for?' asked Jenny, impatient. 'A cover story? No one, so far as I can see, needs a doctor...'

'Yet,' said Charles.

Geneviève pointed at the sky. The question mark was a spiral now.

'Margery, I am sure you can be counted on to bring the ball to a successful conclusion with no one any the wiser. We shall leave now.'

Catriona, Geneviève and Jenny got into the Bentley. Huntstanton and Mr Esse took to their driving seats.

Margery bade Charles good night.

'Not much night left,' he said, looking at his watch again.

Master Wuh sat up front, next to Huntstanton.

Charles got into the back of the Bentley. The ladies made room for him. He pulled the speaking tube and gave an order.

'To the Tower.'

XII: 'Guinness is Good for You!'

The Night Flier turned out to be a Norton motorcycle, an all-black, 600cc, four-gear exemplar of British precision engineering, custom-built for Dr Shade. A prow-like steel cowl welded to the front column would ram through anything less sturdy than a brick wall and usefully turn aside projectiles or pedestrians. Extra tanks under the pillion, containing a noxious mix of petrol and brimstone, fed either the CamShaft One engine or a flexible nozzle fitted above the fishtail exhaust. An oily machine-gun, like a fighter plane's, was built into the prow.

Edwin would have to be careful which switches to throw.

It was a kick-start model. The key Dr Chambers had given him unlocked an ingenious hobbling device he assumed was to prevent unauthorised persons driving the beast away. What a wary, suspicious soul Dr Shade must be! Edwin couldn't imagine thievery of such hard-to-fence vehicles would ever become an epidemic problem. If such conditions ever came to pass, this odd contraption—three iron bars and a padlock, which disabled the engine and locked the wheels—might find a market.

He straddled the bike and stamped down on the starter-pedal. The engine growled instantly to life. He bent low and aimed the throbbing bike at the slope which led up from the underground garage to the street. The machine seemed to know what was required and tore off, prompting Edwin to hang on tight. The Night Flier crested the slope and leaped across three feet of pavement, landing smoothly on the road. He leant into a sharp turn, and drove down Harley Street, startling cats and a courting couple.

The Norton handled better than a Sopwith Camel.

Apart from lorries carrying the early editions and a horse-drawn milk-cart in Cavendish Square, there wasn't much other traffic about. Edwin sped across Oxford Circus, down Regent Street, into Piccadilly Circus.

A few all-night waifs and strays huddled around Eros, in the dazzle of eternal neon. Two or three fellows in bedraggled evening clothes stretched on the pavement, at the frazzled end of a rag which must have begun with a tipple at the Drones and ended with forced ejection from the Criterion Bar. Their natural predators would be at the Pick-Pockets' Ball—so this was the safest night of the year to lie drunk in the centre of town, with a note-case full of fivers, pockets overflowing with small change and grandfather's gold watch dangling on a chain. It had rained earlier. Slick, wet tarmac glittered with reflected highlights from advertisements for Bovril, Sandeman's Port, Schweppes, Gordon's London Gin, Army Club cigarettes and C.B. Cochrane's annual review. By the Guinness Clock—*Guinness is Good for You!*—it was nearly four o'clock.

He ought to be at the Tower before dawn.

In Haymarket, something like a scarecrow clung three quarters of the way up a lamp-post. It turned to stare as the Night Flier passed. The roughly human figure was wrapped in an oversized ulster which hung like folded wings. The face was a scowling leather mask, eyes blazing with blue light. For a moment, Edwin thought it might be Dr Shade, wondering who was warming his saddle. The creature leaped from its perch, coat-skirts flaring to show long, grasshopper-like legs. It slammed onto pavement, body concertinaing like a coiled spring, then launched into space with a mighty hop, arms outspread, kukri knives flashing in each gloved hand.

It was another fugitive waxwork—Spring-Heel'd Jack, the Terror of London. A bad one. Last time the original had bounced around town, it had taken all of the Splendid Six, plus Granite Grant and the Green Archer, to bring him down to earth—and the Splendids weren't in business anymore. Surprisingly, the Night Flier didn't seem to be equipped with a bow and arrow.

The demi-demon soared overhead, aiming heels against a wall, and bounced off—flying well ahead of the Norton, landing, arms outspread, in the middle of the road. He tossed the kukri knives and Edwin weaved to evade the blades. Jack drew a brace of pistols from holsters under his arms. Closer now, Edwin tucked his head down and drove straight at the villain.

Edwin's thumbs were against switches. He aimed the bike and pressed the right switch.

A burst of controlled gunfire, strangely quiet, struck the road. Jack had jumped above the fire.

As Edwin drove under him, Jack seemed to hang in the air, calmly aiming his guns.

A bullet spanged against the Night Flier's prow, striking sparks. When Jack landed, he was behind the bike, with a clear shot at Edwin's unprotected back.

If the right switch was the gun, then the left must be the nozzle above the exhaust. Edwin pressed.

A jet of flame coursed out of the rear-nozzle.

He looked back and saw Jack's mask burn away from his face, which melted. His ulster caught fire, but that didn't stop him leaping, on whatever mechanisms were really built into his heels. On wings of flame, the Terror of London flapped in the Norton's wake, following Edwin into Cockspur Street and across Trafalgar Square. Wherever he touched ground, he left burning pools of wax and cloth. He bounced erratically, then exploded against a Landseer lion, falling to flaming pieces, startling a flock of drowsing pigeons.

Edwin hoped that was the last of the waxworks. Then he remembered that Sweeney Todd was still at large, or at least whoever—Conjurer, presumably—had dressed as the Demon Barber of Fleet Street to slash Sorcerer's throat.

The motorcycle was a perfect machine.

He made a mental note to get in touch with the Norton Company. One of these things could come in handy.

He didn't see why Dr Shade should have a monopoly.

In the moment, he felt considerably better. Wind rushing his face, a downed enemy in flames in his wake, the thrill of speed in his water.

Violence and victory cleared his head.

XIII: 'this is about drawing a line'

The sky was red. The Bentley sped towards the Tower, the Black Mariah close on its rear bumper.

This was another instance in which Charles would have welcomed one of Mycroft's contingencies—an envelope with easy-to-follow instructions, a sheet of paper to trump the runes. Again, sadly, his mentor had failed to foresee this specific eventuality. However, he had a carful of lively minds at his disposal.

'So, ladies,' said Charles, 'suggestions?'

The three women all hesitated, thinking. They knew the problem. At dawn, whoever held any of the seven runes would be killed by whatever Zenf had taken the trouble to summon and bind. To judge from rusty threads in the gutters, these parties were set to appear from the sky in a welter of blood.

'We shouldn't rely on Wizard's counter-spells,' said Catriona, who had made a study of rune-casting for her monograph on the late, unlamented Julian Karswell. 'It's easier to let the dogs loose than call them to heel. No one has ever beat the runes through dispersion, banishment or holding charm. And it's been tried. In '26, Frank Chandler cast a spell to stop time. He simply froze the poor rune-bearer in her place, but scarcely slowed the demons, who happened to be the Devourers From Outside Time. The victim was, well, devoured. Chandu didn't broadcast *that* in his radio memoirs. Last year in Marseilles, the Duc de Richleau managed to *kill* the demon before it got its claws into its appointed victim. I don't want to think about how he managed that. The operation was a success but the patient died. Demon, rune and rune-bearer are mystically linked by the initial summoning. Slay the demon and the rune-bearer goes up in flames. The Duc made a valuable discovery, but looked even more of an idiot than usual. Connaught Drake can spell rings around lightweights like Chandu and de Richleau, but I still doubt he has anything in his tomes to counter a serious rune-casting. Our Great Enchanter is taking his first, best shot.'

Charles took in Catriona's summation. Don't hope for too much from Drake. Yet, this was all about the Ravens—the business with the runes was supposed to make him take his eyes off them.

Their best course still led to the Tower.

'Couldn't the vampire take the runes?' suggested Jenny Chambers.

Geneviève looked aghast. 'I'm not *that* expendable,' she protested.

'No, but technically you're dead already. If the demon is dispelled with the death of the person holding the papers, might the curse not apply to you?'

'I see your point, doctor, but I'm not that sort of vampire. Sorry.'

'Precedents there are unpleasant also,' said Catriona. 'In Alte Strelsau in 1408, Iohannes Meister cast a rune and passed it to a merchant who'd rooked him. However, before his time was up, the merchant was conventionally stabbed to death by another dissatisfied customer.'

'What happened when Meister's demon manifested?' asked Jenny.

'Cheated of its prey, it... well, it was a hundred years before they started work on *Neue* Strelsau.'

'Fair enough. Scrub that. It was an idea, though.'

'Yes, thank you, Jenny,' said Charles.

'Here's a thought,' said Catriona. 'We gather the runes and give them to, say, Ollie Gibberne. She's going to hang in the end, for murder. Being rent limb from limb by fiends isn't *much* more than she deserves.'

'There are practical difficulties, Catriona,' said Charles. 'We've half an hour at the most. Finding your murderess and persuading her to accept a suspicious envelope is liable to take longer.'

'I could do it in two hours. She's frightfully thick. I could tell her it was a mash note from, say, Ronald Colman. Or the King.'

'We don't have two hours.'

Geneviève peered out of the window, looking up into the sky.

'Those clouds are drifting *against* the wind,' she said. 'The red ones that seem to be boiling over.'

'Someone has to say it, so I will,' began Jenny. 'Didn't these three ask for it? They are all petty crooks. Even if one of them is a jolly old bobby...'

'"If you want to know the time, ask a policeman..."' warbled Catriona.

'Yes. "Every member of the force has a watch and chain, of course." Remember what the song is about? Victorian constables were famous for rolling drunks. That's how they got the watches.'

Jenny shared some of her brother's merciless attitudes to law-breakers.

'I was once arrested by Jonathan Wild, the London Thief-Taker,' said Geneviève. 'Now, *he* was a bigger crook than Fantômas, Arsène Lupin and John Dillinger rolled together.'

'We should get them out in the open, then,' said Catriona. 'Limit the damage. Anyone who gets in the way is liable to suffer. A shame about Nosey Parker, though... his mother will be grief-stricken.'

'He doesn't have a mother, Catriona.'

Catriona's eyes goggled. 'It's all lies... !?'

'Not exactly,' Charles explained. 'It's part of his *act*. Pick-pockets are like music hall turns. They have patter, embroidered throughout their careers. Nosey's mother is more like an imaginary friend. Or a comedian's mother-in-law.'

'If one of them—or anyone—ends up with all seven runes, the rest go free,' said Catriona. 'If we can't get someone who really deserves it here, we can at least save two of the three. Despite the mother routine, which I'm still *appalled* by, I vote for Nosey and...'

'Go on,' said Charles.

'Can't decide,' said Catriona. 'Letty's just as obnoxious as the type of fanatical annoyance she poses as... and Ottermole regularly betrays the public trust. I'm sorry. I can't make those decisions. You need Edwin for that. Or Dr Shade.'

'Jenny...' prompted Charles.

'I am, of course, familiar with the concept of triage. Save who you can.'

'Here, we can save almost everyone but must pick one to die,' said Charles. 'Doesn't have to be one of the three dips. Anyone in this car, or the Black Mariah, or at the Tower, or on the streets will do...'

Jenny spread her hands and shook her head.

'I thought so,' he said. 'Good for you, Jenny. You're not your brother.'

Charles saw the Tower up ahead. The bloody clouds were above it, taking solid shape. Wherever the rune-bearers might be at dawn, Southwark or Samara, their deaths would be waiting.

He was determined.

'Ladies, it is decided. We will *not* let this thing happen. It doesn't matter who these people are. It didn't matter to the Great Enchanter when he scattered his runes. Zenf wants to show he can hurt *anyone*. That we can't protect our people. Purse-snatcher or Prince of the Realm, they're all the same to him—and they should be to us. Few may know it, but we're here for the people. We preserve this country from this species of hurt. This is about drawing a line and saying it shall not be crossed.'

Geneviève, Catriona and Jenny looked at him, eyes wide, mouths slightly open.

'What?' he said. 'What is it?'

'It's just... it's just *you*,' said Catriona.

Geneviève leaned over and kissed him on the mouth.

'What was that for?' he asked, bewildered.

'Someone had to,' she explained. 'I elected myself. "Drawing a line". It's so perfect. I see what Mr Mycroft meant about you.'

Charles feared that his face was flushed.

'Don't worry,' Geneviève whispered in his ear. 'In this red light, no one can tell.'

She kissed him again, on the cheek, and sat back. Catriona squeezed his knee. Even Jenny Chambers, who usually only smiled during surgery, was on the point of simpering.

Charles still had no idea what it was all about.

He had puzzled out many mysteries in his long life, but was still on the lower slopes when it came to women.

XIV: 'Peredur Chaffinch Threepence'

Any shepherds in London would have been served severe warning by the dawn skies. From the excessive redness of the clouds, it was to be a bloody, bloody day.

Edwin startled two Yeomen Warders on the early watch. They crossed pikes and braced themselves as the Night Flier roared towards the visitors' gate. He executed a smart turn and used the brakes. The Norton halted smartly.

'Peredur Chaffinch Threepence,' he said.

The code-words signified direst peril to crown and country. The beefeaters stood at once to attention, pikes parted. A trickle of fear-sweat dripped onto one man's ruff.

'You've two more parties arriving,' he told the guards, 'in a Bentley and a Black Mariah. Let them pass. Then lower the portcullis and be ready to defend the Tower.'

'Yes, sir,' said the Warders.

Some thought the duty merely ceremonial, standing about in fancy dress for tour parties, posing for picture post-cards. But the Tower of London was a Royal Residence, a national treasure store, a prison and the old stone heart of William the Conqueror's city. All this made the place a target. Only the best long-term service veterans were eligible to become Yeomen Warders, men proved in battles all over the world.

As Edwin wheeled Dr Shade's bike into the courtyard, there was activity. The full complement of Warders were roused from beds and took defensive positions. It was odd to see beefeaters in their embroidered velvet tunics, knee-britches, floppy hats and half-capes deployed with Thompson sub-machine guns instead of pikestaffs and ceremonial swords. A few of the famous ravens flapped lazily into the air and found perches. Edwin hoped they were used to the chatter of tommy guns. He didn't want to be responsible for scaring off the blessed birds and bringing down the kingdom.

The Keeper of the Ravens was quartered in the White Tower, the oldest part of the fortress. Edwin wondered whether he'd have to hammer on the huge mediaeval door to wake up the Wizard.

'Don't like the look of that sky, Bert,' a Warder told a comrade. 'It'll belt down, sure as eggs is eggs.'

A mild little old fellow in tweeds and an apron, who was scattering feed for the birds, paused with a handful of breadcrumbs, looked up through half-spectacles, and clucked.

'It won't rain,' he said. 'Dear me no. Rain would be a blessing, weather we've been having.'

This was Wizard.

Edwin had expected starry robes and a conical hat, as advertised. Connaught Drake sported a white beard, close-cropped rather than waist-length. His hat was a battered trilby, with a small black feather in the brim.

Edwin opened his mouth to speak.

'Yes... yes... Peredur Chaffinch Threepence,' said Drake, waving away the bother. 'Why we have to make the men learn such rot by heart is beyond me. If it's come to *Peredur Chaffinch Threepence*, then you might as well shout *Woe Calamity Doom*. So, what manner of catastrophe threatens, eh? My birdies have been off their seed for days. So peril must be dire indeed. Tentacles? The Deep Old Damp Ones? No, no, that'd be rising waters, not red skies. The Thames is behaving itself for a change. Bat-wings and scaly tails? It'll be Zenf, then. Continentals think too much of their gargoyles. They think we're still scared of pantomime bogey men with stuck-out tongues and the flaming pitch-forks.'

As far as Edwin was concerned, he *was* still scared. In this business, it wasn't cowardice—it was clear-headedness. Black shapes were in the clouds now. Flapping wings were involved, presumably bat-like.

Something about Wizard rubbed Edwin wrong. He was prepared to concede that he, and everyone he cared about, fell into the category of 'lesser mortals'—but it wasn't quite cricket to rub it in with such high-handed, dismissive irritation. They all had jobs to do, even the Keeper of the Ravens.

Charles Beauregard's Bentley cruised through the main gate, followed by a Black Mariah. When they were in the courtyard, the portcullis came down.

'It's well before visiting hours,' said Wizard. 'We can't be having this, you know. Your Ruling Cabal have a lot to answer for. And the other shower with the black hats.'

It occurred to Edwin that if Wizard was the King Rat, they were now locked in with him.

Huntstanton got out of the Bentley and opened the passenger door. Catriona and Dr Chambers helped Charles out, another indication of the situation's seriousness. The Old Man rarely let anyone treat him like an invalid. Geneviève emerged into dawn light. She didn't shrivel to dust, but hid from the sun with a large green scarf over her hair and blue-tinted tortoise-shell glasses.

A pair of Undertakers were here too, one a half-sized specimen. Edwin supposed that was inevitable, though he didn't have to like it. The Undertaking were mystery-wallahs of the worst kind, and Edwin didn't like the way they went about things.

With Yeomen Warders added to the party, everyone gathered round the Black Mariah. A heavy rock whistled down from the sky, and smashed nearby, exploding to flinty shrapnel. A beefeater was wounded, shards stuck into his cheek and shoulder. Dr Chambers got close to him, tweezers out. With distracted irritation, Connaught Drake snapped his fingers. Black fragments extracted from the Warder's wounds and flew past the startled doctor. The beefeater's tunic was ragged where he'd been blasted, but his skin healed over instantly. He put a hand to his face in disbelief. Dr Chambers clacked her tweezers. After whirling around ostentatiously, the splinters reassembled into a well-behaved stone cherub's head.

Everyone was impressed, but Wizard didn't take applause.

'Which of you is Beauregard?'

Charles stepped forward, leaning heavily on his stick, extending a hand which Drake didn't take.

'Surrounded by women, I see,' said Drake. Edwin was astonished that the Old Man looked sheepish. 'Says something about your character.'

Geneviève bristled a little, like a French cat considering where best to scratch. Good for her. Dr Chambers harrumphed.

'Margery Device speaks highly of you,' Wizard admitted, testily. 'And she speaks lowly of everyone. Now, what *is* all this *bother?* Why have you trooped here in force at the crack of dawn to disturb the birdies and haul the beefeaters out of bed? Zenf's raised some imps, I presume. Do you perchance have *runes* about your person?'

'Not me, Keeper,' said Charles. 'We have three afflicted souls in here.'

Everyone shrank from the van, except Connaught Drake.

'Let's have them in the light, then,' he said. 'Take a look at them. Chances are they won't stay long, so we should get to know them while we can. Horrid business, rune-raising. Underhanded and cowardly. Not British. *Merlin* never cast runes.'

Mr Esse, the adult Undertaker, unlocked the back of the Black Mariah. A beefeater subtly pointed his tommy gun at the doors, as if expecting hungry lions.

'The *event* is set for dawn,' said the Old Man.

'Best be quick, then,' said Drake. 'Get it over with before breakfast. This being Thursday, it's kedgeree.'

The doors opened and three miserable people climbed out. Edwin assumed they were pick-pockets, though one was a police constable and another a pinch-faced woman wearing an 'Abjure Strong Drink' sash. The third was Alfred Parker—who certainly *was* a pick-pocket. Everyone knew Nosey. His larcenous fingers had been used in the service of the Club. Once, by purloining an Eurasian courtesan's deadly steel fan, he had saved Edwin's neck.

'How's your mum, Nosey?' he asked.

Nosey shook his head, in sorrow. 'H'it's 'er h'arches, Mr Winthrop. Fallen like h'ancient Rome.'

'I'd like to talk about Nosey's mother,' said Catriona, in middling-high dudgeon. 'According to Mr Knows-All-Tells-Little here...'

'This may not be the time,' interrupted Charles.

Catriona shut up, which—as far as Edwin was concerned—was another Sign of the Apocalypse.

'Now, you three,' said Drake, sternly, 'turn out your pockets...'

None of them looked happy, and no wonder.

'Come come,' said Drake, 'I'm not a policeman or a schoolmaster. I wish to save you discomfort.'

His tone of voice was convincing.

'You can keep all your loot except some scraps of paper with funny writing. Of no value whatsoever. Nothing you could fence. Yes, Miss Strong Drink, those are what I mean, hand them over...'

The woman parted reluctantly with three runes. They were twisted into little shapes.

'Congratulations, you're not doomed anymore,' said Drake, rolling the runes together.

'Hey, that's mine,' said Dr Chambers, reclaiming her stethoscope.

The temperance woman looked as if she were the victim of a severe affront, and about to set the law on an impertinent false accuser. That must be her act.

'I have no idea how that came to be upon my person. It must have been planted by a malicious individual. Almost certainly in the employ of the perfidious purveyors of alcoholic beverages.'

'Give it up, Letty,' said the constable. 'It's a fair cop.'

The policeman and Nosey came up with two runes apiece. Nosey seemed fascinated by his little strips of deadly paper.

Catriona pointedly took back her silver retracting pencil, without comment. She was in a pet with Nosey Parker.

'That's the lot?' Drake asked.

Charles nodded.

'Such *fuss* over so little,' mused Wizard.

Nosey was the last to part with his strips.

There were shouts from Yeomen Warders, about hostiles in the skies. Mr Esse looked up, staring into the sun. In the twin dark mirrors of his specs, Edwin caught doubled glimpses of something angular and swift. It hovered like a large locust with too few legs and too many wings.

Connaught Drake held up a fistful of runes, letting the trailing edges flutter. It was as if the papers were trying to fly away, but Wizard had a firm grip. Large, thick shadows fell on the courtyard.

Edwin didn't know whether to look up or keep his eyes on the ground. Catriona was by his side, clutching his arm. She clutched her silver pencil like a stiletto—it might do for a vampire, but he was doubtful it'd even annoy the coming predators.

Beefeaters on the battlements began firing into the sky.

Wizard made an exasperated, irritated face and nodded an order, which was relayed upwards. The gunfire cut off. Spent bullets pattered on gravel.

'Now,' said Connaught Drake, holding their full attention, 'you're expecting me to be rent limb from limb by seven demons, aren't you? Well, as Robbie Stone is wont to say rather too often, "for my next trick", I shan't be.'

Edwin looked up and wished he hadn't.

XV: 'no h'end of grief from me h'old plates'

Charles held his sword-cane in both hands, several inches of steel showing, catching the red light. It was instinct rather than sense. The sword would be no more use than the beefeaters' bullets.

Connaught Drake, Raven and Keeper of Ravens, held all the runes. Zenf's creatures were coming from the skies, all teeth and talons. They would not return to their infernal aerie until they had shredded the rune-bearer. Yet Drake had announced that he would *not* suffer the consequences. If he could get out of this fix, he'd be a Wizard indeed.

Someone else was with them in the courtyard.

'Mr Parker,' said Drake, mildly, 'isn't this your mother?'

Nosey, goggling, spun round.

Charles was scarcely less astonished. Here, wincing with each step, was Nosey Parker's mythical mother. There could be no doubt of the relationship. She had the same beak, the same oddly-jointed gait, the same oversized eyes. She wore a hat with gauze and dead flowers around the rim and a cloth coat with a fur collar. Her famously troublesome feet were in carpet-slippers.

Catriona was aghast again, but puzzled.

'Mum,' breathed Nosey, tears in his eyes. 'Mum...'

'Close h'up your mouth, H'Alfred,' she said, 'h'or a bee will fly h'into h'it.'

Something large and sinewy landed on the side of the White Tower, stinking of sulphur, claws digging into old stone.

Geneviève showed her fangface. Her nails had grown to knifepoints. Master Wuh was crouched at her feet, holding a stick like a Chinese fighting monk.

'So this is the Tower of London, then,' said Nosey's Mum, looking around. 'H'I 'ope you h'ain't gettin' ideas h'above your station, H'Alfred. We've always been true blue in h'our family. H'ever since your H'Uncle Charlie, 'im what was relieved at Mafekin', was h'awarded by the h'old Queen. So, no stealin' of the Koh-I-Nor or any h'other of them Crown Jewels. Those sparklers belongs properly to 'Is Majesty the King. You find somethin' h'else to nick, or don't come 'ome with your washin' h'at the h'end of the week.'

Nosey was shame-faced, which suggested he *had* seen an opportunity in this irregular visit to the Tower.

'Mrs Parker,' said Drake, 'if you will take these off my hands.'

He offered her the runes.

'Certainly, ducks,' she said, opening her purse. Drake folded the papers into it, and pressed its catch shut. 'H'I'll willingly take responsibility.'

She patted the purse and slipped it into her pocket.

Drake snapped his fingers and a comfortable chair appeared behind Nosey's Mum. A padded, red-flock armchair with gilt feet.

'Would you care to sit down?' he suggested.

'Cor, thanks, luv,' said Nosey's Mum, sitting down with relief. 'H'it's me feet, you know. No h'end of grief from me h'old plates...'

'It would be best if we all withdrew to a safe distance,' said Drake, to everyone but the old woman. 'It was a pleasure to meet you, Mrs Parker.'

'Don't mention h'it, dearie.'

Geneviève pulled Charles away. He couldn't help but look at the new arrival. She was no illusion. He thought he understood how she had come here. Drake was guardian of the *stories* of London and Nosey's Mum was one of those. Wizard had opened a doorway to the city's shadow, and invited this woman to step through, to be real for a few brief minutes.

They all gave Mrs Parker a wide circle. She raised a cheery hand and flapped it at Nosey.

More creatures alighted. They were big, red-black and indistinct, as if they had their own personal clouds. These things weren't supposed to be seen even in dawn light.

Warders had to put out fires.

Mrs Parker wasn't at all concerned by the seven creatures stalking towards her. She got out some knitting and hummed. The first demon prodded her with a long, triple-segmented finger.

Then, they were on her. In an instant, she was rendered into a red cloud. The chair was torn apart too. In another instant, their purpose fulfilled, Zenf's imps popped out of existence, leaving behind a stench which made Charles choke.

Nosey howled and fell to his knees.

Catriona had a hand over her mouth, horrified.

Most of the warders—and Letty and Ottermole—didn't even know what had happened. It had been too quick.

Wizard pottered about, walking onto the red, white-flecked patch where Nosey's Mum had been. Ravens gathered, settling on his shoulders, pecking at scraps from the ground.

The immediate danger was over. Wizard had bested the Great Enchanter.

'No,' said Catriona, firmly. 'That wasn't fair. That didn't count. You cheated, Drake. You passed the runes. To a real person. An innocent. That's not what you were supposed to do.'

'She took them willingly,' he said. 'She sacrificed herself for the city. She was a true cockney.'

Edwin held Catriona's shoulders. She was furious.

'What about *him?* Nosey? He's broken. If he hadn't believed, deep down *believed*, you wouldn't have been able to fetch her from storyland.'

'No. But it wasn't just him. You *all* had to go along with the stories. And look at him, Miss Kaye. Look.'

Nosey blinked in the sunlight, more baffled than anything else.

'The story is gone,' explained Drake, not unkindly, 'as if it were never told. For him, the pages are blank. For the rest of you, it'll take a few more minutes—until the sun is fully up.'

Charles slid his sword-stick shut.

Dr Chambers took a look at Nosey. 'Doesn't seem to be shock,' she reported.

'H'what's all this about?' said Nosey, deftly extracting a bottle of pills from Jenny Chambers's pocket. 'And h'why are you all lookin' h'at me like that? H'I'm a poor h'orphan, H'I am, h'what never knew 'is Mum and Dad. H'I suffered somethin' h'awful in that 'orrible h'orphanage. H'it'd make a grown man weep...'

A new story was taking shape, to fill the blank page.

The ruin on the cobbles was all wood and cloth and padding and gilt. No other matter. In this world, all that had been sacrificed was a chair.

Catriona was not yet mollified. Charles squeezed her shoulder. At times like this, Edwin's friend reminded him of Kate Reed. Someone had to count the cost, and she was ready to step up—no matter if important persons took offence.

'You'll have to reissue *The Biter Bit*, Miss Kaye,' said Mr Esse. 'With a new appendix. Someone has finally beaten the runes.'

Catriona looked at the Undertaker with disgust.

'Now,' said Drake. 'About this Rat...'

XVI: 'the ravens must be fed'

The ghastly Leticia Hesketh-Stafford was made to give up a cake of soap into which she'd accidentally pressed some keys a beefeater had 'dropped' in all the excitement. After that, the pick-pockets were packed off home.

What had they made of this morning's happening at the Tower? Far-fetched tales would spread through the underworld, refilling the story-pool depleted by Wizard's sacrificial gambit. Edwin knew Mrs Parker had looked exactly as he always imagined her, but the exact image was blurry in his memory now. Wizard had said she would fade. A few minutes ago, he had shared Nosey's hot spasm of grief, but now there was only an after-tingle. He was disturbed at the absence of feelings which had momentarily been real.

An alert came from the guards watching the Thames.

A motor-launch approached, piloted by a tall girl in a reddish-brown body-stocking and moth-winged domino mask. She was an occasional associate of Dr Shade's, and went by the name of Kentish Glory. Margery Device stood next to the woman of mystery, in a tailored sailor suit, ribbons streaming from a jaunty cap. The black, shark-finned boat—presumably another loan from Dr Chambers's brother—slid almost silently up to Tower

Dock. Miss Device stepped ashore as, on Drake's nod, a gate was raised.

The launch sped away from the dock, isinglass carapace unfolding to enclose the skipper. When Kentish Glory was sealed inside, the boat became a submersible and knived under the waters of the Thames.

Miss Device entered the Tower through Traitors' Gate, formerly the Water-Gate.

'You found a way around the rune-casting,' she said with mild congratulation, as if noticing he'd filled in the *Times* crossword double-quick. 'Well done, Conny. I knew you'd spell up some fresh cleverness.'

Wizard looked at Witch and said, 'Who is this at Traitor's Gate? Margery, I don't suppose you've been betraying the Kingdom?'

She seemed delighted at the accusation. '*Moi?* A Queen Rat? You know me better that that, dear.'

'I suppose I do,' he said. 'Still, you had to be asked to your face. At least, to one of your faces. Or aren't we talking about that in public?'

At last, Miss Device was shocked. Edwin had thought she was unflappable.

'You'd all better come into the White Tower,' said Wizard. 'The ravens must be fed, and you can tell me what little you know.'

Connaught Drake rarely had to deal with other people. He was not very good at it. He was probably better with the birds.

Yeomen Warders opened doors and saluted, and Drake led the party up a cramped circular staircase to a large room with niches in the walls, straw on the flagstone floor and open vents in the glass ceiling. The Raven-Cote was airy and sunlit—Geneviève had to find a shadow to shrink into. A shallow drinking fountain burbled pleasantly. Birds arrived in an orderly fashion, and found individual perches and nooks. Wizard unlocked a cabinet and took out several cups, into which he poured birdseed from a packet. He handed cups to Dr Chambers, Catriona and the Junior Undertaker.

'You're the trustworthy ones,' Drake told them. 'Don't give too much, or they bloat.'

He showed how to dribble seeds into smooth depressions in the stone, and his appointed deputies followed suit. The birds came and pecked, not caring whose hand tipped their food.

With a set of long tweezers, Drake doled out special treats—maggots and caterpillars—to favoured ravens. In 1903, he had fed three of the birds with the grubs of the notorious 'worm unknown to science'—they hadn't shown ill-effects and, if rumour was to be believed, were still here at the Tower, having long outlived their contemporaries.

'I have *news*,' said Miss Device. 'It's why I hied myself here...'

'Not more *gossip*, Margery...'

'No, hard information. Marcus has been abducted from Harley Street.'

Dr Chambers was alarmed, and startled a raven with an overgenerous spill.

'I had this from a sweet little fox-child who has lately been cruelly treated,' continued Miss Device. 'Don't fret so, Jenny. Your nursie man was only bopped over the head and rendered unconscious. The Sorcerer-snatcher didn't feel a need to make a point by stringing entrails around the room like Christmas decorations.'

'It has to be Conjurer,' Edwin said. 'He's tried once already.'

The Old Man looked doubtful. 'If Stone could get into the surgery, why not murder Rennes in his sleep without incurring the trouble and risk of spiriting him away? Are we certain it was Conjurer who attacked Sorcerer at the Tivoli?'

'If not Stone, who?' asked Catriona. A raven perched on her knuckle, cooing like a dove. The bird had taken a shine to her.

'Zenf?' suggested Edwin. 'He's kept us busy with runes and pick-pockets. It could have been a deliberate diversion as much as a show of strength.'

'Zenf is the Rat-Master,' said Catriona. 'Stone is his creature.'

'So it seems,' said the Old Man.

'Conjuring tricks,' said Wizard, with disdain. 'All look-here-at-my-waggling-fingers-while-I-stack-the-cards-under-the-table. Scarcely magic. Just an elevated form of *cheating*.'

'Don't mind, Conny,' said Miss Device. 'He's an old fusspot.'

Drake looked as if he was thinking about siccing his ravens on Witch.

Mr Esse stood by the fountain, like a scarecrow in mourning cast-offs. Ravens landed on him. One deposited white birdlime on his top hat.

'So, the Diogenes Club has *lost* two of the Ravens,' said the Undertaker, ignoring the birds. 'This was to be expected. Firmer protective measures should have been taken. Rennes should have been given over into our custody.'

Before Dr Chambers could protest, Beauregard spoke up for her. 'As you well know, anyone who can get past Simon Pure could certainly get into the Mausoleum.'

'It's not that hard to get *out* of,' said Geneviève, teasing a little.

Black fire burned behind Mr Esse's glasses. In daylight, with droppings on his hat and (now) shoulders, an Undertaker wasn't quite so fearsome. Or maybe it was because in this business, they weren't the most frightening players. In that race, the Undertaking would have a hard time placing. Zenf, the Rat, the Ravens, Spring-Heel'd Jack, the waxworks and Dr Chambers's brother (if he counted) were making all the running for the Top Three.

More ravens landed on the Undertaker, overcrowding his shoulders, spreading onto his arms.

'How many birds are there supposed to be?' Catriona asked Drake.

'Fewer,' said Wizard.

Edwin looked up. Black, mean eyes met his gaze. Many more black birds flocked around the vents.

'What's the difference between a raven and a crow?' he asked.

'Strictly speaking, very little,' said Drake. 'They're all *corvidae*. Ravens *are* crows. So are rooks.'

Birds flew in through the vents, and settled on the drinking fountain, the floor and in niches, crowding out the natural tenants with wing-shoves. Catriona protected her new friend from a pecking intruder.

'Ouch,' said Mr Esse. A red flap of skin hung on his bone-white cheek. The bird closest his face pecked him again, cracking the lens of his glasses. He shook his shoulders. The birds lifted off, flapped a little, then attacked him in concert.

Beauregard and Geneviève went to help the Undertaker. Edwin pulled out his revolver—useless, he instantly realised. He shielded Catriona with his body, pressing her against a wall.

He knew she was about to complain.

Then the general attack began.

XVII: 'pest control'

Mr Esse rolled on the flagstones, trying to be rid of the pecking blackbirds. He opened his mouth, and a crow fastened a determined beak onto his tongue. The Undertaker squawked, tears pouring from under his dark glasses, but the crow hung on grimly, wings battering his face.

Charles and Geneviève knelt, frantically picking birds off Mr Esse and batting the creatures away. Charles took hold of the crow which had the Undertaker's tongue in its razor-grip and, at first gingerly, pulled. Mr Esse managed a scream, as if a dentist had just drilled into a nerve. Charles tried squeezing the bird, hard. His wrist took a blow from a wing, which landed as heavily as a police truncheon, and he let go.

Geneviève grasped the raven with fingerpoints, and then extended talons through its feathers into the red meat. That killed it, and it let go of Mr Esse's ragged tongue. The Undertaker's head flopped back, his broken glasses lost. Charles clamped a hand over the open eyes, not wanting them in his mind for the rest of the year. The vampire girl had to remove the dead bird from her fingers, while slapping away its vengeful comrades.

'This isn't how I expected the Diogenes Club to deploy me in the Great Game of Good and Evil,' she said. 'Pest control!'

Charles felt the Undertaker's neck. No pulse. A big, filthy bird on his chest had pecked straight into his heart. Charles took his hand away from the cold face. In death Mr Esse's eyes were ordinary again.

The Raven-Cote was a blizzard of shrieking birds, sharp-beaked, barb-taloned, thick-winged. Charles had been pecked about the ears. Blood dribbled into his collar.

Margery whirled up some defensive spell, hiding inside a personal tornado, and ravens slammed into hard air currents which spun them away from her. Winthrop shielded Catriona, the back of his tuxedo in shreds.

Jenny was under the fountain, hands over her eyes, coat up over the crown of her head. Connaught Drake, Keeper of the Ravens, showed concern for his original birds, stepping in to slap away any intruders who dared molest them.

Some vampires have, or are reputed to have, sway over night-beasts. Crows, at least by their plumage, were as night-associated as wolves or bats. Sadly, Geneviève wasn't of that bloodline.

Her face was torn open from cheek to jaw, to the bone. She pressed a hand to the wound. It closed and healed without a scar even before she had even wiped the blood off. The same happened to scratches on her hands and neck. She at least had that useful trait.

Unlike Charles.

A crow nipped his already-bleeding ear, several times. He couldn't shake it.

Geneviève reached out to him, but the flock—a murder!—of crows was like a thick, thorny hedge between them. Charles felt more shallow stabs. He drew his sword and slashed, not quite at random—several bisected or beheaded birds fell. But his strained knee gave out, and he found himself sprawled over the Undertaker's limp corpse—more immediately pained by his leg and back than by the harrying birds who could kill him. His mouth was full of foul, wet feathers.

A thump came on his chest. The heart-eater bird regarded him with malevolent, quick-blinking black eyes. Its claws hooked into his waistcoat, and its beak aimed at his starched shirt-front. He tried to raise his sword, but a thousand pecks at his hand made him lose his grip.

'Charles!' called Geneviève.

For one quick blink, the heart-eater had Zenf's eyes. Charles knew this killing blow was personal.

Then the crow's neck kinked, broken as if by an invisible whip, and its head hung sideways. Talons relaxed, and the heart-eater fell off his chest.

The other birds on him and Geneviève were suddenly less troublesome. He struggled to sit, ignoring his pains, intent on not being completely useless when she got to his side to help him.

What had happened to the heart-eater?

A niche in the Raven-Cote was entirely filled by Master Wuh, who held the great offensive weapon of generations of British boys, the home-made catapult—a stout forked stick, home-polished, with a length of supple black rubber between the tines. In an Indian hill station, more than sixty years ago, Charles had been a deadly expert with an identical contraption—as many curs, windows, bullies and an *ayah* knew to their cost. With a single pebble, the child had avenged Mr Esse and fulfilled his obligation to protect Charles's life—he doubted Mr Hay was finding Giles Gallant half as useful.

Margery's tornado grew to encompass the whole of the Raven-Cote, spiralling birds up and out through the vents, tearing them away from their intended prey. Her scarf unpicked by beaks, Geneviève's long hair lashed across Charles's face, and she had to gather it up to keep it out of their eyes.

Edwin relaxed and let Catriona free. There were rents scratched in Edwin's overcoat, but he and Catriona were otherwise unharmed. A bird pulled out of Catriona's hand and she snatched it back. It was the bird which had taken a shine to her.

'Don't throw the baby out with the bath-water,' she told Margery Device.

Margery clucked at such ingratitude. She was enjoying her show of weather-witchery.

'Miss Kaye makes an important point,' said Charles. 'If you get rid of the original ravens, the Kingdom is in peril.'

'Oh, pish,' said Witch, in a pet. 'The Kingdom is *always* in peril.'

Nevertheless, Margery shut off the wind. Several birds fell dead. One splashed legs-up into the fountain. A few hardy ravens, mostly with bloody scratches, survived and were not cast out.

Jenny composed herself, opened her doctors' bag, and set about treating scratches. First, she examined Geneviève—whose criss-crossed face healed completely before the doctor could so much as dab at a cut. Unflapped by this miracle, she proceeded to Charles, and took a look at his ear.

'Nasty,' she said, applying something which stung to the wound. 'But you won't need stitches.'

Catriona restored her raven to its prime perch.

'I say,' she exclaimed, 'where's the Wizard?'

XVIII: 'a disappearing act'

If Mr Esse weren't too busy being dead, the Undertaker would doubtless have gloated over the Diogenes Club managing to lose another Raven.

Edwin looked around the Raven-Cote.

'Did anyone see...?' he asked.

Heads shook. 'Someone was in my way,' said Catriona. 'Providing unasked-for-shielding, and practically crushing my poor Hugin.'

Her new special friend was named after one of Odin's attendant birds.

'Next time, I'll let your dressmaker suffer as much as my tailor,' he responded.

He picked his dinner jacket off in ragged strips. He was left with the sleeves, which had to be unpeeled. Catriona helped and tidied his hair while she was about it.

'He was just talking about conjuring tricks,' pointed out Geneviève. 'A distraction of birds, to cover a disappearing act.'

'You think he did this?' Edwin asked the vampire. 'Drake?'

Geneviève gave an unhelpful Gallic shrug.

'Do you think something like this could be done to *him?*' asked Miss

Device. 'If I can snap my fingers and see off the murdering murder, with only my poor witch ways, then surely Wizard—the *Keeper* of the Ravens, who is *fabulously* gifted when it comes to our feathered friends—could have done better?'

Everyone tried not to look at the dead Undertaker.

'Colonel Zenf is arrogant enough to send birds,' said the Old Man, wincing as Dr Chambers fit a large sticking plaster around his gashed ear. 'He wants to best everyone at their own games.'

'I know this isn't going to be a popular observation,' began Catriona, 'but are we *sure* Robert Stone is the Rat?'

Everyone looked at her. Hugin squawked, indignant at the suggestion. She had to chuff neck-feathers to restore herself to the bird's affections.

'Someone had to say it,' she apologised.

Connaught Drake displaced more air by his absence than his presence—like an unnoticed linch-pin suddenly pulled. At least his ravens were still here. Without them, Edwin would have feared that the Tower might tumble and drag the city down with it.

'You can never tell with Conny,' said Miss Device. 'He could have stepped into storyland, written a happy ending—with Zenf turned into a pig and fed to the Royal Family at Christmas—and be back in a trice muttering about the high price of seed and wondering why we're bothering his blessed birds...'

They waited just a few moments longer than a trice.

'Sorry,' said Mrs Device. 'Wishful thinking. Bad habit. Still, wishing can make it so. Sometimes.'

Part of what Witch said made sense. Wizard could have stepped into the city's shadow. Storyland. Catriona had called it that, earlier. Mrs Parker—melted from his memory like ice in the sun—had lived there, and the original Spring-Heel'd Jack. The city's shadow was under attack too, and Drake was its appointed guardian.

'Is it easy?' he asked. 'Stepping into storyland?'

Miss Device was surprised, more at the temerity of the question than its practicality.

Edwin did not miss the flash of pride in Charles Beauregard's eyes as he followed and approved his train of thought. That tiny nod meant more than any medal or honour.

'Not *easy*,' said Miss Device, 'but it's done often. More often by accident than design. Here, in the Keeper's Tower, there are portals and keys. You find others dotted about the city. The London Stone, if used properly. One of those "not for the use of the public" telephone box affairs, I'm told—though that comes and goes. A Highgate antiques shop called Temptations, Ltd. has a minor specialty in permanent doors. You can install them anywhere, and they'll always open into the same place. Some mirrors work like that too. Always risky propositions, though. You never know what's behind a door before you open it. You know the parable of the Lady or the Tiger? It simplifies the situation. In storyland, you might find a tame tiger or a ravenous lady... no offence, Mademoiselle LaVampire... and sometimes there are hungry big cats behind both doors. No, I wouldn't recommend such an expedition to... and again, no offence intended... *amateurs*.'

Miss Device shook her head.

'It's settled, then,' said the Old Man, setting aside everything Witch had said, especially that patronising nonsense about *amateurs*. 'Margery opens a Door. Edwin goes after Wizard...'

'I'll want a change of clothes.'

'Huntstanton has anything you need in the car. I want to borrow Catriona for a few hours, to help me track down Colonel Zenf and, perhaps, one or other of our missing Ravens. If Geneviève would volunteer to accompany you, she might come in handy...'

The vampire girl gave Beauregard an ironic *vive-la-France* salute.

'Jenny,' the Old Man addressed Dr Chambers, 'thank you for your help. You'll want to get back to your surgery and see to Simon Pure. I'll have you chauffeured. It is always a pleasure to see you and I regret—again!—that the circumstances of our meeting should be so troublesome.'

Dr Chambers gave a tight little smile but was grateful to be excused.

Edwin and Geneviève looked at each other. Should he still be wary of the vampire? Charles Beauregard plainly trusted her.

'What should we do in this storyland?' Geneviève asked the Old Man.

'Find Drake and render him what assistance he needs, if he needs it. Then accompany him back here. *If* you judge him to be the King Rat, get him here as soon as possible using whatever means you can. I needn't say that you are stepping into a dangerous world and should exercise utmost caution for, as you know, you are also stepping *out* of a dangerous world. Both planes are in peril, and must be saved.'

'Will do, sir.'

'Good man, Winthrop,' said Beauregard.

XIX: 'a juicy tit-bit'

Margery Device busied herself finding Drake's Door. Winthrop was kitted out with a padded coat and other sundries, including the flying helmet that came with Dr Shade's motorcycle. Geneviève lingered, expectant.

Charles left them to it and sat in the back of the Bentley with Catriona.

'Among our little group, you're the best detective,' he said. 'Which of our Ravens do you think is a Rat?'

Catriona was surprised. She shouldn't have been. She was good at finding things out and, more importantly, working things out. Charles often set her loose on businesses which came under the category of 'mystery'. Unlike the general run of amateur or professional sleuths, she wasn't just a thinking, puzzle-solving machine. She empathised with the people caught up in the conundrum, and sought justice more often than a solution. No wonder Sir Henry Merrivale went purple whenever she was around.

She angled her head in what he recognised as a thinking position.

'Something about this riddle has troubled me ever since Edwin set it out,' she said. 'It's too pat. Four Suspects. One Guilty Party. I mean, it's a bit Green Penguin...'

'Go on,' he said.

'You got this intelligence from Geneviève? She passed on the question—which? Not whether?'

'Mycroft trusted Geneviève.'

'So do I, for what it's worth. But...'

Catriona hesitated. Charles prompted.

'From my experience,' she said, 'you and I are in a minority. Edwin trusts you the way you trust Mycroft, so he has no trouble *accepting* Geneviève—though our first meeting was startling, to say the least. But the rest of the Ruling Cabal *must* be wary of her, if only because they desperately don't want to believe what she's told us. The same goes for the Undertaking, who can't be happy about her escape from the Mausoleum.'

Charles allowed that she was on the money.

'And—have you noticed?—this business of Rat among the Ravens has gone from a state secret whispered in hushed tones among a tiny circle to being general knowledge. Everyone we meet knows what we're up to and what we suspect. That includes all the Ravens, and a widening circle of our acquaintances. Dr Chambers wasn't surprised. I think she heard something from her brother. It's as if some *gossip* were spreading the word all over town...'

As if on cue, Margery Device popped up at the window and said 'did you miss me?'

Catriona bit her tongue.

'Are you flirting with Charles, young lady,' reproached Margery. 'He's old enough to be your grandpa. And aren't you walking out with that nice Mr Winthrop? Such a juicy tit-bit. No one will believe it.'

Catriona was momentarily horror-struck.

'A little joke,' said Margery, blithely. 'I've found Drake's Door. Opening's in a minute or so. Better get a move on. Portals can get shifty if left to themselves.'

Margery flitted off.

'So,' Charles asked Catriona, '*is* there a Rat among the Ravens?'

'I don't know, but this isn't just Zenf sowing suspicion in our camp. There are big brutes in this jungle, shaking the trees. Geneviève tells us we have *a* Rat, but I'm beginning to wonder—judging from the way the Ravens have acted in the last day or so—whether there's just the one?'

'Two Rats?' he said, thinking it over, chill seeping up his spine.

'Why not three? Or four?'

XX: 'Our Man in Storyland'

Beyond Drake's Door was a sea of white fog. Real London pea-soup was yellow-green and foul. The fog of Shadow London was more like thick mist, odourless but damp, arranged in artful drapes.

Edwin kick-walked the Night Flier through the Door. Geneviève sat on the pillion, hands on his shoulders, nails sharp but sheathed. He let the engine growl, but kept the motorcycle on a leash.

When they were through, the Door was gone.

He had never visited Drake's domain before. Shadow London had roughly the same geography as the real city, but famous or infamous buildings and streets were more solid, more defined, than lesser-known byways and districts, which blurred behind thicker curtains of fog.

'I didn't know it was so easy to come here,' said the vampire. 'Or I'd have considered moving. Sometimes, I'd feel happier as a story than a real person.'

'Our Witch makes the near-impossible seem easy, and she only kept open the door Drake made. Usually, there's a high cost to passing over. Jack the Ripper got here by committing five murders...'

'A ritual?'

'Not exactly. The point was to become part of the fabric of *story*. That, he managed.'

'Who was he?'

'No one. That was his problem. He had a name once, and Mycroft at least knew it, but with his final murder, it was wiped out of our world completely. The files are blank. A pathetic, vicious little man became a legend. Even that was an exchange. This place got the Ripper, but Spring-Heel'd Jack crossed the other way. I ran into a fair simulacrum of that bounder last night. Leaping Jack began as a whisper and drunkards' tales, but took on substance when Bloody Jack joined the company of phantom fiends.'

They were still in the courtyard of the Tower of London. Ravens the size of condors nested on the battlements. A wailing sounded through the fog. A wide-skirted, child-sized figure slushed across cobbles towards them.

Edwin turned on a searchlight-bright head-lamp.

A screech came from a mouth located somewhere to the side of the figure's hip. A white, pinched, angry face shrivelled and a seven-fingered hand clapped over the eyes.

'It's Anne Boleyn,' Edwin exclaimed.

'"Wiv 'er 'ead tucked underneaf 'er arm",' Geneviève quoted. 'She waa-aa-alked the Bloody Tower!'

The butchered bride had seemed child-sized because her head wasn't on her shoulders. Blood wept from her neck-stump, staining her enormous ruff like some unknown species of chrysanthemum.

The poor spectre was no threat, and simply kept wailing as she shuffled out of the light. Other, bulkier figures walked through the fog—mostly dead traitors, he assumed, unrepentant or penitent, lugging severed noggins. They might well be in a mood to do some harm. One loose-limbed shadow tumbled and tinkled, whipping streamers of fog with each caper. It wore a belled, three-pronged hat and curly-toed shoes. It was Jack Point, the melancholy fool from *The Yeomen of the Guard*. A keening song shrilled through gloom, 'heigh-dee, heigh-dee, misery me, lack-a-day-dee...'

A rasping sounded, as of a giant, rusted chain unspooling. A portcullis was coming down. Back in the real world, the chains were oiled and Edwin had barely noticed the noise as the gates lowered. Here, the portcullis sounded as he imagined it would.

'Hold on tight,' he told Geneviève, gunning the bike.

Flame shot from the exhaust, which was alarming, and Edwin drove for the gate. He saw the sharpened spear-points of the portcullis, glinting as the Night Flier's beam fell on them.

There was not enough head-room, and it was diminishing by the second.

Trusting to Dr Shade's design, he leaned to the left with all his body, taking the bike and Geneviève with him. His sleeve scraped cobbles and the Night Flier rode on the edges of its tires. At an unnatural angle, they passed under the points and were out of the Tower a second before the portcullis-spears dug into the gravel.

He hauled the Night Flier upright, and the bike did what it was supposed to. He assumed that counter-weights and gyroscopes and balances inside the works assisted stunts like this.

It was exhilarating, bombing through the fog—it was impossible to tell whether it was day or night here—on the marvellous machine.

He shot a look back at Geneviève. Deep parallel scratches on her cheek sliced to the bone around her right eye, tearing her mouth away from glistening fang-teeth.

'The portcullith caught me,' she explained, slushing through her wound. The torn flesh reassembled and healed smoothly. There wasn't even blood, though she licked her lips as if there were. 'That's convenient. I seem to be different here.'

'Careful,' he cautioned. 'I'm told it's addictive.'

As the Night Flier throbbed, he knew he should take the warning himself.

'Where to?' she asked.

'Over Tower Bridge. We've got to liaise with Our Man in Storyland.'

'Who?'

'You'll see.'

Driving almost blind, he took the turn onto the Bridge and cruised under the gothic arch of the North Tower. There was little other road traffic in Shadow London, though a man on a penny-farthing bicycle pedalled the other way across the bridge, lifting a tall hat as he passed.

'Can you hear that?' said Geneviève.

Tiny bells tinkled above. Jack Point had followed them. Edwin wondered whether the embittered jester—'a merryman moping mum, whose soul was sad and whose glance was glum, who sipped no sup and who craved no crumb as he sighed for the love of a lay-dee'—might not be the sort of malcontent easily swayed by the blandishments of the Great Enchanter. Where better to find a treasonable sort than behind Traitors' Gate?

Point had fellows with him—ghosts? traitors? storymen?—on the high-level walkways between the Towers. Back in reality, this section had been closed to the public since 1910. It once had a bad reputation as a haunt of cutpurses, petty thieves and harlots. Here, the bad elements still held that particular high ground.

Now, the road underneath the Night Flier was sloping upwards.

Jack Point was raising the bridge. He must have command over the hydraulic mechanisms that could lift the two hundred-foot, thousand-ton leaves to let shipping pass through.

The bike sped on, forward momentum overcoming the increasing tug of brute gravity.

Through the fog, Edwin saw the edge of the bridge-leaf. The masts of an old schooner, hung with rags, were passing slowly through the gap. Something gigantic thrashed in the waters, making vast eddies in the fog. A sucker-lined tentacle the size of Nelson's column scythed through the masts.

They had bigger things to worry about than a treacherous jester.

The bike slowed as it neared the lip of the bridge. The drag increased as the incline bested forty-five degrees. At maximum elevation, the leaves saluted each other at eighty-three degrees.

'We're too heavy,' said Geneviève, pressing cold lips to his ear. She let go and her weight was whipped from his back.

The Night Flier surged forward, cresting the lip of the bridge-leaf. On instinct, Edwin pressed two red buttons and more flame burst from the exhaust.

Below, a ship was crushed in the thrashing coils of a leviathan, sailors dragged towards a many-toothed beak. A huge, salty eye swivelled as Edwin rocketed across the gap between the two leaves of Tower Bridge.

He didn't have time to mourn Geneviève.

The front wheel landed on the near-vertical incline of the Southern bridge-leaf, and he pulled the bike around. It skidded down on its side, wheelrims striking showers of sparks. Edwin tucked in his knee. The bike was designed to allow such a manoeuvre—his leg neatly fit into a groove in the metal carapace, and his trousers weren't even singed.

At the Southwark end of the bridge, the bike landed with a thump, but kept upright.

He really must write a note of thanks to the Norton Company!

What about the vampire woman? He would have to explain to the Old Man that he had lost her.

He stalled the Night Flier under the arch of the South Tower and looked up.

The bridge-leaves were lowering now. Something hung from the upper walkway.

Laughing, shrieking figures—cutpurses, petty thieves, harlots?—swarmed towards Geneviève, who dangled upside-down like a bat, knees crooked over a cable, hair streaming. Hands reached down and scrabbled at her legs, trying to dislodge her from her perch. Down below, the leviathan still hungered. Maybe only a stake through the heart or a silver bullet in the brain could *kill* a vampire, but Edwin had a notion that being diced by the beak of a monstrous imaginary cephalopod and soaked in its digestive juices might at least severely inconvenience the woman.

From the Night Flier's saddle-bag, he took a bulky, black-painted Verey pistol and shot up a flare. The result wasn't what he expected, which is what he got for using borrowed gear. A purple cloud burst above the bridge, casting a sickly violet glow and forming a shape like a black skull wearing goggles. The gimmick was supposed to terrify those who dared defy Dr Shade. It did the trick on Geneviève's persecutors, who properly cringed and left her alone.

No, only the lesser shadows were seen off. The crooked, bell-tagged Jack Point clung like a gecko to the bridgeworks, spidering under the walkway, teeth bared in his clown grin, working inexorably towards Geneviève Dieudonné.

Edwin drew his Webley and tried to sight on the jester. Jack Point zig-zagged, to avoid being a target or because it was the only way he could move. With a rifle, Edwin might have made the shot. With a pistol, he could as easily shoot Geneviève—and he was loaded with silver.

Gracefully, the vampire swung herself off the cable as if leaping from the trapeze. Jack Point made an ill-judged grab for her, and lost his grip. He plunged through the fog, bouncing and breaking against the guardrail, then sailed, limp, into the thick surface-mists of Shadow Thames. Edwin hoped that was the end of the fool.

Geneviève hung in the air, not clinging to anything.

Edwin was astonished.

She held out her arms and drifted towards him, smiling broadly, enjoying herself too much.

The air was different here.

Dr Shade's giant skull illusion laughed—the Devil knew how that trick was worked!—and evaporated.

Edwin caught Geneviève as if she were his partner in an acrobatic act and set her down.

'Can we do that again?' she asked, breathless. '*C'est incroyable!* Here,

I think I can do all the things they say vampires can do...'

She held up her hand and turned it to mist. The effect spread quickly up her arm, and the shape threatened to drift in the breeze. She had to concentrate to make herself solid again.

'*That*, I didn't enjoy,' she said.

'Focus, Mademoiselle,' he said. 'Remember what I said. It's dangerous here. You can end up as one of the stories. Trapped in one. Like Anne Boleyn, trudging around with her head because it's expected. Or Peter Pan. He lives here too.'

She snapped her fingers and sobered up.

They got back on the Night Flier and drove cautiously through almost-familiar streets. It was a mistake to assume that the topography here was exactly what they knew. Shadows lingered long after buildings fell.

They arrived at the building the Old Man had told him to find.

'There's something I never thought to see again,' said Geneviève. Edwin felt her shudder before she hopped off the pillion. 'It's the Clink.'

'Burned down in the Gordon Riots of 1780. London's most notorious gaol, used for the detention of heretics from the 12th Century, then for the rabble and riff-raff of Southwark. It lingers here because its name is still used as a slang term.'

He got off the Night Flier and propped it up against a horse-trough. He unstrapped his flying helmet. His body still thrummed from the ride.

'I wonder if my cell is still here,' said the vampire. 'I scratched my name on the stone.'

He looked at her as anyone looks at someone who's just admitted to serving a term in prison.

'What were you in for?' he asked.

'Not what you're thinking,' she said, turning with a shy smile. 'No blood-drinking involved. It was *debt*. Twelve shillings, owed to an apothecary. I got by the rules too. Fifty years of needlework, paying off all those pennies. And the interest. I wasn't so accomplished an escape artist back then. And the other prisoners needed me.'

'For what?'

'Doctoring. It's what I've done, mostly. My father before me. I've a couple of medical degrees, taken centuries apart. I knew about blood-types before Jansky and Moss.'

Edwin was surprised. He hadn't considered that vampires might need careers.

'Where's your mysterious contact?' she asked. 'I hope it's not one of those dreary English Jesuits who were clapped up here. Or, worse, a gaoler. The turnkeys were bigger bloodsuckers than me.'

'Our fellow should be *outside* the Clink.'

There, on a bench, sat the Man. A neatly-dressed, nondescript personage in an 18th-Century coat and hat, half-leaning on a stick.

'Ho there,' he called. 'Who approaches?'

'A friend,' said Edwin. 'From the Diogenes Club.'

'I've been expecting ye,' said the Man. 'The Wizard came by earlier. There've been wild rumours. Signs and wonders. Imps and sports. A two-headed calf born in Clerkenwell. Tommy Atkins tells me he's orders to muster in. That's never good news.'

'Geneviève, this is the Ticket-of-Leave Man,' said Edwin.

'Delighted to make your acquaintance,' said the Man, doffing his hat to show a ringlet-fringed baldpate.

'He runs straight now,' Edwin explained, 'but still knows everything that happens in this city, straight or crooked.'

The Man smiled, sadly. At one time, he was a familiar London character: a convict, not exactly released, but trusted enough to be at large; indeed, in such a precarious position, he could be reckoned the most trustworthy man in the city, for he had the most to lose from the slightest step off the path. A sentence in the Clink was not something anyone would wish to resume.

'As a lad, I fell among bad companions,' the Man confessed. 'I chased after the baubles of the wicked world. But I have now repented of that, and serve only the Crown and the cause of Justice.'

The Man set his hat back on his head, which now boasted flowing, grey-gold locks. His nose was longer, with a twist to the side. Now, he had whiskers swarming up his cheeks; now, he was shaven clean. Beauregard had told Edwin about this, but seeing it was another matter. This wasn't any particular Ticket-of-Leave Man, but *all* of them—whether transported to the colonies or lately freed from Clink. There had been a popular melodrama entitled *The Ticket-of-Leave Man*, in which the central figure was a put-upon innocent conspired against by a hypocritical villain. This had transformed the Ticket-of-Leave Man in the popular imagination, taking away an edge of possible menace and setting in stone the notion of a redeemed soul doing his best to make up for past wrongs.

Many citizens of Shadow London were like this—composites of types, rather than individuals. The incarnation of many, many stories, ballads, smoking room jokes, bedtime yarns or fondly held rumours. The Wretched Child Chimney Sweep, the Friendly Bobby on the Beat, the Soho Tart With a Heart, Burlington Bertie From Bow, the Roaring Toff, the Fathead Farmer Lately From the Country (and Ripe to be Rooked), the Mother Ruined by Gin, the Sailor with Six Months' Pay in His Pocket, the Unscrupulous Anatomist, the Irish Labourers Pat and Mike, and other types, archetypes or caricatures.

'Things have not been right round these parts,' confided the Man, talking like a melodrama. 'We have had a Visitor, unwelcome by most, but a dangerous friend to some. You know who I mean?'

Edwin could guess. So, he was sure, could Geneviève.

He saw another layer to the Great Enchanter's gambit with the runes.

To keep Connaught Drake busy while he was trespassing in Wizard's realm. Zenf could evidently gain easy access to Shadow London. Edwin wouldn't put it past the Great Enchanter to manage in an evening as many murders as Jack the Ripper in a long, busy autumn, though he suspected that Zenf could conjure up a Door by other means.

'The Visitor has made allies. Unfortunates, mostly. The unrepentant.'

'We met one at the Tower,' said Geneviève. 'A clown.'

The Man shivered. 'Never could abide clowns,' he admitted. 'Don't see why they're supposed to be funny. Grimaldi's all right, mind. More a weeper than a mocker.'

'What about the Wizard?' asked Edwin. 'Connaught Drake?'

'He's here,' said the Man. 'North of the river. In the City. I've a whisper from a certain Woman of Pleasure that Wizard comes to parlay with the Visitor. He has already offered a sacrifice...'

Nosey Parker's Mum.

'There's great uncertainty in the city,' continued the Man.

Edwin didn't like the sound of 'parlay'. Surely, Drake *couldn't* be the King Rat? If Wizard were in league with Zenf, the war would be over.

'Do you know exactly where Drake is?'

The Ticket-of-Leave Man nodded, and said, 'Thomas Farriner's Bakery.'

Geneviève rolled up her eyes and groaned, 'Not again.'

It took Edwin a moment to make the connection.

To the north of the Clink was the river, and beyond that the City of London. London Bridge was nearby, the ramshackle span which fell down in the rhyme, and beyond that was a bank of pink-tinged fog, as if a giant sun were rising. Shouts and alarums came through the fog, and red-orange plumes darted.

Farriner's Bakery was in Pudding Lane. It was where the Great Fire of London started.

The cries carried over the water, 'City on fire! City on fire!'

'Drake's sold us out,' said Edwin, despair thumping in his chest. 'He's burning the city's shadow.'

'What'll that do to the real London?' Geneviève asked.

'Turn it to ashes and cinders,' said Edwin, '*ashes and cinders*.'

XXI: 'Abracadabra!'

The Quiet Room was anything but.

General Lord Hector Tarr argued the toss with Mr Hay. The alliance of the Diogenes Club and the Undertaking was strained near to breaking.

Charles called 'order'. During the Great War, he'd listened to too much squabbling in operations rooms while ranks of brave men were mowed down in the field. Tarr and Hay were momentarily cowed.

Reports came in from all over London, especially from the area of the

Old City. Buildings had collapsed. Ghosts which walked to a regular schedule failed to appear. Every psychic, swami, seer, fortune-teller, spiritualist medium, prophet, visionary and palmist in the city was struck with raving horrors. At Colney Hatch Asylum and the Purfleet sanatorium, the insane were rioting. Sewer workers and a museum night watchman were missing. A spate of 'tong suicides' had broken out in Limehouse. A backbench MP had spontaneously combusted during a debate on dog licensing; Special Branch and Military Intelligence were scurrying down blind alleys looking for bomb-tossing, black-bearded anarchists.

This, Charles assumed, was overspill from what was happening in the Shadow City.

He looked up at Mycroft's portrait. As usual, he saw something in the eyes, a secret held back. How would the Great Man have handled this?

Catriona rattled the telephone, cut off in mid-call, and tried to get connected again. Charles had her following leads on Rennes and Stone, the missing Ravens. He needed everyone else to cope with small fires and do their best to limit the damage, but it could be that her job was the most important.

Earlier, it had seemed certain Robert Edmond Stone was the Rat. Now the question was open again. Catriona had suggested there might be more than one bad apple in the barrel.

If the Ravens, the city's protectors, stood with Zenf, could they be bested?

Catriona hung up, after another call.

'Simon Pure's recovered from his knock on the head,' she said, 'but has no idea who or what hit him. Dr Chambers is still somewhat short-tempered, and her practice is overwhelmed. A stream of minor casualties has flowed into her surgery. She wonders if we could spare any specialists, but they're all working flat out as it is. Margery got hold of Dr Silence, and he's on his way. I don't suppose it matters whether he sets up shop here or in Harley Street. Harry Dickson promises to get the boat train. The others on the reserve list are casualties, I'm afraid. All our sensitives are screaming. Morris Klaw complains of nightmares. Taverner, Chard and Scarfe are *hors de combat*.'

Charles didn't like relying on the reserves anyway—most were dilettantes and cranks, though he'd be glad of John Silence's help. Jenny Chambers could do with another 'physician extraordinary' on site.

'There is *some* good news,' said Catriona, bitterly. 'The blessed Sir Henry sends his excuses. Apparently, a mystery death in Rutland intrigues H.M. more than the fall of the kingdom. Such a comfort that a few still value the high art of detection above passing expediencies.'

'Anything from Margery?' Charles asked.

'She has her ear out for word on Rennes and Stone,' Catriona continued. 'No luck yet. She hears everything, normally. We have to assume Zenf is deliberately drowning out the usual background chatter. There is currently no echo in the Whispering Gallery of St Paul's. And the Town Crier tried to poison himself with some noxious stuff which burned out his vocal cords.'

'The Ravens must still be in London.'

'Or else things would be worse? I agree. I have a splitting headache, by the way, but I'm putting that down to being awake for thirty-six hours without having eaten.'

Charles realised how tired he was. And hungry.

'I thought so,' said Catriona, diagnosing his condition at a glance. 'I'll send your chimney-sweep down to the kitchens, and have sandwiches and tea sent up. I'm sure even the Undertakers need regular meals.'

Catriona scribbled a note and gave it to Master Wuh, who scuttled off.

As the young Undertaker left the Quiet Room, noise leaked in—a commotion from the supposedly hallowed, silent precincts. Where a rustled newspaper was cause for expulsion and a post-prandial burp once led to a duel with pistols, there was now unholy commotion, with raised voices and a sound horribly like rattled sabres.

The commotion made its way into the Quiet Room.

A gnarly-faced gent in evening dress, complete with silk-lined cape and opera hat, stood there, supporting an identically dressed, insensible fellow whose throat was bandaged.

'Alakazam,' announced the Great Edmondo, tossing Marcus Rennes into the room. He held up empty, white-gloved hands, showing that there was nothing up his sleeves. 'Abracadabra!'

Choking red smoke filled the room.

XXII: 'fetch the engines'

As the Night Flier crossed London Bridge, the whole structure shook. They had to drive between the tall, rickety, mediaeval houses which edged the span, encroaching aggressively on the public right of way. The buildings shook like jelly on a platter. Some collapsed backwards into the river, their fronts floating a moment, doors and windows popped open, before sinking into the Thames.

This was the proverbial London Bridge, the one which was *falling down, falling down.*

A zig-zag crack appeared in the road, showing foaming waters beneath. Edwin jumped the motorbike over the gap, playing hopscotch with the abyss. Geneviève held on tight.

The air was filled with tumult and clanking as iron and steel bent and bowed, wood and clay washed away. Thieves stripped silver and gold from vital support structures. Vikings ravaged the houses—the rhyme dated back to the destruction of a London Bridge by Danes, Edwin remembered—and a long-dressed, white-robed 'fair lady' was dragged by a mob towards an open tomb on the North Embankment.

'Build it up with stone so strong,' Geneviève quoted the nursery rhyme, 'stone so strong will last so long...'

Once they were off the bridge and in the City, fog turned to smoke. Giant towers of flame roared. Many fire-fighters were busy, big red engines with shiny brass trim and human chains of suddenly homeless folk with buckets. A cadre of dancing fanatics threw themselves into the fires.

It was another rhyme, 'London's Burning, London's Burning'.

'Fire fire, fire fire,' quoted Geneviève, 'fetch the engines, fetch the engines, pour on water, pour on water...'

Through great black ropes of smoke, Edwin saw long-destroyed buildings burning again. This wasn't just the Great Fire of 1666, but all of London's fires, past, present, future, historical, legendary and imaginary. Guy Fawkes wriggled atop a burning pyramid stuffed with casks of gunpowder. Along the river, his once-thwarted scheme paid off as the Houses of Parliament exploded in a great, thunderous puff of flame as if a sleeping dragon had belched in its cellars. Obese Zeppelins and vulture-like Gotha bombers soared overhead, dropping incendiary bombs stamped with black eagles as presents from the Kaiser. One of the Martian War Machines from Wells's book waded three-legged through the silt of a dried-up stretch of the river, heat ray ranging against the stock exchanges, law courts and rookeries of Old London. Maddened lamp-lighters, faces clown-like from savage smears of soot and blood, ran from home to home, touching firebrands to dry wood, babies' bedding, curtains, and pots of oil. Cathedral after cathedral fell as if dismissed by an ungrateful or aggrieved deity, spires collapsing upon praying crowds, vast stones raining on the grounds, the honoured dead rudely thrust out of their tombs.

Edwin heard again the big guns of the Somme. For a moment, Dr Shade's Norton was his old Camel. He ached to take to the skies and tear through the whale-hide of a Zeppelin.

Instead, he drove into the heart of the inferno.

Dangerous paths threaded through the burning district. Geneviève patted out flames before they could take hold on their sleeves. Grime built up on his goggles, which Geneviève wiped with her handkerchief. Did vampires have ordinary use for hankies? A watch-tower collapsed behind them, barring the road. Up ahead was Pudding Lane, where the fire started, where Connaught Drake was. The Keeper of the Ravens in league with the Great Enchanter. From now on, if there was a 'from now on', Drake would be known as the Great Traitor.

They halted at a burning traffic light, waiting for curtains of flame to die down so they could pass.

'What are we expected to *do?*' shouted Geneviève.

'Find Drake. Stop him. Take him back. Save the city.'

'Fair enough. How?'

'I'm sure we'll think of something. Ready?'

'As I'll ever be, *mon brave*.'

The fire ahead burned *green*, which he took as a signal to *go*...

The Night Flier shot forward, punching a hole through flame, into an oasis of calm within the city-wide holocaust.

At first, he thought this was an eye of the hurricane, an untouched clearing... then he saw the black buildings. They were charcoal and ash constructions, barely holding the ghost of their former shape. Ash-coated Londoners lay on black cobbles, curled into Pompeii-mummy foetal shapes. Other blasted skeletons, coated with black rags of meat, were Medusa-struck, staring statues.

Connaught Drake sat on a bench outside Thomas Farriner's Bakery, nibbling a currant bun.

'Hello, Winthrop, mademoiselle,' he said, genially. 'Either of you care for one of these? I saved a tray from the flames. Much better than Mrs Lovat's meat pies.'

Wizard indicated a plate on the bench, piled with sweet-smelling, fresh-baked London Buns.

Fire-shapes, phoenix-shadows of Drake's ravens, hopped about. One alighted on the Keeper's shoulder without burning his tweed. He fed it crumbs.

Edwin took off his flying helmet. He drew and pointed his Webley, declaring 'Connaught Drake, I arrest you in the name of the law...'

Wizard chuckled. Edwin had expected as much. Was there a glint of malevolence in the man's mild eye?

'Dear boy, you've grasped the wrong end of the stick.'

Geneviève stood at Edwin's shoulder, showing her best fangface and talons.

'Didn't your mother ever tell you not to pull faces, young lady? You know what'll happen if the wind changes.'

A breeze riffled through Pudding Lane. Charcoal corpses crumbled. Shops and house fell to pieces.

Geneviève wisely pulled her teeth and claws.

'That's better,' said Drake.

'You burned the city,' Edwin accused.

Drake waved the observation away. 'The city is *always* being burned. It *needs* to be burned, just as the bridge needs to fall down. Fire is one of the great forces of London. Once, fire ended plague, cleared the way for... well, the rather overrated St Paul's, but that's by the by. Heed these words: London Can Take It. You'll hear them again, when the air raid sirens shriek. Indeed, London Must Take It. Taking it is what London is *for*.'

Edwin lowered his gun. What did Drake mean?

'Pay attention, Winthrop. We are close to the final working of a clever trick. Better than any of Robbie Stone's, I assure you—though he has helped in a minor sort of way. We've all had our parts to play, including you two.

Just now, you need to do what Beauregard told you to... render me any assistance.'

Fires were dying all around. A parade was coming—rescuers or an invading army? Edwin heard the stamp of marching feet, and cocked his gun. At the head of the parade was a giant nag, which clumped through the embers on huge hooves. On its back sat an imposing figure in a big hat.

'Just the fellow we need,' said Drake. 'Have you met Colonel Zenf?'

The horseman rode into the light, followed by a rabble of Vikings, French infantry, Roman legionaries, ragged cavaliers, fire-spreaders, shaggy Anglo-Saxons, Martian squid-vampires, rowdies from the country and Prussian Uhlans. The Great Enchanter was dwarfish and pot-bellied, gussied up in a too-large uniform with gold epaulettes and a sash. Attached to his sideways-worn hat was a domino mask and a huge, crooked, cardboard nose.

At first, Edwin thought Zenf was dressed as Napoleon... then, he saw that this sham did not represent the historical Buonaparte, but a caricature of the Little Corporal. This was the dreaded *Boney*—a recurring threat, any foreign commander who might boast that his armies would swarm across the Channel, sail up the Thames and put London to the sword.

'Boney was a warrior, way-ay-aye,' he breathed.

'Boney was a warrior, Jean François,' Geneviève completed.

Zenf took off his mask and hat. He looked inordinately pleased with himself. He was waiting to accept a pre-arranged surrender.

Edwin thought he could manage a single shot before the mob got to him. Who best to take out? Drake or Zenf?

'A "very clever trick", you say,' Edwin accused, aiming his Webley. 'Can you manage a bullet-catch?'

'A volunteer from the audience,' Drake told Zenf. 'As for the bullet business, I think that might best be left to my, ah, *lovely assistant*.'

A swift pinch came at Edwin's wrist, paralysing his arm. He dropped his gun.

In a whirl, he was held by cold, strong, fast arms and forced painfully down on his knees. A mouth close to his ear exhaled numbing iciness.

'Sorry,' whispered Geneviève.

He hadn't seen *that* trick coming.

XXIII: 'the worst possible outcome'

When the smoke cleared, Conjurer was on the floor, arms wrestled behind his back and bound with his own cloak. Master Wuh sat on the Great Edmondo.

'Get this incubus off me,' snarled Robert Stone. 'I'm not your Rat.'

'You are the *attack* magician,' said Charles. 'You must expect us to put up a defence.'

'I am addicted to dramatic entrances,' muttered the magician. 'Do I deserve a broken back for it?'

Catriona examined Marcus Rennes. He was unconscious. Slapping didn't wake him up.

'It's not Sorcerer, either,' insisted Stone. 'I had to whip him out the back door of Chambers's clinic while Zenf's creatures were knocking at the front. Good man, that nurse. Stood his ground like Archaeopteryx at the Bridge...'

'I don't think that's the name,' said Giles Gallant. 'If I remember my Classics...'

'B----r your Classics!' said Stone. 'Let me up.'

Charles nodded, and Master Wuh got off Stone's back, then helped him upright—without untying him.

'I do this for a living, you know,' said the Great Edmondo, shrugging free of his makeshift bonds with a flourish. He tried to bring up his hands and found they were still cuffed. Piqued, he shrugged again, and gave the handcuffs to the young Undertaker only to see his wrist now shackled to the boy's. 'This is most irritating and unnecessary,' he said, disappearing the cuffs and pulling coins out of Master Wuh's ears, then dropping them as if they were filthy.

'I've been playing hide and seek with Sweeney Todd and Charlie Peace,' said Conjurer, 'all the way from Harley Street to here. They're both broken now. They weren't wax, by the way. Just wearing wax masks of themselves. They were borrowed from Drake's place, the Shadow City.'

'So it's Wizard after all,' said Charles. 'The worst possible outcome.'

'On some level, I ought to be offended,' said Stone. 'Rennes too if he were awake. Both of us could do a great deal of damage if so inclined. Far more than that fathead Drake. However, I don't think you have anything to worry about from that direction. Or Margery. It's none of us. You should have checked your sources.'

'The leech!' shouted Mr Hay.

'I knew it,' said Tarr.

The two looked at each other, astonished that they agreed on something, then gabbled at once.

'That vampire bitch is in it with Zenf,' said Gallant.

Charles caught a fleeting, instantly suppressed sympathy from Catriona. He felt a chill, a sadness he could not express. It was so *disappointing...*

'I have your attention now,' said Stone. 'This is how magic works. Stage magic, anyway. You were looking in the wrong place. But, just this once, I *have* something up my sleeve... another trick, a trick within a trick, as it were.'

From his sleeve, Stone produced an envelope, which he gave to Charles.

'This was given me when I joined the Ravens,' he said. 'Note the three seals. The red raven is Drake's. The white dove is Stark's. He was Conjurer before me. Slippery b-----d, he was. Could get out of anything. The other one you'll know.'

Charles saw the initials 'M.H.'

'What's it say, man?' prompted Tarr, impatient.

Charles read the legend aloud, 'The Stratagem of King Raven in Rat's Fur, With Notes Upon the Segregation of a Great Enchanter.'

Catriona clapped her forehead, seeing it at once. 'It's all been a lure—a worm on a hook! That clever, monstrous, fat old man! Dead for fifteen years, and still pulling all the strings.'

Charles looked up at the portrait, remembering what it was like to work for Mycroft Holmes, not to see what was intended until the last moment.

He still didn't know what game Geneviève was playing.

XXIV: 'not the usual arrangement'

'Stay down, Edwin,' said the vampire, sadly. 'Let the grown-ups talk.'

He wasn't sure why he was still alive. Geneviève could have opened his throat with a kiss and bled him like human veal. Maybe in the Shadow City, killing wasn't liable to take. He wouldn't rise as *nosferatu*—for that you had to exchange blood with a vampire, drink from their veins as they drank from yours—but he might find himself playing this scene over and over, one of the minor stories attendant upon the Fall of London. The Betrayed Knight, or the Blockhead of Bloomsbury. Old St Paul's burned twice nightly with matinees Wednesdays and Saturdays. And don't forget Edwin Winthrop, starring in Backstabbed by a Bloodsucking Biddy.

'Don't struggle,' she said. 'It'll be all right. Trust me.'

'Trusting you hasn't worked well so far.'

Colonel Zenf was enjoying his moment. He looked about the blackened, after-fire skeleton of Pudding Lane. He poked a wall, and an entire row of bakers' shops crumbled silently, resolved to ash and cinders.

'Amusing,' he observed. 'Just the lightest touch of my finger, and... *pouf!* A fortress of blanc-mange, scarcely worth the conquering. And yet, what a magnificent achievement. The greatest city of the world in flames, at my feet. I am humbled with delight, and quite giddy at the prospect of what to do next...'

Connaught Drake indulged the Great Enchanter. Edwin couldn't imagine what Wizard was thinking. What could Drake possibly *want*?

'I assume you have some symbol of surrender,' said Zenf. 'A key to the city?'

Wizard shrugged.

'Of course, this is but a shadow, but when one holds the shadow, the real thing must follow.'

'That's not the usual arrangement,' said Drake, dryly.

Zenf chortled. 'I suppose not. But we are *unusual* persons.'

'Not that unusual, old thing.'

A crack appeared in Zenf's preening.

Geneviève's grip relaxed, deliberately. 'Be ready,' she whispered in his ear. 'There's everything to play for.'

Edwin could have reached for his dropped pistol. But he was interested now. How would this play out?

Like Edwin, Zenf had got it the wrong way round. When Shadow London burned, it was not weaker, but stronger.

'Feh,' said the Colonel to Drake. 'I was going to kill you anyway.'

The Great Enchanter reached into his coat.

'Now,' said Geneviève, letting Edwin free.

They leaped on Zenf, securing his arms. A contraption like a sextant, covered in runic writing, fell from his grasp. The Great Enchanter struggled against them, but they held on fast.

Edwin took an elbow in the face, but sank a knee into a paunch. Geneviève raked nails across Zenf's piggy cheek.

Drake began to laugh, and the Wizard War was over.

Zenf took a few moments to catch up. His pomp leaked away, leaving a prissy, absurd little man in a comic opera uniform. Edwin and Geneviève held him between them.

The Great Enchanter looked about for his invading army.

In the shadows stood redcoats with muskets, knights in armour, tommies in tin hats, roundheads and cavaliers shoulder to shoulder, bloods and blades, pearly kings and queens, costers, tarts, loafers, brawlers, football fanatics with scarves and rattles, the *haut ton* and the *demi-monde*, air raid wardens, firemen, peelers, bobbies, Bow Street Runners, Chelsea pensioners, dandies, strollers and—yes!—Dick Whittington's Cat. The unconquered and, indeed, *unconquerable* of London.

'A word about tactics, old chap,' Drake said, mildly. 'Upon walking into the enemy's camp to accept surrender, make sure it's actually on offer.'

'But you're...'

'A Rat? Perhaps.'

'It was *revealed*. A Rat among the Ravens.'

'A Rat to whom? A turncoat and betrayer, of course. Tell me, Colonel, don't *you* feel betrayed?'

Zenf shook his head. He still didn't see how he'd been gulled.

Edwin still hadn't completely caught up, but a picture was beginning to form. How much of this had Geneviève known?

A Pearly Queen—*the* Pearly Queen—emerged from the crowd, a thousand luminous teardrops studding her padded jacket, flat cap and long skirts. It was Margery Device.

'Did you get *a little whisper*, Colonel? You should never trust gossip.'

Darkness rose in Zenf's face. Crimson fury stood out on his forehead. He made fists. He raised shadows from the ground. He was still the Great Enchanter, and could summon an army of fiends. Edwin remembered the waxwork horrors... the things that had come after the rune-bearers... the flock of pecking birds... the clowns of Shadow Tower... the worse things that waited.

An ogre loomed over Drake, one of Zenf's 'frightful fiends'. At his touch, it fell to ashes like the shops Zenf had puffed away.

'Not here, old fellow,' said Wizard. 'Sorry.'

'This is our city,' said Witch. 'And you are a prisoner. You came for the key, and all we have for you are chains...'

Zenf was done.

'Well played, Mr Winthrop, Mademoiselle Dieudonné,' Miss Device said to them. 'This couldn't have been done without you.'

Edwin burned, a little. A pat on the back seemed slightly insufficient.

'Cheer up,' said Geneviève. 'We've won.'

Edwin looked at the smoking ruins.

'You're right,' said Wizard. 'It is a mess. But that can be fixed.'

Drake gestured, in distinctly Wizardy fashion, summoning great and powerful forces. In the wake of fire came rebirth. New shops sprung from rubble, a cathedral rose, stones rearranged into fresh edifices. Streets ran straight or crooked, cobbled or tarred. And the river flowed fast and deep, a bloodstream through the heart of the city.

Wizard experimentally touched a petrified fire victim, a lad with a tray of pies. He came to life, crying 'fresh from the oven', hawking his wares. The lad was at the centre of a crowd, spreading the effect. It was like a vivid colour wash over a pencil sketch, turning shrivelled corpses to lively Londoners, fresh from the oven, hale and hearty, hustling and bustling.

Edwin's mouth hung open. Geneviève popped a slice of plum pie into it.

Suddenly, even ashes tasted sweet.

XXV: 'frustrate their knavish tricks'

'Charles,' began the letter, 'you must to steer the Diogenes Club into this new age. Wars will be waged on a scale scarcely imaginable. The coming conflicts between Britain and her allies and Greater Germany can not be averted. It will be the business of the whole world, fought in the open, on battlefields, in the air and on the seas. I hope you come through these particular fires, though at my age—and, frankly, at my weight—it seems certain I shall not.

'However, these "world wars" do not most concern me. As I write, the dreadful business of Persano's Worm has just been concluded. We came closer to ruin than I allowed anyone to know. The purpose of the Stratagem I have set in motion is to prevent a recurrence of such peril. Isidore Persano's wits are fled, and with them his status as Great Enchanter. Others yet unknown or unborn will assume that mantle. We can do nothing to prevent the rise of such person or persons, but we can take steps to cope with them, to— as our National Anthem has it—"confound their politics, frustrate their knavish tricks".

'I have conferred with Rennes, the Greenwich Sorcerer. The augurs suggest a time of danger some twenty-five to thirty years hence. An Enchanter will make his debut, and the forces at his command will be more potent, aggressive and malevolent than at any time in history. Fat ticks bloated on the human misery poured out on the battlefields of Europe will swarm to his cause. Our enemies—human and otherwise—may have their Napoleon, their Bismarck, their Arthur. If this prodigy of wickedness—a successor of Mary Braxton, Isidore Persano and Leo Dare—manages a coup early in his tenure, there will be dire consequences.

'So, in consultation with the Ravens, I intend to nip that man's career in the bud. An agent, at present unknown to you, will—when certain conditions have been fulfilled—allow a rumour to spread. I regret the necessity for deception, but for the Stratagem to succeed, *you must yourself believe this rumour*—which is why this is to be delivered only after an outcome has been achieved. I know you will take actions to oppose the Great Enchanter, by launching a hunt for the Rat Among the Ravens. Our enemy—as yet unknown, and perhaps unmade!—is to be convinced that an opportunity has arisen for him to make a great pre-emptive strike against us. It is my intention that instead he will deliver himself into our hands.

'With the Great Enchanter off the board, dangers will remain—the city may still burn, again—but I am satisfied greater calamities will be prevented. If our enemy survives the affair, use can be made of him. As long as he is alive and in his right mind, *no other can rise to take his place*. Interrogation of Persano has yielded little, but it is my hope our next Great Enchanter can be taken in his right wits, then *turned* to our ends, tapped for what he will know.

'It is a matter of regret to me that I have had to keep you and my other agent apart, for your abilities and temperaments are a perfect complement. It has always been my intention that you and she should *together* carry on the work I have begun.

'Other details of the Stratagem, and the parties who will inevitably be involved, are enclosed.

'Your servant, Mycroft Holmes.'

Charles set down the letter and looked at the faces around him.

'Well...' prompted Catriona.

Charles riffled through the other pages, which detailed the Stratagem. Most of it he had guessed at once, from the heading.

'Geneviève's with us,' he said. 'And so are all the Ravens.'

'There was no Rat?' said Mr Hay.

Charles shook his head. 'Just a Rat-Trap.'

XXVI: 'magic, I expect'

The judge hadn't quite had the temerity to don the black cap while sentencing the Countess of Chelm, but Olivia Gibberne would be in prison until at least

1956—so Catriona was in a good mood.

Edwin, Catriona and Geneviève sat in the Café Royal.

Upon their entrance, the gentleman and ladies of the Diogenes Club had received a polite smattering of applause. Ivor Novello sent over a magnum of fizz, which even the vampire enjoyed. No one quite knew what they had done, but everyone knew it was something grand.

Even in their night-world, things had moved on. Margery Device whispered that the partnership of Dr Shade and Kentish Glory was on the rocks; now, Jonathan Chambers was running around town with a girl reporter, Penny Stamp. Edwin had received a bill from the Norton company, for minor repairs to the Night Flier. With no reigning Great Enchanter, troublesome elements were in a high state of confusion—which served to make some even more troublesome. Geoff Jeperson was back from California, with a disturbing report on the resurgence of the Esoteric Order of Dagon. Lesser warlocks and would-be black magi were feuding and murdering each other in a contest for the unattainable title, and quite a few innocent persons were caught in the crossfire. The one and only original Spring-Heel'd Jack was back, working with Zenith the Albino—and half of Kensington was terrorised. Sweeney Todd was returned to the Shadow City Chamber of Horrors, but no one had caught Charlie Peace yet. The Ruling Cabal were officially 'very concerned' about most of Herr Hitler's ambitions for Europe.

'I'd love to have seen Ed's face when you bit him,' said Catriona.

'I didn't bite him,' responded Geneviève. 'I *held* him. Otherwise he might have shot the Wizard. With a silver bullet. Which I take as a personal slight, by the way.'

The women laughed.

Edwin still shivered at the moment. It had very nearly all gone wrong, and it needn't have.

'You must have known all along there was no real Rat?' said Catriona.

Geneviève sighed. 'Mr Mycroft preferred to complicate things. I no more knew what was in his mind than Charles did. I was told to begin the Rat Hunt. Not in so many words. I was directed to listen for intelligence, and it came to me. When I was in the Mausoleum, I believed it all—one of the Ravens was a traitor, and the city would fall. Then, I was spirited out of gaol...'

'By Stone?' prompted Edwin.

'Yes, Conjurer. I still don't know how it was done. Magic, I expect. Stone had a letter for me, from Mr Mycroft. Sealed orders. I was given a little more of the Stratagem, but the outcome, the purpose, was as much a surprise to me as to anyone. And I thought the whole plan in ruins when Rennes was attacked. It seemed there might be a Rat after all. Robbie Stone was the only Raven not in office when Mr Mycroft drew up his plans, so he *could* have been a random factor. When Conjurer gave me the letter—and, of course,

seals mean little when you're dealing with professional prestidigitators—
it might have been a masterstroke, a Rat telling me there was no Rat. Mr
Mycroft's Stratagem was based on convincing Zenf—whom he didn't even
know—there was Rat among the Ravens. Sorcerer was silenced because he
was the Raven who scanned the horizon. Zenf would want him out of play,
but so would our imaginary Rat. I was on a knife-edge of doubt and belief.
But Charles tipped it for me. We are both creatures of Mr Mycroft. He never
steered us wrong. And, even after his death, he hasn't now.'

Catriona whistled. 'We all did our parts,' she said, 'as if they were written
for us. It's astonishing. I can't wait to look at the documents.'

'Private files, Cat,' said Edwin.

'Membership has its privileges,' she responded. 'Charles has granted
a special dispensation. Of course, anything I write has to go in the private
files too.'

Edwin's champagne was a little flat. Had he left something of himself in
the Shadow City? It seemed to him that slivers of ice had slipped in when he
was on his knees in Pudding Lane, while the 'grown-ups' were talking. He
knew Geneviève had been doing her duty, but...

He had not known Mycroft Holmes, though Charles sometimes said
Edwin thought like the late Chairman—he too planned ahead, set mechanisms
in motion, placed people on the board, devised contingencies. Now, he was
not sure that was entirely a good thing. He hadn't cared overmuch for being
a pawn or a cog.

'What *are* you thinking, Ed?' said Catriona. 'I know that broody brow.
Some scheme is a-hatching.'

'It's nothing like that,' he said. 'It's the Old Man.'

'Charles?' asked Geneviève.

'She likes him,' put in Catriona. 'Cradle-snatching, really.'

'When I grow up,' said Edwin, 'I want to be like Charles Beauregard,
not...'

'Not who?' prompted Catriona, intrigued.

'Anyone else.'

They laughed and clinked glasses. Outside, the sun was down and the
street-lamps on. Londoners bustled to and fro, busy and (for the moment)
safe.

XXVII: 'to judge from the autopsies'

Mr Eye left the room. Since Charles was last here, the crate had been taken
out and a cot put in.

The little man at the other side of the desk seemed absent-minded, all the
wind leaked out of him. He did not look well, though Charles was assured
the Undertaking made sure he got enough to eat and allowed him exercise
and books. His mind was to be as carefully preserved as his body.

'Have you looked in on Isidore Persano?' Charles asked. 'I should think you'd have much in common.'

'Frankly,' responded Zenf, 'I'd rather talk with the worm.'

'There,' said Charles. 'That's your silence broken. A beginning. We trust you'll have much more to say.'

'It wasn't you, was it?' said Zenf, curiously desperate. 'It can't have been. It wasn't Drake, not entirely. There was someone else in it. Someone in deeper shadow?'

'You should know shadow.'

Zenf smiled bitterly. 'So I should.'

Charles allowed a little mercy. 'You are right, Colonel. There was a plan. A contingency. Against you.'

'I knew it.'

The former Great Enchanter was almost flattered. If a man was judged on the quality of his enemies, Zenf was still noteworthy.

'You haven't been replaced,' Charles said. 'Some have tried.'

Zenf snorted.

'Two or three of your, ah, associates have simply disappeared. Others are in morgues or unmarked graves.'

'It was expected. We too have our *contingency plans.*'

'Some deem it sacrilege that lesser lights aspire to your former position. You still have disciples. One particularly devoted follower, to judge from the autopsies.'

Zenf breathed a name, perhaps unconsciously.

Charles caught it. *Vivian.* The woman from the Pick-Pockets' Ball, dressed like a governess. She had retrieved Zenf's ring from the Bishop of Matabeleland. Margery Device would know her full name.

Charles didn't press the point. Zenf had begun to talk. He might not even have realised yet, but now he would co-operate. Now, he would tell all he knew...

Zenf laughed, slyly. For a moment, the Enchanter believed he had power again, and needed to demonstrate it. He was the master, Charles the supplicant. This was as it should seem. In truth, he was a goose, about to be coaxed into laying a succession of golden eggs.

'I know something about those autopsies,' said Zenf, 'something that I believe would surprise you, might even shock you...'

Charles doubted that, but let it slide.

'You see, Miss Vivian has a peculiarity, a secret known only to the dead—and, as it happens, myself. Mr Beauregard, would you care to know what I know?'

Charles nodded, and Zenf began to share his secrets.

KENTISH GLORY:
THE SECRETS OF DREARCLIFF GRANGE SCHOOL

I: A New Bug

A week after Mother found her sleeping on the ceiling, Amy Thomsett was delivered to her new school. Like a parcel.

Amy had hoped the name was misleading. It wasn't. She should have known. Misleading place-names, like Greenland or the Cape of Good Hope, ran the other way—representing desolate, inhospitable climes as pleasant, cheerful retreats. Drearcliff Grange School was precisely as advertised—a rambling, gloomy, ill-repaired estate on top of a cliff.

Waves eternally hammered the base of the four-hundred-foot drop, eroding supporting rock. Chunks of North Somerset regularly sheared from the clifftop. Some time ago, this land-nibbling had reached the Grange. A West Wing, shattered, had fallen into the sea. A gothic tower, complete with crenellations and arrow-slits, stuck up at an angle from the shingles, white froth washing around it. New wings straggled safely, if dully, inland.

Having got off the down train at Watchet Station, Amy was hailed by someone her own age.

'Ho, Thomsett,' said the other girl, sticking out a hand. 'Headmistress has ordered me to slap the bracelets on and ferry you to School. Many new bugs clap eyes on the place and flee for the hills. Men with hunting dogs comb the Quantocks for escapees.'

The girl wore a more lived-in version of the scratchy uniform Mother had bought from the school's recommended dressmaker in Pond Street. Drearcliff kit consisted of grey skirt with black side-stripe, grey blazer with black piping, grey blouse with black buttons, grey socks with black clocks, grey-*ish* straw boater with black band, and bright crimson tie with black-headed pin. On the hankie-pocket badge, a worried-looking woman—Saint Catherine, presumably—hung upside-down on a cartwheel above an embroidered motto, *a fronte praecipitium a tergo lupi*. 'A precipice in front and wolves behind'. If the cliff counted as the precipice, Amy wondered where wolves came into it. Those famous hunting dogs, perhaps?

If it weren't for the skirt, she might have taken the other girl for a young lad. Her ginger hair was cut short flapper fashion, her lips were the same colour as her face, and she had square shoulders. When they shook hands, a strong grip ground Amy's phalanges and metacarpals.

'I'm Walmergrave,' she said. 'Lady Serafine Nimue Todd Walmergrave, in full. All and sundry call me Frecks.'

'Crumpets!' exclaimed Amy. 'Why?'

'Freckles. Used to have 'em. Don't now. Too late to change the handle. This your trunk?'

'Yes.'

Frecks signalled a bent old man, who hefted Amy's luggage up into the back of a horse-cart.

'Joxer's odd-job man and general slavey,' Frecks explained. 'Don't mind him. Shot in the head in the Great War. Came to Drearcliff with the horse, Dauntless. She was in the War too. Charged enemy guns. Not very bright, if you ask me. Say the name—' Frecks mouthed the syllables *Gen-er-al Haig*—'and Dauntless bolts. Runs perfectly amok.'

Joxer had the opposite of a beard; his chin was shaven, but thick brownish-white hair sprouted everywhere else on his face except nose and forehead. Cheek-whiskers teased out to nine-inch points. Eyebrows curled like the heterocera of the *dryocampa rubicunda* or North American Rosy Maple Moth.

On the narrow road to Drearcliff, the cart acquired a train of horn-honking motorists. Frecks smiled and waved cheerily at the angry men, as if they were all in the Lord Mayor's parade. The growling roadsters could not get by the slow-rolling cart. Dauntless ignored beeps and shouts, and kept steady in the middle of the lane. When the cart turned off for the Grange, the motor cars whizzed past in relief. Amy saw fists shaken and lip-read swear words.

The track led to a tall wall. Broken bottles stuck up from a rind of cement running along the top.

'No one knows whether the jagged glass is to keep angry mobs out or hungry girls in,' said Frecks. 'Headmistress emptied all the bottles herself, for personal use. Green was wine. Brown for beer.'

'What about the blue?'

'Poison, my dear.'

They paused at a set of spear-tipped gates. Frecks hopped down and opened them, standing aside to let Dauntless pull the cart through. The girl fastened the gates from the other side, then slipped onto school grounds by a small, almost-hidden door.

'I trust you're giddy from the privilege, Thomsett,' said Frecks. 'You've just passed through School Gate. You only get to do that again when you leave for good. From henceforth, you come and go through Side Door. And Girls' Gate, which is further along. Oh, and over the cliff if you can climb like a monkey or soar like an eagle...'

Considering the way Mother had reacted, Amy thought it best not to mention her floating habit.

They walked down a path between overgrown lawns. On one, a troupe of tall, clumsy girls in wispy Grecian gowns performed energetic leaps and bends under the direction of a large woman who beat time by slapping a horse-crop into a falconer's gauntlet. On the other, a croquet match descended into a scratching, hair-pulling melée as a tiny teacher ineffectually shrilled a whistle. Amy thought she saw blood.

'Unparalleled savagery,' declaimed Frecks. 'That's the Drearcliff spirit. They're shamming the punch-up, by the way. The Fifth have a pool on who can get Miss Dryden to bust a blood vessel by overtooting.'

The path wound through gardens.

'Our grand tour continues,' said Frecks. 'Sixpence for the guide would be appreciated. Dorms are in Old House, the one that's falling off the cliff. I'm to get you settled in our cell later. Ames, the last birdie who had your perch, went to Switzerland for her lungs. I reckon she inhaled ground grit to fake it. I hope you're made of sterner stuff. It's a nuisance having to break in new bugs every twenty minutes.'

Up close, Old House looked no more inviting than from afar. Near the cliff-edge, signs warned against straying too close.

'Don't worry about your things. Joxer will dump the trunk in our quarters. The Witches will go through it for contraband.'

'The Witches?'

Frecks grinned. 'Sixths. Whips. A superior type of she-imp. If you stashed the family silver in with your scanties, Gryce and her Murdering Heathens will have it away. Sidonie Gryce is Head Girl. Wears scalps on her girdle. Did you bring any dollies?'

Amy felt a dread hand clutch at her heart.

'Only Rolly Pontoons... I've had him for ages, since I was little.'

Frecks looked exasperated. 'I assume you *were* warned...'

Father had brought Rolly home from Belgium, on leave. It was the last time Amy saw him. After he was killed, she'd liked to think he left Rolly behind to look after her. Sometimes, she made the big-headed clown float in the playroom, flapping his oversize coat like moth-wings.

'Say goodbye to Rolly Pontoons,' said Frecks, callously. 'The Murdering Heathens have a burning fiery furnace. Like the one Shadrach, Meschach and the other fellow were tossed into. Prophets prosper in flames. Dollies don't, as a rule.'

Amy was determined not to cry.

'Gruesome Gryce will probably dunk you in a horse-trough later, or dangle you out of the East Window. Thinks she's a caution. Best to grind your teeth and get it over with. You can shiv one of the minor arcana later, if you've a mind. It'll either get the Witches off your back for a term, or declare a war which can end only in mutual extermination.'

Amy didn't know what to make of Frecks. At her old day-school, there hadn't been any girls remotely like her.

They passed through a short covered walkway into a quadrangle surrounded by low-lying buildings. In the centre of the grassy square stood a plinth supporting a giant marble foot, broken off at the ankle.

'Some expedition hauled that there tootsie from Ancient Greece. Miss Borrodale, who takes Science, says the rest of the colossus must be *hopping mad*. She's mildly droll, though don't get her on Paleontology or you'll

never escape—and watch out for her thwacking habit. This lump is called
the Heel. Rumour hath it the whole statue was supposed to be Achilles.'

'Death to King Gustav V of Sweden' was written in red on the Heel.

'Don't mind that,' said Frecks. 'Absalom the Anarchist picks on a
different oppressor of the people every week. It's almost educational. Clock
up five Minor Infractions of the School Rules and you have to scrub the Heel
with your toothbrush. I've done it twice.'

'School Rules?'

'Yes, nasty little beasts. Set down at the Diet of Worms in 1066.
Memorise 'em, else you'll be constantly in hot water. In some parts of
School, it's against rules to wear your boater; in other parts, it's against rules
not to. Running from class to Refectory is an Infraction; so is *not* running
from Refectory to class. If a whip slaps you across the chops, you can be
punished for having a red mark on your face. She's entitled to keep slapping
until you cease Impertinent Display. A Minor is whatever one of the Witches
thinks up if she's had a "Dear Jane" from her boyfriend and wants to take
it out on someone who can't jilt her for the butcher's lass. I've been had
for Inappropriate Failure to Whistle. Major Infractions are punishable by
transportation to the Colonies.'

'Buttered crumpets!' exclaimed Amy.

The North side of the quad was taken up by a new, three-storey
building.

Frecks led Amy up to the front steps.

'I go no further, Pilgrim' said Frecks. 'For me to cross this threshhold
would constitute a Major. Like School Gate, you only get the honour—if
honour it be—on your first day. Venture within and see Headmistress, who'll
terrify you for a quarter of an hour. She has degrees in it. If you don't expire
of fright, trot along to Old House and seek out Dorm Three. I'll introduce
you to the Desdemona Damsels. With that, I bid you adieu... oh, and don't
look Headmistress in the eye.'

II: The Headmistress

Amy stepped into a reception room. The opposite wall was three-quarters
covered with photographs of Drearcliff classes and their teachers—starting
in 1887, running up to last year. The wall would be used up by 1944. To one
side, a cabinet displayed sporting and artistic trophies. A grinning African
fetish of evil aspect was lumped in with silver cups and ballerina statuettes.

There was a strong smell of pure alcohol. A burly woman with an
enormous bunch of keys dangling from her belt stood at a table covered with
newspaper, using vaporous astringent to clean a disassembled Lee-Enfield
rifle. She looked at Amy through the long thin telescope of the barrel.

'Go on up, New Girl,' she said. 'Headmistress is waiting.'

The woman nodded to a stairway.

Amy tried to put her foot on the first step, but found she couldn't touch it—as if a hard, invisible pillow lay on top of the carpet. She shot a guilty look at the keys woman, who was absorbed in oiling a spring and didn't notice. This wasn't so much floating as standing on air. It was a slightly sick-making feeling, like pressing bar magnets together when their poles were aligned to repel.

Without thinking, Amy glided up the stairs, toes brushing the steps. She got a grip on the banister and pulled herself hand over hand. She swiftly reached the first-storey landing, and her shoes touched carpet. Her usual weight settled back on, and a floorboard creaked. After floats, she felt heavy, as if Newton were collecting a debt run up when she contravened his Law of Gravity.

A large door bore an engraved brass plate: Dr Mrs Myrna Swan, Headmistress; D. Phil. (Bangalore), D. Eng. (Sao Paolo), M. Script. (Wells Cathedral) & Cetera.

Amy raised a knuckle, but a voice came from beyond before she could rap on the door.

'Enter, Thomsett.'

The door opened by itself. Amy hesitated, looking into a windowless, book-lined study. Across the room, a Eurasian woman of indeterminate age sat behind a desk.

Amy's hand was still up, where the door wasn't.

'You didn't do that,' said Headmistress. 'I did. I am not in the habit of issuing invitations twice.'

Amy stepped into the room.

Headmistress worked a lever on an apparatus which looked a little like a typewriter mated with a sewing machine. The door closed behind Amy.

Above the contraption were several copper tubes which ended in eyepieces like telescopes. Dr Mrs Swan had been looking through one. Amy realised she had seen another tube, with a lens, out on the landing. It must be an array of mirrors, like a triple-jointed periscope.

Dr Mrs Swan's jet-black hair was coiffured in a bun on top of her head, with two pearl-tipped needles stuck through it. Her face was white, but for red beestung lips and a black beauty mark. She had green-gold almond eyes, with tiny lines around them. Amy had seen her before in the class photographs downstairs—over and over, unchanging, all the way back to 1887. Headmistress's age was even more indeterminate than it seemed.

She wore a tight silk dress like a long tunic, green with golden dragon designs. A nurse's watch was pinned like a brooch on her breast. Her black academic cloak hung loosely like a loose shawl; it had sawtooth trailing edges and a flaring demon king collar.

'Thomsett, Amelia,' said Dr Mrs Swan, tapping a folder on her desk. 'Third, Desdemona, Talented.'

Amy understood half of that.

'Desdemona is your house,' Headmistress explained. 'Drearcliff has five. Ariel, Viola, Tamora, Desdemona and Goneril. Had you arrived at the beginning of year, you would be Ariel. In the circumstance, you fit where you must. Desdemona was down a girl. As for your Talent, your mother wrote about "incidents" at home. Footprints on the ceiling. *She* trusts you will grow out of it...'

Amy blushed like a fire-engine.

'I know you will not,' said Dr Mrs Swan. 'Nor should you.'

Amy was astonished. This was not what she—or, she knew, Mother—expected. Mother had tried cold baths, vinegar, weighted pinafores, prayer, long walks, hobbling boots and a buzzing, tickling electric belt. Leeches and exorcism were in the cards. The whole idea of packing Amy off to Drearcliff was to clamp down on *floating*.

'We have a tradition of Talents at Drearcliff. Myrna Swan's Special Girls. No doubt you've heard of Lucinda Tregellis-d'Aulney...'

The Aviatrix. Britain's flying heroine. She didn't just float, she soared. Amy followed her exploits in *Girls' Paper*. The Aviatrix was the only woman in the Splendid Six, the country's most unique and remarkable defenders. Lady Lucinda was currently prominent in the illustrated press. The Aviatrix had just brought to justice Jimmy O'Goblins, the coiner-necromancer who manufactured lightweight sovereigns which caused escalating misfortunes each time they were spent.

'Tregellis-d'Aulney passed out in '16. She has made a name for herself. So have other Special Girls. Irene Dobson, the medium. Cressida Hervey, the Australian opal millionairess—a dowsing Talent. Sylvia Marsh. Ghost Lantern Girl. Helena Strangways, who survived hanging in Montevideo last year. Yuki Kashima. I take pride in my girls' achievements, whichever direction their enthusiasms take them. You have, I trust, an *enthusiasm?*'

Shyly, Amy admitted, 'I like moths. Not collecting them. I don't believe in killing jars and pins. I've sketched three hundred and twelve distinct live specimens. Mostly British Isles, of course. I'm nowhere near finished. There are over two thousand British moth species alone.'

'That is *not* what I mean by an *enthusiasm*, Thomsett. Still, it's early days yet. Can you, ah...?'

Dr Mrs Swan gestured with her flat palm, lifting it up over her desk.

Amy looked at her toes. She had worked so desperately *not* to float, she couldn't unclench whatever it was that held her to the ground. This was like the School Rules—in Headmistress's Study, she was required to comport herself in a manner which would earn punishment elsewhere.

She strained, eyes shut, making noises inside her head.

'You are trying too hard, Thomsett. Nothing good comes of that. You must *let go*, not *hold tight.*'

Amy nodded and stopped trying. She rose an inch or so from the floor, and wobbled—then pressed down again.

Dr Mrs Swan raised an eyebrow. 'Promising.'

Amy was exhausted. She wondered whether the Aviatrix—who grew temporary wings of ectoplasm—had started like this, with tiny floats? Or waking up thumping against her ceiling, blinded by the bedspread tented around her?

'I shall keep my eye on you,' said Headmistress, tapping her copper tubes. 'We shall see what can be done with your Talent. Pick up your Time-Table Book from Keys.'

Amy knew who Headmistress meant.

'*Dismissed*,' said Dr Mrs Swan, depressing a lever.

The door opened. Amy backed through it.

III: Dorm Three

Outside Old House, Amy found four Seconds performing an intricate skipping ritual to a never-ending rhyme about dead black babies in a terrible flood. She asked where she could find Dorm Three. They stopped in mid-chant, staring as if she were a person from Porlock—as it happens, only a few miles away—interrupting Coleridge in full flow. The solemn adjudicator pointed up at the top of Old House, then crossed herself and snapped her fingers to order resumption of skipping and chanting. The terrible flood had to drown many more black babies.

Inside the building, which smelled of rain on rocks, Amy found a tree of signs pointing to destinations as diverse as 'Refectory', 'Stamp Club', 'Timbuctoo' and 'Nurse'. A broken-necked Mr Punch dangled from the Nurse's sign in a hangman's noose, pricking Amy's fears for Rolly Pontoons. Higher branches indicated that Dorms were on the upper floors.

Amy had to climb a winding stone staircase. Names and phrases and dates were scratched into the walls. At her old school, boarders slept in something like a hospital ward or a barracks—a big room with beds lined up opposite each other. At Drearcliff, Dorms were long, dark corridors with doors off to either side. Amy didn't know where to go from the landing, so she opened the first door. Four beds fit into a room the size of the one Lettie the maid lived in at home. A girl with two sets of extra-thick spectacles— one in her hair like an alice band—was putting together a tiny guillotine from lolly-sticks and a safety razor-blade.

'New bug,' she said, without looking up from her labours, 'you want Frecks's cell. End of the line. You'll whiff it before you see it. No mistaking Kali's herbal fags. Now, push off will you... this little beast has to be in chopping order tomorrow, or I'm for a roasting from Digger Downs.'

Amy ventured on. From behind a closed door, she heard a quid pro quo quiz in Latin. She caught a peculiar fragrance—heady, a little exhilirating— wafting from an open room at the far end of the corridor.

Sticking her head in, she found Frecks lolled on a cot, perusing a volume with a brown paper cover. She looked up.

'*My Nine Nights in a Harem*,' Frecks explained. 'Fearful rot. Come the deuce in, Thomsett. Meet your fellow dwellers in despair.'

Amy stepped into the cell, ducking to avoid bumping her head against the low lintel. She wouldn't have much room to float.

'Amy Thomsett, this is Light Fingers...'

A small, blonde girl sat in a rocking chair, deftly embroidering a piece of muslin. She held it up to her face—it was a Columbine mask, with fine stitching around eye- and mouth-holes. Little sequin tears leaked from the eyes.

'The fuming reprobate is Princess Kali.'

A slender brown girl with a red forehead dot and a gold snail stuck to her nose sat on a mat, legs folded under her. She puffed a slim cigarette in a long holder as if it were a religious obligation. Her eyes were slightly glazed.

'Me, you know,' said Frecks. 'That's your corner.'

Frecks indicated a neatly made, if somewhat forlorn, miniature bed. A dagger was stuck through the pillow.

'Don't mind the pig-sticker,' said Frecks. 'It's not for you. Was sent to the last girl, before she took poorly. Never did get to the bottom of that 'un. Many were the questions about dear departed Imogen Ames.'

Light Fingers set aside her needlework.

'She's quick,' said Frecks. 'Her register name is Gladys Naisbitt. Her parents are in gaol. Which puts her one up on most of us. We tend to orphans or semi-orphans at Drearcliff. My lot were shot as spies in the War. By the Hun, I hasten to add. All very glamorous and tragic. I was packed off here by my brother. Ralph holds the purse-strings till I'm eighteen and past it. Worse luck, since he's a gambling fool and a fathead for the fillies. I fully expect him to run through the dosh and leave me to make a way in the world by wits alone. He's tragic, but *not* very glamorous. Still, I don't have the worst of it in this cell. Kali's Pa had her Ma put to death for displeasing him. He's a bandit rajah in far off Kafiristan. He's run through dozens of wives.'

Kali rose elegantly, hands pressed together as if in prayer, and stood on one leg like a flamingo. She had masses of very black hair.

'Hya, dollface,' said the Hindu girl, rather musically. 'Whaddaya know, whaddaya say?'

'Kali learned English from American magazines.'

'Ahhh, nertz! I talks good as any other dame in the joint.'

Kali put both feet on the floor and stubbed out her cigarette in a saucer. She had pictures from the rotogravure pinned up over her cot—scowling men in hats: Lon Chaney, Al Capone, George Bancroft, Jack Dempsey.

'I forgot to ask,' said Frecks. 'Are you down one parent or two?'

'One,' said Amy. 'My father. The War.'

'Tough break, kiddo,' said Kali.

'Say no more,' said Frecks. 'Mystery lingers, though. Why've you suddenly been sent here? In the middle of term? There's usually no mistake about whether one is or is not Drearcliff material.'

Amy hesitated. Interest sparked. Frecks and Kali exchanged a Significant Look.

'Light Fingers,' said Frecks. 'You've got competition. She's another Special.'

Denial sprung up in Amy's throat, but died. There was no point. It was out before she was properly here. Mother would be livid.

Light Fingers regarded Amy with suspicion, tilting her head to one side and then the other.

'It's not something you can see,' said Frecks. 'Like Gould of the Fourth and her teeth and nails. Or that Viola girl with gills. It's something she *does*. Hope you're not a mind-reader, Thomsett. They're unpopular, for reasons obvious. Dear departed Ames was a brain-peeper. Didn't make her happy.'

Amy was tight inside. Close to tears, though she kept them in.

'There there, child,' said Frecks. 'We won't hurt. Tell all.'

'C'mon, popsy, cough it up an' ya'll feel better.'

The three girls were close to her now. Amy knew this was important.

'Light Fingers,' said Frecks, 'show her yours.'

The blonde girl reached out and tapped Amy on the chest with her right forefinger, then opened her left hand to show a black-headed tie-pin.

Amy, astonished, touched her tie. The pin was missing.

'How...?'

'Prestidigitation, old thing,' said Frecks. 'As practiced in the Halls by respected conjurers. And in the stalls by disreputable pick-pockets. The hand is quicker than the eye. Her hands are quicker than a hummingbird's wings.'

Light Fingers clapped her hands, and showed empty palms. Amy found her pin back in place. A bead of blood stood out on the girl's forefinger. Light Fingers popped her finger in her mouth and sucked the tiny wound.

'Gets it from her parents. They had an act at the Tivoli. Doves out of hats. Escapes from water-tanks. Also, a profitable sideline: lifting sparklers from nobs in the audience. Got caught at it. Hence, gaol. Captain Rattray nabbed 'em. You know, Blackfist. The big bruiser in the Splendid Six— with the Blue Streak, Lord Piltdown, the Aviatrix and the other two no one remembers. Mrs Naisbitt made a pass for Rattray's magic gem. That was the end of that.'

'They could escape any time they want,' said Light Fingers. 'They get out of their prisons and visit each other. All the time. But they go back for the head-counts. Less trouble in the long run.'

Her finger was bleeding more and her lips were red.

'Ouch,' she said. 'I'm always doing this.'

'It's a miracle she has any fingers left,' said Frecks.

The three girls looked at Amy, expectant.

'A shy one,' said Frecks. 'Probably taught to hide her light under a bushel. We haven't anything else to show. Kali and I aren't Special that way. Just warped. Drearcliff Girls have something extra or something missing. Not just parents. Bits got left out when we were put together. Know what Kali's going to do to dear old Dad when she goes home?'

Kali drew her thumbnail across her throat and made a 'krkkkk' sound.

'Means it, too. She's going to be a Bandit Queen. She's already coloured in her empire on the map. So, Thomsett, *give...*'

It wasn't that easy. In Headmistress's study, she hadn't been able to perform on cue. Not really. It would be the same here.

'She *is* giving,' said Light Fingers, '*look...!*'

Amy was surprised, then glanced down. She was a full six inches off the floor, feet dangling limp. Her head pressed the plastered ceiling.

Kali and Frecks were wide-eyed. Light Fingers looked a little frightened.

Frecks whistled, long and shrill.

'That was an *appropriate* whistle,' she explained. 'Crivens, you're a pixie!'

Amy went inside herself, and thought heavy thoughts. She came down gently, on toepoints, then settled on her heels.

'I am *not* a pixie,' she said.

'But you can fly!'

She shook her head. 'No, I can't fly. I can *float*. It's not the same.'

The Aviatrix could fly. She could flap her wings, zoom along, soar, outpace any land craft. Amy could wave her arms all she wanted, but just went up and up like a balloon. So far, she'd only floated deliberately indoors. Once, she had dozed under a tree like Alice and woke up trapped by low branches. Mother said if she didn't stop it, she'd drift away and be lost in the clouds.

'Still, you're a Special,' said Frecks. 'Headmistress must love you.'

Kali snarled. 'Stay away from the Swan skirt, she's trouble in velvet! A regular cyanide mama!'

'Tell you what, though,' said Frecks. 'Desdemona won't come bottom in netball this term. Not with two Specials. Light Fingers can steal the ball and make an invisible pass. Thomsett can float and pop it through the hoop from above. That'll be a tough rind for the harpies of Goneril to chew. Must get ten shillings down with Nellie Pugh in the kitchens—she's school bookie, don't you know?—before word gets out.'

For the first time, Amy wondered whether Mother was wrong. Maybe floating wasn't entirely wicked.

She was tired of hearing things like 'how are you ever going to get a husband if you can't keep your feet on the ground?'

She wasn't sure about netball though.

A bell sounded, from down below.

'Grub's up,' announced Frecks. 'Form an orderly rabble and proceed to the Refectory. Come on, Thomsett, we'll get you there alive. Then it's down to whether you can survive the worst Cook flings at you. Word to the wise, shun the semolina. I have it on an impeccable authority that it's bat's blood in sick.'

IV: School Supper
The Refectory made Amy wonder whether Old House had begun as Drearcliff Abbey or Drearcliff Castle. The hall had plainly been a place of worship or assembly before finding its true purpose as a feeding trough. It was the sort of area Douglas Fairbanks generally did his sword-fighting in, complete with flying buttresses, depressed arches, ribbed vaults and other features of architectural interest.

Stained glass windows depicted men in armour battling she-demons, who were generally coming out with the best of it. Amy wasn't sure the windows were appropriate for younger girls. Several panels showed dismembered knights roasted on spits by happy, red-skinned devil cooks with extra mouths in their bosoms.

Girls sat on benches at five long House tables, arranged by year. This meant roughly by size, though the odd freakishly tall or stunted specimen broke up any neat arrangement. Thirds had places half-way along the Desdemona table. They could look across at their contemporaries in the other Houses. It was not done to pay attention up-table or down-table, where seniors or juniors sat.

Hundreds of girls talked at once, and clattered to their table-places. The sound of wooden bench-legs scraping on stone was frequent.

Frecks anatomised the Houses.

'Goneril are Sport House,' Frecks explained. 'Win at absolutely bloody everything, from cross-country runs to tiddlybloodywinks. It's *so* tedious. They used to challenge boys' schools at football, but an archdeacon's son got crippled—and his side took a ten–two hammering—so that was stopped. Tamora has the terrors. I josh you not. You'd do well to stay away. The most evil Witches are Tamora. Viola are babies. Blub all the time. The Greek dancing on the lawn shower you saw earlier. Utterly wet and contemptible. Ariel are so stuck up you'd think they were *port over starboard home* through and through. Their people are mostly in trade. We can't stand 'em. Got all that?'

'Sporty, scary, baby and posh, yes. What are we?'

'Desdemona? Red-headed stepchildren. Who don't fit anywhere else. We come second in most things. If we're top it doesn't count because we don't win properly. You'll hear that a lot.'

High Table was set on a dais before a triptych of especially ferocious dragons. It had a white table-cloth and the best china. Also, decanters of spirits and wine-glasses. Girls made do with tumblers and jugs of brackish water, though Princess Kali surreptitiously dripped something fiery from a bullet-dented hip-flask into her tumbler.

Once the girls were settled, they were counted off by Table Captains from each form, with the few absences due to illness listed. Light Fingers was the Third Desdemona Captain. Then, Headmistress made an entrance, cape flapping. Raucous hub-bub ceased. After Dr Mrs Swan was settled in a throne at the centre of High Table, nine women—and three men!—walked in a processional, in identical capes and mortar-boards, and took high-backed chairs either side. The teachers faced out at the Refectory, at once on display and commanding an audience.

Servants rolled trolleys bearing cauldrons up and down the aisles, doling something which was either thick soup or thin stew into bowls. Frecks showed Amy how to hold her bowl up with one hand while taking a bread roll from a platter on the trolley with the other. Light Fingers made a show of being slow and clumsy, not wasting her Talent at supper.

Headmistress made a gesture. A very fat man in a clergyman's collar and a barrister's wig—the Reverend Mr Bainter, School chaplain and Religious Instruction—got up and mumbled a grace in Latin.

'Bow, you savages,' hissed the Fourth captain up-table, exciting suppressed giggles from acolytes.

Grace concluded, everyone tucked in. Talking resumed, and the Refectory filled with din again.

The soup-or-stew was hot and had a distinct, not unpleasant taste. The meat wasn't the best, but the bread was fresh and soaked up the gravy.

Amy took Frecks's advice and spurned the semolina. She ate an apple, instead.

Frecks introduced Amy to the rest of Third. The guillotine-making girl, who only wore one pair of spectacles to supper, was Lydia Inchfawn. A bird-boned, pale American girl with long straight black hair suffered under the name Ticia Frump and planned to marry as soon as possible to alleviate her burden. The names Satin, Houri, Smudge, Peebles and Clodagh belonged to other girls, but Amy couldn't fix which was which. Her head was overstuffed with new names, rules, people and language—dinner at her old school was supper here, sweet was afters, Scripture was Religious Instruction, prefects were whips.

Martine, the humorous Fourth Captain, took note of a New Girl down-table, but her acolytes kept to themselves.

Between courses, a squeaky-voiced, undersized Fifth slipped down-table, with notebook and pencil. She said she was from the *Drearcliff Trumpet* and wanted to interview the New Girl.

'Push off, Shrimp,' said Frecks. 'She's not talking.'

The reporter blinked and retreated.

'Can't let her get their hooks in you,' said Frecks. 'Be wary of Shrimp. Girl's a menace.'

'Don't let her sketch you,' said Light Fingers. 'You'll be faint-headed for a week and she'll be bright as a new penny. We tried smearing her cot with garlic, but no joy.'

'Garlic and Shrimp?' said Kali, elegantly spooning semolina into a concealed bottle for later disposal. 'Sounds like a recipe for moider.'

'Special isn't always good,' said Frecks.

'Mother says it's *never* good.'

'Who's Special?' asked Inchfawn. 'The new bug?'

'Don't get ahead of yourself,' said Frecks. 'No one said anyone was Special. Except Shrimp.'

'She's Special all right,' shuddered Inchfawn.

Questions were thrown at Amy by other girls. She wound up talking about moths. No one was perplexed, like grown-ups were, but no one was that interested either.

'You'll fit in,' said a girl with black Indian braids. 'You're ga-ga already. We all go ga-ga at Drearcliff. After a while.'

When the last bowl was scraped, the servants returned to collect the crockery. Headmistress stood. Girls sat still and quiet again, as for grace. Amy realised that the convention for quiet was not for religious observance but from whenever Dr Mrs Swan rose till she gave a nod for din to resume.

'Girls,' she began, 'we must welcome a new sister among us...'

'Oh no, she's not going to...' began Frecks...

'... a new friend, a special gift to Drearcliff, a veritable *ornament*...'

'She bloody is,' said Frecks. 'What a terror!'

'... a shining beacon of potential, a talent that should be nurtured till it reaches full bloom...'

Amy didn't hear the rest of the speech. The flagstones had opened and she was pulled under the roiling earth. Everyone in the Refectory looked at her. Her face was flaming red.

'Jammy crumpets!' she exclaimed, *sotto voce*.

'Worse luck,' commiserated Frecks.

'Poison Doll might as well a' stuck a target on ya, kid,' said Kali. 'What happens next won't be pretty. Not ah-*tall* it won't.'

V: The Witches of Drearcliff Grange

A First went down on one knee in front of Amy, hands clasped to her chest, ringlets rustling like silenced sleighbells. The little she-beast declaimed dramatically...

'Welcome, oh sister, oh veritable *ornament*, oh...'

Frecks cuffed the chit about the head, and she squeaked like a pig.

'Out of the way, scum, or be mistaken for a carpet and *walked over*....'

The theatrically inclined First was between the Dorm Three girls and the stairs. The little tragedienne's clique had been laughing at her turn but now just laughed at her. In the show business, applause was fleeting.

Frecks and Kali picked Bernhardt *fille* up and slung her to one side. She spat 'I'll be revenged on the whole pack of you' and scurried away.

'That exit line was from *Twelfth Night*,' said Amy. 'She's a Viola?'

'You heard the blubbing,' said Frecks. 'Of course, she's Viola.'

Kali gave the departed thespian's audience the evil eye.

'Any a' youse mugs got complaints?' she asked.

The down-table girls looked duly intimidated. Kali made neck-breaking gestures and they fled.

'This is gonna get monotonous,' said the Hindu girl.

Amy was not reassured.

'It'll blow over when School finds something else to play with,' said Frecks. 'These things pass, like the wind...'

'Wind does damage, sister...'

''Tis true, 'tis true.'

The Dorm Three girls trouped upstairs.

At their landing, Light Fingers made a sign, and they halted.

'Uh oh,' she said. 'We're Belgium?'

'Belgium?' asked Amy, puzzled.

'Invaded and occupied, Thomsett,' said Frecks. 'Likely to be outraged by the Hun. Best get it over with.'

Their cell was already crowded. Amy's trunk took up most of the limited floor-space. It was open, disclosing the rumple of her possessions.

A womanly Sixth sat in Light Fingers's rocking chair, which was much too small for her. She hummed dreamily to herself, as if thinking only the most modest, chaste, *improving* thoughts. Her complexion was healthy cream, brushed lightly with rose petal red on her cheeks. She had merry cornflower blue eyes and rippling golden hair. She looked like the sort of angel you'd never sully by placing her up on a Christmas tree. Her grey blazer had gold piping, the mark of a prefect. Above her school badge was picked out, in gothic script, *Head Girl*.

'Gryce,' acknowledged Frecks.

'Shut your hole, Walmergrave,' said a bony, dark girl whose sallow face was half-masked by a wing of black hair. 'This isn't your bushwah.'

She stood behind the rocking chair, arranged side-on to all comers as if to present a thinner target. She had been poking through Amy's Book of Moths with a long-nailed finger.

Frecks held back, along with Kali and Light Fingers.

Two other Sixths were in the cell, taking up room: a big-shouldered, tubby girl with a face like one big pimple and rope-braids hanging to her waist; and a fey, huge-eyed sprite with a white streak in her enormous cloud of brown hair. They all had gold piping.

These were the Murdering Heathens.

'Amy, *entrez* your cell and *asseyez-tu* on your cot,' said Gryce, sweetly. 'I fervently hope we shall be *les amies eternels*.'

Frecks gave Amy a gentle prod between the shoulder-blades, and she crossed the threshhold. She had to bend and twist to make her way without touching the Sixths or tripping over her trunk. She sat on her cot, knees together, hands in her lap, trying to ignore the hammering of her heart and the lightness of her spine. This was no time for floating. She thought herself heavy, and her cot-springs creaked.

'I am Sidonie,' said Gryce, looking Amy directly in the eyes. 'I am Head Girl. I embody School Spirit. 'Tis my duty to make *filles nouvelles* welcome. If Discipline is necessary, it is my sacred trust to apply the gentle hand of guidance...'

The dark girl snickered. She had fingernails like painted knives. Her uncovered eye was blue with a dash of red.

'If Encouragement is needed, I shall be at your back, urging you to do your *plus que belle* for School. If Praise is merited, it shall not be withheld. That is the Code of Drearcliff. *Comprenez-tu*, Amy?'

'I think so,' said Amy.

'*Bonne*,' smiled Gryce, with a flash of steel in her eyes. 'These are *mes amies* and fellow prefects. Beryl...'

One-Eye.

'Dora...'

White Streak.

'... and Henry.'

Pimple Face.

'You will address us properly as Head Girl, Prefect Crowninshield, Prefect Paule and Prefect Buller. *Comprenez-tu?*'

'Yes.'

Gryce reached over, smiling, and slapped her face, then gave a 'go ahead, try again' nod.

'Yes, Head Girl.'

Gryce bent over and butterfly-kissed Amy's stinging cheek, then made a stroke-it-better gesture without actually touching her.

'You see, *mes filles*, a perfect demonstration of the Method Gryce in action. Gentle Discipline. Firm Encouragement. Deserved Praise.'

'Can I Encourage her, S-s-sid?' said Buller, leaning over and putting her blotched face close to Amy's. Her breath was sweet, like violet pastilles.

'Not now, Henry,' drawled Crowninshield. She gave a shoulder-twitch which briefly lifted her hair—revealing her other eye, which was brown—before it fell back in place.

'Henry's *enthusiasm* is School Spirit,' said Gryce, waving the big girl away. 'Do you have an *enthusiasm*, Amy?'

Amy was not forthcoming.

Crowninshield made a flutter with Amy's book, flapping its covers like wings, flying it around the room like a trapped moth.

'I am a moth,' Crowninshield said, lips shut but throat moving. 'I'm... drawn... irresistibly... *to the flame!*'

Crowninshield fluttered the book into Paule's hair. The Witch who hadn't spoken batted it away with her hands.

'I repeat: do you have an *enthusiasm*, Amy?

'Yes, Head Girl. It's...'

'Did I ask you what your *enthusiasm* was?'

'No, but...'

The hand went up.

'No, Head Girl,' she corrected herself.

'See, you *can* learn. Now, let us *guess* your *enthusiasm*. Henry?'

Buller made fists, and leaned close again.

'Is it bleeding? Bleeding, while trying not to b-b-blub? Bleeding from something that can n-n-never be fixed?'

'No, Prefect Hen... No, Prefect Buller.'

'Beryl?' asked Gryce.

'It's not butterflies, is it?'

'Yes, it's not butterflies, Prefect Crowninshield.'

Crowninshield thought a moment, and was pleased. 'Do you hold the position that butterflies are a separate phylum of lepidoptera, as opposed to a sub-species of moth?'

'Yes, Prefect Crowninshield.'

Lepidoptera are not a phylum, but an order of insects, which are a class of the arthropod phylum. Strictly, Amy acknowledged that moths were what was left of the lepidoptera once butterflies were excluded. She kept that to herself, though.

'The taxonomy is not uncontroversial, though, is it not?'

Amy couldn't unpick the contradictions, but intuited her inquisitor couldn't either, and answered 'No, Prefect Crowninshield' with confidence.

'Paule, Paule, wisest of us all?'

'I can't bear moths,' said Prefect Paule, in a tiny voice.

'That's not a question,' said Gryce. 'That's a statement.'

'It is all I've to say on the subject. Moths are too Thursday for me.'

Crowninshield tossed Amy the book, which she caught before it hit her in the face. She held it shut in her lap.

Crowninshield tapped her own head. Amy realised what was being asked of her. She balanced the book on her head. At her old school, her form mistress had been a fiend for deportment, so Amy knew how to keep the book level.

Gryce smiled on her. She began to rock back and forth in Light Fingers's chair, as if daring it to fly into splinters and give her cause to inflict severe Encouragement.

Frecks and the others were out in the corridor, watching. A crowd of Thirds had gathered. Had they all been through this? Amy was probably getting an extra helping for being a new bug in the middle of term.

'If the book falls,' said Gryce, rocking faster, 'you'll be marked down as Not School Spirit. *Une vraie salope!* Cleaning the Heel is a let-off next to the Encouragement visited upon those who are Not School Spirit. Keep a straight spine, moth-girl. Shoulders back. Eyes up, chest up. No, eyes down, showing *la modestie propre...*'

Amy looked down, and felt the book tip—but she recovered in an instant.

'There only remains the matter of contraband,' said Gryce, signalling to Buller, who reached down into Amy's trunk and pulled out a blue slip. 'What's this?'

'A gymslip, Sid.'

'Not a Drearcliff slip, though. Excluded.'

Buller tossed it in the air, and Crowninshield caught it.

Mother had not bought new gym clothes from Pond Street, knowing that Amy had the proper items—now, it seemed, the *improper* items—already. Her kit bore no emblems associated with her old school, but did not pass.

'Navy is not Drearcliff blue,' Gryce explained. 'Sea-green is Drearcliff blue. *Comprenez-tu?*'

'Yes, Head Girl.'

Yes, you Simpering Witch!

'Don't think of Sidonie like that,' said Paule, quietly. 'She won't like it.'

Amy felt stabbed. Dora Paule was a Special. Mind-reader, of some sort.

Gryce rocked, as Buller raised item after item. Skirts, socks, blouses. The Head Girl didn't even look at them.

'Excluded, Excluded, Excluded, Acceptable, Excluded...'

An old scarf had passed muster, at random.

Amy breathed evenly, trying not to float. She tried to present a bland countenance, tried not to feel anything. This ordeal would soon be over. The Murdering Heathens would not be here all night, could not devote the rest of their year at Drearcliff to this testing of the new bug.

She thought of moths, fixing their distinguishing marks, wing-patterns and antenna shapes in her mind. Moths made sense. *Hepialidae*: *hepialus humuli* (Ghost Moth), *hepialus sylvina* (Orange Swift), *hepialus fusconebulosa* (Map-Winged Swift). Moths were various, but finite. *Cossidae Zeuzerinae*: *phragmataecia castaneae* (Reed Leopard), *zeuzera pyrina* (Leopard Moth). Moths flew, purposefully. *Limacodidae*: *apoda limacodes* (The Festoon), *heterogenea asella* (The Triangle). Moths were hardy, yet delicate. *Tineidae Tineinae*: *monopis laevigella* (Skin Moth), *tinea pallescentella* (Large Pale Clothes Moth), *monopis weaverella...*

Amy was slapped...

She instinctively raised her hands, to catch the book, but Gryce caught her wrists. Amy cobra-necked and the book didn't fall. She made the book light, almost to the point of floating.

'I said, *what is this contraband?*'

Amy moved her eyes only. Crowninshield held up Rolly Pontoons, invading his ballooning clown suit with her hand, waggling his big-nosed, jug-eared head, jingling the bells on his fools-cap.

A tear rolled down Amy's cheek.

She remembered her father making exactly the same gesture. Rolly was as much puppet as doll.

'Are you a little child? A little child who *plays with dollies?*'

'No, Head Girl.'

'Then, what is this vile specimen?'

Amy kept quiet. To speak would be a betrayal.

'Not your *poupée*, then, Thomsett,' stated Gryce. 'You wouldn't care if it were hurt, then?'

Crowninshield tore off Rolly's left arm, trailing stuffing, and dropped it.

Amy felt a sympathetic pain. The book held firm.

Crowninshield made a scream come out of Rolly's open mouth...

'The whip hurt meeeeee, Ameeeeee,' said Crowninshield, in a strange doll-voice. 'You did nothiiiing, you beast. You were supposed to be meee ickle fwend! Meeee not love you anymore. Meee hate you, Ameeee.'

'Don't talk like that to a Drearcliff girl,' said Crowninshield, in her own voice, rapping Rolly on the nose. 'It's not your place...'

'Nooooooo....'

Crowninshield tore off Rolly's right leg, and waved the puppet from side to side, screeching from the back of her throat.

Tears dripped off Amy's chin, now. But she made no sound. And her book held level.

'Give her the wretched thing, Beryl,' said Gryce.

Crowninshield held out Rolly, then snatched him back as Amy reached for it. Then handed him over. Amy couldn't help hugging the mutilated plaything to her breast.

'Now, show School Spirit, Thomsett. Drearcliff Spirit. Can you do that *pour votre amie* Sidonie?'

'Yes... Head Girl.'

Gryce smiled, and sat back in the chair.

'*Then tear that horrible thing's head off.*'

Amy froze.

'You heard me, new bug. Tear That Horrible Thing's Head Off.'

'Nooooo, don't, Ameeeee. Don't kill 'ums. Meeeee soooo saad!'

'Cut that out,' snarled Buller. 'It makes my f-f-flesh creep.'

'There's a lot of it,' said Crowninshield in her own voice. 'Isn't that right, little cripple? Hasn't Auntie Henry got a vast acreage of flesh to creep.'

'Yessums, sheeeeee's as fat as a cow.'

Amy hugged Rolly Pontoons close. She remembered father, in his uniform. His Rolly Pontoons voice was deeper, jollier than Crowninshield's shrill, cracked whine. 'Hello, Amy, I'm your friend from Belgium. Won't we have jolly jolly fun!'

Moths, she thought, getting a good grip on Rolly's neck. *Gracillariidae Gracillariinae: cameraria ohridella* (Horse Chestnut Leaf-Miner). She found stitches weakened by years of night-time hugs and dug her nails in. *Gracillariidae Lithocolletinae: phyllonorycter coryli* (Nut Leaf Blister Moth), *phyllonorycter...*

'Off with its head,' insisted Gryce.

'Pleeese, nooooo...'

'Mind that wobbly book, Thomsett,' said Crowninshield, seeming to talk over herself.

Amy thought she was pulling Rolly's head, but it stayed stuck. She willed herself to tear, but orders weren't reaching her hands.

From inside her blazer, Gryce produced a pair of man's white dress gloves. She put them on, slowly, flexing her fingers, making and unmaking fists. There were scuffs and stains on the gloves.

Amy looked into Rolly's trusting glass eyes.

Jolly jolly fun.

'Noooooo....'

'Okay, that's the limit,' said Kali.

She stepped into the cell and put her hands round the throat of the nearest Murdering Heathen, Dora Paule.

'Read my mind, sister,' she said.

'So angry,' breathed Paule.

'You ain't talkin' horse-feathers. You in the chair, up and out, see. Take a powder. Amscray to Ellhay. Make like a tree and fall down in the forest. I ain't just lip-flappin'.'

Buller lunged across the cell.

Without letting go of Paule's neck, Kali angled her body and kicked out—sticking her shoe into the prefect's wobbling tummy. Buller doubled over.

'Any more want a taste? Head Girl?'

Gryce stood, head touching the low ceiling. She was a foot taller than Kali.

'Kali Chattopadhyay,' said Gryce. 'You are not showing School Spirit.'

'Ain't I? Balloon juice.'

'I have no idea what that means.'

Frecks was in the cell too, now. She stood aggressively close to Beryl Crowninshield.

'Prefect Crowninshield, do Al Jolson. Sing "Mammy".'

Crowninshield gave a half-smile and had to contort herself to get past Frecks. She was the first out of the room. Kali let Paule go, and she helped Buller—whose red face was set in pain—out.

Kali looked up at Gryce, who reached out and pinched her nose-snail lightly.

'Three Minor Infractions, for all girls in this cell... for all girls in this House.'

Groans from out in the corridor. Someone muttered 'I've only got the bloody Heel now'.

'And a Major for you, Chattopadhyay. Report to the Whips' Hut first thing after chapel tomorrow. For Encouragement.'

'I'll be there, dollface. You can be sure of that.'

'Good night, new bug. We'll pick this up when you've settled in. I fear you've made a poor start. *Au revoir*.'

The Witches were gone.

Frecks shut the cell door, barring the rest of the Dorm. Amy stopped shaking, and mopped her face. Kali took the book off Amy's head and put it on a shelf above Amy's cot.

'Here,' said Light Fingers.

Amy looked down. Light Fingers had Rolly's arm and leg in her cupped, open hands.

'I'll get my sewing things,' said Light Fingers.

VI: Broken In

Three weeks later, Amy had almost forgotten what it was like not to be at Drearcliff Grange. The whole of her life before her School was a fading nursery memory.

Rolly Pontoons, repaired if as lopsided as many a flesh and blood veteran of the Great War, was coffined in a shoe-box under her cot, out of harm's way but also set aside. Her mother's letters, fine copperplate complaints about Letty's slackness and the dreadful neighbours, were read once quickly, shorn of stamps—Clodagh FitzPatrick, of the cell across the corridor, collected, and ordinary British issues were currency in transactions with like-minded souls in far corners of the Empire—and filed, envelopes and all, in a commonplace box.

She now nestled in the heart of a Chinese doll of institutions, official and otherwise. Her permanent skins were Frecks's cell, Dorm Three, Desdemona House and School. At times, she belonged to forms, where Thirds of all Houses mixed, and House Middle School sides where a certain lumpage of Thirds and Fourths, along with gargantuan Seconds and stunted Fifths, was acceptable. She stayed away from netball, but was recruited for other sports—cricket and hockey balls were too fast and small to get a mind-grip on, and there were few opportunities for unnatural leaps and levitations. She had taken her lumps and the newness was worn off her. Everyone else had forgotten what it was like when she wasn't at School too.

Her teachers' names, handles, enthusiasms and tells had been learned. Amy had most to do with Mrs 'Wicked' Wyke, Head of Desdemona Middle, who took Classics, Geography and Gym. Despite her ominous handle, Wicked was a sweet-natured pudding, inclined to fluster and fuss and cluck when liberties were taken—which was, as a consequence, frequently. History, Dance and Deportment were taken by Miss 'Digger' Downs, famous for her utter lack of humour, malapropisms and spoonerisms and protracted, fiendishly devised revenges against pupils and staff alike. Mrs Wyke's classes were lively, wild-spirited affairs, but Digger insisted her charges toil in a silence relieved only by the ticking of the classroom clock or the beat of her riding crop. Her especial belief was that Dance was best taught without the frivolous distraction of music. Religious Instruction was the province of the Reverend Mr Percy 'Ponce' Bainter, who used so much pomade and powder that the fancy was he was a recruiter for a white slaver ring. Several times, Amy was warned in hushed tones that Ponce made a habit of shipping off Fourths and Fifths to the Orient to be hooked on opium, raped by Lascars and sold to brothels. Opinion was divided on whether this was a fate worse than death or an acceptable way of meeting a nice Lascar who would probably turn out, like Tarzan or the Sheik, to be an English Lord raised in foreign parts. English, Poetry and Drama were entrusted to Miss Kaye, 'Acting Mrs Edwards', a sensible flapper—if that wasn't a contradiction in terms—who was only on the staff temporarily while the regular teacher was off having a baby.

Sciences were taken by Miss 'Fossil' Borrodale, a deceptively fair-faced young woman who was the object of Desdemona's most notorious crush, the fanatical devotion which burned in the breast of Lydia Inchfawn. Fossil carried a length of rubber tubing, and settled Minor Infractions by calmly offering miscreants a choice between 'the short, sharp shocks' (three thwacks across the open palm) or 'the long, tiresome retribution' (producing a manuscript copy of ten random pages of the *Encyclopædia Britannica*). Offenders almost always chose the shocks, to the teacher's evident delight— when she was administering 'three across the hand', her eyes glittered and she showed her small, pearly teeth. Lydia filled up sketch-books trying to capture Miss Borrodale's expression in these moments, and would willingly take the blame for any unattributed malfeasance in order the savour the short, sharp shocks on her permanently reddened palm. Fossil also commanded the unpronounceably acronymous QMWAACC—the Queen Mary's Women's Auxiliary Army Cadet Corps—which spent Thursday afternoons on coast patrol with wooden rifles, looking for spies and smugglers (and ammonites) along the beaches and cliffs. Fossil maintained that Drearcliff was ever ready to defend Somerset from foreign devils—no matter that the most likely invaders of these shores would have to come by coracle from Wales. Smudge—Verity Oxenford—told Amy that on a disastrous route march in the rain last term, Fossil came close to having three girls shot for desertion under fire—but Amy already had Smudge down as Dorm Three's Leading Exaggerator.

Amy had three Minor Infractions in her Time-Table Book, which girls must carry at all times and surrender to a prefect or teacher who wished to mark down an MI with a Black Notch in the tally-page at the back. Not having the Book on you was good for an additional MI. Amy's first Black Notches came together. Digger wished to upbraid her for talking in class, to wit: asking Light Fingers for a lend of a pencil sharpener. When Amy admitted that her Book was back in Dorm, she was ordered to report with it before Prep. Digger dipped her pen in an inkwell and made two thick, practiced flick-marks on the tally-page. Carrying the Book at all times wasn't in School Rules, which Amy had tried to learn, but was an Addendum of Usage—unofficial, but enforced. Her other MI was malice on the part of Beryl Crowninshield, the wall-eyed prefect, who singled her out of a gaggle of Thirds crossing the Quad between classes, and Black Notched her for 'taking the inappropriate diagonal'. Crowninshield said 'somebody needs a good bottom-kicking' in a deep voice that seemed to come from the Heel— Amy wasn't sure whether the prefect's ventriloquism was a Talent or just a Trick.

Encouraged by her cell-mates, Amy had experimented. In Gym, she made herself light as a feather and pulled herself up a rope, arm over arm, legs dangling so she didn't chafe her thighs like others ordered to perform this exercise. Out with the QMWAACC on manoeuvres, she lifted herself up, with Frecks and Kali holding her ankles, to peep over a high wall to see if the Ariel Squad, with whom they were 'at War', were creeping into positions, and hoarsely calling out the range for the Desdemona potato-mortars, which soon bombarded their deadly rivals into calling for an armistice. Fossil sent the Ariels off on a punitive march across the shingles to teach them not to surrender so quickly. So far, few knew about her Talent. She was keen on keeping it that way, though she realised that if she were to make more and more use of it, her floating would soon be common knowledge—and, therefore, less of an advantage.

On Saturday afternoons, Wicked worked a projector in the Gym and showed flickers to the whole School. The flickers were mostly ancient one- and two-reelers, often parts of long serials screened out of order and never with the opening or closing episodes to explain or wrap up the story. Girls might hope for Valentino as the Sheik, Charlie Chaplin as the Little Tramp or (in Kali's case) Lon Chaney as a gang boss with no legs (Kali described this film, *The Penalty*, over and over after Lights Out, with elaborations— she proclaimed it as the greatest motion picture ever made). However, they made do with 'The Coughing Horror', one of *The Mysteries of Dr Fu-Manchu* with Harry Agar Lyons, or 'The Bruce-Partington Plans', one of *The Adventures of Sherlock Holmes*, with Eille Norwood. These were thought to be 'proper stories', and held in higher esteem than serials of American origin. In these, soppy heiresses were constantly imperilled by villainous uncles and masked masterminds out to obtain their fortunes, and needed often to be rescued by handsome fellows because they were utterly useless. Fossil taught her QMWAACC girls how to slip out of even the most elaborate sailors' knots, but such skills were evidently not part of the education of the average American heiress.

The flickers drew venomous hisses from the audience whenever it seemed the hero was on the point of planting a passionate smacker on the heroine's cupid's bow lips but they chickened out at the last moment and rubbed cheeks instead. Scornful of the breed of ringleted and ribboned Paulines, Elaines and Helens, Kali dared express a preference for the honestly naked crookery of the wicked uncles and clutching hands and yellow perils above the hollow charms of the unmanly youths held up as heroes in these chapterplays. Amy's favourites among Mrs Wyke's flickers were not American or British, but French—especially those which featured an adventuress named Irma Vep who wore a black bodystocking and mask and prowled the rooftops of Paris, murdering and robbing at the behest of a secret society called Les Vampires. It occurred to Amy—though she did not share the thought even with her cell-mates, who were now closer to her than sisters—that her floating Talent might come in handy if she were ever to pursue a career in crime like Irma.

In three weeks, she had seen and sketched twelve new moths, including the nationally scarce *discoloxia blomeri* (Blomers Rivulet), though the grounds of Drearcliff were not especially fine moth country. Her *enthusiasm* was noted by Fossil Borrodale, who—when not thwacking Infractors—was a surprisingly good teacher; she didn't baby-talk like Wicked Wyke or insist on rote copying like Digger Downs. Called after class to see Fossil, Amy dreaded punishment for some unintentional Major Infraction—only to be asked politely whether she would mind showing Miss Borrodale her Book of Moths. The teacher was impressed with the sketches, and admitted she had begun a similar Book of Fossils when she was Amy's age—which she still kept. The School had a collection of mounted lepidoptera in the Biology Laboratory, with many exotic specimens brought back by a teacher before the turn of the century; Fossil said that Amy could examine this treasure if she liked. Though Amy was against killing to collect, she felt a thrill at the prospect—these specimens had grown dusty and ignored, awaiting her or someone else who shared the *enthusiasm* of the long-gone collector. Leaving Miss Borrodale's classroom, she spied Inchfawn peeping round a corner, boiling with envy and hatred. 'It's all right, Inchfawn, I didn't get the thwacks.' That didn't assuage Inchfawn, who darted away, spectacles up in her hair, the heels of her hands pressed to her eyes.

She knew her cell-mates intimately. They were together in classes, at meals, on QMWAACC exercises, between classes, at the flickers, doing prep, rambling in the grounds, playing sports and games and in the cell, talking in the dark after Lights Out. To everyone else, they were Frecks's cell; among themselves, they were the Forus, a contraction of 'the Four of Us'. If School had a language, the Forus had a dialect—a slang or code comprehensible only by themselves. Frecks was skilled at making up new handles or expressions. Each prefect or teacher or girl had a Secret Handle, for use only among the Forus, selected so that there was no obvious connection between the handle and the subject's name or enthusiasm or physical appearance. Miss Borrodale was not 'Fossil', but 'Lilac' (her first name was Violet). Miss Kaye was not 'Acting Mrs Edwards' but 'Janet' (J came before K in the alphabet). Dora Paule, known to her relatively few friends as 'Daffy', was simply 'A' (because she was 'A-paule-ing'). Lydia Inchfawn was 'Inchworm' to the School, but 'Six Eyes' to the Forus. Only they called whips 'the Witches'; the rest of School called them 'the Sisters'. In Forus lingo, Black Notches were 'Stains' (fully, 'Stains on the Escutcheon'), bosoms were 'beakers' (Light Fingers had the best-developed beakers), prep was 'greens' (as in 'have you eaten your greens?'), serving in QMWAACC was 'being ganged' (derived from press-ganged), custard was 'splodge', and someone with a crush was 'a limpet'.

They all had Secrets. Hers was the floating. Light Fingers had a stash of stolen objects, from practicing her hereditary skills. Frecks had a boyfriend in Watchet—a lad named Cecil, who was walking out with her (when they could both escape, which was seldom) though he was supposedly engaged to a little marchioness. Kali wore the snail in her nose at least partially to cover a scar given her by her father—who once took it in mind to stick the point of a dagger up her nostril and rip it free. Amy told the Forus all about Mother, and the uncles she had periodically gained and lost since Father died. Light Fingers admitted she'd drawn up, and tested, five plans for escaping from School Grounds, which were set down in cipher in her Time-Table Book. Frecks said she was smuggling vitriol out of the Science Building a drop at a time, saving enough to throw in the marchioness's face this Easter—using a test-tube she'd managed to get her brother to leave his fingerprints on. Kali was thinking hard about her first massacre—you couldn't be taken seriously as a bandit in Kafiristan until you'd supervised at least one massacre, and she hoped to be the first of her family to use 'a Chicago pianola' and 'pine-apples' rather than kukri knives or strangling scarves.

In books written by grown-ups, there was a lot of guff about school days being either the happiest of your life or a worse ordeal than penal servitude. Headmistress gave speeches about School Spirit, and Wicked Wyke hoped to foment a similar, if more limited, Desdemona Spirit which never quite caught on—though Desdemonas bristled at any suggestion that other Houses were better in any way, except in games where Goneril won so often it didn't count. Amy didn't have the luxury of stepping out of herself and thinking of Drearcliff in terms of Good, Bad or Indifferent. The place was, at times, immeasurably better than her old school (which she could barely recall—she spent twenty minutes nagging at a lost scrap of memory, unable to summon her old school's word for 'greens') and at times far, far worse. She was here, this was (for the time being) her world, and that was that.

She was a Drearcliff Girl.

VII: Kidnapped!

Because she wore specs, Inchfawn was trusted with the map. The assumption was that she'd be good at orienteering, which transpired to be a tragic fallacy.

This Thursday afternoon, they were at War with an unholy alliance of Tamora and Goneril. Ariel, who were supposed to be on Desdemona's side, had capitulated early. Viola were being Belgium, which meant standing in a field and blubbing rather than being bayonetted or ravaged by hordes of the Hun.

The berserkers of Tamora, art room blue paint on their faces and hockey sticks decorated with the skulls of shrews, had broken through the Desdemona lines, with a great whooping, bashing, screaming attack. Amy, Kali, Smudge Oxenford and Lydia Inchfawn, cut off from the rest of the House, fled to a small, wooded area outside School grounds. Inchfawn found an overgrown path she promised was a short-cut back to HQ, but it ran downwards, turning into a small pebble-bed stream, and came out on the beach.

There was a dramatic view of Drearcliff Grange, but no easy way to get up to it.

Floating was an option—but Inchfawn and Smudge weren't in on the secret, and Amy thought it best to keep them in the dark. Smudge, liable to exaggerate, would have Amy zooming about like the Demon Ace with her tail on fire. And Inchfawn was potentially a Problem.

Since Fossil took an interest in Amy's Book of Moths, the teacher's devoted disciple had been at best cold to her and at worst malicious. Jealousy was a terrible, terrible thing. Lydia Inchfawn was rather an unhappy girl, and Amy of course felt sorry for her—but she was a drip and a millstone, a burden to the House and a liability to School.

'Some short-cut, Six Eyes,' snarled Kali. 'Sure you ain't rattin' for Tamora? If there's one thing I can't stand, it's a dirty squealin' rat. If there's two things I can't stand, it's the wrigglin' portions of a dirty squealin' rat after she's been chopped in half.'

That was a bit strong, but Amy didn't pipe up.

She was cold, bruised and tired. Tuck had run out an hour ago. If and when they finally made it back, they were sure to be down for a couple of Stains. Amy was not looking forwards to scrubbing the Heel with her toothbrush—especially since she only had the one, and would have to clean her teeth with what was left of it. At this rate, they might have to surrender to the Tamora murder patrols who were out hunting stragglers. Tamora tended to keep and play with prisoners, not march them to neutral territory to sit out the War with the wets of Viola.

Inchfawn looked at the unrolled map again and shook her head. She offered it to Smudge, who was in Inchfawn's cell, but the other girl wouldn't touch it.

So far, Amy had stayed away from the beach. Shores were generally not good moth country. The most notable landmark was the fallen tower, which was a way off, surrounded by 'Danger—Keep Out' signs. The coast was unevenly eroded, making beach walks fraught with peril. There was always the risk of being cut off by the tide, which had a habit of swiftly transforming open beach into shrinking shingle bays, inaccessible except by boat or climb. Cliff-base caves tempted the adventurous explorer—but they'd been warned against them because, at high tide, the waters washed in and anyone inside would certainly drown.

It was said the caves were used in olden days by smugglers, though Amy supposed smuggling was more likely on coasts facing France or Holland than one in sight of South Wales. A few wave-cut overhangs were on their way to becoming caves or catastrophic collapses. Chunks of rock often detached from the cliffs and fell on the beach. School legend had it that two teachers were squashed during a midnight tryst, dying in a compromising embrace.

Smudge pointed out the exact spot where this tragedy had occurred. She spread her arms to indicate the extent of the human pancake which had been found the next morning.

'We believe you,' said Amy, 'thousands wouldn't.'

Smudge stuck out her lower lip. She was very fond of this story. At different times, she had identified six or seven different combinations of teachers in old School photographs as the doomed couple.

Inchfawn had obviously given up even trying to help.

Amy knew it was down to her and Kali.

They couldn't go back the way they came. They'd had to move quickly to avoid a Tamora patrol commanded by Crowninshield II, ventriloquist Beryl's nastier sister. When she took prisoners, Crowninshield II liked to perform harsh interrogations. Really, what she liked was tying people up. She practiced knots and bonds on naïve Firsts lured to her cell with the promise of lemonade and buns. She might even have got in trouble for it if her sister weren't a whip.

Together, Amy and Kali looked up the cliff.

'There *might* be a path,' said Amy.

'For *you*, maybe...'

'You're a decent climber, Kali.'

They looked at Inchfawn and Smudge.

'If we ditch the baggage, it's a Stain. A whole mess of Stains, doll.'

Amy admitted it. Desdemona didn't abandon its own.

Kali hefted her wooden rifle.

'If this gat were the real deal, we could ventilate 'em a little, put 'em out of our misery.'

Smudge heard that and was alarmed.

'She's just joshing,' said Amy.

Smudge not only spread wild stories, but believed them. It would be all over School tomorrow that Kali had killed several girls and buried them in the herb garden.

Inchfawn sat down and looked at her big clunky wrist-watch. It was her prize possession, handed on from a brother who'd been in the trenches. If the hour-hand was pointed at the sun, it worked as a compass—but the day was as overcast as usual, if not actually raining, and they already knew which direction they needed to take. It was just that they couldn't go that way easily.

Amy's toe turned something out of the shingle. It was an old cricket ball, seams expanded but holding together. The School pitch was near enough the edge of the cliff that balls could be hit for a six into the sea.

Suddenly, they were surrounded.

Kali threw away her useless wooden rifle, and reached under her khaki knee-length skirt to pull a long, straight knife from a holster strapped to her thigh. Not QMWAACC regulation issue. Amy hefted her wooden rifle by the barrel like a hockey stick, hoping to give the enemy a good sloshing.

'Screw off, mugs!' shouted Kali.

Inchfawn had her hands up, in surrender—the weed. Smudge fumbled with her ill-kept rifle, which came to pieces in her hands.

Kali held up her knife and bared her teeth.

A *crack!* sounded. Then, a curtailed ping-*nyeow!*

A shot, and a ricochet.

If Desdemona had knives, trust Tamora to bring real guns.

'I say, you gels are playing rough,' declared Smudge. 'Get things in proportion, why don't you?'—which was rich, coming from her. 'A damsel could get damaged.'

Another shot, and a spray of pebbles kicked up at Smudge's legs.

Amy looked at the enemy and realised there was a mistake. These weren't Crowninshield II's rope-happy Campfire Comanche. There were eight or nine of them. Slight by grown-up standards, but not all—or not *even*—girls. They wore loose black clothes and matching hoods with eye-holes. Several had revolvers, and one held a shotgun.

'Sticky crumpets!' exclaimed Amy.

The one who had shot at them was definitely not a girl. He had a red tuft on the forehead of his hood, a badge of leadership. It looked like a flame, and Amy wondered if it were a symbol of his secret society. He took careful aim at Smudge and she shut her mouth.

Amy wondered whether she had been wrong about the scarcity of smugglers hereabouts. From their outfits, this mob were up to no good. The hoods suggested *organised* illegality. They reminded her of Les Vampires or the bands of desperate minions employed by wicked uncles to abduct soppy heiresses.

Kali gave a battle yell and charged.

Amy's heart clutched and she was sure her friend would be shot. She swung her rifle, which left her hands and cartwheeled through the air until it smacked against a hooded head. A torrent of frightful masculine swearing poured forth.

Kali went for the leader, who sidestepped her charge and cold-cocked her with his pistol-butt.

Two others caught the stunned girl and swiftly bound her with ropes. They were even more practiced than Crowninshield II.

With his gun, the leader indicated that Amy and the others should not interfere.

The prisoner was dragged, a deadweight, along the beach. The fellow Amy had beaned was still angry, but his leader indicated they shouldn't stick around. They had what they'd come for.

Kali.

'You can't do that, you rotters,' Amy shouted.

They didn't reply and kept on doing it.

'You won't get away with this,' she added.

She didn't sound convincing to herself.

The hooded men moved quickly. They were nearly out of sight beyond a cliff outcrop. Amy picked up the old, wet cricket ball and bowled it at the leader's head. He turned to look back and was struck between the eyes.

'*Thrown*, Amy,' applauded Smudge.

The hood must have protected the leader, for he didn't fall down dead. He shook a fist back at the girls. Amy picked up stones in her fists. The leader made a sign, and the man with the shotgun discharged his weapon in their general direction. Pellets pattered on the beach. Then, he took careful aim. Reluctantly, Amy dropped the rocks.

The abductors hustled away.

As soon as they were round the curve, Amy would follow, keeping close to the cliff, hiding, floating if need be. She could not let smugglers take her friend.

Smudge grabbed her arm, holding her back.

'They'll shoot you,' she said.

'I don't care,' said Amy.

'They might shoot Kali,' Smudge argued.

'If they went to the trouble of tying her up and carting her off, I should say not,' Amy reasoned. 'Her father has many enemies. They probably intend to ransom her.'

'It could be Ponce's white slavers,' put in Smudge. 'Not that Kali's white, but, you know, for her I expect they'd make an exception... she's jolly saleable, I should say.'

'I don't care what colour she is,' said Amy. 'She's a Desdemona of Drearcliff. We can't let her be snatched without a fight.'

Amy broke free of Smudge.

'I wish Miss Borrodale were here,' said Inchfawn.

Then, suddenly, she was.

'You girls,' said Fossil, 'War's over. You're casualties.'

VIII: Treachery

Smudge told the story first, which was a disaster.

After confirming that Kali was among the missing, and hadn't turned up back at School, Fossil took Amy, Smudge and Inchfawn to Headmistress's study. Dr Mrs Swan asked Keys to sit in on the interview, so three grown-ups were aligned. Small chairs were brought in for the girls.

'Chattopadhyay is absent,' stated Dr Mrs Swan. 'Tell me what you know about this impertinence.'

In a gush, Smudge got out her version of what had happened on the beach. She had most of it straight, but embellished details. Instead of a sewn-on red patch in the shape of a flame, Smudge said the leader's hood was actually on fire. She said the abductors had popped out of foxholes on the beach—which might have been true, but sounded silly.

The tide was in now, so any evidence—spent shotgun pellets, for instance—would be washed away.

Amy knew that Smudge wasn't believed.

She calmly confirmed most of the story and insisted the police be called at once. The country must be searched, trains stopped, roads blocked, air fields shut down. It was vital action be taken now.

Dr Mrs Swan and Fossil exchanged *looks*. Amy was still a new girl to them. They now thought she showed signs of following the errant path of Smudge Oxenford into the realms of faerie, flight and fancy.

The spotlight fell on Lydia Inchfawn.

Surely, the grown-ups would have to believe three girls telling the same story!

Inchfawn took off her glasses and cleaned them with a hankie.

'Kali ran off,' said Inchfawn. 'She talked about it, then she did it. She said she could get back to School without us.'

Headmistress's eyes nearly closed.

Any girl who knew Kali could tell this was rot, but Amy understood that—to the tiny mind of a grown-up—Inchfawn's version sounded more believable than a wild romance of armed, hooded villains. Especially if the primary source was the School's most famous Exaggerator. Smudge had invoked smugglers, white slavers, anarchists, spies and members of secret orders of demon-worshipping monks so often that patience with her had run dry.

Amy had a spurt of pity for the Exaggerator. She had too casually wasted her store of credibility and was frustrated that the real, true story of crime and terror she had to impart was rendered worthless by her previous efforts.

For Inchfawn, Amy had only cold contempt. She wanted to slap her, but knew it would just make the drip seem even more like the put-upon truth-teller in a nest of verminous fibbers.

Headmistress asked Fossil to escort Inchfawn to Old House, where she was to clean herself up for supper. Inchfawn was a-tremble at being entrusted to her idol, so ecstatic that she ignored the thumb-through-the-fist sign Amy gave her, which promised justice would be extracted. The traitor couldn't cling to Miss Borrodale's skirts forever. Eventually, she must answer for her crimes.

Amy and Smudge remained with Headmistress.

'It is a serious matter to voice untruths in this study,' said Dr Mrs Swan. 'Even in the cause of protecting a House-mate.'

Now, it looked even worse. Kali had run off like a sneak, and her friends were lying to cover up.

'Do you have anything to add to your account of this afternoon's incident?'

Amy and Smudge did not.

'Very well,' said Headmistress. 'This matter will be resumed.'

'Aren't you going to call the police?' asked Smudge.

'We make our own laws at Drearcliff, and keep them too,' said Dr Mrs Swan, softly. 'Keys will find Chattopadhyay.'

Keys nodded. She had a waterproof cape to hand and was set to go out in search of the missing girl. At least something was being done, though it was scant comfort.

Dr Mrs Swan considered the girls, drummed her lacquered green nails on her desk, and said 'you are dismissed.'

IX: The Moth Club

'Keys won't find Kali,' declared Frecks. 'The old trout knows School better than anyone, but hasn't been off grounds this century. When she was a Sixth, she got engaged to a young officer. He only went off and got killed at Khartoum with General Gordon. Keys took a vow not to leave Drearcliff Grange. Graduated from Girl to Staff, and stayed put. Wants to be buried in the cricket pitch. Under the crease.'

'Could hardly make it any lumpier,' Amy commented.

Frecks and Light Fingers tittered at the drollery, then remembered how grave things were.

They were in their cell. Amy had told her friends all.

'The masked blighters will have Kali in an aeroplane by now,' ventured Light Fingers. 'Or a sealed train carriage. She'll be bundled up like an invalid. Bound to have been drugged too.'

Amy wasn't sure about the theory.

'I don't know why,' she said, 'but I believe Kali hasn't been taken far away, *yet*. The hooded men were only after her. If they were white slavers, wouldn't they have taken all of us?'

'I doubt even the most depraved Oriental potentate would offer cushion-space to Six Eyes Inchfawn,' said Frecks. 'She'd have to be a Special Bonus Offer, thrown in with better quality merchandise.'

'She wasn't much use in the pinch,' admitted Amy. 'Poor girl.'

'I wouldn't "poor girl" Lydia Inchfawn,' said Frecks. 'That one has a sly, cunning streak. And a mercenary nature. Brain-peeping Imogen Ames always shied clear of her. Just like Six Eyes to turn yellow in a pickle.'

'Funny thing, though,' mused Light Fingers. 'I was in Inchfawn's tent when we went hiking last year. We got early tea every day because we were always first to the camp site. Inchfawn was a whizz at map-reading. I'm puzzled she should have lost the knack. Her brother's watch has a dear little compass in it.'

Amy snapped her fingers. 'Crumpets!' she exclaimed. *'Her brother's watch!'*

'Do tell,' urged Frecks.

'She snuck a look at the watch, just before the hooded men pitched up out of nowhere. As if she was waiting for something! We wouldn't have been on the beach at all if it weren't for her mucking up with the map, so how did they know where to find us?'

The three girls goggled at each other. Inchfawn was in with the abductors!

'It's a Hooded Conspiracy!' declared Frecks. 'I knew it in my bones!'

Amy found such fearful malignancy difficult to credit, but it solved the riddle of why Inchfawn had fibbed to Headmistress.

'What a cow-bag!' said Light Fingers.

Frecks knotted a dressing-gown cord.

'Kali showed me how to do this,' she said. 'Put a florin in the knot, to give weight. Hey presto—Thuggee strangling cord! Justice will be swift. Show no mercy.'

Frecks snapped the cord, which twanged like a bowstring.

'Whoah, Nellie,' said Amy. 'Let's not go off half-cocked. Yes, Inchfawn's in on a terrible, terrible crime. But knowing she's in it opens the door a crack. We were at a loss. Now, we have a *clue*. If we play this cleverly, we've a chance at doing what we know Keys can't. Find Kali and get her back...'

'... and see off those dastards in the hoods, and all their drippy minions.'

'Minions?' Light Fingers asked Frecks.

'It won't be just Six Eyes. If they've signed her up to the Hooded Conspiracy, who knows how many other girls—teachers, even—are in it? Could go all the way up to High Table. Might even be a pinch of truth in what Smudge says about Ponce Bainter. On principle, we can't trust anyone outside this cell, not until they prove themselves. Smudge is probably sound, from what you say, Amy. Can't see what earthly use she might be, though.

It's down to we three. We must apply ourselves—use our Talents. Without Kali, we're the Forus no longer. To go up against the Hooded Conspiracy, we must form a conspiracy—a secret society—of our own. Now, what should we call it? The League of Avenging Justice? The Three Good Girls?'

'The Scarlet Slippers?' suggested Light Fingers.

Amy had it. 'The Moth Club.'

The others looked at her, puzzled and a little disappointed.

'The Moth Club?' exclaimed Frecks, in disbelief.

'All those other names *sound* like secret societies,' Amy explained. 'The Moth Club doesn't...'

'It sounds *boring*,' said Light Fingers.

'Moths are *not* boring,' said Amy, a little stung. 'But, I admit, my enthusiasm isn't generally shared. If we talk about Moth Club doings, most people will yawn and not think any more of it. Only we'll know it's important. That's a super way to keep a society secret.'

Frecks saw sense, 'The Moth Club it is!'

'I liked The Scarlet Slippers,' said Light Fingers, weakly.

'We'll have another society called that,' said Frecks, kindly. 'A pretend secret, to cover up the real one. A good name should not go to waste.'

Amy felt a sense of purpose. After the worrying, dizzying helplessness of the afternoon, it was a relief, almost an intoxicant.

Something was being done.

Now they had a name, The Moth Club needed a charter. Amy turned her Book of Moths upside-down, and opened the blank last page. She fetched out pen and ink, and wrote 'the purpose of The Moth Club is to study moths in their habitats, to list and sketch any species found on the grounds of Drearcliff Grange School, to defend the honour of moths against the calumnies of the supporters of trivial butterflies and to take steps to prevent the wanton murder of moths by certain boys who stalk them with poison and kill them in jars for the empty achievement of building a collection of dead things.'

'Phew,' said Light Fingers.

Amy pressed pink blotting paper to the page. She held it up, and saw the charter in mirror-writing.

'That's the *official* story,' said Amy. 'Now, pass me that pencil.'

Pressing firmly, writing between the lines of the previous passage, she wrote 'the true purpose of The Moth Club is to oppose the Hooded Conspiracy, no matter who their agents or masters might be, to rescue Princess Kali Chattopadhyay from their vile clutches and return her to safety. We vow not to rest until this purpose has been achieved, and that none of the undersigned shall betray her cell-sisters on pain of death by strangulation. We shall triumph.'

She showed this to Frecks and Light Fingers, who approved.

Then, using an India rubber, Amy wiped away the pencil—rendering invisible the secret charter of The Moth Club. Its imprint remained on the paper and would emerge if anyone were to rub a pencil-nib over the seemingly blank spaces between the lines.

Amy signed her name in ink under the official and shadow charter, and passed the book to Frecks, who signed with a flourish, and Light Fingers, who had to think hard to make her signature.

'We should take code-names,' said Frecks. 'Secret *secret* handles. Moth names. Thomsett, you're the expert. You pick.'

'Where are your people from?'

'Lincolnshire,' said Frecks.

'Willow Ermine,' she said, printing it in small letters under Frecks's swish of a signature. 'Its wings look like little Lord's robes, white with tiny black spots. Light Fingers?'

'I'm not from anywhere. Mum and Dad were theatricals, on tour all the time.'

'Where were you born?'

'The Theatre Royal, King's Lynn. Between houses.'

'Large Dark Prominent.'

'Pardon?'

'It's a moth. Very rare. The only specimen known in the British Isles was bred in Norfolk, near King's Lynn.'

She wrote down the name

'What about you?' asked Frecks.

'Kentish Glory,' said Amy, lettering it under her signature.

'But you're from Worcestershire,' complained Light Fingers.

'So is the Kentish Glory,' she said. '*Endromidae*: *Endromis versicolora*. Catalogued by Linnaeus in 1758.'

She flipped back the pages to show the sketch—mostly in brown pencil— she had made. The Kentish Glory was the rarest moth she had catalogued to date. It had visited her grandmama's garden two summers ago, and held still on a leaf as if posing for Amy's pencils, fluttering off as soon as the sketch was finished.

Light Fingers produced a needle from her sewing box. They all pricked their forefingers, stuck little full stops of blood after their names to seal the pact, and sat on their cots, sucking their fingers.

The Moth Club was founded.

X: Midnight Retribution

The next night, well after Lights Out, the Moth Club crept along the corridor. They presented strange figures.

They reasoned that if their foes were *hooded*, they must be *masked*.

Born and raised—if not well—in theatres and naturally quick with a needle, Light Fingers was an Old Reliable for the Drearcliff Ballet Club, the Viola Dramatic Society, the Arthur Wing Pinero Players (who existed thanks to a handsome bequest from an Old Girl which went to maintain the School Auditorium in a state of acceptable plushness—on the condition that Drearcliff Grange mount annual productions of a work by the author of *The Gay Lord Quex* and *The Second Mrs Tanqueray*), the Ragged Revue and the Christmas Mummers. For every play, recital or presentation, Light Fingers made or altered costumes to order. Therefore, she had knowledge of and free access to the extensive catacombs under the Auditorium. Here, props, scenery and costumes—some dating back at least to the last century—were stored. Smudge said the storage cellars were haunted by a Viola Fifth who had foolishly drowned herself while taking the role of Ophelia too seriously in the '08 Senior Production of Bowdler's *Hamlet*. The theatrical spectre purportedly dripped trails on the floor and wailed her mad scene among hanging doublets and hose. Light Fingers was not afraid of such silly goose ghosts.

On Saturday afternoons, there were no classes. Girls were expected to pursue their *enthusiasms*. Having raided the catacombs for raw materials, Light Fingers worked in their cell—prickling somewhat at the many and contradictory suggestions and comments from her 'customers'—to run up ensembles suitable for the Moth Club's secret missions.

Now, Amy, Frecks and Light Fingers wore wood-nymph body-stockings from some forgotten sylvan ballet, tight-fitting balaclava helmets from an unsuccessful dramatic recital of *The Charge of the Light Brigade*, sturdy dance pumps, and light-weight cloaks worn by generations of 'gentlemen, courtiers, gallants, clowns, & co.' The costumes were set off by moth-shaped domino masks, with feathery pipe-cleaner antennae and trailing wings which covered their lower faces. The cloaks, masks and leotards were appropriate for their code-name species: Kentish Glory was a brownish rust, Willow Ermine white with small black dots and Large Dark Prominent speckled grey-brown.

Large Dark Prominent silently opened the door, and the Moth Club slipped into Inchfawn's cell.

As they entered, someone stirred. It was Smudge. She lifted herself up on an elbow and shoved her hair away from her face. Catching sight of masked intruders in the moonlight, she shoved the edge of her sheet to her mouth.

For a moment, Amy—Kentish Glory—fought panic. She didn't know which of the three sleeping Thirds was their quarry. Then, she saw two pairs of spectacles neatly folded on a small table by one of the cots.

The Moth Club laid hands on Lydia Inchfawn.

Amy pressed a face-flannel into the girl's mouth. Inchfawn was awake, but too terrified to struggle.

Smudge mumbled a quarter-hearted protest. Willow Ermine raised a finger to her mask-covered mouth. Smudge buried herself under the bed-clothes.

Between them, the Moth Club got Inchfawn cocooned in a sheet and carried out of the cell. The other Thirds didn't even wake up. Smudge could tell them what had happened. She'd exaggerate, of course—and spread lurid tales of deaths-head monsters spiriting Inchfawn away to glut their vampire thirsts. Frightening rumours about the Moth Club might serve a purpose. Wrong-doers *should* be afraid of them.

They carried their muffled burden up the back-stairs. Willow Ermine had Inchfawn's head-and-shoulders end, and bumped the bundled-up bonce against walls and doors a little more than was strictly necessary. A door which should have been locked wasn't. Through this, they reached the flat roof. The cloud had cleared off for once, and a full moon bathed Old House in pale light. Perfect for nocturnal lepidoptera. Chimney-stacks throw stark, deep shadows.

The scene had been prepared. Light Fingers's rocking chair was tipped against the low guardrail, with rope-ends prepared for the accused's neck and ankles. Inchfawn was unrolled from her sheet and tied to the chair. Her hands were bound behind the chair-back, and the gag taken from her mouth.

A kick set her rocking.

'You will not scream, *wretch*,' said Willow Ermine. Frecks put on a deeper, more ominous voice. With wind whining in the chimneys and waves crashing on the shingles hundreds of feet below, it was deuced eerie. Amy's hackles rose.

Inchfawn opened her mouth, but swallowed a cry. Without any of her glasses, she looked like a different girl.

'Lydia Inchfawn, Dorm Three Desdemona, you are accused of treason against your house-mates,' declared Amy, finding her own hollow voice for Kentish Glory. 'It is proven that you did collaborate with the Hooded Conspirators who abducted your house-sister, Princess Kali Chattopadhyay. Furthermore, you did perjure yourself before Headmistress...'

'Who is that?' asked Inchfawn.

'Silence, *weasel*,' boomed Willow Ermine. 'You will hear charges.'

'... you did perjure yourself before Headmistress, to hinder attempts to pursue the Conspiracy and rescue Princess Kali. These things are known. Now, sentence must be passed... and *executed*.'

This was the trickiest part of the plan, Amy knew. And it depended on her. Even if Inchfawn guessed who was behind the mask of Kentish Glory, there was a thing she did not know about Amy Thomsett.

She could float, and she could reach out with her mind and make others float.

'Ha ha, very amusing,' said Inchfawn, unconvincingly. 'Now, if you'll untie me, we can all get back to bed... and nothing more will be said, all right? No need to trouble Headmistress—or the whips!—with this raggishness.'

Willow Ermine and Large Dark Prominent hefted up the chair, and set it on the guardrail, holding it steady.

Inchfawn squeaked.

The accused was tilted backwards, over the edge.

There was a strip of grass between the outer wall of Old House and the cliff-edge. Depending on the wind, a person falling from the roof might bounce on that strip or miss it entirely. Whichever, they would plunge to the shingles. It was remotely possible they'd be impaled on the flagpole which still stuck up from the broken-off tower.

Willow Ermine and Large Dark Prominent struggled a little with the weight. Light Fingers had only lent her chair to the Moth Club on the condition it be returned safely. It was a prized possession, one of the few things she had brought with her to School. It had accompanied her to the dressing rooms of all the great theatres of the kingdom. Amy felt a responsibility for the furniture.

She reached out with her mind, feeling the shape and weight of the chair and its prisoner, then took a firm hold on the lump they made together. The chair juddered a little, as if trying to free itself from the other girls' grips. Now, Amy made it *lighter*, and herself *heavier*. Anchored to the roof by her increased weight, feet sinking a little into soft tar, she held the chair as if invisible strings ran from her eyes to its points of balance.

Amy raised her arms—the wing-like cloak Light Fingers had made spread out—and took all the weight on herself.

Willow Ermine and Large Dark Prominent let go of Inchfawn.

The chair wobbled, but did not topple.

Amy let out the invisible strings and the chair tipped backwards.

'No,' screeched Inchfawn, fat tears streaming down her cheeks. 'It wasn't my fault, you beasts! They said no one would be hurt! I was made to do it! It was... a whip, I tell you. A whip!'

Just as Frecks had theorised, the Hooded Conspiracy ran through the School.

The chair was floating now, like a large balloon. Amy didn't think Inchfawn even noticed. If she looked down, she would see the dark sea, and the white froth of waves on the beach. That would be enough to stop most people's hearts.

Amy began to reel the blubbing culprit in.

'What have we here?' drawled a voice, from behind them. 'Such a shocking spectacle,' it continued, from another direction. 'I should say this was unmistakably a Major,' from one of the chimneys. 'What do you think, Head Girl?'

It was Beryl Crowninshield, throwing her voice about. All the Murdering Heathens were here, in matching grey nighties and dressing gowns. They carried hockey sticks or cricket bats. Henry Buller had one of each, hefted on her shoulders like the crossed swords of a barbarian gladiator. Crowninshield II was with them, a cadet Witch, drooling at the sight of a trussed Third.

'I fear very much so, Prefect Crowninshield,' said Sidonie Gryce. '*C'est tres mechant... tres mechant* indeed.'

The surprise jarred Amy's concentration. Suddenly, she wasn't *heavy*. The chair was let go, over the edge.

Inchfawn wasn't the only one who screamed.

XI: In the Ruck

Before snatching Inchfawn from her cot, the Moth Club had prepared the roof. In case of eventualities like this, a stout cord was tied between guardrail and chair-back. The prisoner dropped barely five feet before the rope cracked like a hangman's neck-breaking noose, and the chair scraped the wall. Knots, tied to QMWAACC standards, held. The chair stayed as securely tethered to the rail as Lydia Inchfawn was to it. She might not be exactly comfortable, but she was in no real danger.

Still, her nasty tumble was a useful distraction.

Amy reached out with her mind and tried to float Henry Buller. The Sixth was hefty, and her flat feet were planted firmly.

'I say, g-g-g-girls,' stuttered Buller. 'I've come over queerly...'

Buller's waist-length braids rose as if on stiff wires, and bobbed like charmed snakes. Her crossed bats lifted from her shoulders, seemingly of their own accord, tugging her elbows up sharply. Her eyes almost popped— which wasn't Amy's doing, just a natural reaction.

Dora Paule hissed. A Special herself, she recognised a Talent in use.

'I d-d-don't like this,' said Buller, her croak close to cracking. 'S-s-s-Sidonie, m-m-make it s-s-s-stop!'

The bats were tugged out of Buller's hands. Amy made them dance in the air like dangerous puppets. She let go and the bats clattered, thumping Buller's shoulders as they fell.

Inchfawn, out of sight, was still making a fuss.

'Cut out the yelpage, stoat,' said Willow Ermine. 'Dangle with some dignity, for the House's sake if not your own.'

Seemingly unperturbed, Sidonie Gryce signalled her Murdering Heathens to spread out, cutting off the Moth Club's avenues of escape across the roof. Buller was *hors de combat*, but the Head Girl had other minions. The Crowninshield sisters took flank positions, chins down as if expecting a charge, evil mismatched eyes peeping up through long fringes. Their identical smiles of unhealthy excitement were all the scarier in the moonlight. Dora Paule seemed, as usual, distracted—but was stationed between the Moth Club and the access door to the back-stairs, blocking their escape route.

'How gaudy you look,' commented Gryce. 'I note a dozen Minor Infractions of Drearcliff dress code. Or has there been some *minuit masquerade* to which, by an oversight, we were not invited? In any case, *mes enfants*, the party is *fini*.'

This was worse than facing the Hooded Conspiracy proper. Grown men might shoot at you, but couldn't dish out extra punishments for having the temerity to fight back. If the Moth Club survived and were unmasked, they would be cleaning the Heel with their tongues and have burning bamboo shoved under their fingernails in the Whips' Hut for the rest of their time at School.

'*Mes filles*,' said Gryce, 'let us see which spotty faces cower behind those ridiculous bug disguises…'

The Crowninshield sisters took steps forward. They had rounders bats—Frecks had taught Amy 'only bounders play rounders', since it was for twits who didn't have the patience and poetic soul for cricket. Henry Buller was now superstitiously afraid of her own weapons, but her ham-sized fists were clenched and she could fetch a clout which would do credit to Gene Tunney.

It was going to be a melée.

'Let the Witches have it,' cried Willow Ermine. 'Tally-hoooo!'

Large Dark Prominent, faster than a nocturnal hummingbird, zig-zagged towards Crowninshield, but stepped into a shadow at the last moment, leaving the prefect blinking. Then, swiftly, she came out of the lea of a chimney and tweaked Crowninshield's nose. She could keep this up all night. Willow Ermine stepped under a bat-slosh from Crowninshield II and punched the Third square on the nose, staggering her back. She ripped her opponent's weapon from her hands, and sailed it off over the edge of the roof.

Amy realised she was floating. The thrill of the moment had made her lighter. Her feet hung limply, about nine inches from the rooftop. Using her moth-wing cloak, she tried to swim through air towards an astonished Henry Buller, but found herself flapping in place. The gentle-seeming wind filled her cloak as if it were a sail. She had to resist being borne backwards over the parapet.

She made herself heavy and landed hard. Her ankles hurt.

Buller charged her, snorting like a heifer. Amy wished she had persuaded Kali to teach her Kafiristani jiu-jitsu.

She held out a hand and floated Buller's dropped cricket bat, tripping the girl up.

Then, she took the fight to the Queen Heathen.

Pushing Buller aside, giving the Sixth enough extra weight to keep her sprawled on the roof, Amy ran at Sidonie Gryce. The Head Girl was used to delegating the thumping and scratching to her Murdering Heathens. Amy had an idea she was, like all bullies, at heart wet and a coward.

Amy screeched. This was her moth-cry. She had practiced. She knew it set teeth on edge.

'*Filles*,' shouted Gryce, calling for help. '*Beryl*…'

The trailing mask-wings tickled Amy's mouth as she kept up her war-cry. She saw fear in the Head Girl's eyes. It was welcome.

In this disguise, the Kentish Glory costume, Amy was not a feeble Third, a new bug who could be shoved around. She was a mystery, a creature, a terror to the wicked, an angel to the well-intentioned. Free of the weaknesses of her person and position. Free to strike!

She pushed Sidonie Gryce up against a chimney stack and drummed fists against the girl's chest and face. She grabbed handfuls of the Head Girl's unbound hair and tugged. She screeched in the Witch's face.

Gryce was helpless.

Amy kept up the attack.

Beryl Crowninshield did not come to help the Head Girl. She was dancing around the roof with Large Dark Prominent, tossing her voice to throw off her opponent but too slow to avoid swift slaps and cuffs. Having put Crowninshield II down with a bloody nose, Willow Ermine laid into Buller with the prefect's own hockey stick.

The Moth Club were giving a good account of themselves.

Amy wondered why she had been intimidated by the Murdering Heathens. Gryce was blubbing as badly as any Viola First now.

A hand clasped her shoulder, and a mouth pressed to her ear.

'*Amy Thomsett,*' whispered Dora Paule, 'stop this. *Now!*'

There was a light, and a smell, and the sky changed...

XII: The Real *Head* Girl

The roof was awash with the harsh purple light of three big, shining moons. All was still. Amy's cloak-collar itched and her new costume felt heavy, her domino tacky against her cheeks.

She couldn't hear the sea any longer. Far off, something wailed musically—soft and mournful, but bone-scrapingly *wrong*.

To Amy's surprise, *everyone else* was floating. But they weren't drifting ever upwards, to be lost in the stratosphere—which Amy was always afraid would happen to her. Willow Ermine, Large Dark Prominent and the Murdering Heathens bobbed gently a few inches above the roof, as if suspended in invisible liquid. To Amy, they all looked like waxworks—frozen in mid-air, mouths open, clothes stiff, hair starched. She let go of Sidonie Gryce, and the Head Girl drifted slightly away. Her face was a contorted mask, eyes open but unseeing. Her hands were raised in defensive claws. She looked silly, but Amy wasn't inclined to laugh.

She turned, *knowing* this was Prefect Paule's doing.

Amy had thought Dora Paule wasn't quite there. Now, she knew that was the honest truth.

Paule wasn't a floating waxwork, but she wasn't herself either. At least, not the self she usually showed.

She was like a balloon person who'd been blown up irregularly. The head was five or six times normal size, swollen cranium distinct beneath a vast dandelion clock of hair. The rest of her was undeveloped, with feeble, withered limbs. Her feet trailed on the roof, but her head must be floating—for her spindly body couldn't otherwise support its weight.

The face, though expanded, was unmistakably Dora Paule.

'Good evening, Amy,' she said, mildly. 'This must be a shock. Did you think you were the only Talent? When I first came to School, I did. It's natural. You read about Blackfist, Dr Shade or Jimmy O'Goblins in the story papers, but never think "*they're like me*".'

In this purple light, Dora Paule sounded less mad. That was not comforting.

'Where are we?'

'A step outside,' said Paule. 'I call it the Purple. I'm always half-here, which is why I'm half-gone Back Home.'

'Do you really look like that?'

'In the Purple, yes. Don't take it seriously. You have wings here.'

It was true. The itching tug Amy had felt was not the cloak Light Fingers had scavenged, but a set of moth-wings anchored to her shoulder-blades. She shrugged and they spread in display—but she didn't know how to flutter. It must be a knack you had to learn, like wiggling your ears. Her forehead tingled, where her antennae were rooted. She had smells in her mouth, tastes in her eyes, colours in her ears.

'Why've you brought us here?' Amy asked.

'Not to save Sidonie,' said Paule. 'She can take her lumps. Though she's not who you should worry about. She's no real idea what's really going on. No one does, except me. Looking at Back Home from the Purple is like watching a play with the script in your hand—you can flip back and forth, read the stage directions even, know what's coming. But you can't change the story. For that, you have to be Back Home.'

Amy, fascinated, touched Gryce's frozen face. Her skin was warm, but not pliant.

'So you're claiming Gryce isn't in the Hooded Conspiracy? That Inchfawn was fibbing?'

'Yes and no.'

Amy's antennae prickled with irritation.

'No,' said Paule, picking up her reaction, 'I'm not being wishy-washy, I'm answering both your questions in order. Yes, Sidonie is not party to the kidnap plot. No, Lydia was telling the truth when she said a whip made her dupe you onto the beach. It was Beryl. She's clever. She works at it, like she works on her ventriloquism. She's not a natural Special, but thinks she can make herself one. It's all about money. She hires out. The people you call the Hooded Conspiracy gave Beryl twenty pounds to make sure Princess Kali was on the beach yesterday. That's not important. *We're* important. So's Gladys Naisbitt, if only she'd look beyond the ends of her fingers. We are the School Spirit. You must know what it means to be a Drearcliff girl...'

Tendrils of thicker purple, like the ghosts of eels, wound at ankle-height.

The quality of the light was unpleasant in the Purple. Though there was no heat, it was as oppressive as a boiling summer's day. The wailing was closer and raised Amy's hackles like the brush of razors. Her antennae stung. She felt sparks behind her eyes.

Dora Paule was leaning towards her. Her forehead seemed to be expanding further. Her eyes were the size of apples.

'Why do you think they send girls to school, anyway?'

Amy was taken aback by the question.

'Your mother said it,' began Paule, '"Boys grow up and go out to conquer the world, make fortunes, fight battles, invent aeroplanes and miracle cures and the wireless. Girls get married and have children. Why fill their heads with anything not relevant to that?"'

Once, when she didn't think Amy could overhear, Mother said something like that to her mother. Grandmama had campaigned most of her life for the vote, which Mother had but never used. They had *differences* over Amy.

'School prepares a girl for life,' said Amy, quoting Grandmama.

'Yes, exactly,' said Paule. 'Ordinary schools prepare ordinary girls for ordinary lives. Babies and cakes and wallpaper. Drearcliff is not an ordinary school. We are not ordinary girls. We will not have ordinary lives. Especially you, Kentish Glory.'

Amy's wings stiffened, involuntarily—with something like pride, but also apprehension. She didn't want to know what happened in the last act before the overture was finished.

'Back Home, there's a demand for *educated* girls,' said Paule. 'Not too educated, but enough. It's like white slavery, really. Girls are put on the market, and bought with a wedding ring or a villa in Nice or an endless supply of dear little hats and gloves. Drearcliff girls don't marry masters of fox-hounds and raise the next generation of gallant captains. The men we end up with are different. Special. There are more of them around now than before the War, have you noticed? Men with great and secret purposes. Freakish geniuses and bold explorers in nether-regions. Special men need Special women. Swan realised that when she started here. She saw the need for *Drearcliff* girls. An ordinary fellow wants a wife who serves tea prettily and puts up with mess in the bedroom in order to pop out healthy babies. Other men want a woman who can walk through the walls of the Tower of London with a crown jewel in her mouth, or keep an entire tribe of pygmies on mind-strings under the impression that she's a volcano goddess. Some men want women who actually *are* volcano goddesses or winged creatures or night-gaunts. Those are the lives Drearcliff prepares you for. Who do you want to marry when you grow up, Amy? A curate, or a masked mystery man?'

Amy wasn't sure she wanted to marry anyone.

'You can forget the curate,' Paule continued. 'It's too late for him. Look how you're dressed. Think what you can do. No matter what your Mother wants, you can't cut out the part of you that *floats*. That means you've got no choice but to live in a night-world.'

Amy looked at the other girls, the frozen ones. Light Fingers was Special, in the sense Paule meant; but the rest—Frecks, Inchfawn, the Murdering Heathens—were... well, not Ordinary, not exactly. There was even something odd about Henry Buller, with her mannish arms and stutter, or Crowninshield II, with her knot-making fingers and cruel twist. Special? Not entirely. But they were unmistakably Drearcliff Girls.

'Do you know who sends their daughters to Drearcliff?' asked Paule. 'Criminal masterminds, outlaw scientists, master magicians, clubland heroes. Sally Nikola of the Fourth is the daughter of the Fifth Most Dangerous Man in the world. Did Swan mention that three Drearcliff girls have been hanged since the War? Two for murder, one for treason. We have at least nine girls at present who aren't strictly human. Ten Brincken, the German Sixth, was bred from the ejaculate of an executed criminal. Janice Marsh, the girl with gills, is even odder than she seems. Perky Pinborough, the Second who smiles all the time and never closes her eyes, has been asleep for six months. A parasitic maggot crawled up her nose into her brain and works her like a big puppet. If you have a conversation with Perky, you're actually talking to the maggot. I'm not sure myself if I'm human. I've been kept back while I develop. I came to Drearcliff when Victoria was Queen. Back Home, I've stopped growing, but in the Purple I still have a way to go.'

Paule flapped her flaccid hands, apologetically.

Amy was worried about what the prefect had said.

'Oh, you're human, all right,' Paule reassured Amy. 'You only have wings and antennae because I've brought you into the Purple. Back Home, you'll be you again. But you'll still have the knack of *floating*.'

The tendrils were thicker now. One brushed past Amy's legs, like sandpapery seaweed.

'You'll have to leave soon. Apart from me, no one can stay in the Purple long. Others attract undue attention. That's not pleasant. I learned my lesson after I lost a few visitors. Misplaced, rather. I'm sure they're here somewhere. I'm glad we've had this little chat, though. We should be friends, if you can be friends with the half of me in the Back Home. We are both *in the know*.'

There was something desperate, something *yearning*, in Dora Paule. If she had to keep repeating the Sixth Form—kept behind while other girls left School to get on with the lives for which they had been prepared—she must be lonely.

Amy understood that. She had been lonely too. Keeping her secret.

...but she wasn't lonely now. She had Frecks and Light Fingers and Smudge and... and Kali. She had her cell, her House, her School.

She realised something about the Purple. It was a deadly distraction. Here, you thought about what Paule wanted you to. You paid attention to her. This place had three moons, but Dora Paule was its star, its sun.

Back Home, other things were important. Amy concentrated, her antennae taut and curved. She remembered the secret charter of the Moth Club.

'...to oppose the Hooded Conspiracy, no matter who their agents or masters might be, to rescue Princess Kali Chattopadhyay from their vile clutches and return her to safety. We vow not to rest until this purpose has been achieved.'

Paule's head was so large now that her body was like the basket hanging under a Montgolfier Balloon.

'Dora,' said Amy, urgently, *'where's Kali?'*

'Oh, she's Rapunzel, waiting,' Paule said, off-handedly. 'She won't be killed till the third dawn.'

The purple light shut off.

Sidonie Gryce was screaming again, picking up where they'd left off. Amy was a full three feet off the ground, hands grabbing Gryce's lapels. She tugged the Head Girl upwards and plopped her bottom in a chimney. Gryce stuck fast, arms and legs lashing out, yelling like a dervish.

Amy landed on the roof, better this time, bending at the knees.

Dora Paule, regularly proportioned, stood aside.

'What did you mean?' Amy asked her. 'Rapunzel? Killed?'

'Mean? I'm not mean. I don't mean. I... oh, good night...'

Willow Ermine, breathing heavy, wings torn, tugged at Amy's cloak, and made for the open door, dragging Amy away from Paule, who fluttered her fingers in a distracted farewell. Light Fingers was already on the back-stairs.

The Murdering Heathens clustered around the Head Girl, wondering how to get her out of the chimney without being hurt by her kicking feet or flailing fists.

The Moth Club rattled back to their cell, divesting themselves of their costumes en route.

A thin voice sounded from outside the window. Inchfawn dangled still.

'That reminds me,' said Frecks. 'Light Fingers, go rouse Wicked Wyke. She'll be up early, since it's Sunday Chapel at seven, Lord help us! Report that some larcenous harlot has stolen your rocking chair! Best shift any oncoming blame onto persons unknown, eh? Say it was probably one of Ariel's well-known not-funny japes.'

Light Fingers got into her dressing gown, and hurried off.

Frecks was abuzz, exhilarated at the Moth Club's first outing. While Amy had been in the Purple, no time at all passed for the others.

Amy didn't know what to tell Frecks.

Rapunzel? *Killed!*

'Crumpets,' she exclaimed. 'Calamity and crumpets!'

XIII: Chapel

Sunday Chapel at Drearcliff was more about mystery than enlightenment. All School—no excuses accepted, including deathly illness—filed in and took their pews. Miss Dryden, of the futile whistle, improvised at a wheezy organ, pumping stately, presumably devotional music with an occasional shrill screech or dramatic detour. Frecks claimed that Dryden sometimes played 'Yes, We Have No Bananas!' so slowly it was nearly unrecognisable.

Most of the Staff—and not a few of the Fifths and Sixths—looked as if they'd spent the night at a cock-fight in an opium den followed by an orgy in a gin-house, then come straight the Chapel without going to bed. Gryce was pretty and perfect, as if fresh from eight hours of innocent sleep, but Crowninshield and Buller showed a satisfying collection of cuts and bruises. Paule was distracted, as usual. Amy wondered whether she even properly noticed what happened outside the Purple, much less remembered what she'd said last night.

'*She won't be killed till the third dawn.*'

If Paule meant the third dawn after Kali's abduction, that would be first thing Monday. Tomorrow morning! In a terror-spasm, Amy envisioned a scimitar held up to catch the sun's first rays and Kali's lovely neck stretched on a chopping block.

Miss Dryden's straining organ rose in a crescendo, giving the Reverend Mr Bainter his cue. The chaplain had to hide behind a curtain while Staff and Girls took their pews. He emerged, wearing a peculiar tricorn mitre with candle-tassels which burned like slow fuses and smelled like Kali's joss cigarettes.

With his hair-slickum, cheek-powder and a lotion which whiffed powerfully of aniseed, Ponce Bainter took to the pulpit like an ageing prima donna to the stage. Amy had thought all clergymen orthodox, respectable and slightly dull. Bainter was more than slightly dull, given to prefacing and concluding sermons with droning Tibetan chants, but was far from orthodox and, as all the girls were certain, quite the reverse of respectable. He seldom mentioned Our Lord Jesus Christ, an important figure in the sermons Amy had heard elsewhere, and his vestments and altar-cloths were embroidered with symbols not found in other churches—mediaeval scientific implements, monocular starfish, bipedal goats, wavy lines, the constellation of the Plough and snarly-face suns. The upside-down woman on the wheel, as represented on the school badge, featured heavily.

The text for today's sermon was the school motto, *A fronte praecipitium a tergo lupi.* Amy, incapable of concentrating on Bainter's windy talk, still didn't find out where the wolves came into it.

Mentally, she wrestled with a different text, '*Oh, she's Rapunzel, waiting.*'

Amy was stumped as to what Paule could have meant. Kali didn't have especially long hair or (so far as Amy knew) a devoted swain intent on

spiriting her off. The whole School whispered that she'd eloped with Ivor
Novello, but that was tommyrot: Kali detested matinee idols, and preferred a
mug with a snub-nosed 'gat' in his fist to a gent with a high-pitched serenade.
Kali was a Princess, but Rapunzel was practically the only fairy tale heroine
Amy could think of who wasn't. Technically, Rapunzel probably became
a Princess after the story was over—provided the Prince who climbed up
her hair did the decent thing and married her. Wondering why Miss Kaye
obviously skipped or altered passages in reading aloud to the class, Amy had
looked up the original Brothers Grimm version; in that, the Prince caddishly
got Rapunzel preggers and was blinded for it. Rapunzel was famously a
prisoner in a tower, so maybe Paule meant Kali was being held captive.
Rapunzel's gaoler was her stepmother, but Kali's father went through wives
so rapidly that no stepmother was around long enough to plot against her.

'You, Amy Thomsett, Desdemona Third,' shouted Bainter, raising his
voice, pointing a finger. Girls edged away, putting clear space between them
and Amy.

Had Ponce known she wasn't paying attention? If so, why single her out?
If anyone in Chapel *wasn't* thinking of something other than the sermon, it
would have been a miracle.

'Answer the Question!'

Amy ummed. She had no idea what the Question was.

'"With a precipice in front and wolves behind, what would you do?"'
rasped Frecks out of the side of her mouth.

Amy said the first thing that came into her mind.

All School tittered, except Ponce—whose eyes bulged with fury.

Amy caught herself. She had said 'I'd *float* over the precipice...'

Dr Mrs Swan, eyes firmly shut throughout Bainter's sermon, blinked
alert and clapped once, silencing laughter.

'...the wolves would rush over the edge,' continued Amy, hoping she
could claim she was trying to be funny, 'and be dashed to death on the
jagged rocks below.'

'And *you*, Thomsett, where would *you* be?'

'Ah, away with the fairies?'

Thunderous laughter. A note was passed along the pew and pressed into
Amy's hand.

She looked. It read MAJOR INFRACTION, R. Wyke (Mrs).

XIX: At the Heel

Cleaning the Heel wasn't quite as frightful as advertised. It *was* done with
toothbrushes, but Infractors didn't have to use their own. Stout-bristled
specimens, new every week, were provided. Buckets of water and carbolic
soap were also involved. Amy had imagined toiling alone, perhaps with
hobbling weights, but reported to the quad after Chapel to find herself in
with a sorry shower from all Forms and Houses. These miscreants had either

clocked up enough Minor Infractions to qualify for the punishment or—like Amy, convicted of Impertinence in Chapel—gone for the High Jump and got caught in a Major.

School Rules decreed that a Major Infraction automatically got you the Heel, but—in a rare, merciful touch—obliterated outstanding Stains like the three Minors Amy had in her book, so you started fresh next week. Anyone with four Black Notches who wanted to do something appalling might find it almost worth the throw. Unity Crawford of Viola, known to all as 'Vanity', was here for pouring red ink on the dress shirt of a girl who had beaten her to the role of Lucas Cleeve, male lead in the Arthur Wing Pinero Players' production of *The Notorious Mrs Ebbsmith*. Perky Pinborough was here because her constant smile irritated the Witches so much they piled Minors on her in the hope of wiping it off. She was cheerful, if glassy-eyed. Amy remembered what Paule said about the maggot in Perky's brain, and decided to start cleaning at the opposite end. The anarchist Hannah Absalom—who mortified a different monarch, plutocrat, churchman or politician every Monday—was up on her regular Major. She set grimly to scraping 'Death to President Zog of Albania!' off the Heel, cleaning the canvas for next week's message of terror.

This week, the Heel was supervised by Miss Kaye. She brought a lawn-chair and a book, and let the girls get to it. She had a hamper, and promised lemonade at the end of the job. Amy knew they were lucky. When Fossil Borrodale was in charge, she stood over Infractors with her bunsen burner tube and added extra *encouragement* if the pace slackened.

Still, this was a pestiferous bother.

Every moment she was here, scraping grime out from under Achilles' marble toenails, she wasn't looking for Kali. If Paule were right, the Moth Club had to find—and *rescue*—their cell-mate before sun-up tomorrow.

It was done inside an hour. Miss Kaye inspected the Heel, deemed it suitably spotless, and gave the girls—Infractors no longer, their books wiped clean as the marble—lemonade. Absalom refused hers on political grounds.

Miss Kaye—Acting Mrs Edwards—wasn't like other Teachers. She wasn't here for life, and lacked the cowed, cringing attitude even termagants like Fossil had around Dr Mrs Swan. She had read out 'Rapunzel', albeit in edited form—so she might have an idea.

Amy asked, 'Why would anyone say Kali Chattopadhyay was "like Rapunzel, waiting"?'

Miss Kaye was surprised.

'Chattopadhyay's hair isn't long,' she said, touching her own trimmed bob. 'And she didn't wait. She took off. If found, she'll be cleaning the Heel all term. Headmistress takes a dim view of absconders. Though she's been in less of a bate about Chattopadhyay than Ferrers III last term. Funny, that. When Ferrers III went over the wall, the Chief Constable was summoned, notices put in the papers, the countryside combed by search parties and the truant tracked by private detectives to a boarding house in Torquay. I'd have thought a Kafiristani Princess would be an even greater loss. But there's been little fuss.'

Was Dr Mrs Swan trying to avoid bad publicity?

'Kali's father happens to be in London on business,' continued Miss Kaye. 'Buying rifles, I believe. He is due to pay a call on School tomorrow. That will, I imagine, be an uncomfortable occasion. Parents don't generally take it kindly when their precious darlings go missing.'

Vanity snorted. She had the full set of parents, but still felt like an orphan. She acted up fearfully in the forlorn hope of getting their attention. Amy suspected that Vanity regretted not thinking of running away, preferably in disguise, to become the centre of a whirlwind of speculation and gossip. If she scarpered now, she'd be accused of imitating Kali—a severe blow to her reputation as an 'original'. Of course, it wouldn't be plagiarism. Kali had not, despite what Inchfawn swore, gone off on her own accord. She'd been snatched!

'But why "Rapunzel, waiting"?'

Miss Kaye shrugged, not casually. Her eyes showed lively interest. There were some—well, Smudge, inevitably—who said she was a spy. Frecks, who knew about the espionage game, said Smudge wasn't as far off as usual about Miss Kaye. There were 'tells', apparently. After last night, Amy wondered if Smudge wasn't imaginative *enough*—her exaggerations paled beside the unvarnished truth of Dora Paule and the Purple. From now on, she might believe the girl on principle. The verdict was that Miss Kaye was at Drearcliff Grange School for some purpose beyond filling in for the absent Mrs Edwards. Amy felt she could trust the temporary teacher in a way she couldn't trust Headmistress or Ponce Bainter or even Miss Borrodale.

'Rapunzel sat in her tower, waiting for her prince to call "Rapunzel, Rapunzel, let down your hair",' said Miss Kaye. 'The story seems to have gone beyond that in Chattopadhyay's case. Her prince has already come and spirited her off.'

'But, Miss, it wasn't like that. I saw hooded men take her away. Against her will.'

Miss Kaye's eyes narrowed. Amy could tell Miss Kaye had no reason not to believe her and maybe more than reason to doubt Inchfawn's story.

'When Rapunzel was waiting, she was in a tower,' said Miss Kaye. 'With no way in but an upper window.'

Amy had to concentrate hard to keep on the ground.

That was it! The tower! Kali was being held in the tower. The broken tower on the beach, surrounded by 'Danger' and 'Keep Out' signs. What better place to keep a prisoner?

She must tell the Moth Club.

XX: A Meeting of the Moth Club

While Amy was taking her punishment in the quad, the rest of the Moth Club had not been idle. Returning to their cell, she found find Light Fingers picking twigs out of her Sunday pinafore and Frecks in a state of high excitement.

'After Chapel, we spotted Crowninshield and her homunculus sister sneaking off grounds,' Frecks explained. 'Light Fingers tailed them. She can dog a person's tracks without being seen. Useful knack if you can come by it. There's a secret way through the wall, hidden by ivy. Which is nice to know. No more braving the glass spikes.'

Light Fingers had worn her Large Dark Prominent domino, but not the full Moth Club get-up.

'They took a hamper down to the beach,' said Light Fingers. 'Contraband from the kitchens.'

'You'll never guess where they were headed!' declared Frecks.

'I bet I can,' said Amy. 'The tower!'

Frecks and Light Fingers presented studies in bugging eyes and open mouths.

'Good gravy, Thomsett,' said Frecks, 'how the diddle did you tumble?'

Amy hadn't told her chums about the Purple, not to keep a secret but because she didn't think she could explain without coming across as potty. Floating and gills and hummingbird hands fell within accepted realms of Specialty, but Paule's Talent was excessive even for Drearcliff.

'Someone mentioned Rapunzel,' Amy said, weakly.

'Ah-hah,' said Frecks. 'She of the upstairs dungeon. The mists clear!'

'When the weird sisters got to the tower, a rope ladder was let down from an upper window,' said Light Fingers. 'There's no other way in. The hamper was hooked to the ladder and pulled up. I didn't see who was doing the pulling...'

'It *must* have been the Hooded Conspirators,' enthused Frecks. 'If they've got Kali, she's in the tower!'

'Crumpets,' exclaimed Amy.

'I still don't see why they *haven't* spirited her away or done her in,' said Frecks. 'They're running a fearful risk sticking close to School. Perhaps Kali's being held for ransom and Swan's keeping mum?'

'Miss Kaye said Mr Chattopadhyay is coming down tomorrow. Perhaps he's bringing a princess's price with him. Kali's weight in gold coins or blood rubies.'

'*I* wouldn't cross Kali's Dad,' said Frecks. 'He's not the sort to take Hooded Conspiracies with a song and a smile and a philosophical laugh. He's the sort who hunts down enemies and garrottes them, their children, their parents, their friends and their pets. Come tomorrow, I shouldn't care to be a white mouse owned by the sweethcart of a cousin of a Hooded Conspirator!'

'We can't wait for tomorrow,' said Amy. 'Mr Chattopadhyay will be too late. Even if he takes the earliest train from London, Joxer won't get him to School till well after dawn. And that's when Kali will be killed. The third dawn!'

'How do you know this?' asked Light Fingers.

'I feel it in my moth antennae,' Amy explained. 'Really, I do. You'll have to take it on trust.'

That hung there in the cell for the briefest flicker.

'Good enough for me,' said Frecks. 'The word of a Moth Club girl is not to be doubted!'

Frecks stuck out her paw, which Amy gripped. Light Fingers grasped their enlocked hands.

It was already getting dark. Girls drifted towards the Refectory.

'We can't hare off now,' said Frecks. 'If we're marked absent at Supper, they'll raise the whole School after us. It'll be torture sitting and eating as if nothing were amiss, but we've got to be valiant. After nosh, we fly!'

XXI: An Upstairs Dungeon

The moon was just past full, the night sky clear. Wet shingles shimmered and tidal pools reflected constellations as the Moth Club—in full costume—crept towards the tower.

Being off School grounds at any time was a Major Infraction. At this hour, it was probably cause for expulsion and disgrace. Their cots were stuffed with pillows, in case Wicked Wyke sprang one of her occasional inspections.

'Should we call "Rapunzel, Rapunzel, let down your hair"?' ventured Willow Ermine. 'Might give Kali heart to know rescue is at hand.'

Amy—Kentish Glory—shook her head. Stealth was the order of the evening.

The three girls blithely passed Danger! and Keep Out! signs, and climbed the rocks and rubble piled around the base of the broken tower. The footing was unsure, with rubbery, slippery seaweed coating broken, tilted surfaces and deceptive pools populated by scuttling crustaceans with angry eyes on stalks. Up close, there was more of the tower than Amy had thought. What had sheared away with the crumbling cliff was the top of a fortified lookout post, built when Somerset expected invading Welsh warriors any minute. Like Rapunzel's upstairs dungeon, it had no ground-level entrance—and no windows for the first thirty feet or so. Leaning inland at a greater angle than the Tower of Pisa, it was a fluke the remnant hadn't completely collapsed long ago. Smudge said it had been secretly shored up in olden days, used by wreckers to lure shipping to disaster.

Large Dark Prominent indicated the window from which the rope ladder had been lowered. It was near the top.

It was down to Kentish Glory to swarm the tower.

Looking at the window, she made herself light. She floated up two or three feet in a spurt and bumped against the inclining stone wall. Her friends winced in sympathy, but she held her tongue.

The wall was rough enough to afford hand-holds every few feet—too crumbly and irregular for mountaineering, but she was a floater, not a climber. She pulled herself up, careful not to get too far from the wall. She carefully angled her body to avoid scraping her legs. It was like swimming through air. The cloak-wings helped her manoeuvre, and she wondered if she could use them to fly properly. A strong wind blew. She had to be wary of being caught by a gust and borne off into open air.

She had a moment to realise she'd never floated this high before. Then, she was near the window, and the urgency of her mission overcame other concerns.

She heard voices inside the tower. The shock made her suddenly heavier. Gravity tugged and she tumbled a few yards, then flattened against the wall, sticking like a moth, cloak spread around her. It took all her concentration to stay light and hold her position.

The talk was in a language she didn't know. Eastern gabble, she thought. Mr Chattopadhyay must have many enemies in Kafiristan, especially former in-laws. Could this be a revenge plan? Using Kali to lure the bandit king to a spot where he could be assassinated. If someone else killed her father, Kali would be furious.

Amy inched up towards the window. Rather than pop her head over the sill, she climbed beside the opening and listened. The conversation stalled. She detected dim light from inside the tower.

Then, she surged up the final few feet and reached the broken battlements. She hopped over, and made herself heavy enough to put her feet on what turned out to be the rotted timbers of a platform-like roof. Creaking wood began to give way under her. She had to float again, taking her weight off the unsafe roof, and gripped the secure stone. She sat in a notch of the battlements and listened. Her racket had not alerted the Hooded Conspirators.

She looked down and waved. Willow Ermine and Large Dark Prominent waved back...

...when Kali was in the Moth Club, what name would she take? Amy hadn't looked up the moths of Kafiristan, but suspected they would be exotic species.

She hooked her feet around stone and let herself float face-down. At full stretch, she reached the window—and peeped in from the top.

The window let into a small room. No one stood guard here. Amy made out a coiled rope ladder, attached to pitons newly hammered into cracks between the flagstones. She also saw the famous hamper, open and empty. It wasn't large enough for a feast, so she assumed that only two or three Hooded Conspirators guarded Kali. She wondered whether the villains bothered to give their captive anything to eat or drink. It would be just like them not to, compounding beastliness with plain rudeness.

Crawling insect-like, Amy entered the room.

Letting go of the window-rim, she bobbed up against the low ceiling like a balloon. She gradually thought herself heavier, and settled her ballet pumps on the floor.

There was a doorway, which had stout, rusted iron hinges—but no door. That must have rotted ages ago. Beyond the opening was a light. She poked her head out, and saw a winding staircase. She went back to the window and quietly let down the rope-ladder, which Large Dark Prominent and Light Fingers caught before it was flapped away in the wind.

Soon, all three girls were inside the tower.

This time, Frecks had brought a hockey stick for use as a cudgel.

Amy remembered that the Hooded Conspirators had firearms. She wondered whether their Leader was here, the fellow she'd beaned with a cricket ball. She hoped his head was still splitting. He must have a good-sized bruise under his hood.

The Moth Club silently made their way down the spiral stairs.

Then, they heard voices—and froze, a tableau of cloaked, masked figures. On the next landing was a room. Lantern-light spilled out.

'…there, the Princess won't slip from that so easily,' drawled an all-too-familiar voice, Beryl Crowninshield. 'My sis is an expert in these things. Houdini himself couldn't get out of one of her corned beef constrictor knots. Much less Nut-Brown Nancy here.'

Willow Ermine quietly slapped her hockey stick into her hand.

Kali was here! And the worst of the Witches!

'Wriggle all you like,' Crowninshield crowed. 'The rope only gets tighter. Honoria had more badges for knots than anyone in the Brownies, before they court-martialled her for demonstrating grief strangle knots on Brown Owl's Pekingnese.'

'She does look funny, Beryl,' said Crowninshield II. 'I didn't think girls her colour could go red in the face.'

An mmpphing noise suggested that Kali was gagged. The tone of her muted protest indicated dire promises.

'Now, give us some of that bottled beer, like you promised,' Crowninshield demanded of her unknown confederates. 'You chappies may be the most desperate Thuggees in far-off Whateveristan, but you're no match for a Drearcliff whip! It's a wonder Red Flame lets you hang around.'

Red Flame—the Leader of the Hooded Conspiracy!

Willow Ermine was all for charging in, but Amy held her back. They were too close to blow the game by indiscriminate action.

A hooded man came onto the landing. The Moth Club stuck still, hiding in the dark. The Crowninshield sisters trotted after him. Beryl was smoking a black cigarette and wearing make-up. Crowninshield II was fiddling with a cat's cradle.

'Beer's down below, eh?' said Crowninshield. 'Makes sense. Keep it cool in the depths.'

'Drink meeeee-eeeee,' came a tiny, shrill, liquid voice from the lower floor.

The Hooded Conspirator, unused to Crowninshield's vent act, clutched his throat in terror. She laughed, nastily.

'Give all your beeeeeer to Beryl,' said a voice from nowhere. 'Or face the wrath of the Great God Jumbo-Omooo!'

Crowninshield II tittered, nastily.

The Hooded Conspirator produced a curved knife from his loose black blouse, but Crowninshield brushed it aside.

'I say, for desperate characters, you mob are utter clots, aren't you? There are Firsts who wouldn't fall for that. Come on, bucko, let's get that beer!'

Crowninshield prodded the knife-man, with rather more confidence than Amy would have shown around fellows intent on executing a girl at dawn. It could scarcely make things worse if they were to toss a couple of extra heads onto the pile.

The sisters were led downstairs, away from the landing.

In the room, Kali mmmppphhed some more. Amy judged that at least one Hooded Conspirator was left to guard her—but probably no more. These were the best odds they would get.

She gave a low whistle, and the Moth Club sprang into action.

XII: Desperate Rescue

Kali was tied up. Seemingly every part of her was individually tied to a particular part of a stout chair. A white scarf wound round the bottom half of her face, lipstick smile painted mockingly over her mouth. Her exposed eyes were darkly furious.

There was indeed but one Conspirator in the room, not even Hooded. He had taken off his mask to drink a mug of tea, and looked stricken to be caught with a naked face when the Moth Club burst in. He was an Englishman, to judge by his colour—but unthreateningly middle-aged. Hood-wearing had scraped his hair into a funny shape.

Willow Ermine conked the Hoodless Conspirator squarely on the noggin, and he went down like a slaughtered beef. His eyes rolled up and blood came out of his nose, but Amy didn't waste sympathy on him.

Large Dark Prominent patted the prone guard down, and came up with a knife which seemed cousin—if not twin—to the dagger waved by his mate when Beryl Crowninshield was showing off her voice-throwing.

Amy got the gag off Kali's mouth.

'Mother of pearl, that's a relief,' said Kali. 'Who the heckle are youse gals?'

Amy flash-lifted her domino.

'I mighta knowed. Get these strings offa me. I've got pins and needles all over.'

Large Dark Prominent sawed rapidly, severing knots which couldn't be untied.

Kali recognised the swiftness of movement.

'Light Fingers? And the frail with the blunt instrument has gotta be Walmergrave. I'm mightily impressed. I was workin' on a coupla ways out, but this saves time an' motion.'

Kali was free. She stood up, but wasn't steady. Amy supported her.

'The old gams don't take kindly to being bound for days on end.'

Amy helped Kali out of the room. The Hoodless Conspirator groaned, and Willow Ermine gave him an extra love tap.

On the landing, they found Crowninshield II. She had a bottle of ginger beer.

'Ber-ylll,' she yelled, 'it's the Moth Girls, again!'

Kali, arm around Amy, lifted up her leg and planted her foot squarely on Crowninshield II's chest—then gave her a shove which tumbled her backwards down the stairs...

'Oh, ow, oh, ow-www, watch out...'

The Third rolled out of sight and collided with bodies rushing upstairs, summoned by her cries. Crowninshield swore loudly, unintentionally throwing her voice so that oaths bounced back from the walls.

'Exite, rapido,' said Amy.

The Moth Club got Kali up to the window-room and helped her onto the ladder. There was a tense moment as it seemed the ex-prisoner's hands couldn't get a grip on the rungs, but her circulation started flowing again and she scrambled down like a monkey.

Willow Ermine and Large Dark Prominent followed.

Amy watched the doorway.

The Hooded Conspirator charged in. Amy threw herself through the window—simultaneously thinking herself light enough to float. She soared out of reach of the tower, and thumped against the cliff. Kali was about half-way down, legs caught in the rungs. Frecks and Light Fingers were stuck above her.

'Give me that shiv,' said Beryl Crowninshield.

Leaning out of the window, the Witch started cutting rope. The three girls lurched dangerously. Kali got free and started moving down again.

'You're going to faa-aalll,' mocked a voice from the winds. 'You'll be squat flat as a pan-caaake!'

One of the main ropes was severed and the other went tight. Crowninshield got her blade to it.

Amy pushed against the cliff-face and launched herself at the tower, aiming for Crowninshield. Her cloak filled with wind, and she rode the air like a glider.

She held her arms out in front, hands knotted into fists.

Like a battering ram, she thumped into Crowninshield's face. The whip raised her knife, but Amy backpedalled in the air and floated out of slashing range.

Bleeding and hurt, Crowninshield took a moment to be astonished by the flying girl.

Kali was on the shingles; the others not far off.

The rope parted, but too late. Willow Ermine and Large Dark Prominent were on the ground.

The ladder fell in a coil at the foot of the tower.

'Beryl, how are *you* going to get down?' asked Amy, sweetly.

Crowninshield hissed, snarled and flung the knife—inaccurately—in Amy's direction. It thumped against the cliff.

Amy let herself descend slowly—she was becoming more expert—and landed on the beach. The others were well ahead, and running.

She looked up, and saw the trapped Witch shaking her fist.

They would soon be back in their cell. All four of them.

XXIII: A Parental Visit

Next morning, Kali reported herself present to Wicked Wyke. She said she had been abducted, held prisoner and rescued, but claimed truthfully that her saviours had been masked. She did not mention that she knew who they were. Though the outcome had been for the good, Drearcliff was not one to forgive Thirds who were off grounds without permission after Lights Out.

Should anyone be inclined to doubt Kali's narrative, they were welcome to visit the scene of the crime, to wit: the tower. Since Beryl Crowninshield had cut off their only means of egress from the secret hiding-place, the rump of the Hooded Conspiracy were still in residence, stewing mightily. Wicked sent a Second with a note to Headmistress, who detailed Keys to lead a deputation to the scene of the crime. The party consisted of Keys, Mrs Wyke, Kali the Accuser and, in the event that a) there were villains and b) they were inclined to put up a fight, the reassuringly male Joxer. Amy suspected that, of the four-strong expedition, Joxer was least able to take care of himself in a melée.

Amy, Frecks and Light Fingers had to endure Monday morning class as per usual, and missed out on the excitement while listening to Digger getting her Tudors and Stuarts mixed up. It was a wonder a period of history so full of people having their heads chopped off could be made to seem to blindingly dull.

Mid-morning, the Moth Club met up in the quad, between classes. The Heel, clean yesterday, already bore Hannah Absalom's message of the week, 'Death to President Juan Vicente Gómez of Venezuela'.

Kali gave them 'the low-down.'

'Swan's called in the cops—you know, that broken-down Sergeant from

Watchet. The Sadista Sisters are tryin' to make out they was snatched too, the doity bums. They're sellin', but Swan's not buyin'—though she'll let 'em off, since she doesn't want to dish out another multiple expulsion this term. If I were the Crowninshields, I'd take a lengthy spell in the slammer rather than stick around School. Beryl the Vent has had her whip's license yanked, which makes her meat for anyone with a grudge—and you'll find me at the head of the line. The Hooded Creeps ain't squawkin'—they don't know enough to be more afraid of Headmistress than their bosses. They were hired goons, anyway. I got that much out of 'em.'

'You've no idea what it was all about?' ventured Amy.

'Were you up for ransom?' asked Frecks.

Kali shrugged. 'They was tightmouth. Something was gonna happen this morning, though. Something permanent, I figure. I lost my hat in the tussle, and one of the hooded jaspers said I wouldn't be needing one after Monday sunrise. He said a tourniquet might suit me better.'

Kali drew a thumb across her neck.

'You know your father's coming,' said Amy.

Kali looked down. 'Yeah. How about that?'

'I doubt we'll ever get to the bottom of this,' said Frecks. 'Still, no real harm done. Jolly jape, as it happens. Kali rescued. Witches routed. Up the Moth Club, down the Murdering Heathens. Hurrah for School!'

Kali knew all about the Moth Club now.

'It'll be a shame to hang up the moth costumes for good,' said Light Fingers. 'I've ideas how to improve them. But Kali's safe, so our charter purpose is fulfilled.'

Amy thought about it.

'Don't put the costumes where we can't get at them,' she said. 'I've a notion we might need them again. Dora Paule said as much and she's supposed to be able to see the future.'

Amy couldn't help wondering who was behind the Hooded Conspiracy, and whether Drearcliff Grange School had heard the last of them. Red Flame remained at large and unknown.

'Uh oh, here comes the Old Man,' said Kali.

Dr Mrs Swan was coming across the quad, with a tall, dark, dramatically bearded man who wore a white western suit and a cherry-red turban. He had electric eyes, like his daughter's. They flashed as he saw the girls in a gaggle by the Heel.

'Don't get hitched to him, that's my advice...'

'No fear,' said Frecks. 'He's *ancient!*'

'My last stepmother was a year younger than me.'

'Crumpets,' gasped Amy.

'Don't worry, doll,' said Kali, kindly. 'Pop likes 'em fleshier than you.'

It wasn't the prospect of matrimony which had startled Amy. It was the large pink sticking plaster on Mr Chattopadhyay's forehead. The patch barely covered a bruise which looked for all the world as if an accurately-chucked cricket ball had struck him between the eyes.

'Double crumpets,' exclaimed Amy, again.

Moon Moon Moon

'Tell you one thing,' said Major Gilbert Took-Flemyng, 'this will bloody kill *science fiction* stone dead.'

Richard Jeperson glanced away from the television set.

Wednesday the 16th of July, 1969. London: about half past one in the afternoon; Cape Kennedy: oh-nine-thirty-two hundred hours.

The Major quaffed from a brandy balloon the size of a honeydew melon. He was an Ordinary Member, one of a necessary rump of blimps who camouflaged the Diogenes Club as a refuge for the hidebound and unsociable. OMs were selected for lack of perspicacity and absence of curiosity. If they noticed the comings and goings of Extraordinary Members, they never mentioned it. For over a century, OMs had filled capacious armchairs, as much a part of the decor as the cushions under their bottoms and the pipe-fumes above their heads. They radiated unwelcome and disapproval with such wattage the casual visitor—not that there were many—was dissuaded from wondering whether the musty, cavernous building in Pall Mall was home to Great Britain's most secret intelligence agency. Which, of course, it was.

'So this is the teleovision, eh?' muttered the Bishop of Brichester. 'Can't say I'm impressed. It's wireless with lantern slides.'

A newly purchased colour television stood in the hearth of the Informal Room, replacing the grate removed after the 1956 Clean Air Act abolished London's poisonous yellow fog. Several OMs had resigned over the appearance of 'this infernal contraption', and a vote of the full membership was necessary each time it was switched on. It would never be tuned to ITV, lest the sanctum be violated by the Devil's adverts.

The ostentatious 22-inch screen showed a Saturn V rocket, rising over the coastal swamps of Florida on a column of white smoke.

The Bishop nodded off. Like the Major, he'd recently sat in silence to a heavy meal in the club's famously unpleasant restaurant room. Richard had opted to nip out to Crank's in Seven Dials for a salad.

A BBC commentator, in tones of muted enthusiasm usually heard during orchestra tuning of a mid-season proms concert, informed viewers that *Apollo 11* would enter Earth orbit in twelve minutes. After a turn and a half around the world, the S-IVB third stage engine would fire, setting Armstrong, Aldrin and Collins on course for the moon.

'It's curtains for Dan Dare and Jet Morgan,' said the Major.

Richard had heard Took-Flemyng's argument before. Robots had been there, and *Apollo 8* and *Apollo 10* had orbited the moon, but—until today—manned expeditions to the moon had been taken only in fancy: Lucian on a waterspout, Francis Godwin's Gonsales in a chariot pulled by geese, Cyrano de Bergerac on a firework, Baron Münchausen on a silver hatchet, Edgar Allan Poe's Hans Pfaall in a balloon, Jules Verne's Baltimore Gun Club in a capsule fired from a giant cannon, H.G. Wells's *First Men in the Moon* in a diving bell coated with anti-gravity paint, Hergé's Tintin in a red-and-white chequered rocket and Arthur C. Clarke's Heywood Floyd on a Pan-Am lunar shuttle. Once NASA boot-prints scarred lunar dust, would the memory of these shadow-pioneers fade? Clarke, still alive to see how close his guesses would turn out, did not seem unduly concerned he was about to be out of a job.

The city streets were empty and traffic stilled, in a way not seen since England fought Germany in the World Cup Final. Even Crank's, a vegetarian café haunted by hippies who'd rather immolate themselves than suffer the haircuts sported by the military men of the Apollo mission, had a transistor set up so customers could listen to launch coverage. US troop withdrawals from Vietnam, Rod Laver's Wimbledon win, a potential Sino–Soviet conflict and an actual El Salvador–Honduras war were relegated to the deep insides of the newspapers, squeezed in after pages of moon stories. Toyshops were filled with Airfix rockets and child-safe space helmets. People looked up at the skies and claimed they saw rocket-trails. Comedians told jokes about the cow-powered Irish moon mission.

Every magazine in W.H. Smith's had a rocket or a moon or an astronaut on the cover. The same images were silk-screened on the T-shirts sported in the summer weather by everyone under thirty. Richard's one-off tee from Stanley 'Mouse' Miller was an orange psychedelic explosion laid over a still from Georges Méliès's 1903 *Voyage dans la Lune*, with a bullet-shaped spaceship lodged in the eye of an irascible man in the moon. Today, he also wore purple bell-bottoms, red-dyed Chelsea boots, a crushed velvet jacket carried over the shoulder *à la* Johnny Hallyday, a variety of peace sign lapel badges, a shiny-peaked Victorian band-leader's cap and wire-frame mint-green sunglasses, which folded into a pocket-clip case that looked like a fat fountain pen.

Moon songs played everywhere—Frank Sinatra's 'Fly Me to the Moon', Jonathan King's 'Everyone's Gone to the Moon' (which set Richard's teeth on edge—as a 'sensitive', he knew something was badly *off* about Jonathan King), the Marcels' 'Blue Moon' (he couldn't get that 'moon moon moon' backing vocal out of his head), Mel Tormé's 'Swingin' on the Moon', Captain Beefheart's 'Moonlight in Vermont' (from *Trout Mask Replica*, the double album Richard agreed with John Peel in rating higher than any Beatles LP), the Bonzo Dog Band's 'Tubas in the Moonlight'. David Bowie's 'Space Oddity' was climbing the charts. Stanley Kubrick's *2001: A Space Odyssey* was still on in the West End. The opening chords of Richard Strauss's 'Thus Spake Zarathustra', featured in the film, were heard over and over, used by the BBC as a signature tune for its moon coverage.

On television, Patrick Moore and James Burke explained what a

TransLunar Injection Burn was. A diagram anatomised the stages of the Saturn V already shed by the *Apollo 11*. The spacecraft now looked surprisingly like the bullets of Verne or Méliès, though sleek aluminium-steel-glass-phenolic rather than rivet-studded brass. 'Phenolic' and 'TransLunar' were among the new words everyone had learned lately.

A discreet cough sounded behind Richard. Hills, the first steward in the Diogenes Club to wear his hair an inch longer than his collar, had appeared at the door of the Informal Room. Ignoring the fretful glares of Major Took-Flemyng and the few other OMs goggling the box, Richard stood.

'Miss Kaye would like to see you, sir,' said Hills, almost subaudibly.

Even today, someone had to think about the Earth. Catriona Kaye, Acting Chair of the Ruling Cabal, was holding the fort. Edwin Winthrop, Richard's usual handler, was in Houston with a small party of British 'observers' at Mission Control. The Club usually had a presence at epochal events.

Richard assumed Catriona that wanted his report on Brian Jones. He had spent the past fortnight investigating an instant myth. When the ex-Rolling Stone was found at the bottom of his swimming pool, a lunatic magician who called himself 'the Elder Mage of Elgin Crescent' raised a fuss in sorcerous circles, alleging that all currently successful pop groups had contracts with the Devil which required the sacrifice of a key member to stay on top. Richard only hoped someone who was in a band with Jonathan King had the same deal. The whisper was all over the place, which did not necessarily lend it special credence. Most pop stars had contracts with EMI, Decca or Colonel Tom Parker which even the Devil's lawyers might deem excessively weighted against the talent. When it came to the Devil's Music, Richard thought Hell more likely to exacerbate the torments of the damned by piping in 'Donald, Where's Yer Troosers?' or 'How Much is that Doggie in the Window? (Ruff Ruff)' than 'Paint It Black' or 'Sympathy for the Devil'.

The case had taken him from Cotchford Farm in East Sussex, former home of A.A. Milne, to Hyde Park, where Mick Jagger mangled a fragment of Shelley before a free concert. A cloud of white butterflies were supposed to be released in a memorial tribute, but—it being a very hot day—mostly died in their boxes. Careful dowsing of the farm turned up nothing suspiciously Satanic, though Richard wouldn't soon forget the inside of Brian Jones's bathroom cabinet. A casual glance at the *NME* showed the line-ups of the Who, the Doors, the Jimi Hendrix Experience and the Wurzels unaltered by recent suspicious death—though an underground magazine alleged the Beatles had ritually murdered Stuart Sutcliffe and implanted a coded confession of the magickal crime in *Rubber Soul*. Richard was prepared to close the docket, though the original complainant was noisily foretelling another significant drowning before the month was out.

This call was new business.

Catriona Kaye—born 1900, as commemorated in the 1920s song written

about her, 'Century Baby'—looked decades younger than her years. Thanks
to *Thoroughly Modern Millie*, her modified flapper style and bobbed hair
intersected with a current fashion. Entering the Quiet Room, Richard found
her sat comfortably on the edge of Winthrop's desk, shoes dangling above
the carpet. She wore a low-waisted dress the colour of her pearls and smoked
a cigarette in a long, black holder. She made an appealing contrast with
the Club's Victorian founder, who glowered heavily out of a monumental
portrait behind her.

'Richard,' said Catriona, smiling, 'meet Special Agent Gauge.'

He turned, and had a little electric shock in the brain.

Parapsychologists called it 'psychic feedback', but Richard knew it as
a kind of spark. Like him, Agent Gauge was a sensitive, a Talent. Frankly, a
Spook. Richard noticed that before noticing she was a she—and he knew her
sex from the fragrance of Ô by Lancôme lingering in the corridor.

A tall blonde about five years younger than Richard, Agent Gauge had
a figure Hugh Hefner would get excited about and a don't-mess-with-me
stance which gave warning to the most octopus-handed *Playboy* subscriber.
She had big grey-blue eyes and straight, mid-length hair with a pronounced
widow's peak. Her only flaw was a tiny question mark scar under her right
eye—easy to cover with make-up, but she chose not to. She modelled a
powder-blue trouser suit over a fawn blouse. Her wide belt, worn high,
matched the blouse and was fastened with a large circular buckle. Her
jacket, tailored to conceal a shoulder-holster, hung oddly because she wasn't
wearing a gun. That made her an American. So did the fact her title was
'Special Agent'.

She stuck out her hand to be shook, but he kissed it.

'Richard Jeperson,' he said, meeting her eyes.

That spark was now a crackle. Richard felt his hair rise as if he were
touching a Van der Graaf generator.

She took her hand away.

'Special Agent Gauge,' she said. 'Whitney Gauge.'

Catriona slid elegantly off the desk and stood between them.

'Special Agent Gauge is with a Federal Bureau of Investigation.'

Richard caught the use of the indefinite article. By decades of self-
serving flackery, J. Edgar Hoover made the world think there was only one
FBI. Actually, Hoover was merely Director of the Bureau of Investigation
of the United States Department of Justice. At least a dozen other arms of
government had investigative divisions which operated across state lines,
and were thus officially Federal Bureaux of Investigation, among them the
Treasury, the Alcohol and Tobacco Overseers, the Internal Revenue Service,
the Commission of Major League Baseball and whatever misleading title
Whitney Gauge's superiors ('the Unnameables' in spook circles) put on
letterheads if they ever sent letters. Alone among overlooked investigators,
the Unnameables never grumbled about Hoover's publicity-hogging.

'You're a long way off your beat, Miss Gauge. Or is it Mrs Gauge?'

'It's Special Agent Gauge,' she said.

Richard detected a tiny crack of smile.

'Something's come up,' said Catriona, 'and Assistant Director Spilsby has sent our friend to sit in. It involves the moon.'

'So does everything this week.'

Catriona arched an eyebrow. 'Indeed. All the little boys want to grow up to be spacemen now. And girls, thanks to that splendid Soviet lady...'

Whitney Gauge frowned, reddening her question mark in a manner Richard found curiously fascinating.

'When I was a lad, I wanted to be a cowboy,' he said. 'Roy Rogers was my idol.'

He mimed a fast double-draw and fired off his fingers at Whitney Gauge, blowing gunsmoke away from the tips.

'I suppose you wanted to be Eliot Ness?'

'No,' she said, 'I wanted to be a ballerina.'

She made an extraordinarily limber fast pirouette and froze, thigh and calf-muscles tight, with cerulean-painted toes—she wore open-toed sandals—hovering an inch from Richard's Adam's apple. After seconds, she broke the pose.

'But I "overdeveloped".'

To Richard's mind, Whitney Gauge developed just fine. He knew better than to put it like that this early in their acquaintance.

'If you young people have finished flirting,' said Catriona, 'can we get on with business? I've a transatlantic call in to Edwin in half an hour, and he'll need to know you're looking into the threat.'

'Threat?' said Richard and Whitney Gauge, together.

Catriona was apologetic. 'More of a niggle. A loose end, though it flaps more than it ought and deserves urgent attention. Are you sitting comfortably?'

Richard and Whitney Gauge were standing, but that wasn't the point.

'Then I'll begin. Were you aware that a group calling itself the Temple of Domina Oriens circulated a petition to pressure NASA to discontinue the Apollo program?'

Richard looked at Whitney Gauge. They both shrugged.

'Will you stop doing that?' Catriona said, pettishly. 'It's faintly disturbing.'

'Doing what?' asked Richard and Whitney Gauge, together.

'*That.* You're long-lost Corsican twins. I fully understand. I nominate you, Richard, to keep quiet—indeed, to refrain from any gesture. Whitney, if you would respond, when necessary.'

Whitney Gauge said 'yes'. Richard suppressed an urge to nod.

'Now, if I may continue... there have, of course, been voices raised against space exploration in general and the moon mission in particular.

Some argue it's an obscene waste of money, when so many problems on Earth remain unsolved. Others worry about a military/political domination of the solar system by America. The Flat Earth Society fear a precipitous decline in membership. And so on. This week, for obvious reasons, the appetite of the press for moon-related stories extends to anyone who says *anything*, positive or negative, about the Apollo mission. The High Priestess of the Temple of Domina Oriens—which is in Clerkenwell, by the way— holds the moon sacred, and claims setting a foot on her soil is like defiling a vestal virgin. She isn't in favour of that.'

'Who is this High Priestess and how large is her congregation?' asked Whitney Gauge.

'She is called Luna Selene Moon...'

'... that's like being named Moon Moon Moon,' put in Richard.

'... which, as Richard has helpfully pointed out, is gilding the lily. She was born Bridget Gail Tully. It could have been worse. She could have called herself "June Bassoon Moon".'

'Or Luna Ticwitch?' Richard ventured.

Whitney Gauge giggled.

'Very amusing, Richard,' said Catriona. 'Now, if you'd pay attention in class, here's what we have on the silly goose.'

Catriona handed Richard a sheaf of photographs and press cuttings. After a riffle, he passed the folder to Whitney Gauge, who gave the documents a similar quick study. The earliest pictures were sepia studies of a long-nosed thin girl in a see-through shift.

'She was an artists' model just after the War, then turned painter. You can guess her favoured subject.'

A glossy catalogue contained miniature representations of samey pictures.

'She calls them "moonscapes", but they look like fairy pictures to me,' said Catriona. 'The Diogenes Club has had several unpleasant involvements with the little folk.'

In recent press photographs, which went with 'silly season' stories about Miss Moon's curse on NASA, the High Priestess was still thin and long-nosed, but wore more demurely opaque shifts. She had masses of white hair usually bound by a circlet with a crescent moon stuck to it.

'The Temple is fair-sized as cults go, with a few mildly influential members. They're on our List.'

Whitney Gauge raised an eyebrow, exactly the way Richard would have if he hadn't known what the List was.

'We divide Britain's home-grown occult groups into cranks, who aren't on the List, and the potentially dangerous, who are,' he explained. 'By "dangerous", we mean possessed of some sort of verifiable magic resources. You dig?'

'I grok.'

'Children,' snorted Catriona, amused. 'The Temple haven't got a record for human sacrifice or souring the milk or laming the Prime Minister, but they've registered a needle-flicker of power, especially recently. Phases of the moon, I expect. And Miss Moon Moon Moon began issuing veiled threats through the popular press. We'd let it go, except she's suddenly changed her tune. For a few weeks, any hack in Fleet Street hoping to fill a puff piece could get an ominous quote from her about how the *Apollo 11* mission was a sacrilege. Terrible would be the vengeance of the ravaged goddess, woe, woe and thrice woe. She came near as spitting to claiming responsibility for the *Apollo 1* launch-pad fire that nearly scuttled the lunar adventure before it was started. Two days ago, the High Priestess shut up. Pulled out of appearing on something called *The Simon Dee Show*. A big protest outside the American Embassy has been quietly called off. One of the busy bees we have combing the cuttings turned up an old associate who is extremely interesting to us. In 1948 or thereabouts, Miss Moon formed a liaison with a Magister Rex Chalfont.'

Catriona paused, as if the name might ring bells. It didn't.

'What do we know about him?' Richard asked.

'Nothing,' said Catriona. 'Not a thing. Just his name, and rank in academic sorcery. Which is wrong *and* impossible. I mean, we know *everything...*'

Catriona was referring to the secret files of the Diogenes Club.

'Whitney's Bureau know even less about Chalfont than we do,' said Catriona. 'But they're interested now. Enough to fly her over on a military aircraft and put her up at Claridge's on the sort of expenses the Royal Family can't claim. If we don't have a dossier on Chalfont, information must have been *kept from us*. That is very, very difficult to do.'

Richard understood that, as Chair of the Ruling Cabal of the Diogenes Club, Catriona Kaye know the birth-name of the tommy buried in the Tomb of the Unknown Soldier in Westminster Abbey, the present addresses of Ambrose Bierce and Judge Crater and why Borley Rectory burned down in 1939. Come to that, she knew where the woozle went, what songs the sirens sang and how flies land upside-down on the ceiling.

'I am perturbed more by the apparent invisibility of this Magister Rex Chalfont than by the High Priestess's ominous utterances. For the sake of all our peaces of mind, it's been decided you two should look up Miss Moon and see what can be learned about her old beau. Do you think you can do that little thing for me? Good. I'm glad. Call Hills and tell him when you can make a report. Better make it before "touch-down" in the Sea of Tranquillity... *"Touch-down"*? Ugh, what a word...'

Richard and Whitney Gauge looked at each other.

Whitney Gauge saw his scarlet Peel Trident parked outside the Club and laughed. The vehicle had been described as a 'flying saucer on wheels'.

'How do you expect us to fit into that?'

'If three astronauts can get into a capsule, two can ride in a bubble-car,' said Richard. 'Comfortably.'

'They said I was too tall to be an astronaut,' she declared. 'The boys in NASA didn't like being shown up.'

He unclipped the fibreglass chassis and lifted it like a cutaway diagram, disclosing comfortable red leather seats mounted on three go-kart wheels.

'I guess your Bentley is at home?'

'I drive a Rolls, actually,' he said. 'Not very manoeuvrable in Central London.'

The American woman looked up and down the empty Mall.

'It's not like this, usually,' he said. 'It's as busy as New York, with politer beeping and shouting.'

'I find that hard to believe.'

'This is a space-related anomaly, Miss America.'

'You can say that again, Carnaby Street. At least you don't have this thing painted up like a British flag.'

'I considered the option, but we're supposed to be a *secret* service. We try to exercise a little discretion.'

'That explains the way you dress.'

'You're not exactly unobtrusive, Agent Gauge. Six-foot Giselles are scarce in these here parts.'

She ducked and folded herself into the passenger seat, smoothed her hair and crossed her arms so they wouldn't be cut off when the dome closed. With practiced ease, Richard took the driver's seat and pulled the chassis down. The Trident clicked together. The Plexiglas bubble-dome interior was scented nicely with Ô.

'Pre-launch check, Major Tom?' she said. 'All systems go for take-off?'

'Roger Charlie Chester Wilko.'

He pulled the starter. The radio came on—more commentary from Florida. *Apollo 11* had left Earth orbit.

He pulled the starter again. The Zweirad motor turned over, purring like a tiger cub.

'What do you call this roadster? The "Dickmobile"?'

'She answers to "Nanny".'

'Very British.'

The Trident picked up speed, zooming through Admiralty Arch into Trafalgar Square. A plague of pigeons took off in a rapid flutter. No tourists around to feed them. The only people in sight were a gaggle of drivers at the taxi-stand and a couple of policemen—all bent around a wireless cabinet, listening to news from space. Orson Welles would have loved an audience like this. At the top of his column, Nelson was probably lifting his good eye to the stratosphere and waving on the lunar mariners.

Richard could get used to a city empty of traffic and pedestrians. Nanny was modified to his specifications, but he'd never had an opportunity to test her at top speed in an urban daytime environment. He thought he could at least double the ordinary Trident's advertised 45 m.p.h.

'I suppose you drive something the length of a skittle alley with fins and an open top?' he ventured.

'I have a Tucker Tomorrow. Best automobile ever made.'

Turning a corner into Charing Cross Road, Nanny lurched as one of her front wheels lifted from the road, tipping his passenger against him.

'You did that deliberately,' she said.

He supposed he had.

'Don't do it again.'

He was warned. On the whole, he thought Special Agent Whitney Gauge was rather fun.

'So you abandoned promising careers as a ballet dancer and a space-woman,' he said. 'What else did you try before you signed with the Unnameables?'

'I was a Mouseketeer. They took away my ears when I told Uncle Walt I thought his pal Senator McCarthy looked like Monstro the Whale from *Pinocchio*. I appeared in the first *Beach Party* movie, but quit because they wouldn't let "the girls" surf. I can hang ten. Frankie Avalon can barely hang one-half. Do you even know what all this means?'

'I speak fluent American.'

'I passed all the NASA astronaut tests, except the one about not menstruating. Otherwise, Buzz Aldrin wouldn't be Number Two on the moon, you better believe it.'

'Are you Air Force?'

'USAAF Intelligence. Officially retired. Like you, a Spook. I passed the other tests they ran at NASA, the ones with the Rhine cards and the spinning needles. You know what happens when you score high psi. I got seconded to, as I said, *a* Federal Bureau of Investigation. Where you're famous, by the way. They teach a course about the Ghost Train you shut down in the 1950s. How old are you anyway, Mr Chips?'

'Cheek,' he said. 'And I don't know, Gidget.'

'Of course, you have no memory of your childhood. It's in the file. And nobody's been able to find out who you really are. That gives you something in common with Magister Rex.'

'I try not to think about it.'

'Liar. I can tell when people lie. That's not one of my tricks. Just a small-t talent. Comes from growing up near Hollywood agents.'

'So what are your "tricks"? Can you hard-boil an egg with your mind?'

'No, of course not. Active Talents like that are incredibly rare. I'm a Reactive Talent, like you. A psychomancer. You're an empath. That's a weird combo, they say. Not advisable.'

'You have feelings about things, I have feelings about people. Those ought to be complementary.'

They were in Holborn now, whizzing down Theobald's Road. A fish 'n' chip shop chalkboard offered "moon" rock and "loonar" chips.

'Catriona thinks we can work together,' he said. 'I assume Assistant Director Spilsby does too.'

A pause. 'I passed the immediate criteria for this assignment.'

'Which was...?'

'Being in the building at the time the alert came in.'

'You have a duty rota? Intrepid agents ready at all times, like the Minutemen?'

'Not exactly. I was in Spilsby's office.'

'Receiving a commendation after your latest victory over the forces of evil?'

'Submitting my resignation after an eleven-month assignment to the reception desk...'

'I see a pattern emerging.'

'You would. While I was passing all those courses in the Top Three and qualifying as a field agent, do you know who my hero was?'

Richard huffed modestly.

'No, Oh-Oh-707, not you... *her*, your Chief. Catriona Kaye. In the States, the Boys' Club won't let a woman into the field. Here, she gets to sit on the board. And her record makes yours look feeble.'

'Steady on. You're steaming up the Plexiglas.'

'I mean, look at it... Angel Down, the Mummy's Heart, the Blame Game, the Witch War, the Unhappy Medium... she was there, for all of them, in the thick of it.'

'She wasn't alone. A fellow named Winthrop was there too. He usually sits in Catriona's chair.'

'I'd expect you to say that. She's had to fight her whole career against people like you.'

'I'm very fond of Catriona Kaye...'

...who was, in fact, the nearest thing he had to a mother. If Whitney Gauge were cleared to know more secrets, he could tell her Catriona wasn't even the first woman member of the Diogenes Club. Geneviève Dieudonné, Kate Reed, Amy Thomsett and Annette Amboise (whose memory was always a tiny stick-pin in his heart) also figured on the rolls... not to speak of Vanessa, Richard's own ward, currently orienteering in the New Forest, picking up tradecraft between A levels at Cheltenham and a Sociology degree at the LSE. Provisional membership was waiting for Vanessa when she graduated, then she'd be in Nanny's passenger seat on jaunts like this.

'...but...'

'Hmmn, yes, what?'

Richard back-tracked.

'You're absolutely right. Catriona sets a mark few can hope to live up to.

You couldn't choose a better heroine. And... the fact that your AD can't see past your chest just goes to show why our country is better than yours.'

Whitney Gauge's mouth formed a perfect Lancôme Ô.

'Just kidding, Minnie Mouse. Hands across the sea, and all that. This is an Anglo–American operation. Our two great nations are equal partners in the marriage.'

'Only Britain is the chick, right? You do the dishes and have America's dinner ready when it comes home?'

Richard laughed. 'Let's not continue down that path. Besides, we're where we're going. Sekforde Street, Clerkenwell. That's the Temple of Domina Oriens.'

Aside from a gilded plaster man-in-the-moon on the lintel, the building had no distinguishing features. Near-identical premises housed a Socialist reading room and a community centre for Piedmontese exiles, both closed. Trades union activists and Italian mini-monarchists were at home in front of the telly.

'Ready for EVA?' he asked.

'Always.'

He released the catch, and the dome rose. They got out and he shut the car.

'Are you feeling anything?' he asked.

'Relief at being able to stand up and breathe. From the sidewalk, nada. You think I should try the door?'

'Go on, fondle the knocker.'

That came out as rather too *Carry On*, he felt.

'I'd rather grab the knob,' she said, and took hold. She let go again, sharply.

'A shock?'

'You think I'd know better,' she admitted, momentarily pale under her tan. 'The last hand that touched this was dipped in blood.'

He looked at her palm.

'Metaphorically, I mean,' he explained. 'If he got any on himself, I'm sure he wiped afterwards.'

'He?'

'I'm getting a man. In a hurry. And a *lot* of blood.'

Richard pushed the door. It opened.

'Too much of a hurry to lock up behind him.'

Whitney Gauge reached for the gun she wasn't carrying.

'Do you have a nightstick or anything? What do you call it, a truncheon?'

'I am not a policeman,' he responded, with dignity.

They stepped into the Temple. The foyer looked and smelled like the front of house of a small theatre. A tea urn and an assortment of biscuits filled a refreshments corner. A notice board behind the cashier's desk displayed type-written schedules of 'rituals, rites, oblations and obeisances'. A painting of an alien landscape hung prominently. A lush, purplish-green jungle was inhabited by furtive creatures which might be crossbreeds of cockatoo and praying mantis. A gap in the fungoid trees showed a night-sky where the Earth shone amid a sprinkle of stars. He didn't have to be a sensitive to intuit that this was the work of Luna Selene Moon.

'Don't look like fairies to me,' said Whitney Gauge. 'More like bugs.'

'Have you ever met any fairies?'

'No.'

'How do you know what they look like?'

'Imagination.'

'Good answer.'

A set of double-doors opened into an auditorium with a raised stage. The house-lights were on. An altar-cum-lectern was set up in front of a triptych which showed three faces of the moon. The symmetrical triple-moon, repeated on the backdrop and the altar, featured a grinning full moon sandwiched between two cruelly sly crescent profiles. Folding chairs were set out for a congregation or audience. A group of the chairs were overturned or had snapped shut. A person curled up and bled in the middle of the mess.

'Moon moon moon,' he muttered.

It was a middle-aged woman in a white robe with a yellow moon on the front. Luna Moon, the former Bridget Tully. Her long hair splayed around her head like an electrified crown. She had been stabbed or shot through the moon on her robe.

Richard checked for a pulse and caught a last flicker.

Then, he was overwhelmed by visions. He was usually attuned simply to inchoate feelings or moods. Only in extreme circumstances did he pick up anything like an image.

This was the most extreme circumstance.

As the High Priestess departed her earthly shell for parts unknown, pictures crowded into Richard's mind.

Pictures in the style of Luna Moon.

Trees with meaty leaves, greenish spongy craters, sugary glistening webs spun by asymmetric spiders with cherry-glacé eyes. The artist's moon was edible. People in robes or jewelled diving suits frolicked—there was no other word for it—with the cockatoo-mantises or their relations, who looked like walrus-weasels or giraffe-fish. The pictures sped up, flickering like Méliès's moon-shot film.

'Richard?'

He was on his knees by the dead woman, struck by acute ice-cream headache and stabbing chest pain.

He had to let go of her, for fear that his consciousness would be pulled wherever hers had gone.

Whitney snapped fingers in front of his face.

He tried to keep the pictures in his memory. Each was crowded out by the next, like pages falling from an album into a fire.

A final image lingered a few instants longer than the others. A different subject, a different style. An Earthscape, a weathered sign in a country lane. Woods and fields. It was daytime, but the moon was out, rising above the roof of an uninviting, large house.

'Mildew Manor,' he said.

The image was gone, self-destructing in memory.

But in speaking the words on the sign aloud, he had captured them.

'Mildew Manor?' Whitney responded. 'What is that? A place? A picture? A state of mind?'

'A novel by Thomas Love Peacock? I don't know.'

'Peacock wrote *Nightmare Abbey* and *Crotchet Castle*...

'... and *Headlong Hall* and *Gryll Grange*...'

'... but no *Mildew Manor*, so far as I know. He died trying to save his books from a fire.'

'You didn't learn that in *The Mickey Mouse Club*.'

'We have libraries in California, too.'

'Glad to hear it. I thought they'd all been torn down and turned into drive-in churches and no-tell motels...'

Whitney let go of him, and they stood up.

'In case you hadn't noticed,' she said, 'this Olde Englishe Temple is exactly the kind of ridiculous made-up religion you're stereotyping as Californian. Oh, and shouldn't we concentrate on the bleeding woman?'

'She can't help us any more, poor love.'

'She can't help *you*, Richard...'

Whitney knelt, and put her palm to the woman's face.

'...you read people, I read *things*. She's not people any more...'

Whitney made *contact*, as with the door-knob, and juddered as if holding a live wire. She closed her eyes, pressed hard on Luna Moon's face and forced herself to maintain the touch.

Richard was concerned.

She let go, opened her eyes and breathed again.

'I hate that,' she said.

He helped her into the foyer. She sat on a saggy armchair next to a low table piled with mimeographed occult newsletters and glossy art magazines. She flipped open a powder-compact and examined her hairline minutely in the mirror.

'Shall I get you tea from the urn? You need to replenish your electrolytes. Maybe some biscuits?'

'What?'

'Cookies.'

'No, just tea... cold, if possible.'

'Is there any other kind? This'll be stewed.'

He turned a spigot and thick brownish liquid filled a mug. The Temple had their own crockery, with a smiley moon decal.

'Ah,' Whitney said, in triumph, 'there's the slut!'

She had plucked a single, silver-white hair from her head.

'Every time,' she said. 'There's always one.'

She put her compact away and took the cold tea. She drained the mug as if on a dare, trying to get it down without tasting.

He nibbled a stale custard cream.

'What did you get from her?' he asked.

'What do you think, Sherlock? A sharp, stabbing pain in the chest.'

'Fear, annoyance...?'

She shook her head. 'No, that's what you'll have *felt*. Empathy, remember? I just get things. Sights, sounds, processes. Pain is a thing, not an emotion. The last thing she saw was a face, fading to black.'

'Can you describe the murderer?'

She held up her mug and pointed to the decal.

'A moon-mask?'

She nodded. 'Something like that. But weirder. Yellow, hook nose, cratery skin, bulby forehead. Under curved glass, like a TV screen or a biker's visor. No, not a crash helmet, a *space* helmet. No NASA or CCCP logo. It was a *custom* spacesuit. Old-fashioned, if that's possible.'

'Did you get an idea of the weapon?'

'Oh yes,' she said. 'The bastard held it up, showed it to her. A double-edged knife. Silvery. Carvings on the blade and hilt. That triple-moon thing.'

'An athamé?' suggested Richard. He knew she'd know what an athamé was.

'Like that. Though it can't have been a ritual killing. She wasn't on the altar, or I'd have seen ceiling and the blade coming down. She was tapped on the shoulder, turned round and stabbed in the heart.'

'Your moon-faced astronaut murdered her?'

'Definitely,' she said. 'That's what she *saw*. What did she feel?'

Richard tried to remember the impressions he had taken from Luna Moon.

'What I said. Not so much fear, more annoyance. She was *irritated* at being murdered, as if she'd had other things to do today and was more concerned about not ticking them off her list than being killed. I got a lot of *pictures* from her, but not real things. Whatever you think of that—' he indicated the painting on the wall—'she was serious about art. The images in her mind were the ones she painted. Important to her. Pregnant with personal meaning.'

'Mildew Manor?'

'That stood out,' he said. 'All the other things were mental moonscapes. The Mildew Manor picture was Earthly. The English countryside, somewhere.'

'You're sure it's a real place?'

'No, but it's important. Like your "old-fashioned" astronaut.'

'Major Stabby.'

'That's his name?' he asked.

'I doubt it, but we have to call him something. You have to call out someone or something before you go after it. That's good practice in magic, isn't it?'

He agreed.

'Have you got your Girl Scout badge on you?' he asked. She nodded. 'Good. You might have to claim diplomatic immunity. Strictly speaking what we've done counts as tampering with Her Majesty's Evidence in a Murder Inquiry. The plods won't like it, but they'll lump it. Luckily, we have a friend in New Scotland Yard...'

Stumbling over a corpse within an hour of accepting a commission bordered on the vulgar. A telephone was on the front desk. He picked it up. First, he would call Catriona Kaye. Then, the police.

'This isn't what I think of as a hotel bar,' Whitney said. 'Too big, too well-lit, too *classy*.'

'I trust you didn't ring down to ask how to make the bed vibrate.'

She poked her tongue out at him.

Normally, that would have excited disapproval in Claridge's, but even here everyone was only paying attention to the moon voyage. A single barman stayed at his post, while the rest of the staff were in a back-room lit by a television set.

Eight hours into its mission, *Apollo 11* had shed its Saturn V rocket stages and left Earth orbit for cislunar space. *Columbia*, the Command/ Service Module, separated from the third stage and docked with the *Eagle*, the Lunar Excursion Module. Broadcasters were already fed up with the technical chatter tossed between the Apollo crew and Mission Control ('Houston'), but the public still found magic in the curt, arcane, tinny American voices. They were talking from outer space!

Whitney had changed into a hot pink minidress with a matching alice band and go-go boots. Even the Claridge's barman noticed, and Richard was sure the great hotels put something in the staff tea to control natural urges insofar as lady guests were concerned.

The only other people in the bar were a table of drunk young execs in city mod uniform—paisley foulards, Day-Glo shirts, two pieces of three-piece Savile Row suits, shaped sideburns. They were toasting a guy named Roly, who had something to do with the packaging of Sky Ray lollies (a big seller this season). Roly took credit for the visionary spirit of the space age between sudden, rapid trips to the Gents.

None of the execs was so drunk that they didn't shoot looks over at

Whitney Gauge. She noticed. Richard noticed she noticed. She noticed Richard noticing. No one was in any doubt. She had conquered Britain without really trying.

Naturally, Richard had ordered champagne and a platter of fresh strawberries. This was still a business meeting.

Richard had remained on hand at the Temple of Domina Oriens as Inspector Price, the Diogenes Club's liaison with Scotland Yard's Department of Queer Complaints, supervised a team of scene-of-the-crime officers and forensics men as they examined and then removed the body of Luna Moon, and searched the building. The Club and DQC had a policy of sharing information, not always observed. No bloody bootprints or daubed messages were found. Richard gave a reasonably detailed report of what he and Whitney had gathered from the deceased, but Price couldn't make much use of it. His boys were stuck with looking for witnesses, chasing up grasses and hoping for a credible confession. Embarrassingly often, even in Diogenes Club cases, boring old police-work turned up an answer before spookery. And you could take it into court, too.

'Have we been through that rigmarole,' said Whitney, biting down on a big ripe strawb, 'where the cops warn us off the case but we stay on it anyway?'

'It's not our place to catch murderers, love,' he told her. 'Though I daresay Euan Price would be grateful if we turned over a stone and found this one. If finding out who killed Miss Moon Moon Moon leads us to understand why we don't have a Magister Rex Chalfont on the books, we should sleuth away to our hearts' content. If it's a side-issue, we drop it and try something else. Let's face it, it would be just *too bloody easy* if Chalfont were our Major Stabby...'

'Magisters generally leave athamé-work to minions. Unless it's Aztec heart-ripping stuff.'

'In Aztec mythology, the moon is the severed head of the Goddess Coyolxauhqui, murdered—along with four hundred siblings—by her foetal half-brother Huitzilopochtli to forestall Coyolxauhqui's attempt to force their mother Coatlicue to have an abortion. How unlike the home-life of our own dear deity! Chup-Kamui, moon goddess of the Ainu, was so disgusted at having to bear witness to the night-time naughtiness of adulterers she swapped places in the pantheon with her brother and became a sun goddess instead.'

'You've read this up, right?'

Richard admitted it. 'I took this from the Temple, and skimmed it while you were napping off jet lag.'

He tossed over a slender volume. *Moon Myths*, by Enzo Yarikh.

'If you need to tell your Basque Ilazki from your Dahomeyan Gleti, this is your *I-Spy Guide*... they're all moon gods and goddesses. Mostly goddesses. Selene was a Greek goddess. Well, a Titan. Luna was Roman, aka Luna Noctiluca. Humanity has been venerating our satellite since cave-days. There's a Neolithic stone circle in the Hebrides that tracks the risings of the moon in an extremely sophisticated manner. Looking up at the night sky is nothing new. And the moon is the biggest, shiniest thing in it.'

Whitney flicked through the pages.

'No pictures,' she said.

'The moon affects the tides, women's cycles, the proverbial lunatic... and some werewolves, though not as many as Lon Chaney Junior would have you believe...'

Whitney gave him back the book and stretched in her chair like a cat. On the other side of the room, she won enthusiastic reviews.

The mastermind of lolly wrapper design finally got drunk enough to do more than look sidelong at the tall blonde bird. Encouraged by perhaps ill-intentioned comrades, Roly spacewalked across acres of carpet and stood over their table. He had a transparent moustache.

'Is this hippie bothering you, Pink Lady?' he asked Whitney, using the burp-speech recommended for those who have lost a larynx to throat-cancer. 'Because, if he is, I could... ah... take care of him for you.'

The other execs cheered. Roly was unsteady on his feet. Mr Sky Ray Lolly didn't look as if he were in any position to 'take care of' a stick insect on crutches.

'That's very kind of you, hoss—but this is my grandfather. I'm seeing he doesn't get into trouble. He's uncontrollable around women.'

The young exec looked at Richard, trying to focus.

'Have a strawberry, old chap,' said Richard.

'Who are you calling a... what did you just say...?'

Roly unwisely plucked the bottle out of the ice bucket and hefted it like a club. Champagne frothed out of the neck, drenching the cuff of his salmon-coloured shirt. He swung the bottle towards Richard's head.

Whitney quick-jabbed two knuckles into Roly's side, just above the rib-cage. He froze in mid-swing, then—as Whitney innocently sipped from her flute—fell like a tree in the forest. Richard caught the bottle.

It was empty. He signalled for another.

Roly lay, face knotted, unable to move. His friends expressed concern, but none ventured to help.

'How long does that last?' Richard asked.

'About ten minutes, usually.'

The barman summoned someone to take care of the fallen exec. If Roly were not a guest, he'd be discreetly ejected from the hotel. If he were, he'd be asked to leave as soon as his bill was settled.

Whitney shrugged, disarmingly, at the pest's friends and eggers-on.

'What can I do,' she said, raising her voice to carry across the acreage of the bar. 'I'm naturally a knockout.'

Laughter came.

'Roly's not usually that much of a prawn,' said one of his mates. 'It's moon madness.'

Richard understood.

More champagne was produced.

'We'll avoid further altercations if this is sent up to the lady's suite,' Richard told the waiter, palming him a ten-shilling note in a handshake.

'Very good, sir.'

'And more strawberries,' said Whitney. 'Many more strawberries.'

'What are we doing outside Handel's house?' Whitney asked.

'Waiting for a bus,' he told her.

After breakfast at Claridge's, they had walked a little way down Brook Street. London was busier this morning. Most folk who had skived off to watch the launch were back at work. Tourists had emerged to wander distractedly. Richard didn't have to be especially empathic to pick up the epochal beat in the back of everyone's mind.

...we're on our way to the moon...

Whitney wore a lime-green trouser suit and matching sun-hat. She had clever glasses which darkened when the sun came out—a NASA by-product, like non-stick pans and Velcro. Oh, and the orbital death rays America thought her NATO allies didn't know about. Those 'communications satellites' would blow up if activated, thanks to a tiny pre-stressed ceramic component manufactured in Milton Keynes. In trying to cut plucky little Britain out of the loop, the Pentagon underestimated Harold Wilson's capacity for sulky vengefulness.

'There's no stop here,' she said.

'It's not a regularly scheduled service. We're going to a party in a bus.'

'Very stylish. Is it a long ride?'

'As long as you want it to be. I didn't say we're going *in a bus* to a party, I said we're going to *a party in a bus*. Here it is.'

Richard pulled a psychedelic explosion out of his hankie pocket and flapped it, as if flagging a taxi. A red London bus stopped for them. The number and destination displayed were a sideways eight infinity symbol and 'Far Out Scene'. Richard helped Whitney onto the open rear platform.

'Hold very tight please,' said a woman in a tailored black silk conductor's uniform, 'ting ting...'

The conductress rang the bell and the bus moved on.

Both decks heaved with assorted people—fragrant hippies and flower children, pinstriped Establishment types, famous faces from fashion and sport, notable beggars and crooks, popular scientists and unpopular clergymen, a couple of exotic dancers from Soho. Something intriguing if non-sexual was happening under a pile of PVC macs between an angry Liverpool poet, an actress who'd been in a controversial *Wednesday Play* and a middle-aged cleaning woman who'd probably got on the wrong bus by mistake.

Upstairs, Eric Clapton and Andrés Segovia were duetting. The tune they had long left behind was 'Shine On Harvest Moon'. Downstairs, Larry Adler played harmonica while Spike Milligan made up limericks. Luckily, there were many rhymes for 'moon'. Silver-paper stars, planets, satellites and spaceships were stuck up on the windows. It was easy to guess the theme of this bash.

'Richard Jeperson,' exclaimed the conductress, kissing him full on the lips, 'how delightful! And this must be the blonde Yank bird you were glimpsed with in Clerkenwell yesterday afternoon and Claridge's bar last night! Don't tell me, Whitney Gauge. With the, um, secret busybody acronym folks... you're the Girl from A.U.N.T.I.E., right?'

'I'm with a Federal Bureau of...'

'Spookery and Goblinage. How sweet.'

Whitney was surprised the conductress was in on the secret, but Richard knew her of old.

'This is Margery Device,' he said. 'Pronounced "Davis", spelled "De Vice". She's the Witch.'

Whitney noticed the definite article.

'Don't listen to Dickie,' Margery said. 'It's just a title.'

'This party is a grand tradition,' Richard said. 'It's always on somewhere in London.'

'Have a cocktail, dear,' said Margery. 'They're all just invented... Absinthe Apollo, Moon Madness, Space Shiver, Fireball XL-5, Buzz Aldrin...'

'I'll have a rum collins...'

'Not new, but topical—I approve,' said Margery, signalling to a Maltese bar-tender Richard had last seen on an identity parade as a near-lookalike for a trunk murderer. 'Richard...?'

'Tizer. I'm on duty.'

Margery laughed.

The hostess was Queen of London Gossip, which meant she knew everything worth knowing and was prepared to be wildly indiscreet if it amused her. The only secret she never shared was her age. She looked exactly as she had when he first went to her party—then in a sculptor's studio in Brixton—in the mid-1950s. The London Witch held up one corner of a defensive magic square which had seen the city through plague, fire, blitz and rationing.

'Is there somewhere quiet we can talk?' he asked Margery.

'No, of course not, silly boy. There's only somewhere loud.'

Richard sipped his Tizer. Whitney at least looked at her cocktail.

'You'll be here about Bridget Tully, of course. Cross-eyed, you know. Odd in a painter. Had an affair with...'

'Magister Rex Chalfont...'

'No, that's not the name I was thinking of. It was the polar explorer. Not him himself—the fellow who played him in *Scott of the Antarctic*. It'll come to me in a moment. I can see the face.'

'It's Chalfont we're interested in,' said Whitney.

'I daresay you are, my girl. An interesting sort of chap. Not a name you hear every day, either.'

'Not a name some of us have heard *ever*, Margery.'

The conductress gave Richard a sly smile. He hadn't believed she didn't remember the exact name of every lighting assistant and walk-on penguin in *Scott of the Antarctic*, much less one of the principle cast. And he didn't believe her casual assumption they knew as much about Chalfont as she evidently did.

Margery fairly chortled. To the point of crowing.

'Are your filing cabinets coming up short? Did you only drop in to my "happening" to quiz poor old Marge about an information gap you shouldn't ought to have? You'll hurt my feelings.'

Richard laughed with her.

'Fair enough. You win. The Diogenes Club are amateur dabblers beside you, Margery. I don't know why we even bother to get out of bed most mornings. But if you could see your way to help...'

'*Quid pro quo*, Dickie. Payment in kind.'

'As you've pointed out, there's an imbalance. You have all the secrets.'

She coyly chewed the corner of a roll of bus-tickets Richard guessed were impregnated with something lysergic. 'Not *all*...'

'All of *ours*. And all of Agent Gauge's too...'

''Tis true. I'm terribly well-informed. Would you like to know who the first homosexual in space was?'

'Not just now.'

Margery tutted.

'Very well, but you're usually much more fun, Dickie... now, I shall point you in a useful direction, on the condition that...'

Richard waited for it.

'...the lovely Whitney answers one single question. With gory details. Truth or dare, without the dare.'

Whitney shrugged. Richard hoped Margery wasn't going to ask something indiscreet about President Nixon. Or dredge up that old one about J. Edgar Hoover's dressmaker.

Margery leaned over, cupping her hand over her mouth, and whispered in the girl's ear. Whitney looked slightly shocked, then amused. She blushed in penny-sized cheek-spots, like a cartoon character. Margery, eager, turned her own ear to receive—and Whitney whispered into it for what seemed a full five minutes. A smile spread across Margery's face, with pauses for knowing looks at Richard and mocking tuts of sham disapproval.

'I suppose I should have known...'

'All right,' said Richard, 'you've had your fun facts for the day, Margery.

Now... Rex Chalfont?'

'Don't know the man,' said Margery, offhand. Richard groaned. 'But I know *of* him...'

Richard and Whitney listened, intently.

'In 1948, the Chalfont Group offered to conquer the moon. For Britain.'

If Chalfont had a group, Richard didn't imagine they were aiming for the pop charts.

'He was a rocket scientist?'

'No, Dickie. How many rocket scientists call themselves "Magister"? He's one of those interdisciplinary fellows who mix runes and equations. You know what Artie Clarke says about advanced technology being "indistinguishable from magic"? Chalfont responds that magic is indistinguishable from magic too. He promised he'd get to the moon before anyone relying on "Nazi fireworks".'

'So, a nut?'

'A nut we should have paid more attention to,' said Margery.

'Because he had his old girlfriend stabbed?'

'Good heavens, no. Someone would have stabbed Bridget Tully eventually. An art critic, most likely. No, we should have paid attention because he did what he said he would.'

'Conquered the moon?'

'That's the whisper. He did it in 1953. In time for the Coronation. Chalfont has always been very patriotic. I suppose Everest got all the headlines.'

'You're having us on,' said Richard.

Margery looked genuinely offended.

'Have I ever misled you?'

'Not directly.'

'Let me get this straight,' said Whitney. 'In three days' time, the *Eagle* will touch down in the Sea of Tranquillity, Neil Armstrong will clamber down his ladder with a Stars and Stripes, and come across a British flag and... what else? A tea and crumpets stand? A statue of Winston Churchill? Art students holding a "Yankee Go Home" banner?'

Margery was briefly serious. 'I don't think Sexy Rexy will let it come to that. If he's got rid of his High Priestess, who was in the *moderate* wing of the Chalfont Group, he'll have decided to haul down the Union Jack, fly the Jolly Roger and... well, prepare to repel boarders.'

It took seconds for that to sink in.

Whitney looked at Richard. He saw her mouth drop open exactly the way he knew his had. Space-time upended itself and turned inside-out like a sock. Arthur C. Clarke would strongly disapprove.

'In the Lake District,' said Margery, 'about five miles from Scafell Pikes. On the Buttermere Road, you take the turn-off marked "Private Road— Trespassers Will Be Dealt With Harshly". You can't miss it.'

Richard was jolted out of his mind-expanding fugue.

'What?' he said.

'Your next question was, or should have been, "Where is Mildew Manor"?'

Richard supposed they should be grateful Margery had told what she knew, and understood it unreasonable to wish she'd volunteered all this sometime in the last sixteen years. What happened on the moon was irrelevant to her bailiwick. She had enough on her plate looking after London, without worrying about satellites or stars. Still, a quiet heads-up wouldn't have hurt.

'Stop the bus,' he said. 'We want to get off.'

They were in Piccadilly Circus.

Margery rang her bell, and said 'ting ting, please take care while leaving the omnibus, and toodle-oo.'

'How could anyone land on the moon in secret?' asked Whitney. 'In 1953?'

'I don't suppose people looked at the skies as much then,' Richard mused.

'A rocket launch is hard to keep quiet.'

'Ahem, *Sputnik...*'

'We knew about Sputnik,' she said. 'We just let Khrushchev have his big day and pretended to be surprised. Do you know how much the covert intelligence and arcane enforcement budget went up the day after all the Senators and Congressmen found out a red eye in the sky could see into their swimming pools?'

They were in St James's Park, watching ducks on the lake. Defectors, spies, tramps and shady-dealers congregated in twos on the benches. Wardens who picked up litter with spiked sticks here had a higher security clearance than the Secretary of State for Defence. Old government secrets, obsolete weapons plans and two-way mirror compromising filmstrips were always found in the grass—along with bloody Sky Ray lolly wrappers, of course.

'Magister Rex Chalfont doesn't believe in rockets,' mused Richard. '"Nazi fireworks". Ergo, no rocket launch.'

'How else are you going to get to the moon? Build a stairway to Heaven?'

'A diving bell shot out of a volcano?'

She knew this game. 'The chariot drawn by geese.'

'Cavorite.'

'Dew.'

'Astral projection.'

Whitney had pause. 'That's not so lunatic.'

'Ha-ha. Neither is antigravity paint.'

'Chalfont is a magus, right? A sorcerer.'

'A *flying* sorcerer.'

'Not necessarily. Picture this... the great Pooh-Bah—and his circle or group or whatever—sit around omming like lamas and go into a trance. Their spirits leave their bodies, then float to the moon.'

Richard conceded that was more likely than geese or gunpowder.

It was also comforting. There were recognised procedures for dealing with astral projectors. You found out where their entranced bodies were laid up and shouted 'wakey-wakey' in their ears. Not a few snuffed themselves by forgetting to nip home and eat, or secreted fragile flesh in places impregnable to enemies which also happened to be airtight. Most who learned the trick were just nosey parkers, anyway... some nights, three or four at a time collided ectoplasmically in Liz Taylor's bedroom. The odd adept managed to create a semi-solid ghost body, and could use the old 'I was dozing at the theatre in full view of the whole audience when that shadowy wraith stoved in my wife's head with a brick' alibi.

A commotion of some sort was underway on Duck Island, across the lake. Birds in a tizzy. Like the Trafalgar Square pigeons, the St James ducks had gone hungry for days while everyone was watching the telly. Perhaps there was lingering resentment at the abandonment of Francis Godwin's waterfowl-based space program. No ducks, no Duck Dodgers.

'Astral projection to the moon is a new one on me,' he admitted. 'In all known cases of out-of-the-body wandering, a filament connects the projected consciousness—in whatever form it takes—back to the physical corpus. A quarter-million-mile sticky string is, to put it mildly, a stretch.'

The ducks quacked up a fuss on the water now, scrapping over floating crumbs, beating each other with tough wings. The disturbance on the island had spread.

'Didn't some turn-of-the-century mediums claim to be star voyagers?'

Richard remembered the file.

'Yes, that's why it's called *astral* projection. But the Club never took them seriously. If they went anywhere during their trips, it wasn't in our universe. One dotty lady claimed she'd been impregnated by an Arcturan, but the baby popped out human. We kept tabs on the lad, of course. Grew up to be a very useful bowler for Leicestershire.'

'*Now* you're talking mumbo jumbo. As far as I'm concerned, cricket is a chirruping insect. Or that squeaker who bugs Pinocchio.'

'...says the girl from the he-man steak-eating cowboy country whose rugby players need to cower inside six inches of leather armour so they don't hurt their little headsies and toesies.'

They both laughed.

'Actually, you're right about football,' she conceded...

'*American* football,' he corrected.

'Those guys are sissies who can't take competition without throwing a fit.'

'They wouldn't let you play, then?'

'Uh-huh. Not after I broke my brother's leg by accident.'

'Were you playing rough while baby-sitting the little fellow?'

'Not my *younger* brother, Brad. My older brother, Trap. The Marine. He was on leave from Vietnam.'

The ducks were tearing into each other now. Feathers and blood-slicks floated on the lake.

'That's not right,' said Richard.

Whitney saw it too. In the agitated water was a rippling reflection which shouldn't be there. It looked like the moon.

Then the ducks fell silent, stopped attacking each other.

They paddled, turning in sync like a water ballet corps—and wound up looking directly at Richard and Whitney, aimed like the guns of pirate raiders.

'That's definitely not right.'

He had a flash of Sky Ray Roly, the moment his eyes blanked and he reached for the champagne bottle.

Moon madness, again?

Richard and Whitney stood still.

Ranks of ducks advanced, sculling with wing-points. Eyes and beaks glinted in the sunlight.

'Look, Mum,' said a passing child, dripping ice-cream in his paw.

'Come away, dear, and don't bother the nice people.'

'But *Mu-u-um...*'

Mother and son moved on. The first ducks were off the lake, waddling on the grass. The lack of quack was disturbing.

Richard sighed inwardly. He really did not want to be seen running away from a horde of ducks in St James's Park. Margery Device would never let him hear the last of it.

'How did Tippi Hedren get out of this in *The Birds?*' Whitney asked.

'Hard to say. The film has an ambiguous ending.'

They began to back away, very slowly. More ducks made it to land.

'What about in the original story?' Whitney asked.

'That doesn't have an ambiguous ending. That has an apocalyptic ending.'

'So, no help there. Thank you, Daphne Du Maurier...'

'*Dame* Daphne... it was in the Queen's Birthday Honours List...'

'Swell. Remind me to send a congratulation card. Should we turn and run now?'

'Not yet.'

'You really think they might be *friendly* lunatic psycho ducks?'

Richard held out his hand, flat-palmed, and said 'stop!'

It worked, for almost a second. Then the ducks flew at them, and they ran.

The doorman of the Diogenes Club passed no comment on the state of their apparel. Over the years, he had seen worse.

Richard and Whitney were bloodied and shredded, bruised by bills and scratched by webbed feet—who knew duck-feet had barbs? They'd only got away because the birds wouldn't leave the park.

'Really,' said Major Took-Flemyng to no one in particular, as they entered the lobby, 'it's a bloody *disgrace!*'

'Sorry,' said Richard to the Major. 'Bit of a difficult day.'

'Still, to bring a *woman* into the club...'

Richard gripped Whitney's arm. In her current ticked-off and duck-assailed state, she might serve the Major worse than her brother Trap.

'Is there a problem, Major?' asked Catriona. She popped out of the Quiet Room, which was on the first-floor landing, and stood at the top of the broad stairs.

Took-Flemyng's misogyny evaporated in an instant. He revealed dentures in a would-be ingratiating grin and bowed low.

'No indeed, Miss Kaye. No problem of any kind. Might I say how charming you look this afternoon?'

'You might. Now, run along, Major.'

'Of course, Miss Kaye.'

Took-Flemyng trotted into the Informal Room, glowing like a schoolgirl awarded a Gold Star by 'Miss' in front of the whole form.

'If Daphne Du Maurier got damed, why not Catriona Kaye?' Whitney whispered.

'Diogenes Club tradition,' he told her. 'Turning down the K. I've only turned down the M.B.E. Catriona turned down a peerage once. We don't like to clutter our calling cards with letters.'

'If you say so, Galahad.'

Catriona had Hills bring them a change of clothes—a mauve tracksuit with white piping for Whitney, an orange-and-black kaftan for Richard—and personally cleaned and dressed their minor wounds. The Diogenes Club First Aid kit had a few unusual items. Besides iodine, Catriona applied sigils of something herbal to speed the healing.

'Attacked by ducks,' said Catriona, as Richard and Whitney drank tea in the Quiet Room. 'That's not the strangest item today. We've had a rash of incidents. People and animals howling at the moon. Even in daylight. There's a lot of—and I use the word carefully—*lunacy* about. Schoolchildren playing "spacemen and monsters" on a bomb site in Streatham managed to vaporise a builder's hut with plastic rayguns. A horticulturist in Surrey nearly choked to death on the poisonous exhalations of a greenhouse full of man-in-the-moon marigolds. Leaping fish beset an angler on the Trent.'

'Is it all connected?' Whitney asked.

'Almost certainly. Tiresome, isn't it? So, you've been to see the Witch. Any joy?'

Richard passed on what Margery Device had told them.

'I assume Luna Moon was in this Chalfont Group,' he said. 'It might be worth our while running down a membership list. Chalfont is off the books, but if we identify known intimates we ought to get a better picture.'

He expected Catriona to use the antique telephone to ring through to the Archive Room.

Instead, she said, 'I daresay the Chalfont Group found room for a science fiction writer called Mungo Zyle, an explorer named Walter Vereker and a middle-aged drop-out born Lawson Hogg but known as "the Hermit of Taunton".'

She let the names lie.

'You didn't know about them yesterday,' he said. 'What brought them to your attention?'

'They were alive yesterday morning,' she admitted. 'In the afternoon and evening, in quick succession, in locations five hundred miles apart, they were stabbed to death. Probably with the same athamé used to kill Luna Moon. Zyle's wound had traces of *someone else's* blood in it. The assassin didn't even wipe tools between jobs.'

'Can we definitely link them to Chalfont?'

'Only by inference. We can link them to *each other*, though. They were of a like age, fell into the category of "crank", and have criss-crossing biographies. Luna Moon did covers for Mungo Zyle's books. Zyle and his wife Anemone co-authored the *Moonmist Trilogy*. It's all trilogies nowadays. I blame Johnny Tolkien. Vereker was arrested at Glastonbury Tor in 1949, taking part in Druidical erotic hullabaloo involving Hogg and a gaggle of silly women in robes. All our victims have a roundabout or direct interest in the topic of the day. Moon-worship. You'll appreciate this: Hogg's farm makes green cheese.'

'Is the Group wiped out?' asked Whitney. 'Are there any surviving members?'

'We can take a guess at Anemone Zyle, since she's disappeared. In other circumstances, she'd be our favoured suspect. I've got research moles digging for others with connections to one or more of our dead people. They've made some suppositions. There's a publisher named Maurice Nordstrom, who isn't in his office today. I had a nice chat with his secretary. Nordstrom & Haw specialise in science fiction, so you'd think he'd be high on Apollo. In fact, he's been in a sulk for months.'

'There's a theory the moon landing is bad for science fiction.'

'I've heard it. Nordstrom publishes the Zyles, also Vereker's books on mountain-climbing. Vereker used to scale Swiss and South American peaks with a Rudolf Gosling, a nasty piece of work who leads the English Liberation Front—which is a fancy name for yet another fascist party. Their Command Bunker is called "the Laburnums". It's in Acacia Road, Frinton. It has net curtains. The ELF tried to get Enoch Powell to join the cause, and got an erudite earful. Gosling is another of Bridget Tully's old beaux. According to his Deputy Leader, he's too busy to talk with strange women. Speaking of strange women, Hogg's Farm was home to a quantity of loose young persons who helped make his cheese. I imagined hermits lived alone, but evidently this one liked the company. They've all scarpered without trace. So, that's quite a little lot of disappearees.'

'The only one I've met is Rudy Gosling,' said Richard. 'His party symbol is an *eismond*, a moon of ice. It derives from one of Himmler's crackpot notions. We couldn't prove anything, but came away from that Handsworth Thuggee business with a strong sense that the ELF were mixed up in it. I wouldn't put it past him to stick an athamé into anyone.'

'I began one of those *Moonmist* novels,' said Whitney. 'It had a map on the first page, with place-names that were anagrams of brands of detergent. Then a glossary of "moon talk" that went on for *pages*. After that, on the first page proper, the lunar controller was described as "resting her chin on her elbows". I threw the book in the trash.'

'Margery said Luna Moon was in "the moderate wing" of the Chalfont Group,' said Richard. 'I suppose the other victims were with her. Which leaves, what? The radical wing.'

'The nasty wing,' said Whitney.

'As good a label as any. Put it on a T-shirt. Chalfont, or whoever heads the Group, has had his Night of the Long Athamé and cleaned house. So, where have the nasties disappeared?'

'Everyone's gone to the moon?' suggested Whitney.

Richard tried not to hum that song.

'Initially, I think Cumbria more likely,' said Catriona. 'That's the hint Margery was dropping. The Witch is usually on the money.'

'Where the Hell is Cumbria?' asked Whitney.

'Beyond the range of the Trident,' said Richard. 'We'll need the Rolls.'

Catriona picked up the phone and began dialling with the end of her cigarette holder. 'I'm concerned about Margery's "prepare to repel boarders" analogy,' she said. 'I want to make sure you don't visit Mildew Manor— which has a *horrible* history, by the way—without proper covering fire.'

Whitney saluted. Richard could almost hear drums.

Catriona got through to the underground exchange, and played the code-word and response parlour game to clear a classified international line. It took her less time than it would take an ordinary telephone subscriber to reach the speaking clock.

'Houston,' she said, when connected, 'you have a problem...'

'A pick-and-mix landscape, Cumbria,' said Whitney. 'You've got your rocks, your grass, your lakes, your mountains. And, oh, no matter how summery it is, it's wet underfoot.'

'Funnily enough, that's been noticed before.'

Richard's Rolls Royce ShadowShark was parked in a lay-by opposite the chained-off turning. The 'Private Road—Trespassers Will Be Dealt With Harshly' sign Margery Device had described hung from the chain. The 'o' in 'Road' was a stuck-on eismond decal with ELF written across it. It might as well have been a neon sign with 'Secret Lair' on it.

Richard wore baggy jungle camouflage trousers and a padded mint-green cagoule, custom-made army boots with gadgets secreted in heel and sole, a jaunty 'Che Guevara' beret and World War One aviator goggles. Whitney had kept the track-suit and photochromatic shades from yesterday, augmented with an even jauntier 'Bonnie Parker' beret. Richard had turned down several offers of guns, and persuaded a reluctant Whitney not to tool up either. She'd acquired a knobkerrie walking stick—the sort country people said they needed for walking down lanes, but mainly used for beating townies who trespassed in fields—and could twirl it like a baton.

Two army lorries were parked nearby. A platoon of squaddies was having tea around a mobile canteen, wondering why they weren't back in barracks watching the telly. *Apollo 11* was only hours away from lunar orbit. A matching US Army team was due to show up to make this a joint Anglo–American operation. A diversion was in force, steering traffic away from the Mildew Manor area. Fell-walkers were being advised to fell-walk the other way. Anthrax was mentioned, though the cover story was getting whiskery. If you added up the times the British public were warned of an anthrax spill to keep them away from something that would terrify them even more, you'd assume the United Kingdom was knee-deep in the stuff. According to Whitney, the American equivalent was 'experimental nerve toxin'—though when an experimental nerve toxin actually leaked, the no-go area was blamed on foot and mouth.

Catriona insisted that the soldiers were only there to maintain a perimeter. This was a business for specialists.

'Spectacular views all around,' said Whitney, 'except in that direction.'

A thicket of trees lined the Private Road and swelled to a copse.

'You'd think it'd been cultivated that way,' she said.

'A shrewd observation. Successive owners of Mildew Manor have had things to hide. In the 18th Century, when banditti prowled the Lake District, this was the home of the wickedest man in England, Nick Goodman... yes, the irony was noticed in his lifetime... and his equally depraved wife, the dreadful Eithne Orfe. We've got two filing cabinets on them.'

'But nothing on Rex Chalfont.'

'No need to rub it in.'

Catriona had a theory that Chalfont had a government connection, and used his pull years ago to stay out of the files. In London, she was following this up—in the few moments when she wasn't suffering transatlantic phone calls from aggrieved, disbelieving and distracted American officials.

The intelligence was not well-received at NASA, even after Assistant

Director Spilsby endorsed the report. He took the issue more seriously now than four days ago, when he had packed Whitney Gauge off to poke into it. Along with the global epidemic of moon madness, 'developments' in space were troubling. LM Pilot Aldrin's report that he 'saw a light moving which was not a star' was bleeped from television coverage. Anyone who used the term 'unidentified flying object' was liable to summary dismissal. Ranger 8 and Surveyor 5, unmanned probes officially dead since their publicly announced missions, had long since been repurposed as weaponised robots—packed full of gizmos which guaranteed the Soviets a hot-foot if they tried to steal a march on Apollo with their Zond moon orbital vehicle. The probes had gone 'off-line' after broadcasting signals that they were subject to Unusual Uncategorised Stress. Surveyor's last message suggested that it was being 'eaten'. It was hotly debated how seriously spook stuff should be taken. A roomful of technocrats and science guys had a hard time adjusting their worldview to take in a magic threat. Richard suggested telling them the UUS was an anthrax outbreak.

Dusty contingency plans for engaging with 'hostiles' on the moon were hauled out of cabinets and had their seals broken. These turned out to be of no practical use: They were all contingent on either a) an unknown foreign power whose spacecraft had markings in the Cyrillic alphabet having sneakily established a covert moonbase, or b) an aggressive extra-terrestrial intelligence lurking in the craters with rayguns in its tentacles. Whoever was responsible for Plan B didn't take seriously the possibility of it ever being considered for use, and proposed drafting Flash Gordon and Captain Video. Interested parties argued over what to tell the astronauts, awaiting a decision from Senator Edward Kennedy. It turned out Kennedy chaired the Oversight Committee which effectively ran the 'Unnameables'. Even Richard was surprised to learn that. When JFK appointed Bobby Attorney General, he gave his other brother a secret job Teddy had hung on to through successive administrations.

In a lorry designated 'Forward Command Post One', Captain 'Mac' Maitland—who sported a rakish eyepatch, but had a haircut more suited to a Swinging Blue Jean than an officer in Her Majesty's Armed Forces—was on the field telephone.

'The American army took a wrong turn and are up the Old Man of Coniston,' said 'Mac' in cut-glass Sandhurst tones—though Richard had read his file and knew he was the son of a Durham miner. 'Typical shambles. The Yanks can put a man on the moon, but get lost in a tourist attraction. No offence, miss.'

Richard and Whitney weren't supposed to venture near Mildew Manor until Anglo–American combined forces were *in situ*.

'Can we offer you tea?' said 'Mac'.

Richard declined politely.

A flight of birds broke out of the copse, giving Richard harrowing duckpond flashbacks...

...then lighting struck out of a clear blue sky, three times. Close by. Flashes, no thunder. So, not ordinary lightning.

Three lithe figures appeared in the road They wore silver body-stockings, loose but clingy enough to show female form, bulbous spherical fish-bowl helmets, thick silver boots and gauntlets, plates of shiny body-armour and gunslinger belts hung with mystery tools. Their faces were painted bright green. Contoured chest-pieces were numbered in swirly hippie script: One, Two, Five. Richard looked around, but Three and Four weren't here. Their absences made dents in the space-women's formation.

A couple of the squaddies laughed. None reached for rifles.

The space-women all carried knives. Athamés.

'Have you noticed we've been wearing "Attack Me" buttons ever since we visited the Temple of Domina Oriens?' said Whitney.

'Yes.'

Two made the first move, tossing her athamé straight at Richard's eyes. The blade was for stabbing, not balanced for knife-throwing. Whitney swung her knobkerrie and knocked the knife off course—it stuck into the side of Maitland's lorry, inches from his head.

One came at Whitney, high. Whitney bent over as if to cartwheel, kicking out with a straight leg, catching One in her midriff, knocking her over. Her head rattled inside her fishbowl, but she got back on her feet.

The soldiers had guns at hand now, but no idea what to do with them.

Two jumped in the air, as if beginning a somersault, then popped out of space and reappeared instantly behind Richard, grabbing his arms. The country air was heavy with the smell of chemical discharge. Two had a solid hold on him, and he only hurt his head by ramming at her nose and thumping a heavy face-plate. Five advanced, lower lip sucked into her mouth, tossing her athamé from hand to hand like a Teddy Girl with a flickknife. She made teasing, stabbing motions. Now might be a good time for Maitland's men to overcome natural gallantry and fire a warning shot into Five's helmet.

Whitney and One circled each other, short knife against long stick. Both made test jabs.

Lightning struck again, cracking into the copse.

Another space-woman—Three or Four?—was stuck in the tree. Not stuck up it, like a cat—in it, trunk and limbs embedded in old wood, head kinking out like a broken branch, face rough like bark.

Two noticed and let Richard go. She grabbed her own helmet and twisted, but it wouldn't come off. Five was distracted by what had happened to the scrambled space-woman, so Richard took her athamé away.

Lighting *unstruck*—or so it seemed—and Whitney was blinking. One wasn't there any more, though her smoking silver boots were.

Two dropped to her knees, frantically struggling with her fishbowl.

'Help her,' Richard said to Five.

He saw concern in the space-woman's green face. After hesitation, she tried to help Two get her helmet off. Five held out her hand. Richard gave her back her knife, knowing she wanted it to cut through Two's neck-piece, not to stick into his chest. Another practical, everyday use for his Talent. The blade broke and Five threw the hilt away in frustration. If Two's face weren't painted, she'd have gone green of her own accord. Her eyes bulged and her mouth gaped like the little boy in the dire warning public information commercial who 'played spaceman' with a plastic bag over his head.

Though they had arrived by unorthodox means, these were Earthly beings.

Within a minute of their arrival, only Five was still standing. The ducks had been more trouble.

'Mac' rapped on Five's helmet with a pistol. The woman meekly put her hands up.

Two keeled over.

Soldiers looked at Three-or-Four, who was plainly dead. One asked if they should try to get her down.

Whitney skinned silver-foil away from Two's wrist—which was pink and had sunburn scars—and failed to find a pulse.

'Welcome to our planet,' said Richard.

Five made fists and thumped the sides of her helmet. Her faceplate popped open and she unloosed a torrent of foul language in broad West Country.

Richard deduced that the space-women were the flower children from Hermit Hogg's cheese farm.

The helmet came off. Five shook out a long tangle of brown hair. The green on her face had streaked. She rubbed it with the heels of her hands.

She didn't stop swearing—not at Richard and Whitney, but at 'Magister'—for long minutes. She went around kicking things, including One's empty boots and Three-or-Four's tree.

The afterstench of bodged magic was thick. A short-term translocation spell, carelessly done.

Richard didn't think any of the space-women had struck down Luna Moon or the others. Those had been professional, vicious jobs. This had been a throwaway. A delaying tactic.

Five shook her fists at the sky. Whitney slapped her, to get her attention. Five slapped back, instantly. But calmed down.

'You,' Whitney said, 'name?'

'Fan.'

'Fan, do you surrender?'

'Oh yerr, I gives up all roight.'

Maitland ordered his Sergeant to take away Fan's tool-belt. A lot of the gadgets seemed to be toys.

'I knew we shouldn't have stepped in that morris square,' said Fan. 'So did he, Magister. Bloody posh old bastard tosser. Couldn't wait to get shot of us. It were all lies, all the time. I b'aint never going to the moon. And he'm killed Jillie and Jonquil and Bertha. Hannah too, prob'ly. She never popped back. Goddess knows where her bits be spread.'

Maitland wasn't following this. Richard and Whitney were.

'Fan,' said Richard, 'we're here to stop Magister Rex Chalfont.'

''Bout bloody time too.'

'So... take us to your leader.'

Fan led Richard and Whitney down a rutted, tree-lined path. Branches entangled above them. Sunbeams filtered down into the nearly covered way, casting shifting patches of light onto the ground.

'So that's what "sun-dappled" means,' he said. 'I'd always wondered.'

Whitney tugged his arm, to prevent an unwise step. She used her knobkerrie to snap a man-trap that had been left under a carpet of mulch.

'Wrong time of year for falling leaves,' she explained.

An unwholesome country smell turned out to be a dead little man splatted against a stout oak by a giant wickerwork fly-swatter studded with Vietcong-style punji sticks.

'Magister Rex hates they poachers,' Fan explained. 'Leaves 'en up to warn off others.'

Richard got on the walkie-talkie and warned Mac to have his men be careful about following the country code. Stiles in these parts were likely to be booby-trapped and streams might well be full of mines.

From the disillusioned space-woman, they learned that Magister Rex and the Inner Circle of the Temple of Domina Oriens had promised free trips to the moon for their followers. Chalfont claimed to have been there and back many times, but the happy hippie cultie side of things had become strained lately—what with the unsought-for competition from NASA. Fan wasn't in on the politics, but confirmed there'd been a little war in the Group. Those left standing had fallen back to Mildew Manor, the unlikely mission control from which Chalfont promised imminent mass migration to the sacred satellite. According to Fan, the quadrilocating assassin was Gosling—who nipped about via more precise and effective spells of translocation than the Hogg Farm Space Kiddettes. It was all done by morris dancing, apparently— Moon Man's Morris, executed by the Chalfont Group with man-in-the-moon masks and belled sticks, around a square marked with yellow diagrams.

Fan was vague about how precisely Chalfont made his space voyages, but clearly believed that Magister Rex had been traversing cislunar space regularly since the 1950s. Without anyone noticing. Had Chalfont perfected a long-range translocation spell? Jaunting that far was beyond the combined magical prowess of Merlin, Circe, Ali Bongo and Sooty, and Richard couldn't see Magister Rex being top of that class. Not with bloody morris dancing. If the sellotape-and-glue sorcery used to deploy Fan and her gang was an example of his prowess, Richard wouldn't trust Chalfont to pull a rabbit out of a hat without killing a volunteer from the audience. Fan only said Magister went to the moon 'through the Shimmer'.

They got out of the copse alive and came upon Mildew Manor, a big, square gothic revival pile—complete with turrets and towers—in the middle of 18th-century fake ancient ruins and gardens cultivated to seem wild. A single light was always kept burning in the East Tower window, in accordance with a tradition no one dared violate. In the driveway, a minivan with a green cheese man-in-the-moon painted on the side panels was parked next to a jeep with an ELF eismond on the bonnet and a couple of bicycles. No built-in-the-garden-shed rocketship in evidence. No transdimensional police box. No Verne cannon. No antigravity trampoline. No geese.

Fan wouldn't go further.

Richard and Whitney crossed the lawn. A moondial was set on a stone table, abandoned teacups around the rim. A ceramic ashtray was full of aromatic dog-ends.

The front door hung open a crack. Whitney pushed it with her stick. No death-trap sprung.

'Anyone home?' called Richard.

'Could they have zapped themselves into oblivion?'

'We can but hope.'

In the hallway, a large Luna Selene Moon canvas hung askew. Whitney adjusted it, and had an insight. Her tactile intuition again.

'This way.'

Richard felt the *thrumm*—in his fillings, mostly—before he heard the churning, rumbling sound. His nerves were on edge, as if he were standing next to an invisible cataract or inside a giant disguised power station. A lot of energy in the air. He didn't need to tell Whitney to be careful.

The first room they came to was a TV lounge. BBC moon news rolled on, to empty chairs. A well-spoken announcer apologised to those tuning in for *Titch and Quackers*, usually broadcast at this time. *Apollo 11* was in lunar orbit. On-screen diagrams showed how the *Eagle* would separate from the *Columbia*, leaving Mike Collins in orbit as Armstrong and Aldrin descended to the lunar surface. The BBC didn't ask what the whole world was wondering—how pissed off was Collins at going so far, but hanging back at the last moment? Touch-down would happen tomorrow evening GMT, and man would first set foot on the moon in the middle of the night. The schedule was for the convenience of American networks, but the BBC were too polite to complain. The television set was splattered with burst tomatoes, suggesting the Chalfont Group's feelings about the Apollo program.

Richard switched off the television, and the *thrumm* was obvious.

Something big, nearby.

At the end of the hall, double-doors were painted with Luna Moon designs, in the same style as the décor at the Temple in Sekforde Street. The *thrumm* came from beyond the doors.

Whitney, wary of another shock, did not reach for the handles.

Richard pulled open the doors...

The Great Hall of Mildew Manor was stripped of furniture. Tall windows were bricked over. Panelling bowed away from the walls, and had come away from bare brick in patches. Uncarpeted, polished floor strained as if the herringbone tiles were resisting universal *pull*.

In the middle of the room, a sphere of blue-white, crackling energy—about twenty feet from pole to pole—revolved slowly. The Shimmer. It looked like a 3-D projection, the ghost of the moon. Though the Shimmer was transparent, Richard couldn't *only* see the far side of the room through it. Somewhere inside the shifting, semi-gaseous globe of magick hung a giant, animate Luna Moon picture.

Whitney whistled.

One other person was in the hall. A man in a red diving suit lay in a corner, clutching his right arm—which ended at the wrist, stump caulked over with blue-green sludge. Richard twisted off the man's helmet—more brass-bound and Victorian than the Space Kiddettes' silver fishbowls—and recognised Maurice Nordstrom, the publisher. His comb-over flapped away from a flaky scalp. He was delirious with pain and wonder.

Nordstrom thumped himself with his stump, and muttered 'failure, failure, failure...'

Richard understood. Magic devices like the Shimmer depend on faith. Waver for even a second and you end up stuck in a tree or rent apart by dwellers in the outer void. Or it just doesn't work.

Nordstrom had been cautious, tried to test the waters. The waters didn't care for the inference that they were not to be trusted.

It was no use quizzing the man. His mind was gone with his hand.

'I don't suppose there's an off switch?' said Whitney.

'Not this side.'

'That's what I was worried about,' she said. 'So, the Shimmer is a portal? A magic door to the moon. Like a Wonderland rabbit-hole or a Narnia wardrobe.'

'If Chalfont had his physics thinking cap on rather than his sorcerer's pointy hat, he'd call it a Schwarzschild Wormhole or an Einstein–Rosen Bridge.'

'Like I said, a magic doorway...'

'...to the moon, Alice.'

The wall-panels, floor-tiles and ceiling were covered with—as Margery Device had said—runes and equations. Childish scrawls, which shone like teeth and white shirts in a discotheque when ultra-violet plays on the crowds during the chorus of 'Hi Ho Silver Lining'. Richard wondered whether the spell had been touched up since 1953. It was a powerful piece of work—a masterpiece, perhaps the only one Magister Rex had in him. He'd had help, of course. Richard knew the brushstrokes of Luna Moon.

'I still don't believe you can actually get to the moon through that,' said Whitney.

'Neither did Nordstrom.'

'I'm not saying you can't get *anywhere*.'

Richard understood. The Shimmer was more likely a portal to another dimension than another world. Luna Moon's imagination, perhaps.

'What about Aldrin's non-star light?' he asked. 'The breakdown of Ranger and Surveyor on your actual moon.'

'Suggestive, not conclusive.'

He looked at her. And knew that, like him, she was more excited than terrified. But was still terrified.

Their hair was rising again, more dramatically. Whitney had a *Bride of Frankenstein* frizz. His scalp prickled as he sprouted a *Struwwelpeter* afro.

'We're putting it off, aren't we?' he said.

She agreed.

He got on the walkie-talkie, and Captain Maitland relayed him to Catriona in London. He gave a concise report about the set-up at Mildew Manor. She had dragged more secrets out of Assistant Director Spilsby.

'The good news,' she responded, 'is that someone in NASA covered their bottom by incorporating unadvertised defensive capabilities into *Apollo 11*. The rocket has "cold iron" and "bell, book and candle", like all British warships since Nelson fought Cagliostro. So, the—whatchumacallit—BEM *ought* to be shielded from sorcerous attack.'

'What's the bad news?'

'Typically, the shield can only be activated—I'm so dreadfully sorry, I'm mindlessly passing on what Americans have told me, what I mean by "activated" is "switched on"—if certain words are spoken at a certain spot by the man in charge. And he's unavailable.'

'Senator Kennedy? Don't tell me he's been shot too!'

'No, he's answering police questions after driving into a lake with a junior aide who drowned. They'd been at a party. It's not an affair from which anyone will emerge with honour. Frankly, I'm so annoyed with Teddy I could spit. Even if he's let go, we can't get him to the pentacle in the Pentagon to read the riot runes.'

'How long can the astronauts stay in orbit? Surely, Houston won't let them try a landing under these circumstances?'

'Houston's tolerance for, and I quote, "hoodoo voodoo" is at an end. They've all been intent on this since Teddy's brother said there'd be an American on the moon before the end of the decade.'

'JFK also promised to bring the American back safely.'

'Indeed. But NASA is in a risk-taking, seat-of-the-trousers mood at the moment. If they aborted the landing—hideous, term, that—they think it'd be the end of the space program.'

'Being blasted to bits during the descent would probably put a dampener on things too.'

'The boffins are impatient.'

'So it's down to us? Whitney and I?'

'Spilsby wants Whitney on the bench. A platoon of GIs with cruciform tattoos and holy water-pistols are on their way...'

'They're lost.'

'I know. It's a wonder they've not napalmed Grassmere. As far as I'm concerned, it really is down to you two. Richard, I don't need to tell you to come back safe. Don't try too hard to protect the girl. She'll not be grateful and can look after herself.'

'I've noticed.'

'Good. You're getting better at noticing. It bodes well. Gallantry is all very well, but it's nearly the 1970s. Lecture over. Go and save the world. And the moon.'

He told Whitney they had the go-ahead. He didn't mention Spilsby.

In an antechamber to the Great Hall, several pressure suits—not strictly *diving* suits, of course—hung on hooks, with helmets shelved above. It took long minutes to get properly dressed for the expedition. The gear was baggy enough to fit over their Earth clothes, though Richard had to take his boots off and transfer gadgets to flapped pouches on the thighs. Reluctantly, they left their berets behind. The suit-boots were weighted, soled with something like slate, fixed to the trouser-rims with gluey strips. The space-suit was reddish metallic oilskin, and musty inside. Somehow, the helmet did not shut off sound.

Whitney had a similar suit, but opted for silver finish and the plastic fishbowl. She struck a pin-up pose.

'Out of sight, Psychedella,' he commented.

They checked each other for straps, seals and hooks and hoped they'd followed proper procedure. The oxygen bottles were lightweight and seemed too small to be any use.

Richard peeled an eismond off his chestplate.

'I'm not wearing this,' he said. 'It's the badge of an oik.'

Beside the suits was a rack of athamés. The Temple must have got a good price on a job-lot of ceremonial stabbing implements. An array of contraptions with pumps and nozzles which looked like Edwardian fly-sprays could have been moon-guns. Hung by the rack was a clip-board with printed forms and a stubby pencil on a string. Richard flipped over filled-in forms. Suits were checked out to Nordstrom, who they needn't worry about, and Rex, Anemone and Gosling, who would likely be more problematic. Boxes were ticked, signatures appended. He and Whitney didn't bother with the paperwork.

It ought to come down to two against three. Richard knew little about

Rex Chalfont or Anemone Zyle, but Rudy Gosling was a practiced killer—
and, whatever lay beyond the Shimmer, they were up against people who
would be more familiar with the terrain.

When they returned to the Great Hall, Nordstrom was dead. Puffy blue-
green fungus was spreading across his face. It was horribly easy to imagine
the poison gunk covering the whole world.

To be on the safe side, they picked him up between them, gave him a
swing or two and launched him into the Shimmer with the old heave-ho.

Nordstrom flapped in the centre of the globe and disappeared, like a
switched-off TV picture dwindling to a dot. Even the after-image didn't
last.

'I hope he didn't just dissolve in front of our eyes,' said Richard. 'If so,
what we're about to do would be cataclysmically stupid.'

She shrugged.

His impulse was to kiss Whitney Gauge, but knew they would just grind
helmets.

'Ready?' she asked.

They held hands, tightly enough to feel the grip through the gauntlets,
and walked towards the Shimmer. After a few steps, they weren't on the
floor, but above it. The phantom moon exerted gravitational pull.

He tried not to shut his eyes. The rushing noise increased.

He and Whitney clung to each other. Incalculable forces worked on
them. He felt upside-down and inside-out...

And topsy-turvy...

On the other side of the Shimmer was the moon. At least, the parti-
coloured Earth, hanging bright in velvet-black night, strongly suggested that
this was the satellite.

Everything else wasn't as expected.

No expanse of greyish dust plain, pitted with craters. Not even a range of
green cheese. In a screamingly colourful jungle, trees had peacock feathers
and birds had serpent-scales. Thick fire rivulets ran through black crystal
fern. Dew-drops crawled up rock-cracks like liquid bugs. Some trees were
sickly, bursting with the blue-green fungus which had tainted Mo Nordstrom.
Patches of the stuff lay about. Small weird dead animals curled up in it like
undigested carrots in fresh sick.

Richard's brain stopped sloshing in its pan as the trip trauma passed. But
his insides still felt funny, and he was light-headed. Close to tipsy. Tipsy-
topsy-turvy was not a place to be. Not with murderers about, and an official
moon mission in peril.

The Shimmer was here too, but in a negative image—a globular tracery
of sparks revolving in mid-air.

Whitney let go his hand and took experimental steps, making yard-long
leaps between footprints. She squealed, like a kid on a fairground ride.

'Look at *meeee...*'

Richard bounded after her. On the moon, everyone was Peter Pan.

A Victrola gramophone, plumped down on a vegetable outcrop, played 'The Roast Beef of Old England' as if underwater.

A gloved hand had taken root in lunar muck, and grown a spindly green arm, with elbow-buds which opened as eyes. Maybe part of Nordstrom made it through the Shimmer after all. The rest of him was presumably scattered in the void.

'Far out, man,' said Whitney.

A furry balloon-bean the size of a prize-winning marrow floated towards them at shin-height, propelled by raspberries emitted from what looked like a human mouth—complete with Ringo Starr moustache—at its rear. Whitney prodded it away with her knobkerrie. It drifted placidly in another direction.

They were in the lea of a castle.

It took a moment for Richard to recognise the structure as a colossal version of Mildew Manor, grown from moon-coral. Even the light in the Rapunzel room was reproduced, magnified as if a White Star were imprisoned in the tower. Windows migrated slowly across the castle-face, catching Earthlight like message-mirrors. One wing crumbled like a cake left out in the rain, iced with the blue-green mould. An ostentatious ELF eismond banner flapped above the highest ramparts in a gentle lunar wind.

Whitney pointed at the flag with a stick.

'If there's a wind, there must be some sort of air.'

'For God's sake don't try to breathe it.'

'I wasn't considering that. It's just... there's no atmosphere on the moon.'

'There aren't any castles, either. Or gramophones. Or...'

Parked in a beaten-down driveway in front of the castle were a 1920 Type 23 Brescia Tourer, a sleek sit-astride device which might be a resting hover-scooter and a scowling orange *Pon-Pon* space-hopper. In a corral nearby, lizard-horses stumped on kangaroo legs, whinnying and coughing.

'Point taken. This is there, though. The moon?'

He shrugged, and wobbled in the bulky, now lightweight, suit. The weird feeling in his water was reduced gravity, he realised. His arms tended to float up in unconscious semaphore.

'I *suppose...*'

He was reluctant to commit. Could there be another moon, stashed in Earth orbit, so unobtrusive astronomers had never noticed? That was ridiculous—but so were the poodle zeppelins and cocktail umbrella hummingbirds and crab cowpats with human fingers.

'It's magic,' he said. 'You know how it works. It's a short cut. And short cuts don't always come out where you think.'

Whitney raised a glove to shade her eyes from the glare and scanned the lunar skies for *Apollo 11*.

A few minutes ago, back on Earth, the television had shown pictures taken from orbit by the astronauts. That was the moon Richard had expected from the blurry transmissions from those now-bust survey probes—less jagged than the desolate, craggy landscape seen in 70mm in the second part of *2001: A Space Odyssey*, blanketed smooth by aeons of dust, with craters of all sizes everywhere.

'This is literally wonderful,' she said.

'A rare correct usage of the word "literally". Congratulations.'

'We-all did have us prop'r schoolin' down 't the one-room shack between corn-shucking, revival meetin's and lynchin's. And at MIT.'

'Literally wonderful,' he mused. 'Full of wonders.'

A purple cow the size of the Goodyear blimp passed over on moth-wings. It was ridden by bipedal lobsters with Maori paint on their organic armour, who stood up like water-skiers, complicated reins in their claws.

'That's not something you see every day,' she said. 'Even in our line.'

He thought about it.

'If you took every guess mankind has made about the moon, all the way back to the ancients, and mixed them together, you'd get this.'

'Maybe Luna Moon was a realist, Richard. She drew what she saw.'

'Or she saw what she drew...'

Whitney at once caught his drift.

'The Chalfont Group didn't travel to this moon. They... what?... they *made* it?'

'I think we all made it. This isn't *the* moon. Not NASA's moon, or Arthur C. Clarke's. It's *a* moon. It's *all* moons. All the *imaginary* moons...'

Applause sounded.

Three people in moon-suits, without helmets, popped into being around them, holding up those fly-spray gadgets. Anemone Zyle, co-authoress of *The Marquise of the Moon*, had a good seat on the back of a rearing lizard-horse, one hand on the reins, another aiming her moon-gun. A gaunt, blonde-grey woman, her set expression suggested the surgical removal of her sense of humour years ago. Richard recognised the ferret-faced oik with an eismond armband and a top hat as Rudy Gosling, the Frinton Führer. The fellow with the floating cloak and pop-eyes must be Magister Rex Chalfont, King of the Moon. He was the one clapping.

'Very close, very good, Mr Jeperson. But not *imaginary*. Nothing is truly imaginary. *Potential*. And imperilled. This moon is here, accessible through magic, just so long as no one comes the long way and spoils it by saying it's not so. Know what happens if one of those *astronauts* sets his dirty great space-boot here? *Puff!* All gone.'

He illustrated his point, by jabbing a finger at a passing balloon-bean. It burst and evaporated.

'At the South Pole, there used to be an entrance to worlds inside the

Earth. Known of for centuries. Magicians used it. Visited Mole Men, Atlanteans and dinosaurs. Then that boring Norwegian trudged there and the hole went away. Just like that. No yeti has been seen in the Himalayas since Hillary crawled to the top of Everest. We can't have that here, can we? You see that now.'

Richard thought it over. Many phantom moons would be lost when the real one was gained.

'*Richard*,' cautioned Whitney.

'Don't worry, I know he's wrong. I'm just trying to frame a way of making him see that.'

Whitney breathed again.

Richard looked at the Moon People. Closed, tight, grim faces. Reluctantly, he concluded reason was probably not an option. But he had to share an insight.

'The blue-green stuff, the mould,' he said. 'It's recent, isn't it? It wasn't here before your purge?'

Only Chalfont tumbled, and tutted with irritation.

Rudy Gosling raised his fly-spray, spun slowly—he was practiced in this gravity—and fired a puff of fléchettes which spread and tore the Victrola to pieces. Music leaked out of the broken bell for long seconds, then died. Gosling grinned, showing ferret teeth, and brought the moon-gun to bear on Richard and Whitney.

'Hold,' said Chalfont.

'I knew you'd seen it,' said Richard. 'Why didn't you tell them?'

Gosling was furious, but didn't go against his Magister.

'We need them alive,' Chalfont said. 'They're here to stop the rot.'

Richard had an answer to something that had bothered him. He knew why they were still alive when the Chalfont Group could have swatted them at any point in the last two days. Why the catspaws used against them—Sky Ray Roly, the angry ducks, the Space Kiddettes—were non-lethal, when the Temple purge had been carried out so ruthlessly and effectively.

He and Whitney were *needed*.

'The dreams of nasty people are limited,' Richard told Whitney. '"Sick in the head" is the expression. This moon feeds off imagination, and is a hungry beastie. Since 1953, the Chalfont Group have preserved it—by ignoring what you could read in *New Scientist* or see through a telescope. Lately, that's taken a *lot* more effort. To maintain a wonderland, you need inspired loons—and this little lot killed off their big dreamers. Was it Luna Moon? Or Mungo Zyle? Who put the most in, but wasn't noticed till you forced them out? Without them, the place has been sighing and dying. It's *literally* a blue moon...'

Anemone Zyle wanted to shoot them, but didn't.

'I'm *imagining* parasitic moon-rats with a moral compass,' Whitney told

Anemone Zyle. 'Their tiny eggs lodge in the windpipes of the wicked, then hatch into furry, toothy balls which choke their hosts. So, have I thunk them into reality yet, Annie? Can you feel a tickle?'

Anemone Zyle didn't laugh. She desperately stifled a psychosomatic cough.

She was their gaoler in Moondew Manor, while Gosling and Chalfont were off upstairs about important man's business. She didn't much care for the gig.

In a lunar version of the Great Hall, Richard and Whitney were strapped to chairs bolted to the floor in the middle of a morris square.

'If you undo these tethers,' said Whitney, 'we could get down and boogie. I'll bet Mr J has some funky moves on him.'

'Shut up, witch,' snarled Anemone Zyle.

'That's about the standard of dialogue in her books, Richard. I assume she wrote the garbage bits. Mungo was the one with the talent.'

The authoress snarled. She wore a chainmail bikini and a veil-trailing triple-moon tiara. A long, thin athamé was strapped to her thigh. She was gym-toned, with any ounce of flab scalpelled or sweated off—but her skin wasn't healthy, especially in the moonglow inside the Manor.

The blue fungus spread wildly across the walls.

'Annie,' said Whitney, 'tell me something... how can you rest your chin on your elbows? Go on, demonstrate now.'

Anemone Zyle was puzzled.

'I suppose you've written so many clunker sentences you don't remember just one gaffe. I wonder which is your worst book? Some fans say *Ghyslayne, Moon-Elf of Bumph* is the absolute pits, but on consideration, I'd have to pick the wind-up of the *Tomes of the Dragonwing* saga. *Tome the Third: Countess of the Craters*. That one really sucks like an Electrolux! I wouldn't think anything could be more crappily drivelling than *Tome the Second: Seraphim of Satellite Sigma*, but you surprised me again. The only even passable passages are copied out of an old pulp by Otis Adelbert Kline. Which would you say was the worst *chapter* in your worst book? That scene where Blodwyn the Troll-Girl plights her troth to the Peri Prince Pyrcyvyl? Or the pie-fight which disrupts the moon-vow ceremony of the itsy-bitsy nipsies?'

Anemone strode over to Whitney's chair, hand out to clamp over the prisoner's mouth.

Whitney shut up and twisted skilfully in her chair, legs scissoring. Her entire lower body lifted and stretched, anchored by the leather straps which fastened her wrists to the armrests. Her knees hammered either side of Anemone Zyle's neck.

'This'll only take a moment.'

Anemone tried to scratch Whitney's dance-powerful legs.

'That won't help,' Whitney grunted. 'Try using your knife.'

Surprised to be getting sound advice in this situation but too pressed to wonder at its sincerity, Anemone drew her athamé and angled it to stick into Whitney's thigh. Whitney gave a squeeze and the gaoler passed out in an instant. Anemone dropped the knife, and Whitney caught its hilt between chin and chest.

Whitney let Anemone fall in a heap, and resumed sitting position, careful not to lose the knife. She manoeuvred the athamé to slide down her arm, bounce off her inner-elbow and spring into her hand. She reversed it, slipped the blade under the strap and sliced herself free.

'You should have used chains,' she said to the unconscious Anemone.

Whitney cut her other strap, but undid Richard's buckles. Between them, they hauled Anemone into Richard's chair and strapped her in. Richard took off her tiara and gave it to Whitney.

'I thought you'd only read a single page of the Zyles' books,' he said.

'As a grown-up,' she admitted. 'I was a science fiction fan in grade school. I read an enormous amount I've done my best to forget. Ever heard of Varno Zhoule? Keith Winton? Cordwainer Bird?'

'Can't say I have. I prefer mysteries myself.'

Their moon-suits had been taken off to facilitate strapping them down. The air in the mansion was breathable, if heavy with spice smells and an underscent of rot.

Anemone moaned, starting to come round.

Whitney gagged the woman with her own veil. Her furious eyes sparked.

'You've had your say, hack queen.'

Whitney gave Richard the knife and fetched her knobkerrie from a corner where a pile of their stuff had been flung.

'To the battlements,' she said.

Blue mould was turning grey and falling off the walls, dissipating like fluff. Richard assumed that he and Whitney were responsible for that.

How many active imaginations did it take to keep this moon alive?

They climbed stairs. Twice, they stepped on morris squares which entirely negated gravity and floated up between floors. Richard gathered that Chalfont and Gosling were busy up in the tall tower.

They had also hinted it wouldn't be necessary to keep their prisoners alive after their immediate Great Work was done. That had to involve the *Eagle*, now descending from lunar orbit.

How exactly did the moon prepare to repel boarders?

The answer became obvious when they came to the room with the eternal light. Approaching quietly, keeping to shadows, they peered through a doorway and saw figures clustered around a large, fat cannon aimed out at the sky through a big hole in the wall.

Chalfont and Gosling were there. Chalfont wore M&S wizard-robes, a coronet with stick-ons representing the phases of the moon, and complicated multi-lensed spectacles. He held a long taper, flame dancing slowly at its end. Gosling was in black tweed with a red sash, an eismond armband, red wellington boots and a top hat—the uniform of the ELF upper echelon.

The other people in the room were phantasms. They worked on the cannon—manipulating an apparently lightweight but solid giant ball into the muzzle, attaching a fuse, making minute adjustments to an aiming device.

Some were familiar.

'The big-schnozz guy must be Cyrano de Bergerac,' whispered Whitney.

'The one from the play, yes,' Richard agreed. 'The historical Cyrano had a normal nose. With him is Baron Münchausen. The fellow in the toga must be Lucian. The bald Frenchman is Georges Méliès, or at least his character in *Voyage to the Moon*. The bug-faced one is a Selenite, from Wells. The girls in leotards I can't place...'

'*Cat-Women of the Moon*. It's a film. The giant toy spider is theirs. Who's the tall silver goon with pipes in his ears?'

'A Cyberman, from *Doctor Who*. He's British.'

'The big cheerful robot with the hammer and sickle? The one who looks like a giant refrigerator?'

'It'll be from some comrades-across-the-stars socialist realist space epic.'

'The bearded drunk?'

'Captain Haddock, from the Tintin album, *Objectif Lune*.'

'The blonde in riding britches?'

'The heroine of *Frau im Mond*, the Fritz Lang film. Look who she's with...'

'Dr Floyd, from *2001*.'

'Arthur C. Clarke is a magician after all.'

A black monolith stood in the room too.

The workers were not transparent, but showed various degrees of unreality. Some were in black and white, or poorly tinted. Some seemed engraved rather than living.

The cannon was stamped 'Property of the Baltimore Gun Club'.

Captain Haddock looked around, rimmed eyes bulging, and pointed a fat gauntlet at Richard and Whitney.

'Bashi-bazouks!' he shouted. 'Ostrogoths! Shibboleths! Vermiform appendices! A billion blistering blue barnacles!'

Then, they all turned to stare. All the lunar explorers and inhabitants, all the pioneers and colonists, the masters and the monsters. Münchausen doffed his plumed cap.

'I knew that bint was too stupid to be trusted,' fumed Gosling, reaching for a moon-gun.

Chalfont was almost happy to see them.

After living off the books for so long, Magister Rex wanted an audience. It may be his magic *needed* an audience.

'You're going to blast the *Eagle* out of the sky,' Richard accused. 'Using a cannon ball painted with Cavorite.'

'A defensive measure,' Chalfont admitted. 'To keep this moon alive, to keep all these moon people alive.'

'Surely, you can't want to see an end for poor Münchausen?' pleaded the Baron. 'So much would be lost.'

'Miaow,' said a Cat-Woman, expressively.

Méliès mimed, impassioned. His films were silent, of course. The Soviet walking fridge saluted Permanent Revolution. The Cyberman raised a headlamp between handles. Richard recognised it as the BBC props department's improvised Cyber-gun. Cyrano went for his deadly blade.

Whitney raised her knobkerrie, but Richard laid a hand on her arm.

Before resorting to violence, he would appeal to reason.

'Gentlemen, Selenites, Cat-Women,' he began, 'I salute you. On behalf of all mankind, you have done your job with honour. You flew ahead, on fancy, on calculation, on ambition, on a dream. Now, the rest of us must catch up. What's about to happen in the Sea of Tranquillity isn't your death, it's your *glory*. I implore you, in the name of the spirit which seized you all in the first place, please do not do the bidding of these mean-spirited men. It's your moon, not theirs. They made the moon sick, remember...'

One of the Selenites still had patches of fungus around its mandibles. The giant spider's legs were limp, the strings eaten away. Haddock's beard had a blueish tinge too.

'You can't hold this scrap of territory for *them*, you must give it up. You have other homes, where you have other shapes. There's Mars and Venus and Vulcan and Skaro. There's Metropolis and Atlantis and Freedonia and Utopia. And Narnia and Oz and Erewhon and Wonderland. The men coming in their capsule have you in their hearts, much more than these pretenders to magic. Their whole enterprise is built on your example. Dr Floyd, you must understand this. Science is indistinguishable from magic. You should welcome the *Eagle*. It's the keeping of the promise you made.'

Gosling raised his moon-gun, but was caught up short—a ghost blade stuck out of the soft part under his chin. Cyrano pulled his epée free, and the Frinton Führer collapsed. He was not bleeding, not even wounded, but was dead.

Chalfont raised his flaming taper.

The *Eagle* was in his sights, multi-faceted form descending towards lunar ground, landing-pads extended. What did the astronauts see below them? Not Moondew Manor and the populated jungles. The undisturbed dust of the Sea of Tranquillity.

Chalfont touched the taper to the fuse, which began to fizz.

The ghosts swirled around the cannon. Some passed through each other.

Whitney thumped Chalfont with her stick, cracking his coronet and knocking him to the floor.

'Too late,' he murmured.

'No,' said Richard. 'It's not.'

Münchausen—who knew the worth of a good story and a grand gesture—was first. He clambered up into the barrel of the cannon, as was his habit. A Cat-Woman was next, the zip up the back of her leotard sparkling as she curled beside the Baron.

Then Floyd, letting a slide-rule float away from him.

And Haddock, bright blue hair grown past his knees. Lucian. Cyrano. The Russian robot. A two-dimensional square-jawed comic book spaceman. The Grand Lunar. Georges Méliès. Dick Tracy. The Cyberman. All of them.

A conglomeration of ghosts stopped up the cannon.

The fuse burned down, and the tower room filled with light.

The Manor was falling like the House of Usher. Sublunar tremors shook its foundations. Richard and Whitney made their way down from the tower in a hurry.

'Great speech,' said Whitney. 'Off the top of your head?'

'I knew they were better than Magister Rex wanted them to be. The moon-ghosts have more in common with the astronauts than with the Chalfont Group. The *Eagle* is their validation. It means we weren't wasting time dreaming them up...'

'It's all right, you can stop now. We should probably shut up and run.'

When the cannon imploded, Chalfont seemed to have been vaporised. The room was empty, even of ghosts. The *Eagle* was safe, and this dream-moon would change.

Richard believed that when the LEM touched down, this moon would pass away, or withdraw deeper into the realm of imagination, a bywater of dreams rather than a river. That meant there'd be nothing here to breathe.

They had to get back through the Shimmer.

'We should take Anemone,' said Richard.

'If we must...' responded Whitney.

Anemone was still fuming. Richard unstrapped her. Claws came for his face. Whitney stepped in and administered a right jab to the authoress's chin, putting her in a co-operative daze.

They carried Anemone Zyle out of Moondew Manor between them.

The moonscape was melting. Animals had become grey statues. A moth-cow was downed nearby, cocoon forming around her.

Richard saw the *Eagle*.

Toting Anemone, Richard and Whitney ran for the Shimmer. It still sparkled.

They reached the spot where they had arrived. Anemone came round, broke free...

'Come with us,' said Richard.

'You'll die.'

Anemone tore off her gag, and said 'don't care.'

'Jump, you silly woman,' said Whitney.

The Shimmer was contracting. Richard reached for Anemone, but she darted away. Whitney took his arm, and they stepped into the Shimmer...

...unscrambled again, they were back on Earth, in the Great Hall at Mildew Manor. The Shimmer, a hole in space, gave a clear view of the dying moon.

Anemone looked up. In the distance, the LEM descended.

A wireless was on somewhere nearby, loud...

'Contact light!' crackled an astronaut. 'Okay, engine stop. ACA—out of detent.'

'Out of detent,' acknowledged another astronaut.

'Mode control... both auto. Descent engine command override off. Engine arm... off. Four-thirteen is in.'

The rich jungle was gone, replaced by grey desert.

'Houston, Tranquillity Base here,' said Neil Armstrong. 'The *Eagle* has landed.'

Anemone Zyle collapsed, sank into dust.

'What happens if they find her?' Whitney asked.

'She's miles from the landing,' he said. 'She won't be found for years. Not until the moon is covered with colony bases and cities and starship ports. Then she'll be a mystery.'

The Shimmer winked shut.

Captain Maitland came into the room, with an American officer who had finally found his way. They had been following the moon-landing on television.

'We cordoned off the place, sir,' said Maitland. 'Stayed well away from the big blue thing.'

'Very wise,' said Richard.

'They've landed safely on the moon,' said Maitland. 'Just thought you'd like to know.'

'Glad to hear it.'

'Any sign of the hostiles?'

'They're no longer a problem, Captain. Mission: accomplished.'

Teams from an alphabet soup of British and American scientific, paranormal and intelligence agencies were going over Mildew Manor in minute detail, examining every rune and algorithm. Richard suspected they wouldn't work for anyone but the vanished Magister Chalfont. And that there was little use in a magic portal to a wiped-away potential realm.

He'd reported to Catriona, who was politely telling Spilsby to give Whitney Gauge a permanent promotion to field work. She'd probably also be offered a congressional medal or a free ticket to Disneyland or some other honour she'd now feel obliged to turn down in the Diogenes Club tradition. Eventually, someone would pass on the news to Senator Kennedy, if he was still interested.

In Houston, arguments had continued until the last moment. The official story was a '1202 Executive Overflow Alarm' had put the landing in jeopardy, and a technician named Bales was forced to make a snap decision about whether or not to go ahead. The LEM missed its designated landing site, and Armstrong had to fly it sideways, with only a few seconds' fuel, to find a flat, safe spot between craters and a boulder field. Catriona had said everyone was impatient. Armstrong and Aldrin were supposed to take a rest period before the historic moment, but even NASA training couldn't turn people into robots who could sleep at a time like this—so man set foot on the moon earlier than advertised, presumably to the fury of US TV networks.

Early in the morning, the garden was ghostly in cold pre-dawn light. Richard sat with Whitney on a bench by the moondial. The silver, conquered satellite was still bright.

The Man in the Moon didn't have a rocket stuck in its eye. But Richard thought the face looked like a startled, apoplectic Rex Chalfont. Perhaps that was what had happened to Magister.

'I miss the moth-cows,' said Whitney.

'They're still there, somewhere. Harder to reach. Like the monolith, and the ice-pools, and the spider on strings. We can't go there anymore.'

'What would it take to find them again?'

'Time. I daresay if we left the moon alone for fifty years or so, the Selenite forests would grow back—but that's not going to happen, is it? Armstrong took his "small step". Man is on the moon now. There'll be more missions. Mines. Colonies. Probably missiles. That's the moon-dream of 1969.'

'Hooray for us,' she said, a little regretful.

'By the way, congratulations,' he said. 'You beat Armstrong. You were the first American on the moon. That's showing NASA they're wrong about girls.'

'Cool. Will my first words get in the books? What were they?'

Richard laughed.

'You said, "Look at *meeeee*..."'

'Okay,' said Whitney, smiling wickedly. 'I'll stand by that.'

ORGAN DONORS

She came out of the lift into Reception and heard there'd been another accident outside. Beyond sepia-tinted doors, a crowd gathered. People kneeled, as if pressing someone to the pavement. Heidi was phoning an ambulance. A man crouched over the fallen person, white shirt stained red, head shaking angrily. The picture was silent, a gentle whir of air conditioning like the flicker of a projector. Sally walked to the doors, calmly hugging file folders to her chest. She looked through heavy brown glass.

Without shock, she knew it was Connor. She could only see feet, still kicking in the gutter. White trainers with shrieking purple-and-yellow laces. His furry legs were bare. Tight black cycle shorts ripped up a seam, showing a thin triangle of untanned skin.

A gulp of thought came: At least their where-are-we-going? lunch was off. She choked back relief, tried to unthink it to limbo. Then craziness kicked in. She dropped her folders and waded through paper, pushing apart the doors. Outside in Soho Square, noise fell on her like a flock of pigeons. Everyone shouted, called, talked. A siren whined rhythmically.

A dozen yards away, a van was on its side, a dazed and bloody man being pulled free. The bicycle was a tangle of metal and rubber. In the broken frame, she saw, squashed, the yellow plastic drinks container she'd bought him. A satchel of video tapes lay in the gutter.

'Connor,' she said, '*Connor!*'

'Don't look, love,' someone said, extending an arm across her chest.

People shifted out of her way, parting like stage curtains. Heat burst in her head, violet flashes dotted her vision. Her ankles and knees ceased to work. The ground shifted like a funhouse ride. Connor's head was a lumpy smear on the pavement, tire track of patterned blood streaking away. She was limp, held up by others. Her head lolled and she saw angry blue sky. Buildings all around were skyscrapers. She was at the bottom of a concrete canyon. Darkness poured in.

At her first interview, Tiny Chiselhurst had been chuffed by her *curriculum vitae*. Like everyone for the last twelve years, he didn't expect a private investigator to look like her. She told him yes, she still had her license, and no, she didn't own a gun. Not anymore.

Her independence was a Recession casualty. She wound up the Sally Rhodes Agency and escaped with no major debts, but there was still the mortgage. None of the big security/investigation firms were hiring, so she was forced to find another job her experience qualified her for. Being a researcher was essentially what she was used to: phoning strangers, asking questions, rushing about in heavy traffic, rummaging through microfiche.

There were even seductive improvements: Working in television, she could rush about in minicabs and retire her much-worn bus-train-tube pass.

On her first day, she was ushered into the open-plan *Survival Kit* office and given a desk behind one of the strange fluted columns that wound their way up through the Mythwrhn Building. Her work station was next to April Treece, an untidy but well-spoken redhead.

'Don't be surprised if you find miniature bottles in the drawers,' April told her. 'The previous tenant went alky.'

Sally had little to move in. No photographs, no toys, no gun. Just a large desk diary and a contacts book. Her mother had given her a Filofax once, but it was somewhere at home unused.

'Welcome to the TV Trenches,' April said, lighting the next cigarette from the dog-end of the last, 'the business that chews you up and spits you out.'

'Why work here, then?'

'Glamour, dahling,' she said, scattering ash over the nest of Post-it notes around her terminal. The other woman was a year or so younger than Sally, in her early thirties. She wore a crushed black velvet hat with a silver arrow pin.

'They put all the new bugs next to me. Like an initiation.'

Their desks were in a kind of recess off the main office, with no window. Sally hadn't yet worked out the building. It seemed a fusion of post-modern neo-brutalism and art deco chintz. In Reception, there was a plaque honouring an award won by Constant Drache for the design. She suspected that, after a while, the place would make her head ache.

'Need protection?' April said, opening the cavernous bottom drawer of her desk. 'We did an item last series and were deluged with samples. Have some Chums.'

She dumped a large carton of condoms on Sally's desk. Under cellophane, Derek Leech, multi-media magnate, was on the pack, safe sex instructions in a speech balloon issuing from his grin.

'Careful,' she warned. 'They rip if you get too excited. We had the brand thoroughly road-tested. The office toy boy was sore for months.'

Sally looked at the carton, unsure how to react. Naturally that was when Tiny Chiselhurst dropped by to welcome her to the team.

She woke up on a couch in Reception. She saw the painted ceiling, a graffiti nightmare of surreal squiggles and souls in torment. Then she saw April.

'Bender tried loosening your clothes,' she said, referring to the notorious office lech, 'but I stopped him before he got too far.'

April's eye-liner had run but she'd stopped crying.

Sally sat up, swallowing a spasm. Her stomach heaved but settled. April hugged her, quickly, then let her go.

'Do you want a cab? To go home?'

She shook her head. She buttoned up her cardigan and waited for a tidal wave of grief-pain-horror. Nothing hit. She stood, April with her. She looked around Reception. Plants spilled out of the lead rhomboid arrangement that passed as a pot. Framed photographs of Tiny and the other presenters, marked with the logos of their programs, were arranged behind Heidi's desk.

'Sal?'

She felt fine. The buzz of worry-irritation which usually cluttered her head was washed away. All morning, she'd been picking through viewing statistics. Her impending Connor discussion prevented concentration; she'd had to go through the stats too many times, filling her mind with useless figures.

She remembered everything but didn't feel it. She might have had total amnesia and instantly relearned every detail about her life. Her memory was all there but didn't necessarily have anything to do with her.

'Connor is dead?' She had to ask.

With a nod, April confirmed it. 'Tiny says so long as you're back to work tomorrow afternoon for the off-line, you're free.'

'I don't need time away,' she said.

April was startled. 'Are you sure? You've had a shock, lovie, you're entitled to be a zombie.'

Sally shook her head, certain. 'Maybe later.'

Although April introduced Connor as the 'office toy boy', it was a joke. He was tall, twenty-one, and trying to earn enough as a bike messenger to go back to college. Like everyone (except Sally), he wanted a career in television. Zipping in and out of Soho gridlock biking memos, sandwiches, video-tape and mysterious parcels between production companies was his way of starting at the bottom. He was one of the lean young people in bright Lycra who congregated in Soho Square, ever alert for a walkie-talkie call. He was freelance but Mythwrhn was his major employer. There were a lot like him.

Sally first slept with him on a Friday night, after a party to mark the first transmission of the series. It had been a long time for her and she was flattered by his enthusiasm. Besides, he was kind of fun.

As he poked about her flat early next morning like a dog marking territory, she wondered whether she'd made a mistake. She hid under the duvet as he wandered, unselfconsciously and interestingly naked, in and out of the room, chattering at her. He said he was 'looking for clues'. April had told everyone that Sally used to be a private eye, and the Philippa Marlowe jokes were wearing thin.

She checked the bedside clock and saw that it was before seven. Also on the table was the carton of Chums, one corner wrenched open. They'd come in handy after all. It'd have been hard to get aroused if she'd thought of Derek Leech leering off the pack at her. She turned the pack, putting Leech's face to the wall.

Connor jumped on her bed, eager to get to it again, but she had to get up to pee. As she left the bedroom, she realised he must be looking at her as she had looked at him. Last night, it had been dark. Putting on a dressing gown would kill the moment, so she went nude into the bathroom. After relieving herself, she looked in the long mirror and wasn't too disappointed. When she was Connor's age, she'd been almost chubby; with the years, she'd exercised and worried away the roundness. April said she envied Sally her cheekbones.

When she got back to the bedroom, Connor had already fit another condom over his swelling penis.

'I started without you,' he said.

Tiny told her she didn't have to come to that week's production meeting, but didn't mean it. Sally was still waiting to wake up an emotional basket case but it hadn't happened yet. She slept through the alarm more often and had stomach troubles, as if suffering from persistent jet-lag, but her thoughts were clear. She even dealt with mental time-bombs like the travelling toothbrush left in her bathroom. Perhaps after all these years, she was used to weirdness. Maybe she couldn't survive without a stream of the unexpected, the tragic, the grotesque.

Networked on ITV at eight on Friday evenings, *Survival Kit* was an aggressive consumer show, proposing that life in the late twentieth century was frighteningly random and unspeakably dangerous. Tiny Chiselhurst was at once editor and presenter, and the show, in its fifth season, was the cash-cow that kept Mythwrhn Productions, a reasonably successful independent, listed as rising. This series, Sally had helped Tiny, whose sarky humour was what kept viewers watching, expose a crooked modelling agency run on white slavery lines. Now she was switched to something that had little to do with the show itself and so was primarily an ornament at these meetings, called upon to report privately afterwards.

Tiny sat in the best chair at the round table as researchers, assistants, producers, directors and minions found places. He seemed to be made entirely of old orange corduroy, with a shaggy seventies mop and moustache. The meeting room was a windowless inner sanctum, eternally lit by grey lights, a crossbreed of padded cell and A-Bomb shelter. After reviewing last week's program, doling out few complements and making Lydia Marks cry again, Tiny asked for updates on items-in-progress. Useless Bruce, fill-in presenter and on-screen reporter, coughed up botulism stats. Tiny told him to keep on the trail. The item hadn't yet taken shape but was promising. What that meant, Sally knew, was that no sexy case—a ten-year-old permanently disabled by fish fingers, say—had come to light. When there was a pathetic human face to go with the story, the item would go ahead.

Finally there was the slot when people were supposed to come up with ideas. This was where performance could be best monitored, since ideas were the currency of television. She'd begun to realise actual execution of an item could be completely botched; what Tiny remembered was who had the idea in the first place. Useless Bruce was well known for ideas that never quite worked.

'I was talking to a bloke at a launch the other night,' said April. Someone said something funny, and she stared them silent. 'He turned out to be a corporate psychiatrist at one of the investment banks, talks people out of jumping off the top floor when they lose a couple of million quid. Anyway, he mentioned this thing, "Sick Building Syndrome", which sounded worth a think.'

Tiny gave her the nod and April gathered notes from a folder.

'There are companies which suffer from problems no one can explain. Lots of days lost due to illness, way above the norm. Also, a high turn-over of staff, nervous breakdowns, personal problems, *sturfe* like that. Even suicides, murders. Other companies in exactly the same business with exactly the same pressures breeze through with *pas de* hassles. It might be down to the buildings they work in, a quirk of architecture that traps ill feelings. You know, bad vibrations.'

Sally noticed that Tiny was counterfeiting interest. For some reason, he was against April's idea. But he let her speak.

'If we found one of these places, it might make an item.'

'It's very visual, Ape,' said Bender, an associate producer, enthusiasm blooming. 'We could dress it up with *Poltergeist* effects. Merchant bank built over a plague pit, maybe.'

Tiny shook his head. This was the man who'd stayed up all night with a camera crew waiting for the UFOs to make corn circles.

'No,' he said. 'I don't think that suits us.'

'Completely over-the-top,' Bender said, enthusiasm vanishing. 'We're a serious program.'

'Thank you, April,' Tiny said. 'But Bender has a point. Maybe last series, we could have done this paranormal hoo-hah...'

'This isn't a spook story,' she protested. 'It's psychology.'

Tiny waved his hand, brushing the idea away. 'Remember the big picture. With the franchise bid, we mustn't do anything to make the ITC look askance. It's up to us to demonstrate that we pass the quality threshold.'

April sat back, bundling now-useless notes. Sally was used to this: It was all down to Tiny, and he could be as capricious as any Roman Emperor at the games.

Roger the Replacement, one of the directors, had noticed a dry piece in the *Financial Times* about a travel firm considered a bad investment, which suggested that further digging might turn up something filmable. British holidaymakers sent to unbuilt hotels in war zones. Tiny gave him a thumbs-up, and, since April wasn't doing anything, assigned her to work the idea. The meeting was wound up.

In the Ladies, Sally found April gripping a sink with both hands, staring down at the plug, muttering 'I hate him I hate him I hate him hate hate hate hate'.

After her exercise class, they had *al fresco* lunch in Soho Square. In summer, it was a huge picnic area; now, in early autumn, office workers—publishing, film, television, advertising—melted away, leaving the square to tramps and runners. He had sandwiches while she dipped Kettle Chips into cottage cheese and pineapple. Connor always pushed his idea that *Survival Kit* do a week-in-the-life-of-a-wino item, unsubtly pressuring Sally to take it into a production meeting. She'd tried to tell him it'd been done before but his excitement always prevailed. Today he pointed out the 'characters' who pan-handled in Soho, explaining their fierce territoriality.

'You don't notice till you're on the streets, Sal. It's a parallel world.'

On a bench nearby sat two men of roughly the same age, a pony-tail in a Gaultier suit and a crusty with filth-locks and biro tattoos. Each pretended the other didn't exist.

'It's a pyramid. At the bottom, people get crushed.'

He was right, but it wasn't *Kit*. Besides, she was irritated: Was he interested in her mainly as a conduit to the inner circle? With one of his lightning subject-shifts, Connor made a grab, sticking his Ribena-sweetened tongue down her throat. His walkie-talkie chirruped and he broke off the kiss. It was just past two and lunch hour was officially over. He frowned as a voice coughed in his ear.

'It's for you,' he said.

Knowing there'd be trouble, she took the receiver. Tiny had been after her to use a portable phone. She was summoned to the Penthouse. Mairi, Tiny's p.a., conveyed the message. Tiny wanted to chat. Sally assumed she was going to be fired and dutifully trudged across the square to Mythwrhn.

She stabbed the top button and the lift jerked up through the building. Tiny had a suite of offices on the top floor which she hadn't visited since her interview. Mairi met her at the lift and offered her decaf, which she refused. She wondered if the girl disapproved of her and Connor. She had the idea it wasn't done to dally out of your age range or income bracket. At least, not if you were a woman. All the young middle-aged male production staff had permanent lusts for the fresh-from-school female secretaries, runners and receptionists.

Tiny's all-glass office was a frozen womb. He sat behind his desk, leaning back. She noticed again the figurine on its stand: a bird-headed, winged woman, throat open in a silent screech. It was an old piece, but not as old as some.

'Know what that is?' Tiny asked rhetorically, prepared to explain and demonstrate his erudition.

'It's the Mythwrhn,' she pre-empted. 'An ancient bird goddess-demon, probably Ugric. Something between a harpy and an angel.'

Tiny was astonished. 'You're the first person who came in here knowing that...'

'I had an interesting career.'

'You must tell me about it sometime.'

'I must.'

The last time she'd seen a statuette of the Mythwrhn, she'd been on a nasty case involving black magic and death. It had been one of her few exciting involvements, although the excitement was not something she wished to repeat.

Without being asked, she took a seat. Apart from Tiny's puffily upholstered black leather egg-shape, all the chairs in the office were peculiar assemblages of chrome tubing and squeaky rubber. As Tiny made cat's cradles with his fingers, she was certain he'd fire her.

'I've been thinking about you, Sally,' he said. 'You're an asset but I'm not sure how well-placed you are.'

Her three-month trial wasn't even up, so she wasn't on a contract yet. No redundancy payment. At least the dole office was within walking distance of the flat. The poll tax would be a problem, but she should qualify for housing benefit.

'Your experience is unique.'

Tiny's confrontational, foot-in-the-door interviews with dodgy characters put him in more danger in any one series of *Survival Kit* than she had been in all her years of tracing the heirs of intestate decedents, finding lost cats and body-guarding custody case kids. But he was still impressed by a real-life private dick. April said the term was sexist and called her a private clit.

'You know about the franchise auction?'

The independent television franchises, which granted a right to broadcast to the companies that made up the ITV network, were being renegotiated. There was currently much scurrying and scheming in the industry as everyone had to justify their existence or give way to someone else. There was controversy over the system, with criticism of the government decision that franchises be awarded to the highest bidder. The Independent Television Commission, the body with power of life and death over the network, had belatedly instituted a policy of partially assessing bids for quality of service rather than just totting up figures. In the run-up to the auction, battles raged up and down the country, with regional companies assailed by challengers. More money than anyone could believe was being poured into the franchise wars. A worry had been raised that the winners were likely to have spent so much on their bids they'd have nothing left over to spend on the actual programs.

'Mythwrhn is throwing in its hat,' Tiny said.

For an independent production company, no matter how financially solid, to launch a franchise bid on its own would be like Lichtenstein declaring war on Switzerland.

'We'll be the most visible element of a consortium. Polymer Records have kicked in, and Mausoleum Films.'

Both were like Mythwrhn, small but successful. Polymer used to be an indie label and now had the corner on the heavier metallurgists, notably the 'underground' cult band Loud Shit. Mausoleum distributed French art and American splatter; they were known for the *Where the Bodies Are Buried* series, although Sally knew they'd funnelled some of their video profits into British film production, yielding several high-profile movies she, along with vast numbers of other people, hadn't wanted to see.

'Deep pockets,' she commented, 'but not deep enough.'

Tiny snapped all his fingers. 'Very sharp, Sally. We have major financial backing, from a multi-media conglomerate who, for reasons of its own, can't be that open about their support. I'm talking newspapers, films and satellite.'

That narrowed it down considerably. To a face the size of a condom packet, in fact.

'We're contesting London, which puts us up against GLT. So it's not going to be a walk-over.'

Greater London Television was one of the keystones of the ITV net, long-established monolith with three shows in the ratings Top Ten, two quizzes and a soap. In television terms, it was, like its audience, middle-aged verging on early retirement. Mythwrhn had a younger demographic.

'I'd like you to be part of the bid,' Tiny said.

She was surprised. 'I'm not a programmer or an accountant.'

'Your special talents can be useful. We'll need a deal of specialised research. In wrapping our package, it'd be handy to have access to certain information. We need to know GLT's weaknesses to help us place our shots.'

This sounded very like industrial espionage. As a field, IE never appealed to Sally. Too much involved affording the client 'plausible deniability' and being paid off to sit out jail sentences.

'You'll keep your desk and your official credit on *Kit* but we'll gradually divert you to the real work. Interested?'

Thinking of the Muswell Hill DSS, she nodded. Tiny grinned wide and extended a hand, but was distracted by a ringing telephone. It was a red contraption aside from his three normal phones, suggesting a hot-line to the Kremlin or the Batcave.

Tiny scooped up the receiver, and said, 'Derek, good to hear from you...'

'Since the franchise *schmeer*,' April said, a drip of mayonnaise on her chin, 'the whole building has gone batty.'

Sally ate her half-bap in silence. She wasn't the only one diverted from usual duties and hustled off to secret meetings.

'They should put Valium dispensers in the loos.'

When the consortium announced their intention to contest London, GLT replied by issuing a complacent press release. Ronnie Shand, host of GLT's 'whacky' girls' bowling quiz *Up Your Alley*, made a joke about Tiny's ego in his weekly monologue. High-level execs were heaping public praise on programs made by their direst enemies. The dirty tricks had started when GLT, alone of the ITV net, pre-empted *Survival Kit* for a Royal Family special. As payback, Tiny had ordered Weepy Lydia to inflate a tedious offshore trust story involving several GLT board members into a majorly juicy scandal item. In the meantime, the best he could do was give five pounds to any office minion who called up the ITV duty officer and logged a complaint about a GLT show. It had the feel of a phoney war.

'Bender's wife chucked him out again last night,' April said. 'Found him writing silly letters to Pomme.'

Pomme was an eighteen-year-old p.a. who looked like a cross between Princess Diana and Julia Roberts. If it weren't for her Liza Doolittle accent, she'd have been easy to hate.

'He kipped in the basement of the building, blind drunk. Must have walked into a wall by the look of his face. I hope he keeps the scars.'

Six months before Sally joined the company, when April was young and naive, she had slept with Bender. It hadn't done either of them any good.

'Are you all right?'

People kept asking her that. Sally nodded vigorously. April touched her cheek, as if it'd enable her to take Sally's emotional temperature.

The funeral had been yesterday. Sally had sent a floral tribute but thought it best not to go. Connor's friends would think she was his aunt or someone. She had never met his parents and didn't especially want to.

From the sandwich shop, Sally saw the square. A knot of messengers hung about the gazebo, all in Lycra shorts and squiggly T-shirts. Sprawled on benches, they let long legs dangle as they worked pain out of their knees. Some, unlike Connor, had helmets like plastic colanders. Staff at Charing Cross Hospital had a nickname for Central London cycle messengers: organ donors. Scrapes and spills were an inevitable part of accelerated lives. And so was human wastage. Ironically, Connor had carried a donor card: He was buried without corneas and one kidney.

'Come on,' said April, looking at her pink plastic watch, 'back to the front...'

If she had doubts about the identity of the consortium's financial backer, they were dispelled by the front page of the *Comet*, tabloid flagship of Derek Leech's media empire. Ronnie Shand was caught in the glare of flash-bulbs, guiltily emerging from a hotel with a girl in dark glasses. The story, two hundred words of patented *Comet* prose, alleged *Up Your Alley* was fixed. Contestants who put out for Shand (51, married with three children) were far more likely to score a strike and take home a fridge-freezer or a holiday in Barbados. An inset showed Ronnie happy with his family in an obviously posed publicity shot. Inside the paper, the girl, an aspiring model, could be seen without clothes, a sidebar giving details about 'my sizzling nights with TV's family man'. Shand was unavailable for comment but GLT made a statement that *Up Your Alley* would be replaced by repeats of *Benny Hill* while an internal investigation was conducted. Sally wondered whether they'd investigate the allegations or witch-hunt their staff for the traitor who'd tipped off the *Comet*.

Tiny was a bundle of suppressed mirth at their meeting and chuckled to himself as she reported. She'd carried out a thorough, boring check of the finances of GLT's component parts, and discovered that profits from hit shows had been severely drained by a couple of disastrous international co-productions, *The Euro-Doctors* and *The Return of Jason King*. The interruption of *Up Your Alley* was a severe embarrassment. GLT must be hurting far more than their bland press releases suggested.

'If it comes to it, we can outspend the bastards,' Tiny said. 'We'll have to make sacrifices. Congratulations, Sally. I judge you well.'

There was something seductive about covert work. Setting aside moral qualms about the franchise system and relegating to a deep basement any idea of serving the viewing public, she could look at the situation and see any number of moves which would be to Mythwrhn's advantage. Taken as a game, it was compulsive. It being television, it was easy to believe no real people at all were affected by any action she might suggest or take.

'I've been looking at *Cowley Mansions*,' she said, referring to GLT's long-running thrice-weekly soap set in a Brixton block of flats. It was said GLT wouldn't lose their franchise because John Major didn't want to go down in history as the Prime Minister who took away the *Mansions*.

Tiny showed interest.

'I've not got paper back-up, but I heard a whisper that GLT took a second mortgage to finance *The Euro-Doctors* and put the *Mansions* on the block.'

'Explain.'

'To sucker in the Italians and the French, GLT threw in foreign rights to the *Mansions* with the deal. Also a significant slice of the domestic ad revenues for a fixed period.'

Tiny whistled.

'As you know, TéVéZé, the French co-producer, went bust at the beginning of the year and was picked up for a song by a British-based concern which turns out to be a subsidiary of Derek Leech Enterprises.'

Tiny sat up.

'If I were, say, Derek Leech, and I wanted to gain control of the *Mansions*, I think I could do it by upping my holdings in an Italian cable channel by only two percent, and by buying, through a third party, the studio and editing facilities GLT have currently put on the market to get fast cash. Years ago, in one of those grand tax write-off gestures, slices of the *Mansions* pie were given in name to those GLT sub-divisions, and when they separate from the parent company, the slices go too. Then, all I'd have to do to get a majority ownership would be to approach the production team and the cast and offer to triple salaries in exchange for their continued attachment. I might have to change the name of the program slightly, say by officially calling it *The Mansions*, to get round GLT's underlying rights.'

Tiny pulled open a drawer and took out a neat bundle of fifty-pound notes. He tossed it across his broad desk and it slid into Sally's lap.

'Buy yourself a frock,' he said.

In the lift, there was something wrong with a connection. The light-strip buzzed and flickered. Sally had a satisfaction high but also an undertone of nervous guilt. It was as if she had just taken part in a blood initiation and was now expected to serve forever the purpose of Kali the Destroyer.

As usual, there was nothing on television. She flicked through the four terrestrial channels: Noel Edmonds, tadpole documentary, Benny Hill (ha ha), putting-up-a-shelf. Like all Mythwrhn employees, she'd been fixed up with a dish *gratis* as a frill of the alliance with Derek Leech, so she zapped through an additional seven Cloud 9 satellite channels: bad new film, bad old film, Russian soccer, softcore in German, car ad, Chums commercial disguised as an AIDS documentary, shopping. After heating risotto, she might watch a *Rockford Files* from the stash she'd taped five years ago. James Garner was the only TV private eye she had time for: The fed-up expression he had whenever anyone got him in trouble was the keynote of her entire life.

The telephone rang. She scooped up the remote, pressing it between shoulder and ear as she manoeuvred around her tiny kitchen.

'Sally Rhodes,' she said. 'No divorce work.'

'Ah, um,' said a tiny voice, 'Miss, um, Ms, Rhodes. This is Eric Glover... Connor's Dad.'

She paused in mid-pour and set down the packet of spicy rice.

'Mr Glover, hello,' she said. 'I'm sorry I couldn't make...'

There was an embarrassed (embarrassing) pause.

'No, that's all right. Thank you for the flowers. They were lovely. I knew you were Connor's friend. He said things about you.'

She had no response.

'It's about the accident,' Eric Glover said. 'You were a witness?'

'No, I was there after.' When he was dead.

'There's a fuss about the insurance.'

'Oh.'

'They can't seem to find the van driver. Or the van.'

'It was overturned, a write-off. The police must have details.'

'Seems there was a mix-up.'

'It was just a delivery van. Sliding doors. I don't know the make.'

She tried to rerun the picture in her mind. She could see the dazed driver crawling out of the door, helped by a young man with a shaved head.

'I didn't suppose you'd know, but I had to ask.'

'Of course. If I remember...'

'No worry.'

There had been a logo on the side of the van. On the door.

'Good-bye now, and thanks again.'

Eric Glover hung up.

It had been a Mythwrhn logo, a prettified bird-woman. Or something similar. She was sure. The driver had been a stranger, but the van was one of the company's small fleet.

Weird. Nobody had mentioned it.

Water boiled over in the rice pan. Sally struggled with the knob of the gas cooker, turning the flame down.

A couple of calls confirmed what Eric Glover told her. It was most likely the van driver would be taken to Charing Cross, where Connor was declared dead, but the hospital had no record of his admission. It was difficult to find one nameless patient in any day's intake, but the nurse she spoke to remembered Connor without recalling anyone brought in at the same time. Sally had only seen the man for a moment: white male, thirties-forties, stocky-tubby, blood on his face. The production manager said none of the vans had been out that day and, yes, they were all garaged where they were supposed to be, and why are you interested? As she made more calls, checking possible hospitals and trying to find a policeman who'd filed an accident report, she fiddled with a loose strand of cardigan wool, resisting the temptation to tug hard and unravel the whole sleeve.

April had dumped her bag and coat on her chair but was not at her desk. That left Sally alone in her alcove, picking at threads when she should be following through the leads Tiny had given her. She had a stack of individual folders containing neatly typed allegations and bundles of photocopied 'evidence', all suggesting chinks in the Great Wall of GLT. The presenter of a holiday morning kid's show might have a conviction under another name for 'fondling' little girls. A hairy-chested supporting actor on *The Euro-Doctors*, considered to have 'spin-off potential' even after the failure of the parent series, was allegedly a major player in the Madrid gay bondage scene. And, sacrilegiously, it was suggested that the producer of a largely unwatched motoring program had orchestrated a write-in campaign to save it from cancellation. In case Sally wondered where these tid-bits came from, she'd already found an overlooked sticker with the DLE logo and a 'please return to the files of the *Comet*' message; checking other files, she found dust- and fluff-covered gluey circles that showed where similar stickers had been peeled off. So, apart from everything else, she was in charge of Tiny's Dirty Tricks Department. She wondered whether G. Gordon Liddy had got sick to his stomach. This morning, she had thrown up last night's risotto. She should have learned to cook.

Bender popped his head into the alcove. When he saw only her, his face fell.

'Have you seen Ape?'

'She was here,' Sally told him. 'She must be in the building.'

Bender looked as if he'd pulled a couple of consecutive twenty-four-hour shifts.

'No matter,' he said, obviously lying. 'This is for her.'

He gave her a file, which she found room for on her desk.

'She's not really supposed to have this, so don't leave it lying around. Give it to her personally.'

Bender, a tall man, never looked a woman in the face. His eyeline was always directed at her chest. In an awkward pause, Sally arranged her cardigan around her neck to cover any exposed skin. The associate producer was a balding schoolboy.

'We were all sorry about, um, you know...'

Sally thanked him, throat suddenly warm. She didn't know why Bender was loitering. Had April taken up with him again? Considering the vehemence of her comments, it was not likely. Or maybe it was.

'If you see... when you see Ape, tell her...'

There was definitely something weird going down. Bender really looked bad. His usual toadying smoothness was worn away. He had an angry red mark on his ring-finger. It had probably had to be sawn free, and serve him right.

'Tell her to return the files a.s.a.p. It's important.'

When he left, she decided to try work therapy. A minion named Roebuck was reputedly interested in being bribed to let Mythwrhn peek at GLT's post-franchise proposals. He'd contacted Tiny, and it was down to her to check his standing. Being suspicious, she guessed Roebuck was her opposite number in GLT's Spook Dept trying to slip the consortium dud information. She only had a name, and she wanted an employment history. There were several people she could phone and—since everyone in television had at some point worked for, or at least applied to work for, everyone else—her first obvious choice was Mythwrhn's own personnel manager. If he had Roebuck's *c.v.* on file, it might have clues as to his contacts or loyalties.

As she bent over in her chair to reach her internal directory from her bottom drawer, her stomach heaved. Gulping back sick, she hurried to the Ladies.

One loo was occupied but the other was free. Apart from a mid-morning cup of tea, there was nothing to come up but clear fluid. It wasn't much of a spasm and settled down almost immediately. She washed her face clean and started to rebuild her make-up. The lighting in the Ladies was subdued and the decor was off, walls covered in wavy lumps like an ice cave. She supposed it had been designed to prevent loitering.

Pomme came in for a pee. She greeted Sally cheerfully, and, after a quick and painless tinkle, chatted as she made a kiss-mouth and retouched her lips.

'That bleedin' door is stuck again,' Pomme said, nodding at the occupied stall. 'Or someone has been in there for a two hour crap.'

Sally looked at the shut door. There was no gap at the bottom to show feet.

'Have you noticed how that happens in this building?' Pomme said. 'Doors lock when you ain't lookin', or come unlocked. The lifts have lay-overs in the Twilight Zone. Even them security keys don't work most of the time. Must be bleedin' haunted.'

The p.a. left, her face requiring considerably less help than Sally's. Finally, Sally was satisfied. She put her make-up things back in her bag. Turning to leave, she heard a muttering.

'Hello,' she asked the closed door.

There was a fumbling and the 'occupied' flag changed. The door pulled inwards.

'April,' she said, looking.

The woman lolled on the closed toilet, eyes fluttering. She'd had a bad nosebleed and her man's dress shirt was bloodied. The bottom half of her face was caked with dried blood and flecked with white powder. Sally hadn't known she did coke. Or that things could get so bad with a supposedly 'fun' drug. April tried to speak but could only gargle. She pinched her nose and winced, snorting blood.

Sally wondered if she should get two tampons from the dispenser and shove them up April's nose. Instead, she wet a paper towel and tried to clean April's face. Her friend was as compliant as an exhausted three-year-old. Most of the blood was sticky on the floor of the stall.

'Pressure,' April said, over and over, repeating the word like a mantra. 'Pressure, pressure, pressure...'

Sally wondered how she was going to get April out of the building and home without anyone noticing. She told April to stay while she went and got her coat and bag. When she came back, April was standing and almost coherent.

'Sal,' she said, smiling as if she hadn't seen her for days, 'things are just fine up here. Except for...'

Sally tried to put April's hat on her, but she wasn't comfortable and kept tilting it different ways, examining herself in the mirror. Her shoulders heaved as if she alone could hear music and wanted to dance. Sally settled the coat around April's shoulders and steered her out of the loo.

The lift was on the floor, so she was able to get April straight in. If she could get her down to Reception and out into the square and find a cab, she could say April was taken ill. A nasty gynaecological problem would go unquestioned. Those were mysteries men didn't want to penetrate.

She stabbed the ground floor button and the doors closed. If they got quickly past Heidi, she could limit the damage. But the lift was going up, she realised. To the Penthouse. April was almost writhing now, and chanting 'pressure, pressure, pressure' until the word lost all meaning.

She slipped an arm around April's waist and tried to hold her still. April laughed as if tickled and a half-moustache of blood dribbled from one nostril. The doors parted and Tiny got in. He was hunched over in an unfamiliar position of subservience, grinning with desperate sincerity as he looked up to his companion. The other man, a human reptile of indeterminate age and indistinct features, was someone Sally recognised from the front of a condom packet.

'Sally, April,' Tiny said, so overwhelmed by his master's presence that he didn't notice their state, 'have you met Derek?'

Sally prayed to be teleported to Japan. The magnate, who kept going in and out of focus as if it were unwise to look at him with the naked eye, smiled a barracuda smile that seemed to fill the lift. She'd always thought of Derek Leech as a James Bond villain, with a high-tech hide-out in an extinct volcano and a missile silo concealed beneath his glass pyramid HQ in London Docklands. A human spider at the heart of a multi-media web, he sucked unimaginable monies from the millions who bought his papers, watched his television, made love with his protection, voted for his bought-and-paid-for politicians. But in person, he was just another well-groomed suit.

Leech nodded at them. Sally tried a weak smile, and April, snorting back blood and residual traces of nose powder, radiated warmth and love before fainting. She slithered through Sally's grasp and collapsed on the floor, knees bunched up against her breasts.

'That's happened before,' Leech said. 'Embarrassing, really.'

Three days into April's 'leave', Bender went up to the Penthouse while Tiny was out recording an interview about the franchise bid. After voiding his bowels on Tiny's granite-slab desk-top and hurling the Mythwrhn statuette through the picture window, he crawled out through shattered glass and stood on the narrow sill while a crowd gathered below. Then, flapping his arms like the failed Wright Brother, he tried to fly over Soho Square. Ten yards from the persistent smear that marked the site of Connor's death, Bender fell to asphalt, neck broken.

It had not been unexpected, somehow. Sally noticed that people were marginally less shocked and surprised by Bender than they'd been by Connor. The office had a wartime feel; the troops kept their heads down and tried not to know too much about their comrades. Everyone secretly looked for jobs somewhere else.

Roger the Replacement went into hospital after a severe angina attack. He was thirty-eight. While he was away, his wife came to clear out his things and told Sally that he now planned to take a year off to consider his career options.

'What's the point,' the woman said. 'If he's dead, he can't spend it.'

'True,' she conceded.

Tiny took to wandering around chewing his moustache, checking and double-checking everyone's work. Still wrapped up 101% in the franchise bid, he suddenly became acutely aware that Mythwrhn's current product would influence the ITC decision. The consequences of being blamed for failure would be unthinkable. Off to one side on 'other projects', she was spared the worst, but the *Survival Kit* team suffered badly from the sudden attack of caution. Items toiled on for months were suddenly dropped, wasting hundreds of hours; others, rejected out of hand, were re-activated, forcing researchers to redo work that had been binned. In one case, the company was brought very close to Lawsuit County as a hastily slapped-together exposé of dangerous toys named a blatantly innocent designer rather than the shoddy manufacturer.

'I blame Derek Leech,' Useless Bruce said out loud in the meeting room as they waited for an unconscionably late Tiny.

'Shush,' Lydia Marks said, 'this place is probably bugged.'

'Tiny's completely hung up on the bid and *Kit* is suffering. Plus Leech has this Mephistopheles effect, you know. I swear reality bends wherever he stands.'

There were mumbles of agreement, including Sally's. There was something else she blamed Derek Leech for, considering the reputation of his products. She thought she was pregnant.

First, her doctor congratulated her in the spirit of female solidarity; then, interpreting her blank expression, she dug out a leaflet and said that at Sally's advanced age, she could probably justify an abortion on health grounds. So it was official: Thirty-five was 'advanced'. Also, Sally was unmistakably 'with child'. She wondered whether her mother would be pleased. And whether she could stand another upheaval.

There wasn't time to talk with Dr Frazier, since she had to rush from the Women's Clinic to a meet with the GLT Deep Throat. Miraculously, Nick Roebuck seemed to be a genuine defector. He wanted old-fashioned money and a shot at a position with the consortium if and when they took over the franchise. Someone reputedly sharp who knew GLT from the inside was convinced enough the consortium were going to win to gamble his career on it. That should be good news for Mythwrhn.

In the cab, Sally held her belly as if she had a stomach ache, trying to feel the alien lodged in her. A tiny Connor, perhaps, dribbled through a ruptured Chum? Or a little Sally, worm-shaped but an incipient woman? Half the time she thought her body had betrayed her; then she was almost won round by the possibilities. All her contemporaries who were going to have babies had already done so. She'd be the last of her generation to give in.

Roebuck had arranged to meet her at a sawdust-on-the-floor pub in Islington, well off the media beat. The cab cruised Upper Street, looking for the sign.

Sally had seen hard-edged women turn mushy-gooey upon producing a baby. She wondered if she'd ever even met a child she liked, let alone whether she was a fit mother. She corrected herself: fit single mother. Christ, should she even tell Connor's parents? There was some of their son left after all. Did she want to invite those strangers into her life, give them a part of her baby?

The cab drew up outside the pub and she paid the driver. Inside, a few glum men were absorbed in their pints. It was mid-afternoon and beer was half-price to the unwaged. She supposed they called it 'the miserable hour'. A country and western song on the juke-box proclaimed 'If They Didn't Have Pussy, There'd Be a Bounty on Their Pelts'.

She spotted Roebuck at once, at a corner table. Shiny of suit and face, scalp red and glistening under thin strands of cross-combed blond hair. Apart from the barmaid, Sally was the only woman in the pub. She let Roebuck buy her a Perrier (until she decided what to do about the baby, she was off the gin) and listened to him gibber inconsequentially as he fiddled with the satchel he'd brought the papers in. He was nervous to the point of terror, as if he expected GLT shock troops in black balaclavas to burst in and execute him.

'May I?' she said, reaching for the goods. 'Just a taste.'

Roebuck looked appalled.

'It could be old copies of the *Independent*,' she explained.

Reluctantly, he handed over. The satchel was almost a schoolkid's accessory, not at all like the slimly imposing briefcases common in the business.

'I trust this'll go in my favour,' Roebuck said.

'I'm sure the consortium will do well by you.'

She looked at a few sheets. There were authentic audience figures, with alarmed notes scrawled in the margins. A couple of thick documents marked 'HIGHLY CONFIDENTIAL' outlined proposed changes in GLT production and transmission schedules. Without a close examination, she guessed the purpose was to cut short-term production costs to cover the losses GLT would sustain ponying up for a winning bid. She was almost satisfied to find a confidential memo from the board, insisting the company try to buy back its squandered percentages of *Cowley Mansions* before a raider took over completely.

'This seems to be in order,' she said.

Roebuck nodded, face burning. Palpable desperation sweated off the man. He gripped the table to prevent his hands shaking. Sally wondered how low the consortium's unseen campaign would get. Roebuck had looked around throughout the meeting, as if searching for a familiar face.

'It'll stop now,' he said. 'Won't it?'

'I don't know what you mean.'

Disgust bulged through fear for a moment and he got up, barging out of the pub, leaving her with the satchel. A couple of others left almost immediately.

She gathered the papers. She'd win untold brownie points for this coup, but didn't know how much of it was her doing. As she left, she noticed an almost-full pint abandoned on a table by the door. The man who'd sat there had struck her as familiar. Broad, undistinguished, in overalls. With a spine-scrape of fear, she wondered whether he might be the van driver.

Out in the street, she couldn't see Roebuck or the nondescript drinker who could have been following him. So much to think about. She looked for another cab.

A man in a suit was dismantling April's desk, sorting through every scrap of paper and odd object in its tardis drawers. April had a system whereby every unwanted freebie and done-with document was shoved into a drawer until it disappeared. Tiny was either overseeing the job or ordered to be present at the dissection. The suit worked like a callous surgeon, calmly incising closed envelopes and packets. Sally wondered whether he was from the drug squad.

'This is Mr Quilbert,' Tiny said, 'our new security manager.'

Quilbert smiled and shook her hand limply. She instantly pegged him as a cuckoo slipped into the Mythwrhn nest by Derek Leech. He had one of those close-to-the-skull haircuts that disguise premature baldness with designer style.

'We've lost an important file,' Tiny said. 'Bender might have given it to April.'

'I didn't think they were talking,' she said. 'Well, not recently.'

'Nothing scary,' Quilbert said, 'just stats about the building. There was a security survey in there.'

'We can get a copy from the consultants,' Tiny said, 'but it'd be embarrassing.'

Quilbert slit open a packet and slid out a pornographic magazine in Hungarian.

'That's from one of last year's items,' Tiny said. Quilbert smiled tightly and dumped it on the pile.

'Have you tried asking April?' she suggested.

'A bit tricky,' Tiny said. 'She's had a relapse. They've had to put her under restraint.'

She took the file, which she'd sincerely forgotten about, home, hoping it might help her understand the tangle of mysteries. Besides, an evening poring through arcane security lore seemed more comfortable than an evening phoning her mother and announcing a compromised 'blessed event'.

There was a new security guard, in a black one-piece bodysuit, installed in Reception, presumably on Quilbert's orders. She was sure his X-Ray vision would perceive the documents she was smuggling out, but he was too busy trying to cosy up to Heidi. That hardly suggested fearsome efficiency.

She made herself tea and sat on her sofa, television on but with the sound down. The file Bender had given her for April was tied with red ribbon. She let it lie a moment and drank her tea. On the screen, an interracial couple argued their way to a cliffhanging climax on *Cowley Mansions*. The soap's storylines had become increasingly bizarre: Peter, the gay yuppie, was discovered to be 'pregnant', a long-unborn twin developing inside his abdomen; Joko, the cool black wastrel, was revealed to be a white boy with permanently dyed skin, hiding out; and Ell Crenshaw, the cockney matriarch who ruled the top floor, spontaneously combusted the week the actress demanded a vast salary hike. Either the writers saw a Leech take-over as inevitable and were devaluing the property before the new landlord arrived, or GLT had ordered audience-grabbing sensationalism in the run-up to the auction.

After the soap came a commercial for the serialisation of Josef Mengele's Auschwitz diaries in the *Argus*, Leech's heavy paper. Then a caring, sensitive ad for Chums.

Sally undid the ribbon and didn't find a security survey. The first item was familiar: A glossy Mythwrhn press release, dated three years ago, about the redesign of their Soho Square premises. She paged through and found quotes from critics praising the features of the building that now drove people mad. The brochure also profiled Constant Drache, the award-winning architect entrusted with the commission. He'd been an unknown until Derek Leech chose him to construct the DLE pyramid, the black glass creation that now dominated Docklands. In a broody shot, Drache posed in black like the lead singer of a Goth group. A wedge of gibberish about his intentions with the building was printed white on black. It was silly, considering that a lot of Drache's 'severe edges' were now best known for ripping the clothes of passing people, but hardly worth Quilbert's search-and-destroy mission. Drache referred to buildings as 'devices', insisting each have its own purpose and be designed to concentrate 'human energies' towards the fulfilment of that purpose. Cathedrals, for instance, were designed to concentrate prayer upwards. Sally wondered what low ceilings and floor-level lighting were supposed to concentrate you towards, and, before she could stop herself, guessed Bender had probably worked it out.

She zapped to the Leech channel and found a scary scene from one of the *Where the Bodies Are Buried* sequels. A teenager screamed silently as Hackwill, the monster, slashed him with a cake-slice.

Under the brochure was a clipped-together batch of articles from a psychology journal. April hadn't abandoned her 'sick building syndrome' idea, or at least had got Bender to retrieve materials from the files before Tiny pulled the plug. Sally skimmed until her head hurt with jargon. Respectable psychology segued into the *Fortean Times* and even weirder quarters. She found pieces, with significant passages underlined in violet, on 'curses' and 'hauntings'.

The television monster laughed loud enough to be heard even with the sound down. The camera pulled back from a graveyard through which a girl was running to reveal that the tilted tombstones constituted a giant face.

The last items were thin strips of word-processed news copy. A fine print tag at the bottom of each page identified the copy as having been generated for the *Comet*. Sally guessed that for a tabloid these pieces would constitute a heavyweight Sunday section article. She read them through, recognising the style and concerns of the Leech press. Dated a year ago, the article a celebrated major police infiltration of a nest of Satanic Child-Abusers. Naming a few names, the piece was about decadent high-society types turning to black magic to advance themselves. A 23-year-old stockbroker was purported to have made a million on Market Tips From Hell. A top model, who'd doubtless have posed nude for the illo, claimed drinking goat blood landed her international assignments.

It was typical *Comet* drivel but had never appeared in the paper. Each strip of prose was individually stamped in red with a large 'NO' design that contained, in tiny letters, the initials 'DL'. She supposed this was Leech's personal veto. Why hadn't the piece appeared? It seemed a natural for the *Comet*. So, most likely, Leech had an interest in its suppression. She read everything through again and found it. The reference in the copy was to the '£3.5 million modern home' which was the gathering point for the cult. In the margin, in faded pencil that looked as if it had been almost rubbed out, were the words 'Drache Retreat'.

'Where's the goon?' Sally asked Heidi. The security man wasn't at his post.

'Caught his hand in the lift,' the receptionist said. 'Dozens of little bones broken.'

Sally raised an eyebrow. A workman was examining the lift door, screw-drivers laid out on a dustcloth like surgical instruments.

'There was blood all over the floor. Disgusting.'

Carefully, she climbed the stairs, trying keep her elbows away from Drache's 'severe edges'. If the architect had chosen to inset razor-blades into all the walls, the effect might have been more obvious.

The *Survival Kit* offices were depopulated. Pomme told her that everyone was off with a bout of the 'flu. Pomme's perfect complexion was marred by eruptions.

'Bleedin' worry, I reckon,' she said, scratching her blood-dotted chin.

April's desk had been put together again but was stripped clean. There was a padded envelope on Sally's desk, with her name printed on it. She opened it and found a bundle of £20 notes. There was no 'compliments' slip.

She took a giant-size bag of Kettle Chips out of her case and, after a furtive glance-around, ate them rapidly, one by one. She was eating for two. The cash was for Roebuck's papers, she understood. A bonus, blood money.

She had just scrunched up the crisp packet and buried it in her waste-bin when Pomme slid her head into the alcove.

'Remember Streaky?' she said, referring to the office cat who'd disappeared three months ago.

Sally nodded.

'The lift-repair man just found the bones at the bottom of the shaft. Ugh.'

All the black magicians she knew were dead, which was not something she usually found upsetting. She couldn't ask anyone to explain things to her. Nevertheless, she thought she'd worked it out.

It was possible to climb past the Penthouse and get onto the roof. The original idea had been to make it a party area but Drache insisted on a rubbery-leathery species of covering that made the slight slope dangerously slippery.

Sally sat carefully and looked out at Soho Square, thinking. Her hair was riffled by the slight breeze. She wished she had more crisps. Down in the world, the organ donors were waiting to be sent out. Today, things had ground to a halt in the business. It was an Armistice, a pause before the *putsch* of the franchise auction. Thousands would go under the mud in that armageddon, leaving the map of Media London dotted with crushed corpses.

It was almost peaceful. Above the building, she felt a calm which was elusive inside it. The knot of worry which she'd got used to eased away.

'Chim-chim-a-nee,' she hummed. 'Chim-chim-a-nee, chim-chim-cha -roo...'

She decided she'd have her baby. And she'd leave Mythwrhn. There, two decisions and her life was solved.

Hours might have passed. The sun came out from behind a cloud and the roof heated. Should she give her blood bonus away? She'd been taking tainted money so long, she might as well keep this too. Soon she'd have to buy cribs and baby-clothes and nappies. Leech's money was no worse than anyone else's.

A few of the rubberised tiles nearby had been dislodged, and a dull metal was exposed. Beneath was a thick layer of lead, its surface covered in apparently functionless runes. She assumed they were symbolic. She picked free a few further tiles, disclosing more and more lead plates, all etched with hieroglyphs, incantations, invocations.

It confirmed what she had guessed. A cathedral was designed to direct upwards; the Mythwrhn Building was designed to capture and contain. In psychic terms, it was earthed. She hoped she wasn't succumbing to the New Age now that life was developing inside her. But for the past few months, she had worked among enough negative energy to blacken anybody's crystal.

No wonder everyone in Mythwrhn was miserable. They were supposed to be. Misery was the cake, she supposed; all the blood was icing. Drache's Design must extend under the pavement into the street, to catch the drippings from Connor. If Bender had jumped from the roof rather than the Penthouse, would he have escaped?

The Device worked like a scale. All the misery weighed one pan down, thrusting the other upwards. She could guess who would be sitting on the other pan. And what the uplift was for.

Under her crossed legs, the building thrummed with pent-up unhappiness. She was above it all. At once, she was centred. In her condition, she had power.

Over the years, she'd collected a library, mainly by ordering from the Amok Bookstore in Los Angeles, which was dedicated to 'extremes of information in print'. She skipped past William B. Moran's *Covert Surveillance and Electronic Penetration*, G.B. Clark's *How to Get Lost and Start All Over Again* and Colonel Rex Applegate's *Kill or Get Killed: For Police and the Military, Last Word on Mob Control*, paused for an amused flick through one of John Minner's seven-volume *How to Kill* series, then selected Kurt Saxon's *The Poor Man's James Bond*.

Saxon, an extreme right-winger and authority on explosives, had authored a guide for the defence of the USA in the event of a Russian invasion, compiling information on sabotage, home-made weaponry and sundry guerrilla tactics. Although Saxon declared himself 'very pro-establishment and pro-law enforcement' and that he would 'not knowingly sell his more sensitive books to any left-wing group or individual', given the ever-decreasing likelihood of a Soviet invasion, the only conceivable purpose of his work was as a manual for the criminal.

Along with more conservative texts—Seymour Lecker's *Deadly Brew: Advanced Improvised Explosives*, the CIA's *Field Expedient Methods for Explosives Preparations*—Saxon's book gave Sally a wide variety of recipes to consider. She made a shopping list and went out to the chemist's, a DIY shop, a tobacconist's, Sainsbury's and Rumbelow's to buy the easily available ingredients she now knew how to convert into a functioning infernal device. The most hard-to-obtain items were the steel buckets in which she wanted to place her home-made bombs, to direct the blasts upwards. Everyone had plastic these days.

She was in her kitchen, attempting to distil a quantity of picric acid from ten bottles of aspirin, when her mother telephoned to see how she was getting on.

'I'm cooking, Mum.'

'That's nice, dear. Having a guest for dinner?'

'No, just practicing.'

'What's in the buckets?' Heidi asked.

'Live crabs,' she claimed. 'We're doing an item on the crooked pet racket.'

'Ugh.'

'You're telling me.'

The security guard was back at his post, hand mittened with plaster. Sally held up a bucket and he avoided looking into it.

'Careful,' she warned, 'the little bastards don't half nip.'

She was nodded through. On her lunch-hour she went back to Muswell Hill to fetch the other two buckets from her flat and went through the whole thing again.

That afternoon, there was enough blast-power under her desk to raise the roof. She hoped.

There was a confab going on up in the Penthouse, a long-term post-franchise planning session. Sally would have to wait until everyone left. The idea of detonating some of the consortium along with the building was tempting, but she was more likely to get away with what she intended if no one was hurt. If the roof was blown off the Device, the energy should dissipate. She couldn't bring Connor or Bender back or restore April's mind or Pomme's complexion, but she could spoil the nasty little scheme.

As the afternoon dragged on, she pretended to work. She ate three packets of Kettle Chips, shuffled papers around on the desk, phoned people back. She guessed this would be her last day. It'd be a shame to do without the leaving party and the whip-round present. She'd probably have qualified for paid maternity leave, too. Actually, she'd be lucky to stay out of jail.

She had the idea, however, that Leech would not want her talking too much about the motive for her terrorist atrocity. A *Comet* think piece about how pregnancy drives women up the walls wouldn't serve to explain away her loud resignation notice.

The few *Kit* staff around drifted off about tea-time. Pomme invited her out for a drink, but Sally said she wanted to get something finished before leaving.

'You look a bit peaky, Sal,' Pomme said. 'You should get a good night's kip.'

Sally agreed.

'You've been driven to smoking?'

There was a packet of cigarettes on her desk. Sally coughed and smiled.

'Your face looks better, Pomme.'

'Fuckin' tell me about it, Sal.'

The girl shrugged and left. Sally realised she'd miss some of the others. Even Useless Bruce. She'd never worked much with people before, and there were nice things about it. From now on, she'd be alone again. Perhaps she would re-start the Agency.

Alone in the office as it got dark outside, she ate more crisps, made herself tea and sat at her desk with a new-bought occult paperback. She gathered that the building was a magical pressure cooker and the accumulation of 'melancholy humours' was a species of sacrifice, a way of getting someone else to pay your infernal dues. It was capitalist black magic, getting minions to pay for the spell in suffering while the conjurers got ahead on other people's sweat. Obviously, some people would do *anything* to get a television franchise. Since catching on, she had been noticing more and more things about the Mythwrhn Building: symbols worked into the design like the hidden cows and lions in a 'How Many Animals Can You See in This Picture?' puzzle; spikes and hooks deliberately placed to be hostile to living inhabitants; numerical patterns in steps, windows and corners.

Sally divided the cigarettes into five sets of three. Pinching off the filters, she connected each of the sets into six-inch-long tubes, securing the joins with extra layers of roll-up paper. Then she dripped lighter fluid, letting the flammable liquid seep through the tobacco cores. One test fuse she stood up in a lump of Blu-Tack and lit. It took over five minutes to burn down completely. Long enough.

At eight o'clock, she put an internal call up to the Penthouse and let it ring. After an age, Tiny's answering machine cut in asking her to leave a message. She double-checked by opening a window in the office and leaning out as far as possible into the well, looking up. No light spilled out of the Penthouse.

The lift was still out of order, so she had to take the works up the stairs. First she went up and circumvented the suite's personal alarm. With some deft fiddling and her electronic key, she got the doors open. The Penthouse was dark and empty. It took three quick trips to get everything into Tiny's office, and she arranged it all on his desk, working by the streetlight.

She felt ill. Since realising what was going on, she'd been more sensitive to the gloom trapped within the walls of the Mythwrhn Building. It was a miasma. The water in the pipes smelled like blood.

Had Bender been trying to break the Device when he smashed the windows? If so, he'd made a mistake.

There was a hatch directly above the desk, just where it was indicated on the plans she'd borrowed. Above would be a crawlspace under the lead shield. She put a chair and the now-untenanted statuette stand on the desk, making a rough arrangement of steps, and climbed up to the ceiling. A good thump dislodged the hatch and she stuck her head into smelly dark.

She'd assumed this was where all the energies would gather. The cavity didn't feel any worse than the rest of the building and she had a moment of doubt. Was this really crazy?

After ferrying up the four buckets and the other stuff, she jammed through into the crawlspace. Here she could turn on the bicycle lamp Connor had left in her flat. She shone the beam around. She almost expected to find screaming skeletons and the remains of blood sacrifices, but the cavity was surprisingly clean. Meccano struts shored up the lead shield and criss-crossed the plastered ceiling. There was a slope to the roof, so the crawlspace grew from a two-foot height at the street edge of the building to four feet at the rear. If she placed her buckets near the rear end, the blast should neatly slide off the lead shield and dump it into the square. With luck, not on the heads of innocent passersby.

She crawled carefully but still opened her palm on a protruding nail. The floor was studded with spikes, either one of Drache's devilish frills or a defensive feature. Crouching at the rear of the building, she pushed up, testing the shield. It was unresisting. Prominent bolts were spaced around the walls. With a monkey-wrench, she loosened as many as she could reach. She banged her elbows constantly and skinned her right knuckles. Her hair was stuck to her face by sweat. This was not usually prescribed for expectant mothers.

With enough bolts loosened, she tried to push the shield again. It creaked alarmingly and shifted. Sally found she was shaking. She thought she could almost dislodge the lead without the bombs. But it was best to be safe.

She'd hoped the joists would be wooden, so she could screw in hooks to hang the buckets from. However, the metal struts came equipped with handy holes, so she was able to rig up the hanging bombs with stout wire. In each bucket of packed-down goo, she'd used Sexton's recommended dosage for disabling a Russian tank. She stuck the long cigarettes in each bucket and flicked a flame from her disposable lighter.

Once the fuses were burning, she intended to get down to her desk and alert the skeleton overnight staff. She'd say she'd seen smoke pouring down the stairs. With five minutes, she should be able to evacuate the building.

She lit the four cigarettes and wriggled back towards the hatch. Down in the Penthouse, lights came on and voices exclaimed surprise. Knowing she was dead, she dangled her legs through the hatch and dropped into the office.

'What, no Leech?' she said.

Tiny was between the others, shaking and pale. The Device had been eating at him as much as his employees. Sally guessed he was only in the consortium as a Judas goat.

Quilbert was in charge, Drache was along for the ride, and the non-descript man holding Tiny up was the muscle. He was also the van-driver who'd knocked down Connor and the balls-squeezer who'd pressured Roebuck. He looked more like a plumber than Satan's Hit Man.

'Ms Rhodes, what are you doing?' Quilbert asked.

'Raising the roof.'

Tiny shook his head and sagged into his chair. Drache strode around the office, examining his handiwork. He had a black leather trench coat and showy wings of hair like horns.

'The stand should be here,' he said, pointing to the dust-free spot where it had stood. 'For the proper balance. Everything is supposed to be exact. How often have I told you, the patterns are all-important?'

Quilbert nodded to the muscle, who clambered onto the desk and stuck his head into the crawlspace.

'Smells like she's been smoking,' he said.

'It's a secret,' she said. 'I quit but backslid. I have to take extreme measures to cover up.'

'I think I can see... *buckets?*'

Quilbert looked at Sally as if trying to read her mind. 'What have you done?'

'I've forestalled the Device,' she said. 'It was all wasted.'

Quilbert's clear blue eyes were unreadable.

'Only an innocent can intervene,' Drache said pompously. 'You've taken blooded coin.'

'He's right,' Quilbert said. 'You don't understand at all. Everything has been pre-arranged.'

'Not everything,' she said. 'I'm going to have a baby.'

Drache looked stricken but Quilbert and Tiny didn't get it. She supposed they found it all as hard to believe as she did.

'There's something burning,' a voice mumbled from above. 'In the buckets...'

Drache flew around in a cold rage.

'If she's carrying a child, she's washed clean,' he said, urgently. 'It'll upset the balances.'

'What have you done?' Quilbert asked.

Sally smiled. 'Wouldn't you like to know?'

'Put out the fires,' Quilbert shouted up, 'at once!'

She should tell them not to tamper with the buckets in case the burning fuses fell. For the sake of her child, she couldn't die.

'Careful,' she said...

The ceiling burst and a billow of flame shot into the office, flattening everyone. A dead human shape thumped onto the desk, covered in burning jelly. Sally's ears were hammered by the blast. The stench of evaporating goo was incredible. Metal wrenched and complained. Hot rivets rained onto the fitted carpet. She heard screaming. A raft of steel and plaster bore down on Quilbert and Tiny. The windows had blown out, and the air was full of flying shards, glinting and scratching. She felt a growing power deep inside her and knew she would survive.

The cloud of flame burned away almost instantly, leaving little fires all around. Drache stumbled, a bloody hand stuck to half his face, and sank to his knees, shrieking. Sally was flat on her back, looking up at the ceiling. She saw night sky and felt the updraft as the accumulated misery of months escaped to the Heavens like prayers.

They kept her in hospital for weeks. Not the same one as Drache and Quilbert, who were private, and certainly not in the department that had received the still officially unidentified van-driver. She only had superficial injuries, but in her condition the doctors wanted to be careful with her.

She read the media pages every day, following the ripples. In the week before the auction, the consortium fell apart. Mausoleum Pictures, wildly over-extended, went bust, bringing down yet another fifth of the British Film Industry. Tiny promised that *Survival Kit* would be back as soon as he was walking, but he'd have to recruit a substantially new staff since almost everyone who had worked in the now-roofless Mythwrhn Building was seeking employment elsewhere. Most wanted to escape from television altogether and find honest work.

The police had interviewed her extensively but she pled amnesia, pretending to be confused about what had happened just before the 'accident'. No charges against her were even suggested. Mythwrhn even continued to pay her salary even though she'd given notice. After the baby, she would not be returning.

Derek Leech, never officially involved in the consortium, said nothing, and his media juggernaut rolled on unhindered by its lack of a controlling interest in a franchise. GLT, somewhat surprised, scaled down their bid and fought off a feeble challenge at auction time, promising to deliver to the British Public the same tried-and-tested program formulae in ever-increasing doses. On *Cowley Mansions*, Peter the gay yuppie had a son-brother and, salary dispute over, the ghost of Ell Crenshaw possessed her long-lost sister.

Apart from the van-driver and Drache, who lost an eye, nobody had really been punished. But none of them benefited from the Device either. All the gathered misery was loose in the world.

The day before she was due out, April and Pomme visited. April was taking it 'one day at a time', and Pomme had discovered a miracle cure. They brought a card signed by everybody on *Survival Kit* except Tiny.

The women cooed over Sally's swollen stomach, and she managed not to be sickened. She felt like a balloon with a head and legs, and nothing she owned, except her nightie, fit any more.

She told them she'd have to sell the flat and get a bigger one or a small house. She'd need more living space. That, she had learned, was important.

SEVEN STARS

Prologue: In Egypt's Land

All Thebes, all *Egypt*, was filled with the stench. Pai-net'em had bound up his head with linen, bandaging nose and mouth as if wrapping himself for interment. The stench got through, filling his nostrils and throat, curling his tongue.

His eyes were swollen almost shut by weeping boils. Insects clumped around his bloody tears, regathering every time he wiped them away. Eggs laid in the gum around his eyes hatched hourly. New-born flies chewed with tiny teeth.

Progress through the city was slow. The roads were filled with the dead, animals and men. Darkness was relieved only by the spreading fires. Most of the people were too concerned with private griefs to lend their hands to fighting the flames.

Truly, this was the time of calamities.

A priest, a man of science, Pharaoh's closest advisor, he was brought as low as a leper. He could not hold in his mind all that had happened in the last month. Looking at the mottled swellings and punctures on his body, he could not tell the marks of sickness from insect bites, even from the scars left by hailstones.

The Gods must hate Egypt, to let this happen.

Pai-net'em could not number the dead of his household. His grief had been spent on lesser catastrophes, sickening cattle and rioting slaves. Now, with brother and son struck down, his wife dead by her own hand, servants' corpses strewn like stones about his estates, he had no more grief, no more feeling, in him.

A stream of blood trickled past Pharaoh's Palace. Tiny frogs hopped in the reddened water. A living carpet—millions of locusts, flies and gnats—covered the streets, slowly reducing the fallen to skeletons. Insects assaulted the feet of those like Pai-net'em who waded perversely about, fixed like stars on their own courses.

The guards lay dead at their posts, wavering masks of flies on their faces. Pai-net'em passed through the open doors. Even here, inside Pharaoh's house, insects swarmed and gnawed. With the crops and the cattle blasted, many more would die of famine even after the darkness abated.

Lightning was striking all through the city.

Pai-net'em found Pharaoh in his morning room, hunched on his day-bed, face as swollen and distorted as the lowest slave's. The great were not spared; indeed, Pharaoh seemed to suffer more than his subjects, for he had far more to lose. If all who lived under him were obliterated, his name would pass from memory.

The old Pharaoh had done much to preserve his name, built many temples, left many writings. This younger man, so addicted to luxury that he neglected public works, had taken to having his name inscribed on tablets over those of his predecessors. It was a desperate act, a cry against the advance of oblivion.

'Pai-net'em,' Pharaoh said, mouth twisting, tongue swollen. 'What has brought these curses upon Egypt?'

Pai-net'em found he did not have the strength to rise from his kneeling position.

'The Israelites claim responsibility, sire.'

'The *Israelites?* The conquered people?'

'Yes. They say their God has visited his wrath upon Egypt.'

Pharaoh's eyes widened.

'Why?'

'They are a sorcerous people. But their claims are fatuous. They have but one God, a child beside our Gods.'

'This is not the work of the Gods.'

Pai-net'em agreed with Pharaoh.

'We both know what is at the bottom of this.'

'You have it here, sire?' Pai-net'em asked.

Pharaoh got off his day-bed, flies falling from his robes. Blood streaked his legs. His chest was sunken, his skin rubbed raw or bloated with sickness.

Pai-net'em stood, coughing fluid into his mouth-linen.

Pharaoh opened a wooden box. The darkness of the morning room was assaulted by red light. Pai-net'em remembered the first time he had seen the glow. Then, Pharaoh had been slim and swift and powerful. And he had been secure in his own health, his position.

Bravely, Pharaoh took the object out of the box. It seemed as if he had dipped his hand into fire and pulled out a solid lump of flame.

Pai-net'em got closer and looked at the jewel. A ruby as big as a man's fist. Inside glinted seven points of red light, in the shape of the seven stars of the night sky. It had fallen into the Nile, from the stars themselves, and turned the river to blood. It was not a jewel, given in tribute to Pharaoh. It was a curse, spat from above at Egypt. It was the source of all miseries, of the insects and the lightning, of the darkness and the death.

'Such a beautiful thing,' Pharaoh mused, 'to contain such curses.'

Pai-net'em saw the beauty, yet the jewel was hideous, crawling with invisible filth.

He shook his head, thinking with bitter humour of the Israelites' claim. This was beyond the Gods of any people. This was death made into an object. It could not be destroyed—that had been tried, with chisels and fire—only passed on, to the unwitting.

'Take it,' Pharaoh said, tossing the jewel to Pai-net'em.

He caught the thing, feeling its horrid pulse.

'Take it far from here.'

Pai-net'em bowed his head.

He would die in the execution of this task. But he had no other purpose. His name would be remembered for this sacrifice. As long as Egypt endured, so would Pai-net'em.

Outside the Palace, he held the jewel to his chest, cupping it with his hand. He thought himself the calm centre of a storm. All around, insects and death whirled in bloody darkness. Evils flowed from the stone, but he was shielded from them. It was as if he were inside it rather than it inside his fist.

Everything was tinted red, as if he were looking through the ruby. His limbs were heavy and he felt trapped.

He started to run, away from the Palace.

A burning began in his chest, where the jewel was clutched, as if a blob of molten metal had struck him and was eating its way towards his heart.

He let his hand fall, but the jewel was stuck to his torso, sinking in. Agony filled his chest, and he tore the linen from his face, screaming.

But he still ran, wading through the streams of frogs and locusts. The weakness of his legs was washed away. He no longer felt anything.

He knew he was dying, but that the jewel kept his body from falling. He shrank inside himself, withdrawing into the ruby, suspended among the Seven Stars. This was not death as he knew it, a calm passage into a dignified afterlife where his family and servants awaited, but a change of perception. He would remain in the world, but be apart from it. As he had served Pharaoh, so would he now serve the Seven Stars.

From the heart of the red night, he looked down on the devastation that was the Land of Egypt.

And could not weep.

Episode One: The Mummy's Heart

It was the size of a human heart. Charles Beauregard let his hand hover over it, fingers outstretched. He shut one eye but could not quite blot out the jewel.

'Aren't rubies generally smaller than this?' he asked.

Professor Trelawny shrugged. 'So I believe. I'm an Egyptologist, not a geologist. Strictly, a ruby is a pure transparent red corundum, though the term is loosely applied to merely red gemstones, like certain varieties of spinel and garnet. In rock-tapping circles, there's an argument that this isn't a ruby proper. Corunda, as you know—sapphire, emery and so on—are second in hardness only to diamond. The Seven Stars is at least as hard as diamond.'

Trelawny tapped the Seven Stars with a knuckle, touching it with a diamond ring. He did not try to scratch the priceless artefact. Presumably for fear of breaking his ring.

'So it's a red diamond?' Beauregard assumed.

Trelawny's huge eyebrows wriggled. 'If such exists, it may well be. Or mighthap a gemstone unknown to modern science. A variety perhaps once familiar to the Pharaonic Kings, lost to obscurity and now rediscovered, for the glory of our own dear Queen.'

Ever since the cloth was unfolded and the jewel disclosed, Beauregard had felt an urge to touch the stone. But he kept his fingers away. Though it was absurd, he had the impression the jewel would be hot as fire, as if just coughed from a volcano.

'Why is it called the Seven Stars?'

Trelawny smiled, weathered face crinkling.

'Turn up the gaslight, would you?'

Beauregard obliged. The flame grew with a serpent's hiss, casting more light. The basements of the British Museum were divided into dozens of store-rooms, offices and laboratories. Trelawny's lair, a surprisingly uncluttered space, was currently devoted to the study of the Jewel of Seven Stars.

Trelawny pulled on a white cotton glove and lifted the stone. He had to stretch his thumb and little finger to get a secure grip.

'Look *through* the jewel, at the flame.'

Beauregard stepped around the table. Trelawny held the gemstone like a lens. In the red depths, seven fires burned. Beauregard shifted position and the fires vanished. He moved back, and they shone again. Seven pinpoints of light, in a familiar pattern.

'Ursa Major,' he commented.

Trelawny set the jewel down again.

'The Great Bear, Charlemagne's Wain, the good old Plough. Also known, I understand, as the *Septentrionnes*, the Seven Ploughing Oxen, and, to the Hindoo, the Seven *Rishis* or Holy Ancient Sages. Or, as our American cousins would have it, the Big Dipper. What in Hades do you think a dipper is, by the way?'

'A ladle. Do you take an interest in astronomy, Professor?'

Trelawny laughed and indicated the jewel.

'I take an interest in this. The rest of it I got from an encyclopedia.'

'Is it a natural effect?'

'If not, Ancient Egyptian jewellers were possessed of secrets lost to memory. Which is, incidentally, not an entirely unlikely hypothesis. We still don't really know how they managed to build pyramids. I incline, however, to consider the stars a natural, or supernatural, phenomenon.'

'Supernatural?'

Trelawny's eyebrows waved again.

'There's a curse, you see.'

'Of course there is.'

Without the light behind it, the jewel seemed a dead lump, a giant blood clot. There was certainly blood in its history.

'I can't take curses too seriously,' Trelawny announced. 'Every ancient site has been at least thrice-accursed. If you consider its collection of maleficent objects from unhallowed graves, you'd have to deem the British Museum the most curse-plagued spot in the Empire. But hundreds of visitors traipse around upstairs every day without suffering ill-effects. Unless, of course, they've first stopped at the pie stall in Great Russell Street.'

Beauregard thought the professor might be whistling in the dark.

'And yet,' Trelawny mused, 'this little item has its secrets.'

'I assure you, professor, I should not be here if those secrets were not taken very seriously by eminent persons.'

'So I understand.'

Trelawny was an open man, not at all the stuffy professor. He had spent more years in deserts and digs than in classrooms and store-rooms. Beauregard had liked him at first sight. However, the professor was wary of him.

Beauregard must seem mysterious: not a policeman or a diplomat, yet given charge of this delicate matter. When called upon to explain his position, he was supposed to describe himself as a servant of the Queen and not mention the Diogenes Club, the adjunct of the Crown to which he was attached.

'Since the Seven Stars was discovered...'

'In the Valley of the Sorcerer, two years ago,' Trelawny footnoted.

'Nine men have died. In connection with this stone.'

Trelawny shrugged. Beauregard knew that most of the dead had been the professor's colleagues.

'Nothing mysterious in that, Beauregard. The jewel is of enormous academic interest but also great value. The traditional tomb-robbers believe that Egyptologists are, so to speak, poaching on their preserve. To us, these remnants of the past are miraculous glimpses of lost history, but generations of *fellahin* have seen the tombs of the long-dead as a field of potatoes, to be dug up and sold.'

Beauregard's gaze kept returning to the jewel. It was one of those objects that had the power of fascination. Even without the light behind it, there was a fire there.

'It was found, I understand, *inside* a mummy?'

Trelawny nodded. 'Not common practice, but not unknown. The mummy was that of Pai-net'em, of the household of Merneptah II. From the fragmentary records, it seems Pharaoh relied on him much as our own dear Queen relies on Lord Salisbury. An influential advisor, Merneptah, a wastrel, left the duller administrative chores to men like old Pai-net'em.'

'Was he the sorcerer for which the valley was named?'

'Almost certainly not. Pai-net'em was squeezed in among many tombs. His place of interment is modest, especially considering his importance. By rights, he should have been buried in the Theban version of Westminster Abbey. At first, we believed the mummy to be one of Pai-net'em's servants but evidence—not least, the Seven Stars—later revealed the body as the man himself.'

'The jewel?'

'We shipped the mummy here for examination. When Sir Joseph Whemple and I supervised the unwrapping, it was as if fire exploded from its chest. A trick of the light, but startling. It's a unique find. The Cairo Museum of Antiquities started hemming and hawing and asking for *their* mummy back, oh and the jewel of course. Lord Cromer convinced the *khedive* the most apt course of action would be to make a gift of the Seven Stars to the Queen, in honour of her Jubilee.'

'Sir Joseph was subsequently murdered?'

Trelawny nodded.

'Some devil cut his throat. In his office. Four doors down the corridor. With a dull knife. It was as if his neck were clawed open.'

'But the jewel was safe?'

'*In* a safe, actually. We have vaults for items of especial value.'

Beauregard had seen the police reports. Half the Egyptian scholars in London had been ungently interrogated, suspected of membership in some fanatic cult. No arrests had been made.

The death of Sir Joseph brought the Seven Stars to the notice of the Diogenes Club. Mycroft Holmes, of the Ruling Cabal, had clipped the report from the *Times* and predicted that the affair would be forwarded to his department of service.

'Has the mummy been returned to Cairo?'

Beauregard was relying on a favourite tactic, asking a question to which he knew the answer. Mycroft taught that facts themselves were often less significant than the way facts were presented by individuals.

'Now there's a question,' Trelawny said, brow crinkled. 'Whoever killed Sir Joseph stole the mummy. It was a light enough carcass. Still, not an easy item to get past our stout night watchmen. And of little worth in monetary terms. Mummies are ten a penny. Most were robbed of their funerary ornaments thousands of years ago. If the jewel hadn't been *inside* Pai-net'em, the robbers would have had it along with the rest of his grave goods.'

'Certain occult practitioners have use for the ancient dead,' Beauregard commented.

'Good Lord, what for?'

'Charms and potions and totems and such. Ingredients in arcane rituals.'

Trelawny said nothing. At Oxford, he had been a member of an occult society, the Order of the Ram.

"Eye of mummy, toe of dog', that sort of thing,' Beauregard prompted.

Finally, Trelawny snorted.

'Some dunderheads do take an interest in that sort of rot,' he admitted. 'In my student days, I ran into a pack of them myself. The sons of the clods I knew probably still pay through the nose for crumbled horse manure passed off as the ashes of the mages of Atlantis. Pai-net'em's poor bones might fetch something on that singular market. I trust the police are pursuing that avenue of inquiry.'

'So do I.'

Beauregard looked back at the Seven Stars.

'I shall not entirely be sorry to see the jewel go to the Tower,' Trelawny said. 'The death of Sir Joseph rattled me, I don't mind telling you. The scientist in me says I should cling to the stone until its mysteries are exhausted. But the cautious man tells me to let the next fellow worry about it.'

'And I'm the next fellow?'

Trelawny smiled, sadly. He dropped a cloth on the Seven Stars.

'From Merneptah to Pai-net'em,' the professor said. 'And now from Abel Trelawny to Queen Victoria. From pharaoh to sovereign in just three thousand years. Perhaps that'll be the end of it. For my part, I certainly hope so.'

He made his way upstairs. Late in the afternoon, the crowds were thinning. He touched his hat-brim to Jenks, the Diogenes man who wore the uniform of an attendant and had been working here, keeping an eye out, ever since the murder of Sir Joseph.

The Hall of Egyptian Antiquities, always popular, was almost empty. A noseless giant head dominated the room, eyes eerily impassive. Beauregard wanted to take a look at some mummies, to get an idea of what was missing.

Under glass was the bandage-wrapped corpse of a young girl.

He thought of his late wife, Pamela. She was buried in the hill country of India, a world away. Would she find herself on display millennia hence, a typical specimen of the 19th-Century Anno Domini?

He felt an instant of connection. With the girl.

The plaque said she was unknown, but the daughter of wealth. *Ushabti* mannikins were found in her grave, to be her servants in the afterlife. Her bindings were an intricate herringbone. Her nose still had definition under ancient cloth.

Beauregard had a sense that he was a moment in history, a pause in a story which had begun long before him and would continue well past his death. People came and went, but some things remained, eternal.

He thought of the Seven Stars, undisturbed for three thousand years.

And who knew how old the jewel was when buried inside Pai-net'em?

A chill crept up his spine. He felt eyes upon his back, but the only reflection in the glass of the display case was that of the blind stone head.

He turned, and saw a woman with a pale face and smoked glasses. Almost a girl, fair and fragile. He thought for a moment she might be blind too, but she was watching him.

He almost said something; then, very swiftly, she was gone.

In another life...

He looked at the mummy again, wondering why he was so stirred inside.

He bade Jenks a good day and left the museum.

Pall Mall was half-decorated. London was disappearing under cheerful swathes of patriotic bunting in honour of the Queen's Diamond Jubilee. Her sixty years on the throne had seen unimaginable changes in Britain and her Empire. The Queen had weathered constitutional crises, setting an example in conduct that many of her subjects, from her own children down, could not match.

He had taken an open cab from the British Museum, enjoying the early June evening. The Jubilee, not yet fully upon the city, encouraged an opening-up. People wore sashes and ribbons in celebration of a Queen who ruled through love, not the fear Merneptah and his like had wielded like a lash.

In years of service, he had seen the Empire at its best and worst. He hated the pettiness and cruelty that existed as much in this city as in the farthest outpost, but admired fiercely the aspirations to decency and honour embodied in Victoria's great heart. To him, the Union Jack was not the trade-mark of some gigantic financial concern or the territorial stink of a bristling bulldog but a banner which meant the innocent were protected and the helpless defended.

He entered the lobby of the Diogenes Club and was discreetly admitted to the chamber of the Ruling Cabal. Mycroft Holmes, the huge spider at the centre of the nation's intelligence web, sat in his custom-made leather armchair, plump fingers pyramided, brows knit in thought. He did not greet Beauregard for a full minute, as he finished some mental calculation.

'Beauregard,' he said. 'This is a delicate business.'

Beauregard agreed.

'You've seen the bauble?'

'It's considerably more than that, Mycroft. A ruby as big as my fist.'

'It's not a ruby.'

'I fail to see how the geology is germane to the affair.'

'One should consider a jewel from all angles, the better to appreciate its many facets. This is a jewel like no other.'

'I couldn't agree more.'

'It won't attract as much attention as the *Koh-i-Nor* or the Moonstone or the Green Eye of the Yellow God. But it's the more remarkable.'

'It's washed in blood.'

'All great gems are.'

'This one looks like it.'

'Tell me, Beauregard, what of the points of light?'

'The Seven Stars. Exactly in the configuration of Ursa Major. That's an uncanny feature. As if the stone were a star map.'

'Stent, the Astronomer Royal, has suggested the Seven Stars fell to Earth as a meteor. Maybe it is a message from those stars.'

Beauregard shuddered again. He didn't like to think of a red streak nearing the Earth, millennia ago.

'It's a strange thing,' he admitted.

'And what of the murder of Sir Joseph Whemple and the theft of the mummy?'

Beauregard considered the little he had learned.

'Trelawny went out of his way to pooh-pooh a suggestion that the mummy might have been stolen for use in magical rituals. Yet he was, admittedly as a youth, involved in such rites himself. It's my consideration that he suspects as much, but does not dare propose the theory strongly lest his past be looked into too closely.'

Mycroft's fat face crumpled in mild irritation. 'We know much about Abel Trelawny and the Society of the Ram. Have you heard of Declan Mountmain?'

'The Fenian?'

'Not strictly. We came close to gaoling him for that dynamite business at Lord's but he slipped through the net, found subordinates to take the blame.'

Beauregard remembered the atrocity. It was a wonder no one had been killed.

'Mountmain is a crank,' declared Mycroft, 'but a dangerous one. Most advocates of Irish Home Rule distance themselves from him. The Fenian Brotherhood regard him as a loose cannon of the worst sort. He wrote a pamphlet which was suppressed as obscene, alleging prominent cabinet ministers and churchmen constitute a cult devoted to the pagan worship of a goddess incarnated as our Queen. Apparently, we are given to snatching drabs from the alleys of the East End and ritually disembowelling them in a temple beneath Buckingham Palace.'

Beauregard found the suggestion disgusting.

'Mountmain himself believes none of it. He is merely trying to project his own methods and manners on those he deems his foemen. He is an adept in occult sciences, and remains the Great Pooh-Bah of the Order of the Ram. His beliefs are a mixture of paganism and Satanism, with a little Hindoo or Ancient Egyptian tosh thrown in. He blathers about Atlantis and R'lyeh and the Plateau of Leng and Elder Gods from the Stars. All very arcane and eldritch, no doubt.'

'You believe this Mountmain to be behind the attempts on the Seven Stars?'

'I believe nothing that cannot be proven. Mountmain has an old connection with Trelawny. He is a collector of weird artefacts. He has a fortune at his disposal, augmented by funds extorted from supporters of his dubious political cause. He is by no means the only blackguard of his stripe—you've heard me remark that the mountaineer Aleister Crowley is a young man worth watching—but he is currently the worst of his shabby crowd.'

'Should I make some discreet inquiries about Declan Mountmain?'

'If you think it worthwhile.'

As usual with Mycroft, Beauregard felt he had been led through a maze to a foregone conclusion. It was the Great Man's knack to draw his own ideas out of other people.

'Very well. I think I know where to start.'

A mere hundred yards from the Diogenes Club were the offices of the *Pall Mall Gazette*. He strolled casually, pondering the two sides to his immediate problem.

When Mycroft mentioned Declan Mountmain, he knew he would have to bring Katharine Reed into it. She was a reporter, the sole woman in regular employment at the *Gazette*, at least when she wasn't in jail for suffragette agitations. Kate knew as much about the Irish Home Rule movement as any man, probably because she was in it up to her spectacles. She also had a knack for finding out things about prominent personages that did them no credit. He was certain Kate would know about Mountmain.

The other side of the coin was that Kate was insatiably curious and as tenacious as a tick. Every time she was asked a question, she would ask one back. And trade answer for answer. With her disarming manner and steel-trap mind, she might latch on, and follow him to what she imagined was a story worth printing. The Diogenes Club prided itself on being the least-known arm of the British Government. Mycroft had a positive distaste for seeing the organisation's name, let alone his own, in the papers. Such things he left for his more famous, though less acute, brother.

Kate had been a friend of Pamela's. She shared with his late wife a trick of looking through Charles Beauregard as if he were a pane of glass. And he was about to recruit her for a confidential mission.

He thought, not for the first time, that he must be mad. He knew where Kate's cubby hole was, but would have been able to identify it anyway. By the shouting.

A large, well-dressed man, neck scarlet, was blustering.

'Come out from that desk and be thrashed!'

He recognised Henry Wilcox, the financial colossus.

He guessed at once that the *Gazette* must have carried some story under Kate's by-line that revealed an irregularity on Wilcox's part.

'Shift yourself, coward,' the colossus roared.

Wilcox was standing over a sturdy desk. He lashed it with a riding-crop.

The desk shook.

Kate, Beauregard gathered, was underneath.

He wondered whether he should intervene, but thought better of it. Kate Reed didn't care for it if other people fought her battles for her, though she was herself practiced at pitching in to any brawl that came along.

Wilcox savagely whipped a type-writing apparatus.

The desk heaved upwards and a small woman exploded from her hiding-place.

'How dare you!' she shouted. 'Henry Wilcox, you have a great deal to be ashamed of!'

The colossus, as imposing physically as he was financially, was given pause. Kate, red-haired and freckled and often hesitant in polite company, was in a fine fury. Up on her toes, she stuck her face close to Wilcox's and adjusted her thick spectacles.

'This piece which names me,' he began.

'Do you deny the facts?'

'That's not the point,' he snarled.

'I rather think it is. Maybe we should print a follow-up article. You want your side of it to be given. Well, Mr Wilcox, now is your chance.'

Kate set her chair upright and fed a sheet of paper into her type-writer.

'First of all, there's the question of the girl's age. What was your initial estimate?'

'I didn't come here to be insulted.'

'Really? Where do you go to be insulted? I understand the house which employs your young associate offers many varieties of satisfaction.'

'Your manner does not become your sex.'

Kate Reed looked as if she was about to breathe fire.

'I suppose seeking Biblical knowledge of children is a noble and worthy occupation for the mighty male gender.'

'That's libel.'

'No, that's slander. It is only libel if we print it. And if it's proven untrue.'

'She'd never furnish proof.'

'Your soiled dove? How much would you wish to wager on that?'

Wilcox's entire face was red. Beauregard wondered if the colossus were not on the verge of a coronary. From what he gathered, the man was an utter swine.

Kate typed rapidly, fingers jabbing like little knives.

'Would you care to take the address of the *Gazette*'s solicitors with you? Your own can get in touch with them when this piece runs.'

Wilcox muttered a word Beauregard had hoped never to hear in a lady's presence. Kate, unblushing, kept on typing.

The financial colossus put on his hat and withdrew, pushing impatiently past Beauregard.

'Stupid little tart,' he said.

'The girl or me?' Kate shouted after him.

Beauregard replaced Wilcox in Kate's line of fire, standing by her desk. She looked up, smiled a little, and kept on typing.

'Charles, good day to you. What trouble am I in now?'

'You seem more than able to find enough on your own.'

'That man buys children for unspeakable purposes. And yet he'll probably wind up with a knighthood.'

'I doubt that.'

'Others have before him,' she broke off typing, and looked at him. 'Oh, I see. Words in the right ears. A name crossed off a list. Closed ranks. Nothing in the open, you know, where it might upset the rabble. Just an understanding. Some things aren't done, you know. He has money all right, and the house, and the prospects. But he's not a *gentleman*. You can probably do it. I don't underestimate your shadowy influence. But getting him blackballed isn't the scope of my ambitions for the monstrous thug. I'd rather see him de-balled.'

Beauregard was shocked. Kate was habitually forward, but he'd never heard her voice such an extreme sentiment.

She softened, and rested her elbows on her desk. Her hair had come undone.

'I'm sorry. I shouldn't rail at you. It's not your fault.'

Beauregard pulled the paper from the typewriter. Kate had been typing a nursery rhyme.

'Mr Stead won't publish anything more about Wilcox,' she admitted, referring to the editor. 'He's a crusading soul, hot on exposing "the maiden tribute of modern Babylon", but to be frank our solicitors aren't up to the level Wilcox can afford. Stead wants to stay in business.'

Kate took the sheet of paper, crumpled it into a ball, and missed a wicker basket.

Beauregard wondered how best to broach the subject.

'What are your plans for the Jubilee?' he asked.

'Are you offering to escort me to that little ceremony at the Tower I'm not supposed to know you're arranging? If you were, I'd suspect you were only luring me there so I could be clapped in irons and penned in the deepest dungeon.'

'As a reporter, I thought you might be interested.'

'She's a nice enough old girl, the Queen. But I don't think she ought to be ruling over my stretch of the world. Or quite a few other patches of red on the map. I was imagining I'd celebrate the Jubilee by cosily chaining myself to some nice railings and being spat on by patriotic crowds.'

Beauregard couldn't miss the seam of self-doubt in Kate's calculated outrageousness.

'Can I depend on your discretion?'

She looked at him with comical pity.

'Of course I can't,' he said, smiling. 'However, needs must when the Devil drives. What do you know about Declan Mountmain?'

Anything comical was wiped from Kate's face.

'Charles, *don't.*'

'I don't understand.'

'Whatever involves Mountmain, don't pursue it. There are fools and blackguards and rogues and monsters. He's all of them. Beside Mountmain's sins, Henry Wilcox's are mere errors of judgement.'

'His name has come up.'

'I want nothing to do with it. Whatever it is.'

'Then you won't want to be my guest at the Tower. To see the Jewel of Seven Stars.'

'That's different. I accept that invitation. Thank you, kind sir.'

She stood up and leaned over the desk to kiss his cheek.

'What shall I wear? Something green?'

He laughed. 'Don't you dare.'

She giggled.

The deepness of her feelings about Mountmain shadowed their gaiety. Uncomfortably, Beauregard suspected that Mycroft had set him on the right road, and that he would not like where it was leading.

There were policemen in the courtyard of the British Museum. And a light burning behind one set of tall windows. He realised that the illuminated room was the Hall of Egyptian Antiquities.

He had been summoned from his house in Chelsea by a cryptic message. Before being shaken awake by his manservant, Bairstow, he had been dreaming an Egyptian dream, floating down the Nile on a barge, pursued by the hordes of the Mahdi—which had actually happened to him in this life—and of the Pharaoh of Exodus—which certainly hadn't.

In the Hall, caped constables stood over a sheeted form. A small, whiskered man in a bowler hat fretted.

'Good morning, Lestrade.'

'Is it?' the policeman asked. Dawn was pinking the windows. 'Seems like the start of another long bloody day to me.'

There was a lot of damage about. The case of the mummy he had looked at earlier was smashed in, broken shards of glass strewn over the Egyptian girl. Other exhibits were knocked over and scattered.

'I needn't tell you how unpleasant this is,' Lestrade said, nodding to a constable, who lifted the sheet.

It was Jenks, throat torn away.

'We thought he was just a keeper,' Lestrade said. 'Then we found his papers, and it seems he was one of your mob.'

'Indeed,' Beauregard said, not committing.

'Doubtless poking around into the last business. The Whemple murder. Behind the backs of the hard-working police.'

'Jenks was just watching over things. There's a crown jewel in the basement, you know.'

'There was.'

The phrase was like a hammer.

'The vault was broken into. Nothing subtle or clever. Looks like dynamite to me. The blast woke up every guard in the building. The ones who slept through this.'

'The Jewel of Seven Stars is gone?'

'I should say so.'

Beauregard looked at Jenks's wound.

'Is this what Whemple looked like?'

Lestrade nodded. 'Ripped from ear to ear, with something serrated and not too sharp.'

Beauregard had seen tiger-marks in India, crocodile attacks in Egypt, lion maulings in the Transvaal, wolf victims in Siberia and the Canadian Northwoods.

'Could have been an animal,' he said.

'We thought of that. With Whemple, there was nothing missing, if you get my drift. Ripped this way and that, but not chewed, torn off, or eaten. Animals don't do that. They always at least try to eat what they've killed.'

For some reason, he thought of the woman in smoked glasses, who had been here when last he saw Jenks. In his memory, she had teeth like a dainty cannibal, filed to points.

'It's unusual.'

'I don't like the unusual ones, sir. They always mean that poor old coppers like me get pushed aside and clever fellows like you or the chap from Baker Street are let loose on my patch. What I like is a murderer who gets drunk and takes a cudgel to his wife, then sits down blubbing until the police turn up. That's a proper murder. This is just fiendishness.'

'Your murderer has made two bad mistakes tonight, Lestrade. In taking the Seven Stars, he has robbed the Queen. And in killing Jenks, he has aroused the ire of the Diogenes Club. I should not care to exchange places with him.'

Declan Mountmain's London address was a Georgian mansion in Wimpole Street. Just the lair for a viper who wished to nestle close to the bosom of Empire.

Beauregard deemed it best to make a direct approach. It would be interesting, considering last night's business at the Museum, to gauge Mountmain's condition this morning. Were his ears ringing, as if he had been in the vicinity of an explosion in a confined space?

He knocked on Mountmain's sturdy front door, and waited on the step for the butler to open up.

'Mr Mountmain isn't receiving visitors, sir,' said the sharp-faced servant. 'He has taken to his bed.'

'He'll see me,' Beauregard said, confidently.

The butler hesitated.

'Are you the doctor, sir? The *confidential* doctor?'

Beauregard looked up and down the street, as if suspecting he was being followed. As it happens, there was a suspiciously human-sized bundle in a doorway a dozen houses distant. This was not a district in which gentlemen of the road sleeping under the stars were much tolerated.

'Do you think you should mention such matters out on the street where anyone might hear you?'

The butler was chastened, and—unless Beauregard wildly missed his guess—terrified.

The door was pulled open wide, and Beauregard allowed in. He tried to project from within the impression that he was a disgraced physician on a hush-hush mission of dark mercy. Such impersonations were surprisingly easy, especially if one didn't actually claim to be who one was pretending to be but merely let others make assumptions one did not contradict.

Mountmain's hallway was dark. The windows were still curtained. A line of wavering light under a door revealed that one of the rooms was occupied, and low voices could be made out. The butler did not lead Beauregard to that door, but to another, which he opened.

A single lamp burned, a dark lantern set upon a table. A man lay on a divan, a sheet thrown over him. He was groaning, and a black-red stain covered a full quarter of the sheet.

The butler turned up the lamp and Beauregard looked at the man. He was deathly pale beneath grime, teeth gritted, pellets of sweat on his forehead.

Beauregard lifted the sheet.

A gouge had been taken out of the man, ripping through his shirt, exposing ribs.

The wounded man gripped Beaureagard's arm.

'A priest,' he said. 'Get a priest.'

'Come now, Bacon,' boomed a voice. 'Have you so easily turned apostate and reverted to the poor faith of your feeble fathers?'

Beauregard turned.

In the doorway stood the man he knew to be Declan Mountmain. Short and stout, with a high forehead growing higher as his black hair receded away from the point of his widow's peak, Mountmain was somehow an impressive presence. He wore a Norfolk jacket and riding boots, unmistakably blooded. Not the sort of outfit for lounging around the house before breakfast, but ideal wear for an after-midnight adventure in larceny and murder.

Bacon's wound was irresistibly reminiscent of the fatal injuries suffered by Jenks and Whemple.

'Who might you be, sir?' Mountmain asked. 'And what business have you poking around in young Bacon's open wound? You're no damned doctor, that's certain.'

Beauregard handed over his card.

'I wished to consult you in your capacity as an expert on occult matters.'

Mountmain looked at the card, cocked a quizzical eyebrow, then landed a slap across the face of his butler, slamming him against the wall.

'You're a worthless fool,' he told his servant.

'This man needs medical attention,' Beauregard said. 'And, by his admission, spiritual attention too.'

Mountmain strode over.

Beauregard felt Bacon's grip strengthen as Mountmain neared. Then it was suddenly limp.

'No, he needs funerary attention,' Mountmain said.

Bacon's dead hand fell. There was blood on Beauregard's sleeve.

'Very tragic,' Mountmain said, deliberate despite his rage. 'A carriage accident.'

According to Mycroft, people who volunteer explanations as yet unasked-for are certain to be lying. Beauregard realised that Mountmain's contempt for others was such that he did not even take the trouble to concoct a believable story.

Mountmain's jacket was dusty and odiferous. Beauregard recognised the Guy Fawkes Night smell that lingers after a dynamite blast.

'There will now be tedious complications as a result of my charitable taking-in of this stranger. I should be grateful if you quit this house so I can make the proper, ruinously costly, arrangements.'

Beauregard looked at the dead man's face. It was still stamped with fear.

'If I can be of assistance,' he ventured, 'I shall report the matter to the police. I am in a small way officially connected.'

Mountmain looked up at Beauregard, calculating.

'That will not be necessary.'

'The young man's name was, what did you say, Bacon?'

'He blurted it as he was carried into the house.'

Mountmain spread his arms and looked down at his blood- and dirt-smeared clothes. He did not say so outright, but implied he was in this condition because he had hauled an injured passer-by off the street. Now his rage was cooling, he showed something of the canniness Beauregard expected of such a dangerous man.

'The business upon which I called...'

'I can't be expected to think of that,' Mountmain said. 'There's a corpse ruining the furniture. Put your concerns in writing and send them to my secretary. Now, if you will be so kind as to leave...'

Mountmain's door slammed behind Beauregard. He stood outside the house, mind swarming around the problem.

He glanced at the doorway where the vagrant had been earlier, but it was unoccupied. He half-thought the bundle might have been Kate, pursuing a story. She was certainly not above disguising herself as an urchin.

A man had died in his presence.

No matter how often it happened, it was shocking. Death struck deep in him, reaching that portion of his heart he thought buried with Pamela. All death took him back to the hill country, to his wife bathed in blood and their still-born son. Then, he had wept and raged and had to be restrained from taking a sabre to the drunken doctor. Now, it was his duty to show nothing, to pretend he felt as little as Mountmain evidently did. Death was at worst a rude inconvenience.

He concentrated. His hands did not shake. He walked away from the house with even steps. An observer would not think he was about business of great moment.

Mountmain and Bacon, and who knows how many confederates, had been at the Museum last night, and had certainly set the charges that blew the safe. The man had a habit of meddling with dynamite. He must be after the Seven Stars, though it was not yet clear whether Mountmain's interest in the stone was down to its monetary value, its political import, or an as-yet unknown occult significance.

Beauregard paused casually and took a cigar from his case. He stepped into the shelter of a doorway to light the cigar, turning and hunching a little to keep the match-flame out of the wind. He paused to let the flame grow the length of the match, and lit up the doorway. A scrap of rag wound around the boot-scraper, some grey stuff brittle with dust.

He puffed on his fine cigar and picked up the rag, as if he had dropped it when taking his matches from his pocket. It almost crumbled in his hands and he carefully folded it into his silver cigar case.

A hansom cab trundled by, looking for custom. Beauregard hailed it.

Trelawny was in shock at the loss of the Seven Stars. His room was turned upside-down, and the corridor outside blackened by the blast. Beauregard had the impression Mountmain had overdone the dynamite. Lestrade's men were still pottering around.

'Ever since the Valley of the Sorcerer, it's been like this,' Trelawny said.

'Blood and shot and death. In Egypt, you expect that sort of thing. But not here, in London, in the British Museum.'

'Do you know a man named Mountmain?'

'Declan Mountmain? The worst sort of occult busybody. Half-baked theories and disgusting personal habits.'

'Were you not close to him at Oxford? In the Order of the Ram?'

Trelawny was surprised to have that brought up.

'I wouldn't say "close". I took a passing interest in such concerns. It's impossible to get far in Egyptology without trying to understand occult practices. Mountmain and I quarrelled without relief and I broke with him long ago. To him, it's all about *power*, not knowledge.'

'I believe that last night Mountmain stole the Seven Stars.'

Trelawny sat down, astonished.

'He has many low associations. He would know the cutters and fences who could deal with such booty.'

Trelawny shook his head.

'If it's Mountmain, it's not for the money. I believe I mentioned that the Seven Stars was as hard as diamond. Actually, it is far harder. I doubt if it could be broken into smaller stones for disposal. It would probably be a blessing if that were possible, though the process might well merely disperse the ill fortune throughout the world.'

'If not the money...?'

'The magic, Beauregard. Mountmain believes in such things. For him, they seem to work. At Oxford, he had a fearful row with one of the professors and cast an enchantment on the fellow. It was a terrible thing to see.'

'He sickened and died?'

'Eventually. First, he lost his position, his standing, his reputation. He was found guilty of unholy acts, and claimed that voices compelled him.'

'The Seven Stars?'

'...would be of incalculable use to Mountmain. There are references in certain books, the sort we keep under lock and key and don't allow in the index. Though lost since the time of Merneptah, there are references to the Jewel of Seven Stars. It has a shadowy reputation.'

'Mountmain would know this?'

'Of course.'

'He would wish to employ the stone in some species of ritual?'

'Indubitably.'

'To what end?'

Trelawny shook his head.

'Something on a cyclopean scale, Beauregard. According to the *Al Azif* of the mad Arab Al-Hazred, the last time the jewel was the focus of occult power was in the thick of the Plagues of Egypt.'

Beauregard took out his cigar case.

'What do you make of this?'

Trelawny looked at the scrap of cloth.

'Is this part of the debris?'

Beauregard said nothing.

'I'd heard one of the mummies upstairs was damaged. This looks like a funerary binding. It's certainly ancient. I say, you shouldn't just have picked it up as a souvenir.'

Beauregard took the rag back and folded it again.

'I think I'll hang on to it for the moment.'

Kate hadn't got all of the story out of him, but he had doled her a few of the less arcane facts.

They were in Covent Garden, at a café. The awning was draped with flags. A portrait of the Queen hung proudly in prime position.

'You believe Mountmain has this gem? In his town house? And he has a dead man on the premises?'

Beauregard sipped his tea and nodded.

'If Ireland and dynamite are involved, such niceties as due process and search warrants usually go out the window. So why hasn't Lestrade descended on the scene with a dozen flatfeet and torn the house apart?'

'It's not quite that simple.'

'Yes it is, Charles. And you know it.'

'I don't mind telling you, I didn't much care for your countryman.'

Kate almost laughed.

'"My countryman". I suppose you wouldn't mind at all if I habitually referred to Blackbeard, Charlie Peace, Jonathan Wild and Burke and Hare as "your countrymen".'

'I'm sorry. And Burke and Hare were Irish.'

'I believe in Home Rule for the people of Ireland, and Egypt and India come to that. Mountmain's interest in the country of his birth involves replacing the muddled and unjust rule of England with the monstrous and tyrannical rule of Declan Mountmain. Have you read any of his pamphlets? He claims descent from the Mage-Kings of Erin, whomsoever they might be. If he ever has a Diamond Jubilee, it will be celebrated by ripping out the beating hearts of Wicklow virgins. Distasteful as all this Union Jackery might be, Vicky doesn't insist her ministers cut throats at the Palace. At least, not since Palmerston.'

'You wouldn't happen to have been passing Mountmain's town house this morning, in the borrowed clothes of a tramp?'

Kate's eyes went wide.

'Wherever did you get that idea?'

'Something glimpsed out of the corner of my eye.'

'What are you going to do about your blessed jewel?'

Beauregard considered the matter.

'I rather thought I might try to steal it back.'

Kate smiled, eyes crinkling behind spectacles. She was much more appealing than generally reckoned, he thought. A face made beautiful by character (and wit) wore far better than one made beautiful by nature (and paint).

'Now that's a lovely notion. Charles, I always admire you most in your all-too infrequent excursions into larceny. Do not even consider embarking on such a venture without me.'

'Kate, you know that's absolutely impossible.'

'Then why did you mention it? You know me too well to think I'd just flutter my handkerchief and let you bravely go about your business while I fret the night away in fear of your life. Make no mistake, Charles, that young fellow you saw wasn't the first corpse to be found in the immediate vicinity of Declan Mountmain.'

He could give in now, or he could argue the afternoon away and give in around tea-time. Or he could give in now, and tell Kate that the burglary was set for tomorrow night, then make the attempt this evening.

'By the way,' she said. 'If you're thinking of telling me you intend to do your house-breaking later than this very night, I shall not believe you.'

'Very well, Kate. You may come with me. But you will not come into the house itself. You shall wait outside, to alert me to any danger. By whistling.'

'We'll discuss the specifics when we come to them.'

'No, now. Kate, promise.'

Her nose twitched and she looked everywhere but at him.

'I promise,' Kate said. 'I'll be the whistler.'

He raised his cup and she clinked hers against it.

'To larceny,' she said, 'and the ruin of rogues of all nations.'

After arranging with Kate to meet later, Beauregard took a cab back to Chelsea. He wished to call on one of his near neighbours in Cheyne Walk. The occult wasn't his field of expertise, and he wanted a little more knowledge before venturing into Mountmain's lair.

Mr Thomas Carnacki, the celebrated 'ghost-finder', admitted Beauregard to his comfortable sitting room.

'I'm sorry to interrupt.'

Carnacki had been entertaining an actorly-looking man. He waved aside the apology.

'Machen and I were just yarning. You know his work, of course.'

Beauregard was unfamiliar with the author.

'I am pleased to meet you, Mr Beauregard,' said Machen, offering a bony hand to be shaken. There was a little Welsh in his accent, thinned by London.

'I've come to make inquiries on a matter relating to your speciality.'

'Machen might help, as well,' Carnacki said.

The dapper little man offered Beauregard brandy, which he declined. He wanted to keep his head clear for the rest of the night's business.

'Have you heard of the Jewel of Seven Stars?'

Carnacki and Machen said nothing, in the distinctive manner of people reluctant to venture onto shivering sands.

'I see that you have. I assume you know of its recent discovery, inside a mummy.'

'I had doubted its authenticity,' Machen said. 'It's a fabled object.'

'Professor Trelawny is convinced that it is the genuine gem,' Beauregard said to Machen. 'It is certainly as old as the mummy. Three thousand years.'

'That merely means that it's an old fake. Made in imitation of an item that probably never existed.'

'There's a curse, of course,' said Carnacki.

'Of course,' Beauregard agreed.

'One might say, the curse of curses.'

'Trelawny mentioned the Plagues of Egypt.'

'Frogs, locusts, boils, blood, gnats, and so forth,' Machen chanted.

'There's been blood.'

'I hardly think we need to fear the plagues of Egypt. Pharaoh, after all, held the Israelites in bondage. All are free in our Empire.'

Carnacki swilled his brandy, beaming. To him, this was a parlour game. He prided himself on never being rattled.

'It is a mistake to take Exodus, as it were, as gospel,' Machen commented. 'Egyptian records make little of the tribes of Israel. And the plagues are almost totally expunged. Of course, the Egyptians believed that to forget a thing or a person was to revoke their very existence. To blot the plagues from the histories would mean they could be averted, as it were, in retrospect.'

Beauregard wondered whether Mountmain might not see himself as Ireland's Moses. He decided to drop the name.

'Do you know Declan Mountmain?'

As vehement as Kate's reaction to the name had been, Carnacki's and Machen's were more extreme. The ghost-finder spat a mouthful of brandy back into his glass, and Machen's thin lips pressed together in disgust and rage.

'He's one of your occult fellows, isn't he?' Beauregard prompted, disingenuously.

'Mountmain wants to bring things back,' Machen said. 'Old things. Things best left in the beyond.'

'Is he after the Seven Stars?' Carnacki asked. Beauregard had forgotten that the little man had the instincts of a detective. 'They'd make a deuced combination.'

He distracted himself for the cab journey by running through the plagues of

Egypt, in order. First, the waters of the Nile turned to blood. Second, hordes of frogs. Third, the dust became swarms of gnats. Fourth, an infestation of flies. Fifth, the cattle struck dead. Sixth, an epidemic of boils. Seventh, lightning and hail struck the crops and livestock. Eighth, locusts. Ninth, darkness covered the land for three days. And tenth, the death of all the first-born throughout the country.

In Exodus, the story reads strangely. It's all down to the Lord and Pharaoh. The suggestion seems to be that the Lord visits the plagues on Egypt but influences Pharaoh to ignore them, 'hardening his heart' against letting the tribes of Israel go free. Beauregard remembered officers in India who were like that, alternately inflicting hideous punishments and encouraging the offenders to defy them, as an excuse for continuing with the punishment.

On the whole, it wasn't the sort of behaviour one expected from a proper God. One of Mountmain's eldritch and arcane Old Ones, perhaps.

Carnacki seemed to suggest that the Israelites didn't really come into it. The point was the plagues.

The effect of all ten must have been devastation on a vast scale. In the aftermath, with no crops or cattle, most people maddened by disease or bereavement, the chaos would take generations to pass away.

If he had been Pharaoh, Beauregard would have felt he had a legitimate complaint that disproportionate sentence had been inflicted.

He had the cab drop him off in Cavendish Square.

Kate turned up on a bicycle. She wore britches and a tweed-cap. He thought better of asking her if she were disguised as a youth.

They walked up Wimpole Street.

'Where do you think Mountmain has the jewel?' she asked.

'I don't expect to find it. I just want to get the lie of the land. Consider this an exploratory expedition. Later, Lestrade and his stout fellows can go through the place and recover the swag.'

'You make a poor cracksman.'

'I should hope so, Kate.'

'Is that the address? It doesn't look all that foreboding.'

Mountmain's house was dark. Beauregard did not make the mistake of assuming it therefore empty or the household a-bed. He had the impression that the Irish Mage conducted much of his business away from the windows. The room in which Bacon had died was windowless.

'Do you favour the first or the second storey for your illicit entry, Charles?'

'Neither. I hope to go in through the basement.'

Iron, spear-topped railings stood in front of the house. The steps to the front door rose above a row of windows at ground-level. He assumed that these led to the kitchens or the wine cellars.

'Have you noticed the device on the arch-stone above the door?'

Beauregard looked up. Inset into the stone were what looked like polished nail-heads.

'Ursa Major,' he said.

The glints were in the form of the constellation. He looked up at the cloudless sky. Despite the warm glow of gaslight, the stars in the heavens shone.

'This all leads back to the Great Bear,' Kate said. 'To the stars.'

'I'm going. Remember, if there's trouble, whistle. If I don't come out, alert Lestrade.'

'And the Diogenes Club?'

He was uncomfortable hearing the name on her tongue.

'Them too.'

'One more thing,' she insisted.

He looked at her. She kissed him, standing on tip-toes to peck at his lips.

'For luck,' she said.

He felt a great warmth for Kate Reed. She was a kindly soul. He squeezed her shoulder and scooted across the street, deftly vaulting the railings.

The first window he tried was fastened. He took out his penknife and scraped away old putty. A pane came away entire, and he set it to one side. The black curtain wafted inwards with the rush of night air.

He slid himself through the curtain, setting his rubber-soles down on a flagstone floor about six feet below the level of the window. Glass crunched beneath his boots.

The room was dark. He stood still as a statue, continuing to hear the crunch as if it were a volley of shots. His breath was even and his heartbeat regular. He was used to this sort of night-creeping, but it did not do to get too cocky.

Had someone dropped something?

He chanced a match and found himself in a store-room. It was as cold as a larder, but the jars and vials on the shelves lining the walls did not suggest domestic arts. Free-floating eyeballs peered at him.

If he had tried the next window along, he would have found it broken. Some mischance, or a less professional cracksman, had smashed it in.

A tiny scrap hung from a spar of glass still in the frame. It was a fragment of cloth, similar to the stuff he still had in his cigar case. He thought of a man-shaped huddle, and shuddered. The match burned his fingers. He shook it out and dropped it.

The after-trail of flame wiggled on the surface of his eyes. He had a fix on the door, and took a grip of the handle. He had a lockpick in case he found himself shut in. He pulled, and the door moved more easily than he expected. He felt the jamb and realised the door had been locked, but forced. The lock itself was torn out of the wood, but the metal tongue was still out, fixed.

He stepped into a passageway. His eyes were used to the dark. He proceeded down the passage, trying doors. All were broken in, locks smashed.

He took out his revolver.

Someone had invaded this house before him.

The rooms were all like the one he had been in, stores for arcane items. He recognised certain occult implements. One room, a windowless hole, was given over to ancient books, and had been torn apart. Priceless volumes were strewn on the floor, leaking pages like flesh from a wound.

Upstairs, there was a thunderous knocking at the door.

It couldn't be Kate. She would have whistled.

Light leaked down. The gas in the hallway had been turned up. There were footsteps, and offensive shouts.

Mountmain answered his own door. He had probably discharged the butler.

Beauregard couldn't resist a smile.

The light showed a set of double doors, of some metal, at the end of the passageway. They had been abused and wrenched around the locks.

'What the Devil do you want?' Mountmain roared.

'The Seven Stars,' boomed a familiar voice.

'What are they? And who are you?'

'You know that as well as I do, Declan. I haven't changed so much since Oxford.'

It was Trelawny.

'Get out of the house, or I shall summon the police.'

'Very well,' Trelawny called Mountmain's bluff.

'Seven Stars, you say?'

'And the mummy! Where's Pai-net'em?'

A tiny hand took Beauregard's sleeve and tugged.

His heart spasmed and he turned, raising his revolver and aiming directly at a startled face.

Kate whistled, almost soundlessly.

He did not waste words in protest. She had disobeyed him and come into the house. She must have seen Trelawny barge in.

Mountmain and Trelawny continued their argument. It sounded as if blows would soon be exchanged. Mountmain was unlikely to hear them moving about beneath his feet.

He nodded to Kate, and proceeded to the double doors.

After a breath, he pushed the doors open.

The room was large, and dimly lit by Aladdin-style lamps. Kate gasped at the obscenity of the bas-reliefs that covered the walls and the altar. Fishy chimerae and alarmed nymphs coupled with joyless frenzy.

Beauregard was surprised to see the Jewel of Seven Stars laying in the open, on the altar. It held the lamp-lights, and its stars burned.

Kate gasped at her first sight of the jewel.

Another item of stolen property lay on the floor, stretched out face-down before the altar. Its bandages were unravelled around its ankles and arms, and it was broken into a scarecrow pose, crucified rather than curled up at rest.

The mummy of Pai-net'em.

Kate stepped over the mummy and looked at the Seven Stars. Her fingers fluttered near it, tips reddened by the stone's inner glow.

'It's a beauty,' she said.

Beauregard had not bargained for something as easy as this.

'Should we just take it and leave?' Kate asked.

Beauregard hesitated.

'Come on, it's one in the eye for Mountmain.'

She took a hold of the jewel, and screamed.

A spindly arm had shot out, and a sinewy hand grabbed her leg, pulling her down.

It couldn't be the mummy. It was someone wrapped in mouldering bandages, a grotesque guardian for the jewel.

At the scream, Mountmain and Trelawny stopped arguing.

The mummy man rose up, loose-limbed and faceless, and threw Kate away. Her cap fell on the floor, and her hair tumbled loose. The jewel cast a bloody light across the mummy's sunken chest.

Living eyes looked out of the dead mask.

Beauregard caught Kate and hugged her. He kept the mummy man covered with his revolver.

Mountmain charged into the room and was struck dumb by what he saw.

'What in the name of Glaaki!'

Underneath ancient linen, a lipless mouth smiled.

Trelawny was at Mountmain's shoulder. He barged past the Irishman and towered over the mummy man.

'Stay back, Professor,' Beauregard warned.

Trelawny reached for the Seven Stars. The mummy launched a claw-fingered hand at the professor's throat, and ripped it away. A rain of gore fell onto the jewel and seemed to be absorbed.

Trelawny fell to his knees, still trying to draw air into his lungs through his ruptured throat. He pitched forward, dead. The mummy hung his head, almost in tribute.

Beauregard put three shots into the monster's chest, about where his heart should have been. He saw dusty divots raised in the cloth-wrapped flesh. It staggered but did not fall.

Mountmain was backing away from the altar.

'Interfering fool,' he snarled at Beauregard. 'Are you content now?'

'What is that?' Beauregard indicated the mummy.

'What do you think? It's Pai-net'em, wanting his jewel back. It's all he's ever wanted.'

The mummy stood over the altar.

Beauregard saw he had been wrong. It couldn't be a man dressed up. The legs were too thin, like shrouded bones. This was an ancient, dried thing, somehow animate, still imbued with soul.

'He's the saving of your rotten world,' Mountmain said. 'But he'll rip you apart. My design may not be accomplished, but you'll get no joy from my thwarting. Mr Beauregard, and whoever you might be, young sir, I bid you good-bye.'

The Irish Mage stepped back through the doors and slammed them shut.

They were trapped with Pai-net'em.

'"Young sir"!' Kate sneered. 'The cheek of the man.'

The mummy had killed Whemple, Jenks, Bacon and Trelawny. And others. All who stood between it and the Jewel of Seven Stars. Now Mountmain thought it would kill Beauregard and Kate.

The mummy bobbed a little, like a limber puppet. Flesh gobbets still clung to its claw-hand. It hovered by the altar, where the jewel was fixed.

Beauregard was prepared to throw himself to Pai-net'em, to protect Kate. He did not think he could come out best in a wrestling match. And clearly his revolver was useless against this dead-alive thing from an ancient grave. Had he lain for three thousand years, seven sparks inside the jewel to keep him warm?

Through the thin bandage, Beauregard saw Pai-net'em's snarl.

'Take it,' Beauregard said, indicating the jewel. 'It was robbed from you. On behalf of my queen, I return it to you, with honour.'

Did Pai-net'em listen? Could he understand?

The mummy snatched up the jewel and held it to his breast. The Seven Stars sank in and the hole closed over. A red glow seemed to throb in Pai-net'em's chest. He slumped, dormant.

Kate let out a breath, and clung to Beauregard.

He kissed her hair.

By dawn, Declan Mountmain was in custody, apprehended at Victoria Station attempting to board the boat train. With two corpses (three, counting the mummy) in his house, he would be detained for some time. The Seven Stars, Beauregard had decided, should remain where it was. It did not strike him as a fitting addition to Her Majesty's collection, and he had taken on himself to relinquish it for the nation. He had an idea Victoria would approve.

Kate, who had to keep out of the way while Lestrade was poking around, sat on the front steps, waiting for him.

'The house is full of stolen property,' he told her. 'Manuscripts from university libraries, impedimenta from museums. There are even body parts, too repulsive to mention, which seem not to be of ancient origin.'

'I told you Declan Mountmain was a bad 'un.'

'He'll trouble us no longer.'

Kate looked at him oddly.

'I wouldn't be so sure of that, Charles. We can't exactly stand up in court and honestly tell the tale, can we?'

Kate scratched her ankle, where the mummy had grasped.

'I'd love to write it up, just to see Stead's face as he spiked the story.'

She stood up, linked arms, and walked away from Mountmain's house. It was the Day of the Jubilee. Flags were unfurled and streets were filling, as London began its great celebration.

'I shall not get to go to the Tower,' Kate said. 'And I had a dress picked out.'

'It's always possible you'll end up in the Tower.'

She punched his arm.

'Get away with you, Charles.'

'I'm afraid the best I can offer is a trip to the British Museum, to see Pai-net'em returned to his sarcophagus. I doubt he'll go on exhibition. My recommendation is that he be misfiled and lost in the depths of the collection.'

Kate was thoughtful.

'Nothing's solved, Charles. The Seven Stars remains a mystery. We're not closing the book, but leaving the story to be taken up by the as-yet unborn. Is that not always how it is?'

Episode Two: The Magician and the Matinee Idol

The February chill made Catriona Kaye wish hemlines weren't being worn above the knee this season. Her bobbed hair, tucked under a cloche hat, left her slender neck bare, prompting her to wrap her fur collar tight around her throat.

Born with the century, now just twenty-two, she sometimes felt that her obligation to follow the fashions of the times was a curse. Her father, a West Country parson, was always on at her about the scandalous way she dressed, not to mention her cacophonous American tastes in music. Edwin never chided, sometimes claiming in his lofty manner that she was a useful barometer: When she was up, so was the world; when she was down, calamity was in the offing.

Presently, she had much in common with the Grand Old Duke of York's Ten Thousand Men. She was neither up nor down. The wind blowing down Baker Street was winter, but the clarity of the air—no fog, no rain—was spring.

Things were about to change.

Two elderly matrons nearby had noticed the celebrity. They were frankly goggling, like children at the circus. Catriona thought them rather sweet about it.

The celebrity had just stepped out of a door which bore a famous, and famously hard-to-locate, address: 221B. He wore a fore-and-aft cap, and a checked ulster of Victorian cut. He turned to cast a hawk-like gaze at the distance, sharp profile distinct and distinctive, and raised a magnifying glass to his eye.

'Isn't that...?' began one of the matrons.

The object of their amazement was accompanied by a shorter, plumper, huffier man, in a bowler hat and moustache. He held a revolver.

'I do believe it is,' the other matron agreed. '*John Barrymore!*'

The Great Profile turned full-face to the admiring dears, one eye hugely magnified by his glass, flashed a thin grin, and gallantly doffed his deerstalker. One matron swooned in the other's arms.

Catriona couldn't help but giggle.

A short man with a megaphone began shouting, chiding the matinee idol for 'playing at the rear stalls'.

'I'm afraid I shall never get the hang of this film business,' Barrymore lamented.

Catriona understood that the actor was mostly concerned with his impending *Hamlet*, and had little concentration left over for this photoplay of Mr Conan Doyle's *Sherlock Holmes*, or rather Mr William Gillette's celebrated stage drama. From what she'd seen of the 'shooting', Barrymore's sleuth had quite a bit of the gloomy Dane about him and spent a great deal more time making goo-goo eyes at the heroine than plodding over the scene of the crime with Good Old Watson. Mycroft Holmes would be revolving— very slowly, and with great gravity—in his grave.

Edwin, her 'whatever', affected to be interested in the intricacies of the camera, and spent his time interrogating the crew on tiny technical points. She knew that trick of his, to pretend one overwhelming enthusiasm in order to winkle out all manner of other unconnected information from those he was politely and unnoticeably interrogating.

Not for the first time, she felt a lot like Good Old Watson. She and Edwin were a partnership, but too many people—though not Edwin himself— thought of her as a decorative adjunct to the genius of a Great Man.

Admittedly, she wasn't expected to pen adulatory accounts of the exploits she shared with Edwin Winthrop. In most cases, the principles would certainly not care to find their confidential affairs written up in the popular press. The bally Baskervilles can hardly have been delighted to have the whole nation privy to their nasty squabbles, come to that. There were also, in some instances connected with Edwin's shadowy employers in the late War, questions of state secrecy to be considered.

Barrymore was annoying the director, a man named Parker, with his diffidence. When disinterested in his work, he tended to ignore his Prince's sound advice against 'sawing the air'. She noticed that Roland Young, the cove playing Good Old Watson, was managing with extremely British tact not to be annoyed, in such a manner that his actual feelings were plain. Now that was real acting.

After two days of hanging about as the American film crew took location 'shots', she was used to being mistaken for an actress or even one of the Great Profile's surplus mistresses. Remembering Edwin's advice, she took pains never to contradict or confirm assumptions.

As their occasional government commissions went, this was hardly momentous. Their business was usually with the living who are being bothered by the dead; in this case, they were here to protect the interests of the dead against slander. Edwin was doing an unofficial favour for the Diogenes Club, the institution which had found him official employment during the Great War and which still had occasional need to call on his services.

Mycroft Holmes, the consulting detective's less famous but more perspicacious brother, had once sat on the Ruling Cabal of the Diogenes Club, in the seat now occupied by the somewhat slimmer-hipped Mr Charles Beauregard, to whom Edwin reported.

Last year, Edwin and Catriona had been involved by the Diogenes Club in a row involving a phantasmal samurai who wielded a very substantial sword in the Japanese Embassy, lopping off the heads of several uncomplaining staff members. The bloody business was eventually brought to a satisfactory conclusion, with human deviltry exposed and psychic shenanigans explained away. She was now the only girl she knew with a personal scroll of commendation from the Emperor of Japan in her dresser drawer.

This was far more routine. It came down to reputation. Though never under the command of the Diogenes Club, the Great Detective had once or twice assisted his brother with problems much as Edwin and Catriona now assisted Beauregard. It had been the cause of something of a rift between the Holmes Boyos that Good Old Watson and Mr Doyle had written up a few of these bits of business, going so far as to mention the institution in print and giving some hint as to Mycroft Holmes's actual position in the British government.

That was all blown over now. But Beauregard, as much out of respect for the memory of his old chief, wanted the cloak of obscurity habitually worn by the Diogenes Club and all its operatives to fall heavy again.

'It will almost be a holiday,' Beauregard had said. 'Mingling with show-folk. Just make sure they stay away from the facts.'

Parker was on at Barrymore again about his famous moustache. It was still not shaven off. Apparently, it would not show in 'long shots', but would have to go for the 'close-ups'.

Catriona wondered whether Edwin's moustache was only coincidentally identical to the actor's. He professed to disdain fashion when he was making fun of her kimonos or shaven hackles, but he could be a touch dandyish in his own appearance.

'You'd be fastidious too,' he would say, 'if you'd spent four years in a uniform stiff with mud.'

The War excused a lot.

Parker stormed away from the actors. Barrymore, treating the wide step of 221B as a stage, gave a bow for the gallery. The onlooking crowds applauded mightily. The director glared in frustration and muttered about cracking the whip when the company got back to the States.

'You, technical advisor,' Parker addressed her. 'What's wrong with that scene?'

'I don't like to mention it really,' she said.

'It's what you're here for, isn't it? It's that blasted lip-fungus of John's.'

'He could be in disguise,' she said, trying to be generous.

Parker laughed bitterly.

'It's the address,' she piped. 'The front door would just have 221 on it. A and B and, for all we know, C would have doors on the landings.'

Parker shook his head and stalked off.

'I am right,' she told his back.

Though they lived—together! in sin! scandalously!—in the Somerset house Edwin had inherited from his disreputable father, they were more often found these modern days in their London *pied-a-terre*, a nice little flat in Bloomsbury, which Catriona officially kept as a residence to allow her father to avoid a heart attack by believing she lived apart from Edwin. This evening, with Paul Whiteman's 'Whispering' on the gramophone, they discussed the day's work as they danced, occasionally dropping the odd inconvenient item of clothing.

'Old Beauregard has nothing to worry about, Cat,' said Edwin, almost directly into her ear. 'Along the chain that leads from Holmes to Watson to Doyle to Gillette to Barrymore, anything that might be taken as real or referring to reality has been stripped away.'

'The Diogenes doesn't figure in the film scenario?'

One hand firmly in the small of her back, Edwin dipped her over, supporting her weight. She often felt on the point of losing her balance, but Edwin would pull her back just in time.

'No.'

They kissed. The song ended. They occupied themselves upon the divan.

Afterwards, propped up among Turkish cushions, drawing on a cigarette through a long holder, kimono loose about her shoulders, she thought again about the errand.

'Surely, after all these years, no one actually cares about the dratted Bruce-Partington Plans anymore.'

Edwin laughed lazily. He was drifting towards a doze as she was becoming more awake. He claimed to be catching up on all the sleep missed through four years of shelling day and night.

'It's the principle, poppet. Secrecy. If everybody knew everything, there'd be mass panic.'

She wondered about that.

'Darkness has become a habit for too many, Edwin.'

'You shall cast light, Cat. You are a beacon.'

He stroked her leg. She considered stabbing him with her lighted cigarette.

'Rotter,' she snorted.

Edwin sat up, unconsciously passed his fingers over his (John Barrymore) moustache, and paid attention.

'Old secrets, dear,' she said. 'There are too many of them. And new ones piled on top.'

'We only need dawdle about the kinema wallahs for a few more days,' he said, taking her hand. 'Then, I promise, we can find a nice ghost story, a bleeding nun with ghastly groans or a castle spectre with clanking chains. We shall explain it away with the shining light of science and rationality. Bit by bit, we shall banish the darkness from these isles.'

She biffed him with a cushion.

Mostly, the darkness was subject to banishment when they applied themselves. But sometimes...

'What more do we need to know about this silly film?'

'Nothing, really. I telephoned Beauregard and passed on all that we've ferreted out. He particularly asked that we be present at the next "location", to represent the nation's interests.'

'The *nation's* interests?'

'Indeed. The Goldwyn Company has secured permission to take film in the private recesses of the national collection, in the basements of the British Museum—some confrontation between Holmesy and that mathematics professor of sorry memory—and we're to be there to see they don't break anything. They will be "shooting" at night, after everyone has gone home.'

She shook her head.

'I'm a serious person,' she announced. 'A scientific inquirer. My field, in which I am widely published and hailed even at my tender age, is psychical research. I do not mind, under certain circumstances, serving my country as a more-or-less secret agent. However, I draw the line at working as an unsalaried night watchman!'

He embraced her, and she knew she'd give in eventually.

'Haven't you ever wanted to find out what's *really* kept in all those vaults? We shall get to root about among artefacts and manuscripts forbidden to the public.'

That was not fair. He knew she couldn't resist that temptation.

She kissed him, hungry again.

'You shall shine in the dark,' he said.

The cellar was vast, a vaulted ceiling above a crate-filled trench. Though the tiled walls were cold to the touch, the cellar was remarkably free of damp. At one end, an uncrated Easter Island head, crown scraping the ceiling, surveyed the scene. The statue was as long-faced and beaky as the unprepossessing original currently impersonated by the classically handsome actor grappling centre stage with an ersatz Napoleon of Crime.

'This looks like an underground railway station,' she commented.

'Exactly, Clever Cat,' Edwin agreed. 'Built as a stop for British Museum, but never finished. The company was bankrupted. Most of the line caved in, but the Museum has kept this as its deepest store-room. Some things are too huge to stack in an ordinary basement.'

'How silly,' she said. 'Plainly, the underground railway should be operated by a single company for the benefit of the nation, not by competing and inept rival factions who'll honeycomb under London until the whole city falls in.'

He did not give her an argument.

Parker called 'cut!', his megaphone-amplified voice booming through the cellar.

Barrymore—lip shorn at last, not entirely to the detriment of his looks—stood up, and a girl dashed in to re-apply grease-paint to his cheeks. The site of his battle with Moriarty was now swarming with 'crew', all intent on some tiny task.

A youth in knickerbockers assisted 'Moriarty' to his feet. The Prof was impersonated by an authentically frightening-looking fellow with ragged hair, eyes like corpse-candle flames, and a thin-lipped sneer. An assistant director who, she realised, was slightly sweet on her, said Moriarty's impersonator was an Austrian by the aptly villainous name of Gustav von Seyffertitz. He had signed himself with the absurdly Yankee alias of 'G. Butler Clonblough' during the late unpleasantness.

Barrymore could switch his Sherlock off and on like an electric lamp, melodramatic when the camera was cranking but larking outrageously between 'takes'. Von Seyffertitz, whom Barrymore liked because he made him look even more handsome by contrast, seemed always to be 'on', and occupied himself by skulking villainously as the director shouted at Barrymore.

She nudged Edwin, and nodded at 'Moriarty'.

The actor was drifting out of the circle of artificial light, towards the pile of crates, as if drawn to worship at the chin of the Easter Island head.

'That's odd,' Edwin commented.

'You're just jealous.'

So far, they hadn't been able to take advantage of this opportunity to root about among forbidden treasures. The priceless and ancient artefacts were just backdrop, and heaven help anyone who strayed accidentally into the camera's line of sight. The director might well have the powers of instant trial and execution granted to battlefield commanders.

Von Seyffertitz was definitely looking for something. Through pince-nez, he peered at runic marks chalked on the crates, tutting to himself.

'Old Beauregard told us to be on our guard down here,' Edwin said. 'There was some bad business to do with the Museum in his day, round about the Jubilee. He's a bit cranky about it, if you ask me. Long and distinguished service and all that.'

Ever since descending from street level, Catriona had felt a chill that was more than the cold. Beyond the fragile light, the shadows were deeper than they had any business to be.

'Mr Beauregard is rarely mistaken,' she reminded Edwin.

It was time for the antagonists to tussle again. Parker called the 'crew' clear, and pulled Barrymore and von Seyffertitz together as if refereeing a boxing match. The Austrian seemed reluctant to leave off his poking-around for something as insignificant as doing his job.

'I'll bet that fellow gets fed up with being defeated,' Edwin said. 'I've seen him as the villain in a half-dozen flickers.'

Like her, Edwin was secretly devoted to the newest art. They attended the kinema far more than the theatre, and had an especial fondness for the serials made in Paris, *Fantômas* and *Judex*. When she had occasion to use an alias herself, Catriona often picked 'Irma Vep', after the ambiguous villainess of *Les vampires*.

'I wonder if he is ever tempted to fight back properly, and best the hero. Just once.'

She saw what Edwin meant. Moriarty was giving a strong account of himself for an elderly mathematics professor—in actuality, exactly the sort of person it is supremely easy to toss off a waterfall—and Sherlock was taking all the knocks.

Von Seyffertitz weaved and punched like a far younger man, landing a few potential bruises on the famous face. Barrymore was in a bit of a sweat. Had the Professor forgotten the scenario? He *was* supposed to lose.

Von Seyffertitz got a wrestling hold on Barrymore and threw him to the floor. The director called 'cut!' Concerned people descended in a swarm. The star was bleeding. Moriarty mouthed an insincere apology.

'My face, my face,' wailed Barrymore, theatrical voice filling the cellar.

Edwin nodded that she should take a look.

She ventured near the actor, handkerchief out.

Blood trickled from both nostrils, replacing the shaven moustache with a red imitation.

'Is my dose broken?'

She staunched the flow of blood, and felt for give in Barrymore's nasal cartilage. She thought his valuable fizzog was not seriously damaged and told him so.

'Thank heavens,' he declared, kissing her forehead, fulfilling the dreams of a million matinee-goers. She felt a sticky, unromantic discharge in her hair and discreetly scraped it off and onto a wall.

'I must save myself,' the actor muttered. 'This doesn't matter.'

Barrymore was relieved beyond proportion. She realised he had been afraid for his long-awaited *Hamlet*.

'Bless you, child,' he said. 'For the merciful news. One cannot play the Prince with a patch of plaster in the middle of one's face. To have lost that for this penny dreadful would have been too much to bear.'

Actors were a rum lot.

Parker called an end to the night's 'shoot'. Until Barrymore's nose recovered, there was no point in going on. An assistant gleefully totted up how much this delay would cost.

'Tomorrow night, I want you to thrash that blasted Austrian within an inch of his ugly life!' demanded Parker.

'You have my word,' Barrymore said, sounding better already.

The equipment was dismantled, and the company began to withdraw on the double.

Edwin touched her elbow and stepped into shadow, encouraging her to join him.

'Something's wrong,' he said, trench-nerves a-tingle.

She nodded. He was right. She felt it too.

The film lights were turned off, leaving deep darks and illusory afterimages. But there was another light, a reddish glow, almost infernal.

Was there a whiff of brimstone?

Equipment and persons were being crammed into a cage lift that was the easiest access to the surface.

The glow was coming from behind the Easter Island head. A shadow, like a man-sized stick insect, moved on the face of the head, clinging to the hatchet-nose.

'Look, Cat. You can see that the tunnel extends beyond that statue. It must be shored up and used as extra storage space.'

The shadow detached itself from the nose and slipped around the head, briefly blotting the crimson glow, and disappeared into the tunnel.

'That was a man,' Edwin said.

'Was it?' she ventured, unsure.

There was something in the way the shadow moved.

'Come on, Cat.'

Edwin was after the shadow. She hesitated only a moment and followed him. He had produced a revolver from under his coat. This was no longer a holiday.

She wished she had dressed for this.

The film folk were busy leaving. Only a few remained, and they were intent on their business, noticing nothing. Edwin paused at the end of the platform and looked at the Easter Island head.

'I wonder how they got it down here?' he mused.

The face seemed to snarl at them.

Edwin led the way, climbing around the head by using the pendulous earlobe as a grip, and dropping to the cinder-strewn bed of the tunnel. She followed, fearing for the state of her silk stockings and white pumps.

In the tunnel, the glow was stronger. Definitely a red lamp somewhere, beyond the array of dilapidated crates. It was also much colder here. She shivered.

These crates were stacked more hap-hazardly. Some were broken, spilling straw onto the tunnel-bed. Some of the damage looked recent.

Edwin was attracted to a crate that lay open. Straw and African masks were strewn nearby, as if thrown out to make way for some new treasure. He lit a match and tutted. She stepped over to look in.

An elderly man, dressed in his unmentionables, was crammed into the crate, unconscious. She checked his breathing and pulse. Edwin lowered the match, to cast light on the man's face. It was von Seyffertitz, a chloroform burn around his mouth and nose.

'He's been here for a while.' she said.

'Then who was playing the Prof?'

She shivered, not with the cold.

'I say,' boomed a familiar voice, 'who's there? What's going on?'

It was, of all people, John Barrymore.

'It's Miss Kaye, isn't it? The angel of nasal mercy. And you're the lucky fellow who knocks around with her.'

'Edwin Winthrop,' Edwin introduced himself.

'Are you sneaking off to, um, spoon?'

Edwin shook out the match too late. Barrymore had seen von Seyffertitz in the crate.

'Good God, a body!'

Edwin glumly lit another match.

'It's Gustav the Ghastly,' Barrymore said.

'Someone has been impersonating him,' Edwin admitted.

'I shouldn't wonder,' Barrymore said. 'He's easy to "do". I can look like him myself. A grotesque face is far easier to hide behind than a handsome one. When I played the uncanny Mr Hyde...'

Edwin waved the actor quiet.

Barrymore became aware of the ruby light. He caught on at once that there was something strange about here.

Among the African masks was a white shock of hair. The wig 'Moriarty' had worn. The pince-nez and a false nose were in with the mess.

Their quarry was so intent on his business that he didn't mind leaving a trail. That suggested an arrogance or confidence that was not comforting.

'Come on,' said the matinee idol, striding forwards like a proper hero, 'let's get to the bottom of this.'

Edwin took Catriona's arm, smoothing her gooseflesh, and held up the match as they walked towards the glow. When the match went out, there was enough light to see by. Somehow, that was more frightening than the dark.

A large brass-bound trunk blocked almost the entire tunnel as if it were a dead end. But red light outlined it, revealing that there was a space beyond.

They crept up and pressed themselves to the wall, to look past the trunk.

It was hard to make sense of what they saw. An area had been cleared and a design marked on the cinder-floor in white powder or paint. At various points of the design stood Arabian Nights lamps, burning redly. Catriona could not at first discern the shape made by the lines and the lights. It was not the familiar magic circle, or a pentagram.

There were seven lamps, spread not quite in a line. She moved her head a little, and saw it.

'The plough,' she whispered.

Edwin's grip on her arm momentarily strengthened.

'Clever Cat,' he said, proud.

The lamps made up the Seven Stars. The constellation of Ursa Major.

An open case—not a wooden crate but a coffin-shaped metal container—was in the middle of the design. A point of red glinted within the case. She fancied she could see it even through the metal side.

And a thin figure stood over the case, arms spread wide, muttering in an unfamiliar language. The frock coat of Moriarty still hung from his shoulders, lifted by an otherwise-unfelt wind.

Some species of ritual was in progress. With every atom of sense in her body, Catriona felt this was Evil. She knew Edwin and Barrymore were as aware as she of this, and were struck quiet.

The man who had been Moriarty took a dagger from his inside pocket, and addressed the points of the constellation, tapping the tip of the dagger to his forehead and then pointing it at the individual star-fires. Then, he let his loose sleeve fall back and swiftly carved a series of symbols into his left arm, raising lines of blood that dripped down into the crate. Switching hands, he as deftly repeated the carvings on his right arm, allowing a red rain to fall.

Barrymore squeezed into the space between the crate and the wall, drawn into the drama like a star pulled from the wings. Edwin let Catriona go and took hold of the actor's shoulder, holding him back. All three were now jammed into the small space.

She saw that a body lay in the case, a light burning in its chest. Blood sprinkled a papery face and arms.

The ritual-maker was not a young man. His face was as sunken as that of the actor he had impersonated, if not as that of the mummy he was incanting over. He was almost completely bald, and stringy in the arms and throat.

Barrymore got free of Edwin and stepped into the makeshift temple. The ritual-maker saw him and halted, dagger pointed now as a weapon rather than a magic tool.

'Back, play-actor,' he said. 'I've waited too many years to be interrupted now. This has to be done precisely, as I once learned to my cost. It's not easy to separate Pai-net'em from his treasure.'

The ritual-maker spoke with an Irish accent.

Edwin and Catriona stood either side of Barrymore.

'Three interlopers,' the ritual-maker sneered. A drop of his own blood sparked at the tip of his dagger. 'You'll stay well back if you know what's good for you.'

The light in the mummy's chest was pulsing.

'Twenty-five years a convict,' the ritual-maker declared, 'and months of waiting for a chance to come down here. This new wonder of the age, the cinematograph, was just stirring when I went into Princetown Jail. Now, it has opened doors, just as I am opening a door now, a door that will mean the ruination at last of England and all it stands for.'

He was more than a madman.

'I know who you are,' Edwin said, quietly. 'Declan Mountmain.'

The ritual-maker was shocked.

'So, I'm not forgotten after all. I had thought all the others long dead. Evidently, England remembers its foes. Who set you upon me?'

Edwin gave no answer, but Catriona thought to herself that this was no accident. Charles Beauregard and the Diogenes Club had foreseen something like this.

She had heard of Declan Mountmain. Some sort of magician from the last century. His reputation was not of the best.

'Your prison didn't kill me,' Mountmain said. 'And now, at last, I shall have my prize. The magicking is complete. Pai-net'em is bound. I may take the jewel. I'm glad of an audience, as a matter of fact. I might even let you live through the deluge to come, to tell the tale.'

He knelt over the mummy and plunged the dagger into its chest. The corpse's eyes flew open and glared redly. But only the eyes moved, blazing with ancient frustration.

'Tied you proper, you Egyptian fool,' Mountmain chuckled. 'You'll walk no more.'

The magician sawed at the mummy's chest, cutting around the glow like a butcher. He thrust his hand into the hole he had made and pulled out the source of the light.

Catriona could only gasp. She felt dizzy.

It was a huge jewel, burning with an inner light.

'With this, I shall bring down a cataclysm whose memory will last when the sun has turned cold.'

Edwin raised his revolver and shot Mountmain.

The magician laughed. She *saw* the bullet strike him in the face, make a ripple as if in a reflection of a face on the surface of a pond, and disappear. The shot embedded itself in the brickwork of a wall a dozen feet behind Mountmain.

'The Jewel of Seven Stars has accepted me,' the magician announced. 'As it once accepted this dead thing.'

Mountmain brought his boot heel down on the mummy's head, crushing it in its bandages. The eyes no longer moved.

'I am become the Destroyer of Empire!'

Mountmain's laughter filled the tunnel. His eyes shone, each reflecting the Seven Stars.

Whatever else the jewel had done for him, it had transformed him into the incarnation of the melodrama villain he had been impersonating. Mountmain was acting exactly like a Drury Lane dastard, threatening to evict the heroine's mother into the cold, cold snow unless she bent to his wicked will.

The jewel reached out to them.

Catriona felt its pull. She resisted the impulse to faint, as if she were turned into the feeble girl who would be tied to the railway tracks.

'O villainy!' Barrymore thundered. 'Ho! Let the door be locked! Treachery, seek it out!'

Edwin fired another useless shot, this time at the jewel itself.

John Barrymore leaped upon Declan Mountmain.

The indecision of Hamlet was thrown aside, and he was Sherlock incarnate, incisive brain directing instant action.

She saw how surprised Mountmain was at this attack, how almost amused...

Barrymore's hands went to Mountmain's throat.

They grappled together, as if tottering on the brink of the Reichenbach. Mountmain fought back fiercely, as he had done when the camera was rolling. He clubbed Barrymore's head with the mighty jewel, causing flashes of bloody light to flood the tunnel.

Barrymore had Mountmain's dagger, and was gouging at the magician's wavering chest.

'The point envenomed too,' Barrymore quoted. 'Then, venom, to thy work.'

The dagger seemed to affect Mountmain more than the bullet had.

Edwin was calculating the odds.

'The Seven Stars isn't for the taking,' he said. 'It has to be fought for. It has to be earned.'

As usual, Catriona was annoyed that things were being kept from her. But she got the drift of the situation.

Barrymore and Mountmain fought like tigers. A lamp was knocked over, fire spreading along the white lines of the constellation. Shadows danced on the walls, and writhed on the contorted faces of the magician and the matinee idol.

'Here, thou incestuous, murd'rous, damnéd Dane, drink off this potion...'

'Pull down the stars,' Catriona said.

Edwin understood at once.

Mountmain had drawn power from his design. It was a condition of the ritual. She kicked one of the lamps out of place, and it shattered against a far wall in a splash of burning oil. She did the same for another.

Edwin stamped on the burning lines, kicking the diagram to pieces.

Barrymore had Mountmain bent backwards over the case, pushing him down onto the mummy's bones. The jewel was trapped between them. There was blood on both men's faces.

Catriona kicked aside the last of the lamps.

Fire spread, but the constellation was gone.

Barrymore and Mountmain cried out together. It was as if needle-fingers scraped Catriona's bones. There was something inhuman in the shared scream.

Edwin held her.

Mountmain lay broken across the coffin-case, one of the mummy's arms around his chest. A last sigh escaped from him, with a wisp of smoke from his mouth.

Barrymore staggered to his feet, slowly. His shirt was torn open, and a great red wound showed on his chest.

'I am dead, Horatio,' he declaimed.

'You that look pale and tremble at this chance,

That are but mutes or audience to this act,

Had I but time—as this fell sergeant Death

Is strict in his arrest—O, I could tell you—

But let it be Horatio, I am dead,

Thou liv'st. Report me and my cause aright

To the unsatisfied.'

As he spoke, Barrymore's voice grew in strength. His wound pulsed, not with flowing red blood but flowing red light.

'It's *inside* him,' Edwin breathed.

The flesh closed over the light, and the red was in the actor's eyes.

'O God, Horatio, what a wounded name,

Things standing thus unknown, shall live behind me!'

Then Barrymore stopped doing Hamlet, stopped doing Holmes. He stood still. His skin was smooth where his wound had been. Catriona thought she saw a faint light inside, as if his heart glowed. The jewel was gone.

Edwin picked up the dagger and looked at the stricken man.

Was he going to cut it out? As Mountmain had from the mummy. If so, would the jewel be his—with whatever that entailed—as it had been the mummy's?

Edwin thought it through and dropped the dagger.

Barrymore shook his head, as if he had just walked on stage without knowing his lines or his role.

The fires were burning out. Edwin arranged Mountmain in the coffin, tucking in his arms and legs, and put the lid on it, fitting it firmly into place.

Barrymore looked around with a 'where am I?' expression.

'Let's get him out of this place,' Catriona said.

Edwin agreed with her.

John Barrymore looked at the spectre, eyes bright with fear and love.

'Angels and ministers of grace defend us!
Be thou a spirit of health or goblin damned,
Bring with thee airs from heaven or blasts from hell,
Be thy intents wicked or charitable,
Thou com'st in such a questionable shape
That I will speak to thee...'

Catriona's hand closed on Edwin's. From their box, they could see the spots of sweat on the star's face. This was the opening night of Barrymore's greatest triumph. He seemed fairly to glow.

At last, she understood what the fuss was about. This was how her father must have felt when Irving gave his Dane. How the first audiences at the Globe Theatre must have felt.

The business under the British Museum was months gone, and they were an ocean away, in New York at the invitation of the star, his debt to them repaid with tickets to the opening of the century.

As the play went on, she wondered about the light in the actor's eyes, and thought about the jewel in his chest. He had been good before, but he was great now. Had the jewel anything to do with that? And was there a price to pay?

Then she was caught up in the drama, swept from her box back to Elsinore, when ghosts walked and vengeance warped the heart and soul.

Episode Three: The Trouble With Barrymore

'You are a private detective?' asked the little pop-eyed man with the Peter Lorre voice. 'Yes?'

'That's what the sign says,' I quipped.

My caller stepped nervously around the office door, and giggled the way he did in the movies. He *was* Peter Lorre.

'Can you be trusted with a confidential matter?'

'If I couldn't, I might be tempted to fib about it.'

His giggle became a laugh. The laugh you usually heard when he was torturing someone. It made a person nervous.

'I should have thought of that. You are an astute fellow.'

'In my business, it sometimes helps to be honest. If I weren't, would my office look like this?'

Lorre looked at my filing cabinet, and took in the fizzing neon sign out in the street too close to my window. The sun was just down, and night people were rising from their Murphy beds and coming out of their holes. My place of business did not look much like the elegant suite Bogart has in *The Maltese Falcon*. Then again, Sam Spade was a San Francisco dick.

'You were recommended to me by Janey Wilde.'

That figured. They had been in a *Mr Moto* movie together, two years ago when Hollywood could make films with Japanese good guys. I hadn't seen Janey since I handed back her missing child three months ago. She had called me in on a case I didn't like to think about, a case that didn't jibe with the way I had always assumed the world went.

If she had sent the talking screen's premier sadist to my office, I had a suspicion that the world was about to take another kink. I'd crossed that line once, from the place where mysteries can be wrapped up and the bodies stayed buried, into *Weird Tales* country.

'She impressed upon me your abilities at locating and returning missing persons.'

Besides everything else, I had got her back her baby. That made me a hero, I guess. She'd given me a big bonus but, what with the war and everything, the town had forgotten to throw a parade and give me the key to the girls' locker-room.

'Who's walked away?' I asked, hoping to jog Lorre out of his circumlocutory flirtation.

'"Walked" is not such an apt expression. You have heard, of course, of the Great Profile, John Barrymore.'

He pronounced it 'pro-feel', which—judging by what I had heard of Prince Jack—was not inappropriate.

'He died last week,' I said.

I was sorry as hell about it. I'd never met the man, but he had great talent and had drank it away. It was hard not to feel something about that.

'I hope you don't want me to investigate a murder. That's the cops' business and they'd rather I left them to it. Besides, I understand Mr Barrymore succumbed to what might best be called "natural causes".'

Lorre shrugged.

'John Barrymore is dead. There is no doubt about that. As dead as Sessue

Hayakawa's career prospects. But he is also a missing person. I want you to find him, and bring him back to the Pierce Brothers Mortuary on Sunset Boulevard. For this, I will pay one hundred dollars.'

'For this, you will pay twenty-five dollars a day. Plus expenses. My fees are not on a sliding scale.'

Lorre spread his hands and hunched his shoulders, accepting my terms.

'Someone has snatched Barrymore's body?'

'Regrettably, that is so. I am ashamed to confess that I am that someone. Do not think me callous. I am a European as yet unused to the brutalities of this frontier culture. I was suborned into the act by a well-respected father figure, the director Raoul Walsh.

'As an amateur of psychology, I have been conducting extensive self-analysis for years. I recognise in myself a lamentable need to accept the authority of a patriarch. It is a common European failing, most tragically represented by the general adulation of Hitler. He offered me a high position in the Reich film industry, despite my "mongrel" Hungarian background. I wired him that Germany had room for only one mass murderer of his talents and mine.

'I digress. I'm sorry. It is through embarrassment. Mr Walsh, a forceful individual who is in a position to advance my career should he so choose, suggested I join him in a cruel practical joke at the expense of his friend, Mr Errol Flynn.'

Lorre wandered around my tiny office as he spoke, picking up and putting things down, as if given bits of business by the director. I wondered if, after years of self-analysis, he realised he was repeating his act from *The Maltese Falcon*.

'Mr Flynn was greatly upset by the passing of Mr Barrymore. He also has a tendency to idolise father figures, and saw in Barrymore perhaps the end result of his own dissolution. He organised a wake at the Cock and Bull, a bar catering to the more theatrical type of alcoholic. John Carradine recited speeches from *Hamlet*. David Niven recounted anecdotes of dubious provenance. A great deal of liquor was consumed. Flynn himself told stories of Barrymore's genius and tragedy. He became extremely intoxicated and was struck with a fit of melancholy. At that point, Mr Walsh suggested a somewhat macabre practical joke, which we hurried to put into action.'

Lorre paused. I was following the story. Working in Hollywood, you get used to the name-dropping.

'At the end of the evening, Flynn was incapable of returning to his home unassisted. A taxi-cab was arranged. With drunken difficulty, he opened the front door of his house and switched on the lights, to be confronted with John Barrymore, unembalmed, sprawled in a chair in his hallway. The effect must have been considerable.

'You see, while Flynn was drinking, Walsh and myself surreptitiously left the Cock and Bull and made our way to the mortuary, where we bribed an attendant. We borrowed the body and transported it across town in Walsh's car, broke into Flynn's house, and propped up the corpse where he would find it. Imagine the ghastly sight it presented. Corpses have an unhealthy, pale glow in the moonlight. And Barrymore's face, empty of life, was a puffy mask of his former self. A truly grotesque thing.'

This sort of thing happens more than you'd think. As Lorre said, Hollywood is a frontier town. Nobodies are elevated to positions of wealth and power in a few short months and then transformed back into nobodies again. Every prince has his court of hangers-on, jesters, assassins, freaks, witch doctors and courtesans.

'So Barrymore is at Flynn's house?' I deduced. 'Why don't you just go over there and snatch him back. Flynn must be out cold by now.'

Lorre smiled again. His teeth were not good.

'Naturally, that was our plan. But when we returned at dawn this morning, we found Flynn's front door hanging open, the chair knocked over, and no sign of either Flynn or the *corpus*. Various of our party have been searching the predictable sinkholes of vice and depravity all day, but we have reached the end of our resources. It has been decided that you are to be commissioned to bring this regrettable matter to a swift, happy and most of all unpublicised conclusion.'

I sensed that under all the irony and his *mysterioso* screen image, Lorre was pretty much disgusted at what he had done. Then again, ninety-nine out of a hundred actors in this town would french kiss a leper if a bigshot director like Walsh suggested it. Father figures and idolatry aside, it made sense to keep happy someone who could turn you from a drunken Tasmanian pretty boy into Errol Flynn.

'You think Flynn still has the corpse?'

Lorre shrugged again. 'It is most likely. Unless both have been kidnapped by another party.'

'You've left someone at Flynn's house? In case he comes back.'

Lorre nodded. 'Of course. Mr Walsh took charge, and made sensible arrangements. He is a man of action.'

Lorre gave me a hundred dollars as a retainer. It came in whisky-circled five- and ten-spots, with a few crumpled singles, probably from a bar room whip-round. I imagined Walsh not having small enough bills on him to contribute.

We shook hands on it. I had a client. I had a case. I had a headache.

'Hold, sirrah!'

A long-legged figure, cloaked in darkness (and a cloak), stood tall in Errol Flynn's hallway, an accusing foil pointed at my breast-pocket. He had shoulder-length hair and a Buffalo Bill beard. His eyes were watery with a whiskeyish tinge. I recognised John Carradine.

'I'm the detective,' I said. 'Peter Lorre sent me.'

He stepped back, and saluted, slapping his long nose with the edge of his foil.

'Enter freely, friend. Thou most worthy servant of the higher law.'

Flynn lived in a big house up on Mulholland Drive. I'd heard the stories and expected *boudoir* decor, complete with velvet curtains and pictures of fat little naked people on fat little naked cushions. In fact, the place was in disappointingly good taste.

He even had books. Not sawn-off spines glued together to make a novelty door for a hidden cocktail bar. Not privately published, gorgeously-illustrated pornography. Proper books, by fellows such as Shakespeare, Scott, Stevenson and Conrad.

On its side in the hallway was a comfortable armchair. I imagined it stood up, with a dead actor sprawled in it. Not a lovely image.

Carradine bobbed around like a scarecrow on strings as I inspected the scene of the crime. Like Lorre, he knew how to cast himself. In his life, he was a courtier. Others might be Hamlet or Claudius, but he was down for Horatio or Osric. He knew when to put in a 'fie on it' or a 'message, sire!' and could swish his sword with the best of them. At this precise moment, he was getting in my way more than was advisable.

There were two possibilities. Flynn had taken the body and run off, either in a fit of insanity or as a joke to get back at Walsh. Or someone had intervened and snatched the both of them.

Actually, there was a third possibility. Three months ago, I'd have ruled it out altogether. But on a derelict gambling ship out in the Bay my opinion of the world had taken a tumble. Barrymore could have got up, and taken Flynn with him to the world of the dead.

To Flynn, Barrymore might be Jacob Marley. His fate was a hideously plausible prediction of the destination at the end of the road the younger man was taking. Was Flynn even now being shown the drunken ruination he could expect if he didn't reform?

No. That sort of thing didn't happen.

In books and movies, the supernatural has a point. The ghosts teach Scrooge a lesson. My experience was that nothing could be learned from the inexplicable. Like in the cartoons, pianos sometimes fell from the sky and squashed random people into pancakes.

There was no point in trying to make sense of this. If Barrymore were dragging a dead leg around the Hollywood hills like Tom Tyler in *The Mummy's Hand*, was that any more insane than the idea of propping up a dead matinee idol in a movie star's hallway just for laughs?

I looked around, for clues. The door-lock was smashed in, showing raw wood where the mechanism had been wrenched away. That didn't square with what Lorre told me.

'When they planted the body, how did they get in?'

Carradine hung his head to one side in a posture classically intended to display thought to the gallery.

'French windows at the back,' he said.

Lorre told me Flynn came home and, with drunken difficulty, unlocked his front door. But Lorre hadn't been there. He was imagining the plan as Walsh intended it. Had Flynn been so drunk that he decided not to bother with keys and smashed down his own front door?

It depended on what kind of drunk he was. If he were so soused he couldn't use a key, he would most likely be incapable of the physical task of kicking in a door—not an easy thing off the screen, even if you are Captain Blood and Robin Hood in one. In any case, it was more probable that Flynn would go round the back and get in easily through the French windows (as demonstrated by Walsh's body-snatching party) or take the easy option of sleeping it off in the garden.

I examined the lock. It had been professionally broken. A hefty shoulder had been applied. And a tell-tale black gouge suggested the involvement of a crowbar.

So someone else had broken in after Walsh. Someone better at smashing down doors but not as familiar with the property.

I reconstructed the crime, crossing the Flynn threshold and imagining myself as the wobbly movie star.

Dropped off in his drive-way, he weaves his way up to his front door and finds it broken in. Lorre, in his reconstruction, imagined Flynn coming face to face with the dead Barrymore. That was possible. But he must be alerted by the broken lock to the fact that something is wrong. That percolates through even the most drunken brain. He steps warily into the hallway, imagining himself the hero of his movie, too drunk to be as cautious and cowardly as anyone who didn't think he was Errol Flynn would be.

Standing in his doorway, in a sort of vestibule between the door and the hall, I thought it through. There was a table by the door. In a bowl on the table were a bunch of keys, a money-clip well-filled with bills and a five-hundred dollar watch. Flynn goes through the ritual of divesting himself of these items after stepping into his house, all the while trying fuzzily to think about the broken door. Is there danger inside?

I stepped out of the vestibule and reached out. I touched the lightswitch he must have flicked. I turned the lights off and then on again.

Flynn's eyes would be dazzled.

And he sees?

Barrymore, certainly. Maybe Walsh's joke goes as planned, and Flynn is terror-struck by the apparition. A puffy-faced, bloodless corpse.

But someone else—most likely, several someones—is there too, about their own business. Probably ill-doing of some sort. This place stank of it.

'Something is rotten in the state of Denmark,' I opined.

'You can say that again, buddy,' Carradine nodded sagely.

As I drove to the Pierce Brothers Mortuary, I thought about the case. The most likely and comforting solution, ridiculous as it sounds, was that Walsh chose to play his prank by coincidence on the night some entirely unconnected thieves decided to break into the Flynn mansion. The thieves get a surprise when they find Barrymore and are themselves surprised by a returning Flynn, and flee the scene, kidnapping the living and the dead.

It didn't play in Peoria. No matter how spooked they were by the body-snatching business, I couldn't imagine thieves who specialise in homes of the rich and famous but leave behind several thousand dollars of untraceable notes and an expensive watch. Not the sort of oversight you expect of the larcenous professional.

That meant the two break-ins at the Flynn place were connected. The second was a consequence of the first. The unknown persons were after Barrymore's body.

I wondered about the more fanatical fans. All the women who supposedly committed suicide when God took Valentino away. With a queasy stomach turn-over, I remembered whispers about corrupt morgue attendants who took back-handers to let ghoulish busybodies peer and pry and poke at celebrity corpses. There were stories about Jean Harlow you don't want to hear.

This was California, central clearing house for cults. Mostly harmless kook groups, but there were others—I had shivery memories of the Esoteric Order of Dagon in Bay City—who were deeply dangerous.

Did some crazed John Barrymore worshipper out there have enough *tana* leaves to bring him back for one last private performance?

It was a fine spring night. With the windows of the Chrysler rolled down, I could smell orange blossom and gasoline on the Los Angeles breeze. There was a war on, of course. But there were always wars on.

The Mortuary was a single-story structure with a lot of stucco, and a couple of palm trees in the sidewalk outside. They had a marquee, presumably to announce their big funerals. Barrymore, lucky to get work in Bulldog Drummond 'B' pictures these last few years, was back on top again, name in big black letters. This was the last place a star wanted to get billing. Though when Carradine went, he'd be lucky to rate a mention on the 'Also Dead' roster posted outside.

There's a guy who always plays mortuary attendants in movies. A little, skinny, bald, pockmarked character with a voice that reminds you of Karloff and eyes that light up when he thinks of a nice, cold grave. His name is Milton Parsons.

I could swear he moonlights at Pierce Brothers. He was behind the desk, a bellhop in a mausoleum, reading a funeral directors' trade magazine. The cover story was about a shortage of coffin materials, what with the war effort claiming most of the nation's lumber and brass. Wasn't that just like the government, making the undertaker's job difficult at the same time it was supplying him with more corpses?

I showed him my badge. It's very impressive.

'I've come about Barrymore,' I said.

I didn't have to ask whether he was the attendant Walsh had bribed. He gulped, Adam's apple bobbing over his wing-collar. He looked sallow and guilty.

'I was assured by Mr Walsh...' he began.

'That's okay, fella. There's a war on. Rules don't necessarily apply.'

He smiled, displaying a creepy slice of dentition that made his face even more skull-like. I wondered how much he'd have charged for a feel of Jean Harlow. I tried to keep my stomach down.

'Have there been any other unusual inquiries concerning Mr Barrymore?'

His eyes glittered. 'A great many have called to pay their respects. Several studio heads...'

None of whom would have given him work last week.

'... and a remarkable number of ladies.'

Barrymore had been famously profligate in that department since the turn of the century.

'If I might say so, it is becoming an embarrassment that the star is not, as it were, appearing on stage. An understudy will not suffice.'

'I'm doing my best to get him back.'

'I should hope so.'

I imagined Barrymore laughing. Wherever he was.

'Since Walsh took him away, have there been any other *insistent* inquiries?'

'Oh, all of them.'

'Unusually insistent. Groups of people, not single mourners. With perhaps a hefty member of the party, a chauffeur or bodyguard.'

I was thinking of the type of muscle used to smash in doors.

'Maybe of an occult bent. You know, creepy types?'

He thought about it. He shuddered.

'Yes, sir. Indeed. Groups of that description have called. Two of them.'

I closed my mouth. 'Two?'

'Shortly after Mr Walsh and Mr Lorre departed, an Irish fellow demanded to be allowed to see the corpse. He offered quite a considerable emolument.'

The attendant must have been sick to have gone with the first offer.

'He became quite abusive when we were unable to strike an agreement. He was accompanied by two unusual individuals. I didn't get much of a look at them, but they struck me as *wrong* somehow. I had the impression that they wore rather too much scent. To cover another smell, perhaps.'

'This Irishman. I don't suppose you got his name?'

The attendant shook his head. He did not enjoy remembering this encounter. I had hit upon something that spooked him.

Imagine how that made me feel.

'Didn't he give you some way to get in touch with him, when the corpse was returned, so you could do business?'

The attendant froze, and clammed up. I filled it in for him.

'You told him about Walsh. You told him who had the body. He paid you.'

He didn't contradict me.

'You said Barrymore was at Errol Flynn's house.'

'No,' he admitted. 'Is that true?'

'Did Walsh have much of a start on the Mystery Man?'

'An hour or so.'

It was impossible that the Irishman had tailed Walsh. Somehow, he had homed in on Barrymore. Did the dead actor come equipped with some sort of beacon?

My head was hurting more.

'And the second group?' I asked. 'You said two suspicious groups made inquiries.'

'I told them nothing.'

'So they weren't paying. Who were they?'

'An Englishman, a French-accented woman and an American who claimed to be a federal agent. The Englishman did most of the talking. He left his card.'

He left that up in the air. I didn't reach into my pocket. There was no need to put a bribe down to expenses yet.

'Do the Pierce Brothers still own the mortuary?' I asked. 'And are they aware of your sideline?'

The attendant scowled and pulled the card out of thin air like a conjurer. He handed it over.

I knew the name before I saw it.

EDWIN WINTHROP. THE DIOGENES CLUB. LONDON.

He had been around the Janey Wilde business also, along with a French woman named Geneviève Dieudonné and a fed called Finlay. I had the impression that Winthrop's special field of interest was *Weird Tales* country.

There was a telephone number on the back of the card.

'Because no money was involved, you didn't tell Winthrop about the Irishman, did you?'

The attendant looked down at his shoes. I shook my head, almost in admiration.

If Edwin Winthrop was surprised to hear from me, he didn't betray it in his even, chatty tones. I mentioned that I was looking for an actor, a recently deceased one, and that his name had come up in the investigation.

'In that case, you better pop out here for a chat. We're holed up in Coldwater Canyon. Just a couple of houses down from Boris Karloff.'

He laughed that off. If Bela Lugosi was involved in this, then all the screen's bogeymen would be represented. That wasn't my kind of movie.

I took the address, which was on Bowmont Drive.

'Careful how you go,' Winthrop advised me. 'The turns get a bit sticky. And a lot of the signs have been taken down, to fool Japanese invaders."

I knew that.

I drove out to Coldwater Canyon. This was going to be an all-night case. It seemed to me that everyone involved slept only in the day, like Dracula. Except Barrymore, and he was supposed to be sleeping all the time.

I knew next to nothing about Winthrop. He had some official position, but wasn't keen on specifics. There were worse things waiting man than death, Hamlet had said—and John Carradine would agree with him—and that was something princes and governments had always known, and always done their best to conceal from the rabble. I knew that all governments must have people like Winthrop—or our own Special Agent Finlay—to take care of those things, discreetly and without public honour. I didn't like to think how busy they might be.

I couldn't spot Karloff's house, and it took me a while to find Winthrop's hide-out. The whole street was ordinary. It was an ordinary house. A Filipino houseboy led me out onto the patio, where a group of people sat around the swimming pool. The moon was bright, and the only artificial light came from the glow-worm ends of cigars and cigarettes.

Winthrop wore a white dinner jacket and was smoking a foot-long Cuban cigar. A black cat was nestled in his arms, blinking contentedly. Winthrop grinned to see me.

Geneviève Dieudonné, who wore something silvery and clinging that suggested a resistance to the quiet cool of the night air, arose elegantly from a recliner and gave me a dazzling smile. She said she was pleased to see me again.

A grunt from the other man I knew, Special Agent Finlay, suggested he disagreed with his French associate. He waved a paw at me, sucked his cigarette dead, then lit another.

There were other people around the pool. I would have thought them a party, but the only drink in sight was tea, served in mugs, not the best china. This was a meeting and, from the slightly electric air, I guessed an urgent one.

Winthrop introduced me around.

A behemoth of a man whose weight was barely supported by a reinforced deck-chair was Judge Keith Pursuivant, a jurist I had never heard of but who greeted me in oratorical Southern style. He wore a voluminous cloak and a wide hat, and might have been Carradine inflated to the size of a dirigible.

Also present were a fellow called Thunstone, an academic named Leffing, a little Frenchman whose name I missed, a physician named Silence, and an American with too many Gs in his name to be credible.

'Have you heard of the Jewel of Seven Stars?' Winthrop asked.

'A racehorse?'

Winthrop laughed, and chucked the cat under the chin. 'No. A gemstone. One of the treasures of Ancient Egypt. An item of immense occult significance.'

'*Nom d'un nom*,' cursed the Frenchman. 'A psychic *bombe*, of incalculable magnitude.'

'Let me guess, someone else has it, and you want it?'

'You see through us entirely.'

'It's for the war effort,' Finlay said, dourly.

'We're throwing stones at Japan now?'

Strangely, nobody laughed at that. Which gave me a chill. This group might have its comical aspects, but they were deadly serious about their fabulous jewel.

'If it comes to that,' Geneviève said, 'the War might be well lost.'

'Set against us in this business are a crew of very dangerous characters,' Winthrop explained.

'An Irishman?' I ventured.

'You are up on this. Yes, Bennett Mountmain is the man to watch. A worse dastard than his uncle, if that's possible.'

Bennett Mountmain. I had a name.

'He was kicked out of Ireland by the priests. He still claims to be the rightful king or some such rot. We know he's been knocking about in bad places. Haiti, Transylvania, Berlin. Like that swine Crowley in the last show, he's been working for the Huns. He's in close with Hitler's crackpot mages. And he's after the jewel.'

'We think the Nazis have the spear of Longinus. Combine that with the Jewel of Seven Stars, and they might trump our Ark of the Covenant. We'd need Excalibur *and* the Holy Grail to beat that.'

'And the Maltese Falcon?' I asked.

'Oh, that's real too. The Knights Templar still have it. By now, it might be charged with some minor power. We don't need to bother with that. Do we, Gees?'

The fellow with all the Gs nodded. These people had a complex private history I didn't want to go into.

You might not think it to look at me, but I do know what the spear of Longinus is. Also known as the *heilige lance*. And everybody's heard of Excalibur and the Holy Grail. From that, I could deduce the sort of item this Jewel of Seven Stars was supposed to be.

'Mountmain has the jewel,' Judge Pursuivant boomed. His tones were impressive enough to disturb coyotes out in the canyon. 'All is lost.'

'He may have the jewel,' Winthrop said. 'But that's not the half of it. Getting it out of its vessel is notoriously a sticky business. We know that it is to be done at dawn, and in this mysterious White House of the prophecy. Mountmain's uncle couldn't manage it, which is why we're here all these years later. And the last twenty years will have shaped its aura in all manner of configurations. When you think of the life John Barrymore has lived. The heights, the depths, the triumphs, the humiliations, the genius, the despair. How much was Barrymore and how much the jewel? And how has all this *experience* affected the stone?'

Winthrop was excited, whereas the rest of his company was scared. Maybe he was a man of greater vision than they. Or maybe he was mad.

'We should be in Washington,' Finlay said, gloomily. 'We've missed the thing here. We should be there at dawn. The President himself might be in danger.'

Winthrop wasn't convinced.

'We have Washington covered. And North Africa. And *Maison Blanche* in New Orleans.'

Finlay killed another cigarette.

'This jewel,' I asked. 'You say it's in a vessel?'

Winthrop nodded, happily.

'What kind of vessel?'

'Why, John Barrymore's body, of course.'

About midnight I was back in my office in the Cahuenga Building, telephoning hospitals and morgues, asking whether a surplus stiff might have washed their way, one that seemed oddly familiar if looked at from the side. It was proper detective work, and as tedious and pointless as hell.

Someone—most likely this Bennett Mountmain bird—had John Barrymore, and inside the Great Profile was a rare and fabulously valuable jewel. Of course, if Mountmain hacked out the Seven Stars and dumped the body somewhere I could find it, then I'd still be living up to the letter of my mission. Lorre wanted the body back, not some priceless MacGuffin hidden inside it.

I was not yet suspicious enough to wonder whether Lorre had known about the Jewel of Seven Stars. He was only a sinister conspirator in the movies.

After the call-round was finished, I hit a few bars where newsmen hang out and invested some of Lorre's money in buying drinks and pumping for information. You can imagine the sort of newsman who has to stay behind in Los Angeles while all the decent writers head off to become war correspondents, and who also happens to be an after-midnight boozer.

I knew a lot of fellows like that.

Having struck Milton Parsons, I wondered if I'd come across a convenient squealer who was the spitting image of Elisha Cook, Jr, a shifty, sad-eyed little man who had the secret of the plot and was willing to swap it for a pathetic sliver of conversation. Of course, if I found an Elisha it was most likely he would wind up horribly dead by dawn, as an example.

Sometimes, it doesn't work out like that.

Nobody had even heard of Bennett Mountmain.

I got back to my office at about three, and found men waiting for me. I walked right into trouble. A fist sunk into my gut before I could get my hat off. Someone tried to take my coat off without unbuttoning it, yanking it from my shoulders to improvise a strait-jacket. I heard my spiffy coat rip as I was trussed.

The manhandlers were a couple of blank-faced goons in shabby overcoats. They smelled like Tijuana whores, but I didn't get fairy vibrations off them. They wore the scent to cover another smell. That was a familiar note.

In my chair sat a man with a gun. It was a very nice gun, an automatic. He showed it to me without actually pointing it anywhere, twirling it by the trigger guard. I happened to notice that the safety catch wasn't on. My visitor was a locked-room murder mystery waiting to happen.

'Twenty years I've waited,' my visitor said.

He had an Irish accent, soft but sinister. I knew who this was, but didn't say so.

'And before that, my uncle wasted a lifetime. To be so close to the achievement of such a purpose and have it snatched away. Do you have any idea, you foolish little detective, what that kind of frustration can make a person do?'

I was just deducing something when the gun went off. A bullet spanged off my filing cabinet, putting a dent in it and ringing the mostly-empty thing like a coffin-shaped bell. The bullet ricocheted my way, and thunked into the meaty shoulder of one of the men holding me.

He didn't say a thing. He barely even moved. I saw a slow trickle of dark blood seep into his sleeve. The man's lack of complaint frightened me.

Mountmain was pointing the gun now. At me.

'Where is it?' he asked.

'This is where I say, "I don't know what you're talking about", and you sneer, "but of course you do, foolish little detective"'—I liked the phrase—'and try to beat it out of me for an hour or two. The flaw in your plan is that I really don't know what you're talking about.'

There was no harm trying it on.

'You are working for the Diogenes Club,' he sneered. His favoured mode of expression was the sneer.

'I am working for Mr Moto.'

Deliberately, he shot the man he had wounded. This time, he put a bullet in the man's forehead. His hat blew off in a red cloud. No matter how John

Barrymore looked, this fellow looked worse. The trickling hole between his eyebrows didn't help.

'That's someone I rely on and, in a strange sort of way, am fond of,' Mountmain said. 'Now imagine what I'll do to you, whom I've never met before and to whom I've taken an intense dislike.'

'This would have something to do with a recently deceased Sweet Prince?'

'Give the man a goldfish.'

'And a rock?'

Mountmain's sneer verged on a snarl.

'A rock? You could call it that. If you were a very stupid person indeed.'

I did my best to shrug. Not easy.

Until five minutes ago, I'd assumed Mountmain had Barrymore. Certainly, that was what Winthrop thought. And he had read the program, which gave away all the story I had missed.

Not so.

'Your response time is excellent,' I said. 'I only started asking about you two hours ago.'

Mountmain sneered away the compliment.

'Ten thousand dollars,' he said. 'If you lead me to the jewel. If not, you'll be tortured until you tell what you know. In unspeakable ways.'

'I've never been tortured in a speakable way.'

'Americans are such children. You always "crack wise". But you don't know what wise means in Europe.'

He took my letter-opener from my desk. He flicked his cigarette lighter, raising a flame. He held the flame under the blade, looking from it to me.

'I'd have taken the ten thousand dollars,' he said.

'You've waited twenty years for something. If you wouldn't put up with torture after that, then you're not the man I think you are.'

He almost smiled.

'Very cleverly put. Indeed, I'd endure anything. But that's because I know what's at stake.'

The blade was red.

'You, *ma cushla*, know nothing.'

I tried to wrestle free, but the two goons—if that was all they were—held me fast. Mountmain stood up. He put his lighter away and spat on the red-hot blade. There was a hiss.

My office is on the sixth floor. Behind Mountmain was the window, and beyond that the irritating neon light. A face hung upside-down at the top of my window, a fall of blonde hair wavering.

I was impressed. Geneviève had either climbed up from the street or down from the roof.

She clambered like a lizard, her arms and torso visible through the window, and lunged forwards, breaking through the glass.

Mountmain turned as her arms went around his waist. He stabbed with my letter-opener, and she grabbed it with her bare hand. I smelled burning flesh and heard the sizzle. She bared sharp—unnaturally sharp—teeth and hissed, but did not scream. Mountmain bent backwards.

He shouted words in a language I didn't know.

I was let go, and the goons rounded on Geneviève.

The office was too small for much of a fight. Geneviève took hold of the first goon, the one with the holes in him, and stuffed him out of the window. He fell like a stone. I felt the building shake as he smacked against the sidewalk.

The other goon hung back.

Mountmain scrambled to the doorway and tipped an invisible hat, sneering another command in old Irish or whatever. Then he left us with the goon.

This was a bigger specimen. It had an acre of chest, and eyes like white marbles. Geneviève made a face at it.

'It's been around too long,' she said. 'The binding is coming loose.'

I had no idea what she was talking about.

Come to that, I was only just taking in the subtle changes in her. She still wore the evening gown, and had even scaled the building in heels, but her face was a different shape, sharper somehow. She had pointed teeth and diamond-shaped claw-nails.

We were in the world of the weird.

Geneviève held out her wounded hand. I saw the weal shrivel and disappear, leaving her white palm unmarred. The goon lurched towards her.

She knelt down, scooped up the letter-opener, and stuck it into his head. He halted, like a statue, but his eyes still rolled. He fell over, rattling the floorboards, and lay on his back.

'Do you keep food-stuffs here?' she asked.

'Is this the time to eat?'

'Table salt. I need salt.'

She was on the mark. I've had too many meals in the office, while working odd hours. I have a hoard of basic groceries stashed in the bottom drawer of the filing cabinet, below the liquor. Without questioning her, I found a half-full bag of salt. It must have been there for years.

She smiled tightly as she took it, never looking away from the goon. With a pointed finger, she yanked his jaw open. Then she poured salt into his mouth, filling it entirely until trails spilled out.

'Needle and thread would be too much to ask. Do you have an office stapler? A first-aid kit?'

There was a small box of pills and salves. She took a roll of bandage and wound it around the lower half of the goon's head, mummifying the salt inside his mouth. Then, she stood up.

The goon shook, and came apart. He dissolved into what Mr Edgar Allan Poe once described as a 'loathsome mass of putrescence'.

'Zombies,' she spat. 'Hateful things.'

I drove, with Geneviève beside me, legs up on the seat like a child. She chattered and I interjected, and we tried to figure it out.

'Mountmain must have had Barrymore, but lost him,' I said.

'He'll have him again soon. More importantly, he'll have the jewel. I'm surprised he bothered to call on you. It shows an impatience that is not good for him.'

'How did he find Barrymore in the first place? The mortuary attendant couldn't have known where Lorre and Walsh took him.'

'That's a nasty business. Scrying. It involves disembowelling a cat. Twice in one night would be pushing it, but my guess is that having failed to get what he wanted from you, he'll be here-kitty-kittying in some alleyway.'

'He can find Barrymore by gutting a cat?'

'Magic. Hocus pocus. It works, you know.'

'With so much at stake, couldn't you find a cat willing to give its life for the war effort?'

'It's not as easy as that. You have to be steeped in black magic for it to work. And that's not a good thing to be. It has long-term implications.'

'But Mountmain doesn't care?'

'I should think not. That's why black magic is a temptation. You get ahead easily, delaying the pay-off until it's too late.'

'What are you, a white witch?'

She laughed, musically.

'Don't be silly. I'm a vampire.'

'Blood-sucking fiend, creature of the night, accursed *nosferatu*, coffin-dwelling undead...'

'That sort of thing.'

I let her go with it. Obviously, it wasn't worth arguing.

'Where are the rest of you? Winthrop and the others?'

'I'm afraid we have certain differences among ourselves. The War makes for odd alliances. I have a distaste for government work, which has been set aside for the moment. I've been keeping track of the Jewel of Seven Stars since its rediscovery. Edwin is a servant of the crown. The Diogenes Club, and its equivalents in the allied nations, wants to get hold of the Seven Stars to use as a weapon of war.'

'How can a jewel win the War?'

'Think of it as a lens. It can focus intense destructive power. It seems to have a specific purpose. It is a device for destroying empires.'

'Like Germany and Japan? Sounds good.'

'You don't mean that. You haven't thought through what it means. It's not enough to win. You have to win without tainting yourself, or you're just piling up debts future generations will have to pay. Edwin can rationalise that; I can't. Of course, it's likely I'll be around to go through whatever future generations have to put up with.'

'Mountmain wants the jewel to help Hitler?'

'And himself. His family believes in a destiny. He is the head of something called the Order of the Ram. It is foretold that the Ram will reign over the last days of the world. You know who Nostradamus is?'

'Fortune teller?'

'That's the bimbo. In his suppressed quatrains, Nostradamus is surprisingly specific about the Mont-Mains. An expression disturbingly equivalent to "thousand-year reich" crops up quite a lot.'

'Errol Flynn has the body,' I said.

She was quiet, and thoughtful.

'He's the only player left in the game. Mountmain wouldn't have taken him seriously, a drunken hero. He got hold of the body and escaped. Then, Mountmain must have revised his first impression and assumed Flynn was acting to a deliberate plan rather than careening at random. He'd start looking around for confederates, and that would lead to the person rattling his cage, to wit: me.'

'I loved him in *The Adventures of Robin Hood*,' she said. '"It's injustice I hate, not Normandy!"'

'But where is Flynn? It's a shame your prophet didn't say where we could find him.'

'Michel de Nostre-Dame wasn't always accurate. Sometimes, he didn't understand what he saw. Sometimes, he filled in with nonsense. He does describe a crisis, but his suggestion is absurd. He says that the jewel is to be found at the White House. Edwin has someone in Washington. And Finlay is on a plane, racing the sun. Just in case the jewel is spirited across country by dawn.'

'*Dawn?*'

'Two hours away. That's where the quatrain is highly specific. Even allowing for changes in the calendar since 1558.'

I shook my head.

'There are white houses in California.'

'To be frank, it could mean anything. The expression Nostradamus uses is "Maison Blanche".'

I stopped the car. We were outside the Warner Brothers lot. Lorre's home base. And Errol Flynn's. The pre-dawn light was already turning the water tower into a Martian War Machine.

I laughed out loud.

This was what it was like. When you saw it, and nobody else did. This was what made a detective.

'It's here,' I said.

'How can you know that?'

'*Variety*. The trade paper. Most of my work is related to the studios. I keep up with the industry. Peter Lorre's shooting a film at Warners at the moment. With Humphrey Bogart and Ingrid Bergman.'

Geneviève was prettily puzzled. Her face had settled down to her ingénue look again.

'I don't see...'

'It's called *Casablanca*, Geneviève. *Casa Blanca. Maison Blanche.* White House.'

She looked across the lot, to the sound stages.

'Not the White House in Washington, not the city in North Africa. Here, *Casablanca*, Hollywood.'

I drove onto the lot.

There were night watchmen around, and a few early-arriving or late-staying technicians. I asked a uniformed guard if he'd seen Flynn. The man didn't want to say anything.

'I know he's on a bender,' I said.

Finally, he nodded to a stage.

'He'll be sleeping it off now,' the guard said. 'He's a good lad, and we don't mind covering for him. The stories you hear don't mean anything.'

I thanked him.

I could not resist a little triumph when I told Geneviève I had been right.

We walked rapidly to the stage and found an unlocked door.

Inside was an Alice world. Half the stage was converted into a nightclub, with ceiling fans, a beat-up piano, twenty-five yards of bar, a back-room full of gambling equipment and row upon row of bottles of cold tea. Glasses and guns and hats were strewn around, each precisely in the spot they would need to be for shooting to resume. There were black cameras, like huge upright insects, halted where the club carpets gave way to bare concrete. Unlit lights hung from frames above.

In the centre of the set were two men, slumped over a bottle.

Flynn was so drunk and scared that he was drinking cold tea as if it were best bourbon. Barrymore was dead, but moving. The supposedly dark set was lit by a ruby glow from inside the dead man's chest.

Flynn raised a glass to his idol.

'What's it all for, Jack?' He asked. 'All this mess, this nightmare, this fantasy, this horror? Is it just for play, just a game? To be packed up and put away by some snot-nosed kid who's lost interest?'

He slammed his glass down.

'I don't want it like that. I want Hamlet and Sherlock Holmes and Don Juan and Robin Hood and Custer. I want us to be heroes, to save something worth saving, to respect maidenly virtues and reflect manly ones. We shouldn't just be pathetic, whoremongering drunks, Jack.'

Barrymore was nodding.

There was no life in him. At least, none of his own. It was the Jewel of Seven Stars, animate. Geneviève took my arm, and gripped like a vice.

'To the glorious damnéd,' Flynn toasted, tossing his glass away, wreaking hell with the continuity.

Barrymore's starched shirt was open and his chest was bulging. A cinder glowed inside his translucent flesh, outlining the black bars of his ribs.

'If Flynn takes the jewel, he'll be John Barrymore all over again,' Geneviève said. 'Personal triumph and degradation. But only personal. It will be shielded from the world. Rather, the world will be shielded from it.'

'But it'll kill him,' I suggested.

Geneviève nodded.

'Everybody dies,' she said.

'Except you.'

In a tiny, long-ago frightened little girl's voice, she repeated, 'Except me.'

Streaks of sunlight were filtering through the unshuttered glass roof of the stage. I wondered if Geneviève Dieudonné would shrivel at dawn, like the salt-stuffed zombie in my office.

A shot sounded.

Geneviève yelped. She looked down at a scarlet patch on her silver chest. Blood spread and her eyes were wide with surprise.

'Except me,' she said, crumpling.

I turned, my gun out.

Bennett Mountmain strolled onto the stage.

He wore a stinking cat's skin on his forehead and upper face, like a caul, eyeholes ripped in the blood-matted fur.

'Silver bullet,' he explained.

Geneviève moaned and held her wound. She seemed for the first time helpless. She was muttering in French.

Mountmain walked past me, with contempt.

Flynn stood up and barred his way, shielding Barrymore.

'You again,' he snarled. 'The treasure-hunter. You'll have to fight your way past my cold steel to snatch Cap'n Blood's doubloons for your coffers.'

Wearily, Mountmain held up his gun.

'Go ahead, varlet, and shoot,' said Flynn. His face was red and sunken, but he was twice the hero he seemed on the screen. He appeared to grow, to have some of the ruby glow, and he threw open his mouth and laughed at Mountmain.

The Black Magician fired, and his gun exploded in his hand.

Flynn's laughter grew, filling the stage, setting ceiling fans whirling. There was a demonic overtone to it. He stood with his legs apart, hands on hips, eyes shining.

Barrymore tipped forward, and a large stone fell out of his chest onto the prop table.

The light of Seven Stars lit up the *Casablanca* set.

Mountmain was on the floor, rolling in agony, weeping tears of bloody frustration. Geneviève was trying to sit up and say something. I knelt by her, to see what could be done.

There was blood on her back too. The bullet had shot right through her. The holes in her were mending over and coming apart again as I looked. Her blonde hair was white. Her face was a paper mask.

'Take the jewel,' she said. 'Save Flynn.'

I crossed the room.

Flynn looked at me. He was unsure. He had recognised Mountmain for what he was. But not me.

'Pure and parfait knight,' he said.

That was just embarrassing.

He stepped aside. I picked up the Jewel of Seven Stars. Tiny points shone inside it. I expected it to be warm and yielding, but it was cold and hard. I wanted to throw it into the sea.

'You've found it,' a British voice said. 'Good man.'

Winthrop had left his scrying caul outside, but his forehead was still smeared. As he wiped the last of the blood away, I remembered the cat he had been cradling in Coldwater Canyon.

'Edwin,' Geneviève said, weakly, shocked. 'You haven't...'

'Can't make an omelette without breaking eggs,' he said, unapologetically. 'You don't approve, of course. Catriona wouldn't either. But you'll thank me for it in the long run. May I?'

He held out his hand. I looked at the jewel. I wanted to be rid of it. Flynn was still there. I sensed an attraction from the gem to the star. The sun was not yet up. I could plunge the stone into Flynn's chest and hide it for another generation. At the cost of a man's life.

Who's to say Errol Flynn wouldn't ruin himself without supernatural intervention? Plenty have.

Mountmain yelled hatred and defiance and frustration. He was bleeding to death.

Winthrop's hand was still extended. It was my decision.

People were pouring onto the stage. Winthrop's colleagues, cops, studio guards, Warners staff, uniformed soldiers, uniformed Nazis. I saw Peter Lorre, and other famous faces. Everybody was in this movie.

'Catch,' I said, tossing the jewel up like a bridal bouquet.

Mountmain stood up, extending his ruined hand. Judge Pursuivant landed on him, crushing him to the floor.

Winthrop made a cricketer's catch.

'Owzat,' he said.

Geneviève sighed through pain. I think she had stopped bleeding.

Someone asked in a loud Hungarian voice what the dead body of John Barrymore was doing on his set. Lorre breathed soothing sentiments, and a couple of grips removed the untenanted vessel from the site. Flynn, now merely drunk, further infuriated the director with cheery idiocies. That part of the story was swept aside. Hollywood hi-jinks. They happen all the time.

It came down to Winthrop, Geneviève and the jewel.

And me.

'We must be wise, Edwin,' Geneviève said.

The Britisher nodded.

'We have a great responsibility. I swear we shall not misuse it.'

'We may not have the chance to decide. You can feel it, can't you? As if it were alive?'

'Yes, Gené.'

Mountmain was dead, his spine snapped by Pursuivant. It had all come back on him, the black magic. Just as Geneviève had said it would.

Winthrop seemed sobered, shaken even. He couldn't get the last of the cat-blood off his face. He had done his duty, but now he was asking himself questions.

I hated that. I knew I'd be doing the same thing.

A soldier was beside Winthrop, with a lead box.

'Sir,' he prompted.

Winthrop dropped the Jewel of Seven Stars into the box, and the soldier hesitated, eyes held by the red light, before clamping shut the lid. He marched off, other soldiers trotting at his heels, drawing Pursuivant and the others.

Winthrop helped Geneviève onto a stretcher. She was fading, bare arms wrinkling like a mummy's, face sinking greyly onto her skull.

'What wash that?' someone asked me. 'The red shtone in the boxsh?'

I turned towards the star of *Casablanca*, a man satisfyingly shorter and older than me.

'That,' I said, 'was the stuff that dreams are made of.'

Episode Four: The Biafran Bank Manager

On the road to Somerset, Richard Jeperson drove into an anomaly. It was after midnight, a clear night in May. Behind the leather-covered wheel of his Rolls Royce ShadowShark, he mulled over the urgent message that had brought him from Chelsea to the West Country.

Then the quality of the dark changed.

He faded the dashboard-mounted eight-track, cutting the cool jazz theme that had underscored his drive. He braked, bringing the wonderful machine to a dead halt within three yards.

He heard no night-birds.

'Weirdsville,' he mused.

After slipping his flared orange frock coat over a purple silk shirt, he got out of the car.

He was parked on a straight road that cut across the levels. The stars and the sliver of moon were bright enough to highlight the flat fields of the wetlands, the maze of water-filled rhynes that made a patchwork of the working landscape.

Nothing wrong there, on the dull earth.

But in Heaven?

Tossing his tightly curled shoulder-length hair out of his eyes, he looked up.

An unaccustomed spasm of fear gripped him.

He saw at once what was anomalous.

He skimmed the constellations again, making sure he had his bearings. The North Star. Cassiopeia, the seated woman. Orion, the hunter.

Ursa Major, the Plough, was gone.

A black stretch of emptiness in the universe.

He had chanced on wrongnesses before, but nothing on such a cosmic scale. This could not be a localised phenomenon. If the seven stars were really gone, then the whole universe had been altered.

He found himself shivering.

The moment passed. He looked up, and the constellations were aright again. The Plough twinkled on, seven diamond-chips in the Heavens. Richard was cold, with a heart-chill that was more than the night. The world was not aright just yet.

He got back into the ShadowShark and drove on.

Two hours earlier, he'd been in the basement of his home in Chelsea, meditating. He was half-way through a ritual of purification involving a week of fasting. He had gone beyond the hunger that had chewed his stomach for the first three days. He had shifted up a plane of perception. Strength was pouring into him, and his mind was forming pearls of understanding around grits of mystery.

Against all his express orders, Fred—one of his assistants—had interrupted his meditation, calling him to the telephone. He didn't waste time in protest. Fred had been selected for his reliability. He'd not have broken in unless it was something of supreme importance.

After exchanging a few words with Catriona Kaye, Richard had ordered Fred to get the Rolls out of the garage and despatched Vanessa, his other associate, to pick up three portions of cod and chips wrapped. Throughout the drive, he had been working the wheel and gear-shifts one-handed, while feeding himself with the other. He could not afford the physical weakness of fasting. His stomach knotted as he stuffed himself. He overcame the side-effects of such a sudden imposture on his body by mental force alone. By breaking off the ritual, he lost much. Wisdom leaked from his mind as fish and chips filled his belly.

It was a haunting. Normally, he'd have taken Fred or Vanessa with him. But this was not one of his usual exploits on behalf of the Diogenes Club, the venerable institution that referred many problems to him. This went to the heart of his whole life. Now, the Diogenes itself—or rather, its most respected elder statesman, Edwin Winthrop—was under siege from forces unknown.

He drove with both hands now. He had a sense of the enormity of the interests at stake.

Geoffrey Jeperson, the man who adopted him—a boy with no memories—from the rubble of war, had served on the Ruling Cabal of the Diogenes Club with Winthrop. Richard had been brought up with stories of Edwin Winthrop's secret services to his country. He had taken his first tentative steps into the arcane as Winthrop's most junior assistant. With old Mr Jeperson dead and Brigadier-General Sir Giles Gallant retired, Winthrop was the last serving member of the Cabal that had seen the Diogenes through the tricky post-war years, when its many enemies had worked to see its ancient charter revoked and its resources dissipated.

Winthrop, nearly eighty, took little active part in the working of the club that was more than a club. He knew well enough to withdraw and let younger men have the reins, just as he had taken over from his own mentor.

Richard wondered whether Winthrop entirely liked or trusted the people who now belonged to the club. The likes of Cornelius and King, who puffed *kif* in the smoking room, and toted transistor radios, where an inadvertent cough was once grounds for instant expulsion, to keep up with the cricket. The new generation, among whom Richard counted himself, seemed to dabble in the occult like dilettantes, rather than marching into the darkness like Victorian explorers or mapping plans for the conquest of the unknown like imperial generals.

But Winthrop had been a firebrand before he was a blimp. He still had his secrets.

Now those secrets were crawling into the open.

The anomaly convinced Richard that the haunting was even worse than Catriona, Winthrop's lifelong companion, had indicated.

The ShadowShark cruised into the village of Alder. All the farmhouses were dark. The Manor House was a little way out of the village, on its own grounds. Richard drove past the small church and the Valiant Soldier pub, then took the almost-hidden road out to Winthrop's family home.

The car tripped an electric eye and the wrought iron gates swayed open automatically. Lights burned on in the house, which seemed bigger after dark than Richard remembered it.

Catriona Kaye was waiting for him on the porch. A small, pretty woman, as old as the century, she seemed fragile, but Richard knew her to have a rugged constitution. Now, she seemed her age, nervous and worried.

'Richard, thank God you've come.'

'Peace, Cat,' he said, hugging her.

'It's worse than you think.'

'I think it's pretty much as bad as it can get. Sometimes, stars are missing.'

'You've noticed?'

They looked up, reassuring themselves. The Plough was there.

'How often?' he asked her.

'More and more.'

'Let's go indoors.'

The panelled hallway was empty. Richard noticed at once that the Turkish carpet had been taken up and was rolled into a giant sausage against one wall, like a record-breaking draught excluder. The floor was polished wood tiles, in a herringbone pattern, discreet charms of protection carved in corners.

Catriona gasped in horror.

'It was here,' she said. 'Moments ago.'

She scanned the floor, dropping down on her knees, and feeling the wood with gloved hands.

'Just here,' she said, almost at the foot of the main staircase. It was still carpeted, a claret weave held down by brass rails.

Catriona began tugging at the stair carpet, wrenching tacks loose. Richard went to her and helped her stand. Her knees popped as he got her upright. She was alarmingly light, as if she might drift away.

'Lift the carpet,' she said.

He took out his Swiss army knife and used the screwdriver to extract the bottom five rails. Like a conjurer whipping a table-cloth out from under a complete dinner service, he pulled the carpet loose, popping tacks, and tossed it back in a great flap onto the upper stairs.

Catriona gasped again. Richard knew how she felt.

Burned into the bare wood of the stairs was the black shape of a man, like a shadow torn free and thrown away. It seemed to be crawling up to the landing, one hand reaching up, fingers outstretched, the other poised to overreach its fellow, pulling the bulk of the shadow upwards.

'It was on the ground floor just now,' Catriona said. 'Before that, outside, a burnt patch on the lawns, the drive-way—on *gravel!*—the front steps. It lay under the mats on the doorstep.'

'You've seen it moving?'

'Watched kettles, Richard. I've sat and stared for hours, keeping it still, keeping it at bay. But look away for a moment, and it shifts.'

He sat on the stairs, just below the man-shape. The outline was distinct. The light wood around the outline was unaffected, a little dusty, but the shape was matt black. It seemed like a stain rather than a brand. He touched it with his fingertips, then laid his flat palm where the small of the man's back would have been.

'It's warm,' he said. 'Body temperature.'

It was as if someone with a high fever had lain there. He looked at his fingers. No black had come off on them. He flipped the longest blade out of his knife and scored across the ankle. The black went into the wood.

'There are others, out on the moor, gathering.'

He turned to look at Catriona. The woman was strung taut, and he knew better than to try and soothe her. She'd been around the weird long enough to know how serious this was.

'It's an attack,' he said, standing up, brushing dust from the knees of his salmon-coloured flared trousers. 'But from what quarter?'

'Edwin won't talk. But it's to do with the War, I'm sure.'

When people said 'the War', depending on their age, they meant the First or Second World War. But Catriona meant a greater conflict that included both World Wars. It had started a great deal earlier, in the mid-19th Century—nobody could agree quite when—but finished in 1945, with the defeat not only of Germany and Japan but of an older, not entirely human, faction that had used the axis powers as catspaws.

Outside of the Diogenes Club, almost no one understood that War. Richard, who had no memory of his childhood, had lived through the aftermath. He'd heard Edwin's account of the War, had examined many of the documents kept in the secret library of the club, and saw all the time the lingering effects, written into the ways of the world in manners untraceable to most of humankind but as glaring as neon to the initiate.

'He says it's not over. That we made a great mistake.'

Richard looked into Catriona's pale blue eyes, struck breathless by their lasting loveliness, and sensed her controlled terror. He embraced her and heard her squeal of shock.

'We looked away,' she said.

He turned back, still holding Catriona by her shoulders.

An orange score-mark, where he had scratched the wood, shone in the stairs. The shape's feet were on the next step up, its head and arms were under the still-attached carpet.

'If it gets completely under the carpet, it'll be able to move like lightning. Once it's out of sight, it's free.'

He left Catriona and started working on the stair-rails. In minutes, he'd exposed the shadow's head and skinned the carpet up to the first floor landing.

'I'll stay here and watch,' she said. 'You should go and see Edwin. He's in the *camera obscura*.'

Two staircases led up from the first floor landing. One was the ingress to an attic apartment mysteriously occupied by an ancient female dependent Edwin in happier times referred to as 'Mrs Rochester'. The other led to the *camera obscura*, a large space in which an image of the house and its surroundings was projected by an apparatus of reflectors installed around the turn of the century by Edwin's father.

Richard paused on the landing. It was carpeted by a linked series of Indian rugs, which could be easily pulled up. The far staircase, to Mrs Rochester's rooms, was in shadow. He thought he could hear her breathing, as he had often done twenty years ago. Most boys would have had nightmares about the asthmatic invalid, but Richard had no dreams at all, no memories to prod his night-thoughts to fancy.

He climbed up to the *camera obscura* and stepped into the dark room.

Edwin stood, leaning under a giant circular mirror, looking down at the mostly shadowed table. The distinct shapes of the house, the grounds, the village and the moor were outlined. By moving the mirror, Edwin could spy further afield.

Nothing was moving.

'Shadows,' Edwin said, his voice still strong. 'Reflections and shadows.'

He dipped his hand into the image, waving through the church, scaling his skin with old stone.

'Richard, I'm glad you're here.'

'It's not a happy place, Edwin.'

Edwin's dark face twisted in a smile.

'How would you put it, "a bad vibes zone"?'

'Something like that.'

'It's a Hiroshima shadow.'

'Yes.'

At the sites of the atom bomb detonations, vaporised people left such shapes on the walls and streets, permanent shadows.

'I'm to pay for what I did.'

'You weren't the only one, Edwin. You're not even the only one left.'

'But I'm special. You see, I played it both ways. I had two chances. The first time, I was wise or cowardly and let it go. The second time, I was foolish or brave and took hold of it.'

'There was a War on.'

'There was always a war on.'

'Not now.'

'You think so?'

'Come on, Edwin. This is the Age of Aquarius. You more than anyone should know that. You helped throw the foe back into the outer darkness.'

'You've grown up being told that, boy.'

'I've grown up knowing that.'

The darkness that lay like a veil in his mind, blacking out the first years of his memory, throbbed. Things were shifting there, trying to break the surface.

'Do you want to see something pretty?'

Edwin Winthrop did not ramble. Even at his age, he was sharp. This was not a casual question, addressed to a child who had long grown up.

'I love beauty,' Richard said.

Edwin nodded and touched a lever. The table parted, with a slight creak.

Red light filled the room.

'It's the Jewel of Seven Stars,' Richard said.

'That's right.'

The gem lay on black velvet, its trapped light-points shining.

'The Seven Stars. They weren't there earlier. In the sky. That's not supposed to happen.'

'It's a sign, boy.'

'What isn't?'

'Very good. Everything is a sign. We won the War, you know. With this, essentially. People cleverer than I looked into it and saw a little of how the universe worked.'

Richard looked behind him. In the darkened room, shadows could glide like serpents.

'And I gave this to them. Not the Diogenes Club, me. Just as twenty years earlier, I let the jewel go. The club has always been people like you and I, Richard. We like to pretend we're servants of the Queen or the country. But when it comes to this bauble, we're on our own. As far as it belongs to anyone, it's mine now. Can you imagine Truman letting Oppenheimer *keep* his bomb? Yet the club let me take this souvenir when it was all over.'

'Men can be trusted, Edwin. Institutions change. Even the Diogenes Club.'

'Do you want this?'

Edwin indicated the jewel.

It seemed to pull on Richard's gaze, sucking him into red depths. A moment's contact made him squirm inside. He broke the spell, and looked away.

'Very sensible. It can bring great gifts, but there are prices to be paid. A talented man was once elevated to genius by it, but his life dribbled away in waste and pathetic tragedy. We won a War, but we changed so much in the winning that I'm not sure we even came through it. I don't just mean Britain lost an Empire. It's more than that. Mrs Rochester told me I took too many short-cuts. So I must pay. You've always seen the dark in me, Richard. Because, through no fault of your own, there's a dark in you.'

Richard shook his head, vigorously. He could not let this pass.

'I'd have died in a concentration camp if it were not for the Diogenes Club, if not for men like my father and for *you*, Edwin. I was a boy with no memory. You've given me more than life. There's been a purpose.'

'I've a terrible feeling we've just left a mess for you to clean up. All these, what do you call them, "anomalies", all these wrongnesses in the world. Think of them as fall-out. And the other horrors, the ones everyone notices—the famines, the brushfire wars, the deaths of notable men. When I laid my hand on this'—he grasped the jewel, his hand a black spider over the red glow, flesh-clad bones outlined by the gem's inner light—'I took the worst short-cut, and I made it acceptable. There used to be, in Beauregard's time, an absolute standard. I destroyed that.'

Richard did not want to believe his old friend. If there was chaos where once there had been order, he was a child of that chaos. Where Edwin had gone by intellect, he ventured with instinct.

'Now, I must pay. I've always known.'

'We'll see about that,' Richard said, determined.

A flash of light filled the room. Not from the jewel. It was lightning, drawn into the *camera obscura* from outside. Violent rain drummed the roof. A storm had appeared out of cloudless night sky.

Down below, in the hallway, there was a hammering.

As they emerged onto the landing, light fell onto Edwin's head. Richard did not have time to be shocked by the new lines etched into his friend's face.

They made their way to the main staircase.

Catriona lay in a huddle on the stairs. The shadowman was gone. The front doors stood open, and someone stood on the mat, looking down.

The polished floor of the hallway was crowded. A dozen shadowmen, overlapping, reaching out, were frozen, swimming towards the foot of the stairs.

The house was invaded.

'Ho there above,' shouted the newcomer at the door, a woman.

Lights flickered as thunder crashed. Rain blew into the hall, whipping the woman's long coat around her long legs.

Richard was by Catriona, checking her strong pulse. She was just asleep. He looked at the woman in the doorway. The door slammed shut behind her, nudging her into the hall. She stepped gingerly onto the tangle of shadows.

She had a cloud of white hair, medusa-snaked by the storm, with a seam of natural scarlet running through it. Despite the white, her face was unlined. The flicker of the lights made her freckles stand out.

The woman was of Amazon height and figure, well over six feet, extra inches added by her hair and stacked heels. Under a deep-green, ankle-length velvet trench coat, she wore a violet blouse, no bra, frayed denim hot pants, fishnet tights and calf-length soft leather pirate boots. She had a considerable weight of jade around her neck and wrists and pendant gold disc earrings the size of beermats.

Richard, though immediately impressed, had no idea who this woman was.

'All in this house are in grave danger,' she intoned.

'Tell us something we don't know, love,' he replied.

She strode across the chaos of shadowmen, slipping off and shaking out her wet coat. Her arms were bare. High up on her right upper arm was an intricate tattoo of a growling bear, with the stars of the constellation picked out in inset sequins.

'I'm Maureen Mountmain,' she announced, 'High Priestess of the Order of the Ram.'

'Richard Jeperson, at your service,' he snapped. 'I assume you know this is Miss Catriona Kaye and the gent whose house you are invading is Mr Edwin Winthrop.'

'There's someone else here,' she said, looking up at the ceiling. 'I sense great age, and a strong light.'

'That'd be Mrs Rochester. She's sick.'

Maureen laughed open-mouthed. She was close enough for Richard to catch her scent, which was entirely natural, earthy and appealing. Maureen Mountmain was extremely attractive, not just physically. She had a fraction of the magnetism he'd felt from the Jewel of Seven Stars.

'I don't know her real name,' he admitted.

'It's God-Given,' Maureen said. 'Jennifer God-Given.'

'If you say so, love.'

'I told you my name was Maureen, Richard. Not "love", "darling", "honey" or "pussycat".'

'I stand corrected, Maureen.'

'Do people call you Dick?'

'Never.'

'There's always a first time, Dick.'

There was a tigerish quality about Maureen Mountmain. The claws were never quite sheathed.

'Mountmain,' said Edwin, shakily. 'I know that name.'

'Do not confuse me with any of my family, Mr Winthrop. My Uncle Bennett and my Great-Uncle Declan, for instance. I believe you were present at their happy deaths. Mountmain men have always been overreaching fools. The women-folk are wiser. If you heed me, you might live out the night.'

Richard wasn't sure whether he wanted to trust Maureen. He knew about the relatives she'd mentioned, from Edwin and from a comprehensive study of dangerous crackpots. If she was as well up on the War as he thought she was, she might fancy herself the Witch Queen of the Western Isles.

Come to that, she might earn the title.

'Don't just stand there gaping, idjits,' she said, indicating the shadowmen at her feet. 'You have other visitors. This is serious.'

Catriona stirred. Richard helped her sit up.

'Very well, Miss Mountmain,' Edwin said, a little of his old iron back.

'Welcome to the Manor House. I am pleased to meet you.'

Edwin slowly made his way down the stairs, past Richard and Catriona. He stood at the foot of the stairs and held out his hand to Maureen.

'There's been bad blood between the Diogenes Club and your family,' he said. 'Let it be at an end.'

Maureen looked at Edwin's hand. It occurred to Richard that the woman could snap Edwin's neck with a single blow. Instead, Maureen Mountmain embraced Edwin fiercely, lifting him a little off his feet.

'Blessed be,' she announced.

Richard felt Catriona's fur rising. A feud might be over, but enmities lingered.

'I remember Declan Mountmain,' Catriona said. 'An utter bastard.'

'Quite right,' Maureen said, releasing Edwin. 'And Bennett was worse. If either of them had been able to make use of the weirdstone, there'd be precious little of the world left by now.'

Catriona stood, daintily, and nodded a curt acceptance of Maureen Mountmain.

'What Declan and Bennett wished for may still come about,' Maureen said, urgently. 'They were bested, and the greater forces who used them checked, by the rituals your Diogenes Club used in the War. But you woke up the Seven Stars, bought a short-term victory at the cost of long-term trouble.'

Edwin nodded. 'I admit as much,' he said.

'Do not bother justifying your actions. All men and most women would have done the same.'

'*Most* women?' thought Richard.

'And you could have done it earlier, when victory would have seemed even cheaper and been far more costly. For that, the world owes you, Miss Kaye, a debt that'll never be understood. Your influence, a sensible woman's, tempered this man's instincts. Like my uncles, Edwin and, I intuit with certainty, Dick here, are fascinated by the weirdstone. To them it is like a well-made gun that should be fired or a showoff's automobile that must be driven. Men never think that guns have to be fired *at* something or cars driven *to* somewhere.'

Richard bristled. This bedraggled demi-goddess had the nerve to barge into someone else's home and deliver a lecture in occult feminism.

'Women have faults too,' she said, in his direction. 'Men like guns and cars, women like men who like guns and cars. Who is to say which is the more foolish?'

'What's happening here?' Richard asked.

Edwin looked down. Maureen stepped in.

'A crisis, of course.'

'It's coming for the Seven Stars,' Edwin said, 'swirling about the house, converging on the gem.'

'What is coming?'

'The Biafran Bank Manager,' Edwin chuckled, blackly.

'*What?*'

It was a strange thing to say. But Edwin was no longer the firm-minded man Richard remembered.

'A joke in poor taste,' Maureen explained. 'He means the Skeleton in the Closet.'

Richard had heard it before, a reference to a television advert. It was one of a wave of desperate jokes made in response to the heart-breaking photographs of starved men, women and children that came out of Biafra during the famine. Any disaster that couldn't be contained by the human mind spilled over in sick humour, graveyard comedy.

'Why now?' Richard asked.

'It's been coming a long way, my boy,' Edwin said, 'for a long time.'

'He's been building you up for this,' Maureen said. 'Your life has been a series of initiations.'

Edwin looked at her sharply, with new respect.

'I've had to teach myself, old man. But I've been coming along too.'

'It's true,' Edwin said. 'Richard, I knew I wouldn't be capable of facing what is coming. I thought, almost hoped, I'd be dead by the time the changes really got underway, and you were the one we chose to take over. You're stronger now than I ever was. You have talents. We had to work for things which are easy for you. I know that's no comfort.'

Richard felt a deep resentment. Not at the way his life had been shaped, but that the great purpose he had always sensed was imperfectly revealed to him while an outsider, the daughter of old enemies, had understood.

Thunder crashed again, and the lights went out. They came back again and the shadowmen on the floor were crowded around the foot of the stairs, black fingers reaching upwards. The quality of the light was different, wavering. Filaments fizzed at the end of their tether.

It was the anomaly again, and they were inside it.

The lights strobed, leaving photo-flash impressions on his eyes. The periods of darkness between the periods of light lengthened. The shadowmen were in motion, revealed by a pixilation of still images. They crowded together as they swarmed up the stairs, passing under Richard and Catriona. A fresh wave spread out from under the closed front doors, scrambling around Maureen's boots. Richard held Catriona and tried to gather his spiritual strength, controlling his breathing, feeling the focus gather in the centre of his chest, preparing for an assault.

The shadowmen flowed up onto the landing, gathering around Edwin, arms seeming to lift from the floor, as insubstantial yet sinewy as steel cobwebs.

From inside his jacket, Edwin took the Jewel of Seven Stars.

The lightbulbs all exploded at once. Glass tinkled onto polished wood. The shadowmen were frozen.

Red light filled the hall, spilling down from the landing. Edwin held the jewel up. The Seven Stars shone, like the ones no longer in the Heavens. The constant light held the shadowmen back.

'So that's it,' Maureen said, awed. 'I never dreamed.'

'You feel it, like everyone,' Edwin said. 'The *temptation*.'

'I can't blame you,' she admitted.

Edwin set the jewel on the floor. Once out of his hand, the jewel changed. Its light, fuelled by the wielder, dimmed. The shadows around Edwin grew. A thin arm, like a black stocking on a wind-whipped washing line, wrapped around Edwin's leg. He sank to one knee, pulled down. Another shadow latched onto his arm.

Catriona broke free, suddenly strong, and ran up the stairs, Richard and Maureen at her heels. They hesitated at the landing.

Edwin lay on the floor, twisted. Shadowmen twined around him, pinning him down, growing tight. The lightpoints of the jewel, lying nearby, glowed like drops of radioactive blood.

Catriona released a single sob, and clung to the banister. Richard felt Maureen's strong hand on his arm, sensed the warmth of her body close to him. This was entirely the wrong time to be aroused, but he had no control over his surging blood.

The shadowmen wrapped Edwin like a mummy's windings. He disappeared under black, elongated forms. The shadowmen coalesced into one man and flattened, leaving a final Hiroshima shadow.

'It took him,' Maureen said.

The anomaly wasn't passed. It wasn't over.

Maureen stepped past him and reached down for the jewel. Richard took her arm, holding her back, feeling the warmth of her bare skin, fighting the fog of desire in his mind, torn by a deep need to throw her aside and take the jewel for himself. With Edwin gone, it was up for grabs.

'No,' he said, finding his strength.

Maureen's outstretched fingers curled into a fist.

'No,' she agreed.

They separated and stood either side of the jewel. It was changed, somehow. Edwin had passed into it or beyond it.

'It'd make a novel doorstop,' he suggested.

She laughed, with an appealing edge of hysteria.

Catriona still stood, clinging to the banister, eyes sparkling with unshed tears, the life she had shared with Edwin torn away and crumpled up.

'This is like a blasted relay race,' Richard said. 'Do we pick up the baton?'

'We have to do something with it.'

'Take it upstairs,' Catriona said. 'She'll know what must be done.'

'She?' Richard and Maureen both asked.

'Mrs Rochester. Geneviève, her name is. She'll be waiting. I'll be up myself, when I've composed myself. I'd like to be alone now, anyway. Alone with...'

She indicated the last shadowman. This one would stay put.

'Together,' Maureen said.

They lifted the jewel between their right hands. Richard felt Maureen's cheek against his, and the side of her body as they slipped arms about each other. She had a few inches on him. Between their palms, the Seven Stars glowed.

They made their way to the far staircase.

Mrs Rochester—Jennifer God-Given—Geneviève Dieudonné—lay on a narrow, coffin-shaped pallet. A tie-dyed blanket was gathered over her legs. She looked a thousand years old, and was plugged into a standing dripfeed. A bandage was fixed to her side, stained with greenish seepage.

Her million wrinkles arranged themselves into a smile.

'I apologise for my appearance. Your uncle shot me, dear. With silver. If he'd had better aim, I'd not be here.'

'You know who I am?' Maureen asked.

'Madame Sosostris knows all,' Geneviève intoned.

Another name? No, a joke.

They set the jewel down at the old woman's feet. It nestled in the folds of her blanket, like a hot-water bottle.

'Edwin's gone,' Richard said.

'I know. He stepped into the shadows. Against my advice, but it's too late to bother with all that. He was, at heart, a good man. Despite everything.'

Maureen was clinging closer to Richard. For the first time, he had a sense that she too was afraid. Her obvious courage was in need of the occasional injection of bravado.

'Will you die?' Maureen asked the ancient woman.

'No, no, no,' Geneviève chuckled. 'At least, not just yet. You might not think it to look at me, but I'm getting better. The tide of years caught up with me, but it's drawing away from the shore now.'

'Do you need our blood?'

Richard noticed only now the sharp little teeth in the old woman's shrunken mouth.

'Not yet,' Geneviève said. 'You mustn't think of me until you've bound the jewel. We've a chance to damp down the ill effects of its use, just briefly. There's a ritual which will truly end yesterday's War, which will pack back into the stone all the nastiness that has trickled out since we opened it up back in '44.'

'Will everything be... better?' Richard asked.

'Not really,' Geneviève admitted. 'Nuclear reactions will still be part of physics, and you all have to live with the consequences. All the rest of it, you must take responsibility for. The Jewel of Seven Stars didn't make men stupid or venal or mad. It just fed on those things and spewed them out a thousandfold. But with the stone wrapped, the old world will have a chance.'

'Why didn't Edwin perform this ritual?' Maureen asked.

'He'd spoiled himself for it. Something sad about a cat. And Catriona couldn't stand in for you. The participants have to be from both factions. You're a Mountmain, dear. And Richard is the creature of the Diogenes Club. Adversaries whose allegiances run counter to the official history. Churchill and Hitler were equally opposed to Diogenes and aligned with your uncles. There were great villains on Edwin's side and saints tied up with the Mountmains. It's too late to blame anyone. You just have to end the cycle, to make way for that Aquarian nonsense.'

As Geneviève spoke, Maureen took his hand in a tigerish grip.

'This ritual,' he began, 'what exactly...?'

'What do you think?' Geneviève laughed.

Richard looked up into Maureen's eyes, and saw understanding in them.

Magical sex always struck Richard as somehow contrived, requiring the consideration of mathematics in a process that worked best when run on sheer instinct. You had to keep your head full of angles of the compass and meaningless rituals, locked up within your own skull when your body wanted to flow mindlessly into another. And magick rituals tended to be performed on cold stone floors hardly suited to comfort or arousal.

This was not like that at all.

They were together on cushions spread over the *camera obscura* table, the jewel between them. In their own anomaly, they ebbed and flowed like the tides, bloodstreams and bodies pushed and pulled by primal forces. Daybreak brought fields and woods and buildings into the room, patterning their bodies. At the centre of a harmonious universe, energies poured in through their open minds, bound up and redirected by their coupling. Mirrors shone warm sunlight down on them.

Tantric sex, the most common form of sex magic, was all about building up spiritual energy by making love at length but never reaching the dissipation of climax.

This was not like that at all.

They peaked three times apiece.

'The seventh,' she whispered.

They passed the jewel between them, running it over their bodies. Richard looked through the stone, past the stars, seeing Maureen's face rubied with joy. They kissed the Jewel of Seven Stars, and Maureen took it, pressing it to her yoni.

He entered her again, pushing the weirdstone into her womb.

Joined by the jewel, they came again, finally, together, completing the pattern of seven stars.

Then, they slept.

Richard awoke, all sense of time lost. His coat had been arranged around him.

Maureen was gone.

He still felt her, tasted her, scented her.

The Jewel of Seven Stars was gone too.

Dressed, clothes abrading the tender spots of his body, he explored the house.

The Hiroshima Shadow marked Edwin's passing.

Catriona was in Mrs Rochester's room. Geneviève was sitting up, hidden behind a veil of mosquito netting.

'She took the stone,' he said, weakly.

'Her family have been after it for years,' said a voice from behind the netting.

'She visited,' Catriona said, 'after she left you, she came here. She was glowing, Richard.'

'Like a ripe orange,' the voice—so unlike Mrs Rochester's frail whisper—said, 'so full of *life* that she had some to share. Edwin made up for what he did with the stone, and she made up for what her uncle did to me.'

The veil fell.

The woman on the bed was not Mrs Rochester. She was lithe, red-lipped and unhurt. But it was Geneviève, young again.

'Now,' she said, 'the old War is over.'

The anomaly was gone. The War was finished. A great purpose of his life, undefined in his mind until last night, was concluded. But he still had his darkness, the shadowed part of his mind and memory. Because a part of his life was gone, he clung tenaciously to what he could remember, fixing memories like butterflies pinned to a card. Edwin Winthrop was a memory now, and Mrs Rochester. And Maureen.

Their coming together ended something, cleared the stage for many beginnings. But that was it. Her taste would fade. But the memory would stay.

Geneviève got out of bed for the first time in thirty years. Her old woman's nightgown hung strangely on a body barely grown. Underneath her years, she was impossibly young. She hugged Catriona, and Richard. She danced on the points of her toes. The jewel-light shone in eyes reddened by Maureen's blood.

Catriona was bereft, Geneviève reborn.

A fresh cycle would begin.

Episode Five: Mimsy

One day in Spring, the Devil called her.

'Sally Rhodes Investigations,' she said brightly into the phone, trying to sound like a receptionist.

'Miss Rhodes,' he said, voice distorted a little, perhaps addressed to a speaker phone, 'this is Derek Leech.'

She hung up.

The voice had scraped her bones.

She looked from the office half of her front room to the living room half. Jerome, her son, was building a Lego robot, notionally supervised by Neil, her boyfriend, who was curled on the ancient sofa, making notes on a scribble-pad. Neil was still assembling an argument for the book he'd been thinking of starting for three years. Lego structures spread about the floor, weaving around the cat-basket and several of Neil's abandoned coffee mugs.

Normality, she thought.

Kid. Man. Pet. Toys. A mess, but a mess she could cope with, a mess she loved.

The phone rang again. She let it.

The office half of the room was ordered, different. A computer, a fax, files, a desk. This was where she thought. Over there, on the sofa, amid the lovable mess, was where she felt.

She was breaking her own rules.

The ringing phone jarred on her emotions.

At her desk, she was in business. She had to be harder, stronger.

She picked up the phone, but didn't announce herself.

'Miss Rhodes, for every second you don't hang up, I shall donate one hundred pounds to your favoured charity, which is, I believe, Shelter.'

It did not surprise her that Leech knew she supported Help for the Homeless. The multi-media magnate knew everything about everyone. Atop his Pyramid in London Docklands, he had all the knowledge of the world at his disposal.

'Go ahead,' she said.

'Regardless of our past differences, I admire your independence of spirit.'

'Thank you. Now what is this about?'

'A friend of mine needs your services.'

'You have friends?'

She imagined that Leech had only acolytes, employees and possessions.

'The finest friends money can buy, my dear. That was a joke. You may laugh.'

'Ha ha ha.'

'My friend's name is Maureen Mountmain. She has a daughter, Mimsy, who has gone missing. Maureen would like to retain you to find her.'

'You must have people who could do that. If this Maureen Mountmain was really your friend, why don't you turn the dogs loose?'

'You have resources no one I employ could have.'

That was the most frightening thing anyone had ever said to her. Leech let it hang in the air.

'Sally, you've inconvenienced me. Twice. Your life would be much easier if you had chosen not to stand in my way. You have something of the purity of a saint. No one in my organisation can say as much. Only someone of your virtues could handle this job. I appeal to you, as a secular saint, to help my friend.'

She let seconds tick by.

'Do you accept?'

She counted slowly up to ten in her mind, making a thousand pounds for the homeless.

'I'll take the job,' she said, 'on the condition that I'm retained by this Mrs Mountmain...'

'Miss.'

'... Miss Mountmain, and not by you personally or any sneaky subsidiary company.'

'You'll not take the King's shilling.'

'Cursed gold?'

Leech laughed, like ice cubes cracking in a bowl of warm blood.

'Once this call is completed, your business is with the Mountmains. I act, in this instance, only as intermediary.'

She knew there was a hidden clause somewhere. With Leech, nothing was straightforward. His way was to rely on the fallibility of those he dealt with. Despite his stated opinion, she knew she was as likely to be gulled into a moral trap as anyone else.

Jerome pestered Neil for his expert opinion on the robot spider scuttling around the floor.

'My associate, Ms Wilding, will give details of the appointment she has arranged for you with Miss Mountmain. I have enjoyed this conversation. Good-bye.'

The phone clicked, and a woman came on. Sally took down an address and a time.

When she hung up, she realised her heart was racing. It had been a while.

She'd been working on everyday stuff these last few years. As it happened, she'd done a lot of work with runaway children. Though sometimes she walked away well-paid and satisfied from a tearful reunion, she more often traced some kid caught between a horrific home life and an ordeal on the streets, then wound up sucked into an emotional, legal and ethical Gordian knot.

But the weird stuff was in her past.

Even with Jerome and Neil, physical left-overs from that period of her life, in the flat, she'd almost convinced herself she didn't live in that world any more. She had kept up with the inescapable growth of Derek Leech's Earthly dominion, but tried to forget the strange devices at its heart.

Perhaps she was wrong. Perhaps he wasn't the Devil, but just an ambitious businessman. He had used magic in the past, but that was only trickery. Conjuring, not sorcery.

She tried and failed to convince herself.

'Mummy, look, I've made a monster.'

'Lovely,' she said to her son. 'Neil, you're on kid-watch and the phone. I'm out on business.'

Neil looked up at her and waved a cheery paw.

'I accept the mission,' he said.

She kissed them both and left the flat.

The address she had been given turned out to be a Georgian mansion in Wimpole Street. It stood out among perfectly preserved neighbours, showing signs of dilapidation and abuse. By contrast, with polished brass door-trimmings and blue plaques announcing the former residence of the great and good, the Mountmain house looked like a squat. Over the lintel was spray-painted *Declan Mountmain, Terrorist and Devil-Worshipper, Lived Here 1888–1897.*

Maureen Mountmain, who answered the door herself, was tall and thin, with a strange red streak through snow-white hair. She wore long black velvet skirts and a tatted shawl over a leather waistcoat. Her neck and wrists were ringed with jades and pearls. Her face was stretched tight, but Sally didn't see tell-tale face-lift scars. As her shawl slipped, she showed a sparkling tattoo on her upper arm. There was a great strength in her but she lacked substance, as if every surplus atom had been sucked away over the years.

She wanted to ask Maureen how well she knew Derek Leech, and what their connection was, but that wasn't the point.

She was hurried into the hallway, which stank of patchouli. The original wooden panels had been painted over with dull purple. Childish patterns, like the crescent moons and stars on a cartoon wizard's conical cap, were scattered across the walls and ceiling. On a second look, Sally saw that the painting-over extended to framed pictures that still hung, chameleoned, up the staircase.

'When she was little, Mimsy only liked purple,' Maureen said, proudly. 'She can be very insistent.'

'Do you have any pictures of her?'

'At an early age, she heard about the aboriginal belief that photographs could capture souls. She would smash any cameras she saw. With a hammer.'

Sally thought about that for a moment. She wondered whether Mimsy took her hammer with her.

'Any drawings or portraits?' she asked.

Maureen shuddered.

'Even worse. Mimsy believes that art not only captures the soul but distorts and malforms it.'

'She's very concerned with her soul.'

'Mimsy is extremely religious.'

'Did she attend any particular church? That might be a good place to start looking for her.'

Maureen shrugged. As Sally's eyes got used to the gloom of the hall, she noticed just how distracted Maureen Mountmain was. Her pupils were shrunk to black pin-holes.

'Mimsy rejects organised religion. She has declared herself the Avatar of the Ram. She hopes to revive the Society of the Ram, an occult congregation my family has often been involved with.'

'Devil-Worshipper and Terrorist?'

'Mimsy put that up there. She was proud of her heritage.'

'Are you?'

Maureen was unwilling to say.

Sally knew that something had broken this woman. Deep down inside her, there was extraordinary resilience, but it had been besieged and eroded. Maureen Mountmain was a walking remnant. It was too early to be sure, but Sally had an idea how Miss Mountmain had been broken and who had done the deed.

'Might Mimsy be with her father? You live apart?'

Again, Maureen was unwilling, but this time she put an answer together.

'Mimsy doesn't know her father. He is...unavailable to her.'

'If it's not a rude question, do *you* know Mimsy's father?'

For the first time, Maureen smiled. In her wistfulness, she could be beautiful. Sally knew from the flicker of wattage that this woman had once shined like a lantern.

'I know who Mimsy's father is.'

She didn't volunteer any more.

'May I see Mimsy's room?'

Maureen led her upstairs. The whole first floor of the house was a ruin. Several fires had started but failed to take. A medieval tapestry, of knights hunting something in green woods, was half-scorched away, leaving the men in armour surrounding a suggestive brown shape. There were broken items of furniture, statuary and ceramic piled in a corner.

Maureen indicated a door smashed on its hinges.

'You say Mimsy left?' Sally asked. 'You don't think she was

abducted?'

'She walked out of this house on her own. But she might not have been herself.'

'I don't understand.'

'She took with her a precious item. A keepsake, if you will. Something that was important once. It was her belief that this item communicated with her, issued orders. A large red stone.'

'A ruby?'

'Not exactly. The weirdstone is known as the Seven Stars, because of a formation of light-catching flaws which look like the constellation.'

Maureen dropped her shawl to show her tattoo. Seven blue eyes glinted in a green creature, also configured like the Great Bear.

'Is this jewel valuable?'

'Many might pay dearly for it. I certainly did, though not in money. But it's not a thing which can be owned. It is a thing which owns.'

'Mimsy thought this jewel talked to her?'

Maureen nodded.

Sally looked around the room. After the build-up, it was a surprisingly ordinary teenager's bedroom. A single bed with a frilly duvet, matched by all the lampshades. Posters of David Duchovny, Brad Pitt and some pretty boy pop singer she was too out-of-date to recognise. A shelf of books: thick occult-themed paperback nonsense—*Flying Saucers from Ancient Atlantis*—mixed with black-spined, obviously old hardbacks. Outgrown toys were placed like trophies on a mantelpiece: Turtles, Muppets, a withered rag doll.

She tried to imagine Mimsy. Long ago, before all the weirdness, Sally had taken a degree in child psychology. It was just about her only real qualification.

'Imaginary friends are projections,' she suggested. 'Mimsy might have displaced onto the jewel, using its "voice" to escape responsibility. It's more sophisticated than "I didn't break the vase, the pixies did", it's "I broke the vase, but I was obeying orders".'

'Mimsy is twenty-seven,' Maureen said. 'In her life, she has never made an excuse or obeyed orders. It is her belief that the jewel talks. I don't doubt this is true.'

'A subjective truth, maybe.'

'You don't believe that, Miss Rhodes. You know Derek Leech. You know better. There's such a thing as Magic. And such a thing as Evil.'

Sally was off her balance. She had thought this was about a teenage runaway.

'Does she have a job? A boyfriend?'

'She can always get money from people. And she has lovers. None of them mean anything. Mimsy has only one emotional tie.'

'To you?'

'No. To the weirdstone.'

'Neil, pick up,' she told her own answerphone.

She was calling from her mobile, out in the open in Soho Square. Merciless sun shone down, but the dry air was cold.

Neil came on, grumbling.

'I thought you were answering the phone,' she said.

'Jermo and I were watching *Thunderbirds*.'

She let that pass.

'I need you to do some research, historical stuff.'

One of Neil's uses was trawling the internet for ostensibly useless information. He had even been known on occasion to go physically to a library and open a book.

'Write these keywords down. The Jewel of Seven Stars, the Society of the Ram.'

'Dennis Wheatley novels?'

'One's an object, the other's a cult. And see what you can find out about the Mountmain family. Specifically, a fellow named Declan Mountmain from the late 19th Century, and a couple of contemporary women, Maureen—must be in her late forties though she doesn't look it—and Mimsy, twenty-seven.'

'As in Borogoves?'

'Mimsy. No, it's not short for anything.'

'No wonder she ran away from home. Calling a kid Mimsy is semiotic child abuse.'

'There are worse kinds.'

She folded up the phone and thought. Mimsy's father—whoever he might be—was out of the picture, supposedly. She'd accept that for now.

Unconsciously, she had come to the Square to make her call. It was where she had met Jerome's father. Connor had been lolling on the benches with the other bike messengers, waiting for jobs to come in. He had been killed in a street accident, also near here.

She was reminded not to trust Derek Leech.

Mimsy, obviously, was a horror. But how much of one? Spoiled brat or Anti-Christ? She found herself aching for Mimsy's Mumsy. Despite purple panels and hippie scent, and the timid dithering at the memory of her daughter, Maureen was a survivor. Sally wondered whether she was looking at her own future in Maureen Mountmain.

Sally had a tattoo. A porpoise on her ankle. That didn't make her strange. She had worked a case once with Harry D'Amour, an American private detective who was covered in tattoos, which he claimed worked as a psychic armour. You needed armour for what was most vulnerable, and you couldn't tattoo your heart.

'What's up, Sal?'

Her ex-boyfriend sat down next to her. He wore Lycra cycling shorts and a joke T-shirt with a thick tyre track across the chest.

'Hello, Connor,' she said, unfazed.

'I've never thanked you for avenging my death,' he said.

He looked impossibly young in the bright sunshine. He had been nearly two-thirds her age. Now he was just over half her age.

'You look good,' he said.

'I dye my hair.'

'But just a little.'

'Just. You have a son. He's a good kid. Jerome.'

'I didn't know.'

'I thought you might not.'

'She's a strange one, Sal. That's why I'm here. Why I've been allowed to talk to you.'

'This is about Mimsy Mountmain?'

Connor looked sheepish. They hadn't been together long and, baby or not, it wouldn't have lasted. He had always been looking for an angle, less interested in a leg over than a leg up. But she was sorry he had been killed.

Jerome loved Neil—that was one reason Neil had lasted—but had grown up, like Mimsy, without a Dad.

'It's not so much Mimsy, it's this rock thing. The jewel. You're to mind out for it. It can cause a lot of trouble. Not just for you there, but for me here. For us here.'

'Where is here?'

'Somewhere else. You'd be able to explain it. I can't. Sorry, Sal. Gotta rush.'

He stood up and looked around. She wondered if he'd come on his bike.

'Did I ever tell you I loved you?'

'No.'

'Funny that.'

He left. Sally wondered why she was crying.

When she got back to Muswell Hill, she heard the retch of the printer as she climbed the steps to her flat. After her ghostly encounter, she had spent an afternoon getting in touch with old contacts who knew something about what is euphemistically known as 'alternative religion'. Though a few of them had heard of Declan Mountmain as a historical fruitcake, no one could tell her anything about his present-day descendants.

She let herself in, and found Neil and Jerome busy down-loading and printing-out. In the last few months, Jerome had gone from helping Neil with the computer to being impatient with the grown-up's inability to get on as well with the machine as he did.

'There's a lot of dirt, Sal-love,' Neil announced, proudly.

Sally hugged Jerome, surprising him.

'Gerroff,' he said, wriggling.

She laughed. She had needed contact with Connor's flesh-and-bone offspring. It grounded her, dispersed some of the weirdness build-up.

'It wasn't Dennis Wheatley,' Neil said. 'It was Bram Stoker. He wrote a novel called *The Jewel of Seven Stars*. It was made into a Hammer Film with Valerie Leon.'

Like a great many men his age, Neil had encyclopedic recall of the bosomy starlets who appeared in the Bond films, Hammer Horrors, Carry Ons and *Two Ronnies* TV sketches of the early 1970s.

'You know Stoker based Dracula on Vlad the Impaler. He also based this *Seven Stars* effort on scraps of truth. It's about an Ancient Egyptian witch who possesses a modern lass. There was, apparently, a real Jewel of Seven Stars, found in a proper mummy's tomb. It disappeared after a break-in at the British Museum in 1897. Guess who was the number-one suspect?'

'Is this like Jack the Ripper? Pick an eminent Victorian?'

'No. It's highly guessable. I'm talking Declan Mountmain, who was sort of a cross between Aleister Crowley and Patrick Bergin in *Patriot Games*. Half mad warlock, half psycho Irish separatist. He tried to blow up Lords, during a Gentlemen versus Players match. He had a nephew, Bennett, who was by all accounts even worse. He was in with the Nazis in World War Two and was killed in Los Angeles while spying for Hitler.'

'No wonder Maureen's off her head.'

'I've got a great .jpg from a Hippie History web site, of Maureen at Glastonbury in 1968. She's got up as a fertility priestess, body-painted green all over and extremely topless. I had to send Jermo into the other room while I down-loaded it.'

'I saw the rude lady,' Jerome piped up.

'Well, I tried to send him. Anyway, Maureen was not only the Wiccan babe of the Summer of Love but an early *Comet* knock-out, one of Derek Leech's first Page Three girls. Those shots will be on the Net somewhere, but you have to pay a fee to get them. Do you think Leech is this Mimsy's father?'

She thought about it. It fitted together, perhaps a bit too neatly.

'There are other players in this. And the jewel comes into it somehow.'

'I've got a big cast for you, going back a hundred years, snatched from a lot of occult and paranoid conspiracy sites, the type you have to play sword and sorcery games to get onto. Some famous names. But there are interesting gaps. Names rubbed out of the record, like those Pharaohs who were so disgraceful that they were removed from history. I keep coming across these references to "the War" in contexts that make me wonder which one is being fought.'

She looked at the sheaf of printed-out articles for a while, trying to piece it all together.

'It's this bloody stone,' she said, at last. 'That's what's wrong. In 1897, it supposedly disappears. Then it turns up in a treasure chest in Wimpole Street and waltzes off with Mimsy. But there's this one tiny mention of it in the reports of Bennett Mountmain's death in Los Angeles.'

'So he took it on holiday? Maybe it was a talisman of his devotion to the führer.'

'But how does it come to Maureen, and Mimsy? In 1942, this Captain "W" of the deleted name seems to have snatched it back for England. Or Egypt. Or Science. I think the jewel has been stolen back and forth between two crews down the years. The Mountmains and some other shower, the mystery "W"'s bunch. The others mentioned only by initials. Mr "B" from 1897, even this "R.J." from the '70s. We need more about the Initials. Could you spend tomorrow on it? You might have to stir yourself to the British Museum and the Newspaper Library.'

'I'll take Jermo to see the mummies.'

Jerome stuck his arms out and limped across the room.

'How does he know what the Mummy walks like, Neil?' she asked. 'Have you been showing him your Hammer videos?'

'He gets it from *Scooby-Doo*.'

She playfully strangled him.

'So perish all unbelievers who defile the innocent minds of young children,' she intoned, solemnly.

They kissed and cuddled, and Jerome told them not to be soppy.

If a grown-up woman of twenty-seven wants to go missing and not be found, the legal position is that it's very much her business. Here, the abandoned mother might be able to lay a charge of theft against the absconded daughter, but Sally now knew enough about the Seven Stars to realise accusing anyone of stealing it would result in a potentially endless series of criss-cross counter-charges.

Mimsy had walked out of her mother's house a week ago.

Finally, Maureen had coughed up an address book, with Mimsy's friends marked by pink felt-tip pen asterisks.

Sally spent two days making telephone calls.

None of Mimsy's 'friends'—current worshippers, cast-off ex-lovers, bedazzled sidekicks or bitter rivals—admitted any knowledge of her.

But the drudgery was useful.

Everyone she talked with revealed, by their attitude, a bit more about the quarry. The impression Sally had already formed from Maureen was strengthening by the minute.

Mimsy Mountmain was quite a package. In her early teens, she'd made a million pounds as a songwriter. Sally remembered the titles of a few pop hits whose tunes and lyrics had vanished from her mind. Mimsy hadn't needed to work since, but had published a series of slim volumes of poetry in an invented language.

At sixteen, she put a young man into a coma by battering him with a half-brick. The court returned a verdict of self-defence and she was written up, in the *Comet* among other papers, as a have-a-go heroine. Then, under less clear-cut circumstances, she did it again. This time, the cracked skull belonged to a married bank manager rather than an unemployed football fan. She did three years in Holloway, and came out as the undisputed princess of the prison.

Her ex-lovers were all stand-outs. Politicians, celebs, serious wealth, famous criminals, beauties and monsters. Some of them hadn't come through the Mimsy Mountmain Experience without sustaining severe damage.

It might be that Mimsy was more than just missing.

She tried to read one of Mimsy's poems. Without being in the least comprehensible, it gave her the shudders. She had the impression Mimsy was up to something.

'It's not a family,' Neil said, without taking off his coat, 'it's a club.'

Sally looked up. Neil brought Jerome into the flat.

'We saw mummies!' her son said.

Neil flopped open a notebook.

'Ever heard of a journo named Katharine Reed? Irish, turn of the century, bit of a firebrand?'

Sally hadn't.

'She left a memoir, and in that memoir she alludes in an off-hand way to a Charles Beauregard who is almost certainly your Mr "B". The *DNB* has pages on him. Reading between lines, he was something between a spy and a spy-catcher.'

'I know the feeling.'

'He became something high up in the Secret Service, and his protégé was a Captain Edwin Winthrop.'

'Him I've heard of. He co-wrote a book about authentic hauntings in the West Country. Sometime in the '20s.'

'That's the one. And he is your Captain "W", to be found in Hollywood in 1942.'

Sally considered hugging Neil. But the mention of the Secret Service was unsettling.

'Have you a name for the last one, "R.J."?'

'Sadly, 1972 wasn't long enough ago for any of the secret stuff to have been disclosed yet. And a lot of the files on the others, even Beauregard, are sealed until well into Jerome's adult life. He'll have to finish the puzzle.'

'I'm going to be a spy when I grow up,' Jerome announced.

'That'll be useful,' she said. 'What did you mean about a club?'

Neil grinned.

'You'll love this. Remember Mycroft Holmes?'

'Who?'

'Brother of the more famous...?'

'Sherlock?'

'Give the girl a kiss,' he said, and did. 'Yep, Mycroft, whom Conan Doyle informs us "sometimes *was* the British Government", was, as it turns out, a real person. His private fiefdom was a gentleman's club in Pall Mall, the Diogenes. It was a cover for a special section of British Intelligence. When Mycroft retired or died, this Beauregard took over and played the hush-hush game even more seriously. For the best part of this century, the Diogenes Club was Britain's own Department of Weird Shit. You know what I mean.'

'Only too well.'

'Aside from the wonderful Kate Reed, none of the people mixed up in this thought to write memoirs—though I've found references to a suppressed issue of *Black Mask* which supposedly ran a story that gave away too much—which means it's all locked up in Whitehall somewhere. When you sort this out...'

'When!'

'When. I have confidence in you. Anyway, when you sort this out, there might be a book in the Diogenes Club. Britain's *X-Files*. There's a hook. And at this late date, the secrecy issue is long dead.'

'I'm not so sure about that.'

'Come on, Sal-love. It's great stuff. Look, mummy's curses, Sherlock Holmes, Hooray for Hollywood, spies and ghosts, a fabulous lost treasure, Nazi Irishmen, hippie chicks with extremely large breasts, politics and black magic, terrorism, old dark houses, the plague.'

'Think it through, Neil. You say it's all still secret.'

'Just bureaucracy. We can get in there.'

'When the War is over, the secrets come out. We know about that Scottish island Churchill dosed with anthrax. The Eastern Bloc refugees we handed over to Stalin for genocide. All that came out. Why not this stuff about the jewel?'

'Too trivial to be taken seriously. I mean, it's absurd, right? Spooks.'

'When the War is over, the secrets come out. These secrets aren't out. Because the War isn't over.'

'You're being a wet blanket, love.'

She backed off from an argument. Neil didn't like being a dependant, but none of his outside projects ever quite came together. And he resisted being brought into the firm as a partner.

'I'm sorry,' she said.

While she was on the bus, her mobile bleeped. It was Maureen. Sally ran down the list of the people she'd talked with, and floated out some of the material Neil had gathered on the Diogenes Club. Surprisingly, a door opened. Then closed again.

'They're out of business,' Maureen said. 'Have been for a long time. Winthrop, I knew. At the end. That was the last War. This is something new.'

'Is it about Mimsy or the Seven Stars?'

Maureen hesitated.

The bus was stuck in Camden High Street.

'Sally, when you find Mimsy... you won't hurt her, will you?'

She thought of the two coma men. Only one had got better.

'If she doesn't want to come home, that's fine by me. I just want to know if she's all right.'

She had heard that on every missing child case. If Jerome wandered off, she wouldn't be convinced he was all right until he was back home. But Jerome wasn't twenty-seven.

'I think Mimsy can take care of herself,' she said, trying to reassure Maureen.

'The Jewel of Seven Stars isn't important to me.'

After Maureen had rung off and the traffic started moving again, Sally thought to ask herself the question.

So, who is the jewel important to?

A morphing billboard outside the bus shifted from an ad for the new *Dr Shade* movie to one for the *Daily Comet* to one for Cloud 9 satellite TV. All Derek Leech products.

The traffic thickened again, and Sally felt trapped.

Despite what she had told Neil and what Maureen had told her, she had to go to Pall Mall. It wasn't that she thought this Diogenes Club was germane to the investigation, but she wanted to look at it, to cut off that avenue before it took up too much time. Besides, she was curious.

It took several wanders up and down the Mall before she found the tiny brass plate on the big oak doors. All it said was *Members Only*. The building was shuttered and out of use. She hammered on the doors, to see whether she could raise some member from a decades-long sleep. No one came.

She stood away from the building.

The Mall was busy, with Easter Holiday tourists enjoying the country's new climate in short-sleeved shirts and pastel dresses. There might be a drought on, but she could get used to this Californian London. Doommerchants, however, said it was a sign of the end of the world.

A slim blonde girl in white wafted across very green grass, towards her. She wore a wide-brimmed straw hat and dark glasses with lenses the size and colour of apples.

For a moment, Sally thought this was another ghost. It was something about the way the light hit the girl's hair. She reminded Sally of Connor.

'Nobody home,' the girl said.

She was too young to be Mimsy, not yet out of her teens. She had the trace of an accent.

Sally shrugged.

'You're looking for the jewel,' the girl said.

Through the green lenses, tiny red points shone. This pretty waif had enormously hungry eyes.

'I'm looking for the woman who has the jewel,' Sally said.

'Mimsy,' the girl said, head cocked. 'Poor dear.'

'I'm Sally Rhodes. Who are you?'

'Geneviève Dieudonné. Call me Gené.'

'Are you Mimsy's friend?'

Gené smiled, dazzling. Sally realised this girl had an archness and composure that didn't quite fit with her initial estimate of her age.

'I've never met her. But I *feel* her. I share blood with her mother. That was a great sacrifice for Maureen. She was just pregnant. There's a sliver of me in Maureen, left behind like a sting in a wound. And a tinier sliver in Mimsy. Along with all the other stuff. She was conceived around the Jewel of Seven Stars. That's why it speaks to her.'

Gené wasn't insane. But she was talking about things beyond Sally's experience.

'The bauble that causes the trouble, Sally,' Gené said. 'I've danced with the stone, like the gentlemen who used to doze beyond those doors, like the Mountmain Line. Down the years we all revolve around the Seven Stars. Sometimes, years and years slip by and I don't think of the thing, but always it's there, the knowledge that I share the planet with the Jewel of Seven Stars, that it'll be back.'

'That's an odd way of putting it.'

'I'm an odd sort of person.'

'Are you one of Leech's?'

'Good Heavens, no. I've been called a leech, though.'

When Gené smiled, she showed sharp little teeth, like hooks carved of white ice.

'What do you want from me?'

'A partnership. I help you find the girl, and you let me have the jewel.'

'What do you want with it?'

'What do people want with jewels? I wish I knew. Since you ask, I'll tell you. If possible, I'll get rid of it. It was buried for thousands of years without causing too much trouble. If I could securely bury it again, or stow it away on a deep-space probe, I'd do it. It fell out of the sky once. For years, I wondered about those seven flaws, the seven stars. Then, when we launched *Voyager*, I understood. On our rocket we engraved a star map, to show where it came from. The jewel is dangerous, and I want to damp the fire. Satisfied?'

'Not really.'

'I wouldn't be either. You remind me of myself at your age. Seriously, Mimsy—whether she knows it or not, and I think she does and welcomes it—is in danger so long as she has that stone with her. Your job, I understand, is to find Mimsy and make sure she's safe...'

How had this woman known that?

'... and I can help you.'

'If you can find Mimsy, why don't you? Why do you need me?'

'I'm not a solo sort of person. Difficult in my position, but there you are. I work best with a stout-hearted comrade. Someone to keep me down to earth.'

'I like you, Gené. Why is that?'

'Good taste.'

Gené kissed Sally on the cheek, with an electric touch.

'Come on, Sal. Let's get a cab. I think I know where to start.'

Sally was usually sparing with taxi travel. It was still most practical to get around London on the bus and tube, and she had to account for her expenses. But Gené had a handbag full of money, in several different currencies. She got them into a black cab and ordered the driver to take them to Docklands.

'You rattled a lot of webs when you went through Maureen Mountmain's address book,' Gené explained. 'Bells rang, and I hopped on a plane from Palermo. I've read up on you. You're good. They'd have liked you at the Diogenes Club, though they were funny about women.'

It was evening, now. Not dark yet, but the light was thin and cold. They were venturing into Docklands just as most people were leaving. The '80s *moderne* office buildings were unnaturally clean in their emptiness, life-sized toys fresh from their boxes.

The black glass pyramid caught the last of the sun.

'It's coming back to Leech,' Sally said.

'Not really. But I think you'd have come here yourself soon.'

'If I can help it, I stay away.'

'Understood. But you've covered Mimsy's human connections with no luck. You're drawing back and looking at the whole picture. That's what made you go to the Mall. What you have to do is think of yourself as part of the pattern, to see how you fit in, where you can be triangulated.'

Sally saw what Gené meant.

'I'm in the pattern because of Leech. He doesn't do anything for no reason. This isn't a favour to a friend. This is part of a plan.'

Gené clapped.

'I'm the last person Leech loves. He said—and he's always annoyingly truthful—that only I could do this job. He wants me to find Mimsy.'

'And the Seven Stars.'

'There's a link between Leech and Mimsy. It's broken, or at least played out to its full length. Is he after the jewel?'

'Leech's dominion is of this world,' Gené said. 'He only wants what I want, to keep the Seven Stars out of circulation. I'm not happy to share a common cause with him, but there you are. This business scrambles all your allegiances.'

'I thought Leech might be Mimsy's father.'

'Good guess, but no. That was Richard Jeperson, one of the Diogenes fellows. Mimsy is unpredictable precisely because she is the fruit of an opposition, the Mountmain Line and the Diogenes Club. And whatever I threw in didn't help. Whatever havoc she wreaks, we can all take the blame.'

Gené had the cab stop a few streets away from the Pyramid.

When it had driven off, the road was empty. The last of the light was going. It was a cloudless night, but the blanket of sodium orange street-lighting kept the stars at bay.

'One of the reasons I like you, Sal, is that you believe me. Over the years, almost no one has. Not at first. But you've stepped into the dark enough times to know the truth when you hear it.'

They looked up at the Pyramid.

'The Jewel of Seven Stars is a tool for ending empires,' Gené said. 'It ended the rule of a Pharaoh. Declan Mountmain wanted to use it on Britain. Bennett Mountmain thought he could win the War for Hitler. Edwin Winthrop turned it on Germany and Japan. It could be used on that Pyramid.'

Sally imagined Leech's empire in ruins.

'But there's a cost. The world is still living with the consequences of the way Edwin and the Diogenes Club wound up the last War. I think Leech is one of those consequences. If the times weren't out of joint, he wouldn't have taken hold and grown like a cancer.'

'Leech thinks Mimsy is a *threat?*'

She couldn't believe it. But it made sense.

'A mad woman from a long line of mad people? Armed with a chunk of dubious crystal? Do you have any idea of just who Derek Leech is? Of how far beyond human reckoning he is?'

'Why you, Sal? Why did he pick you?'

'He said I was a saint.'

Gené spread her arms and opened her hands.

'I'm not a saint. I'm a single Mum. I'm kissing forty. My life and business lurches from crisis to crisis.'

'*Twice*, you've stopped him, Sal. You've saved people from him.'

'In the end, that meant nothing. He had other plans.'

'No one else has ever stopped him. Not once.'

Sally saw what Gené meant.

'So I'm the only person he can think of who could stand between him and Mimsy.'

'Not just Mimsy.'

The night was all around. Gené took off her dark glasses. Her eyes were alive and ancient, points of red burning in their depths.

They had spent the night by the Pyramid. Nothing had happened. Her instinctive faith in Gené's inside knowledge was fraying. It would have been much more convenient if Mimsy had turned up in Derek Leech's lobby, brandishing the Jewel of Seven Stars like a *Star Trek* phaser.

Red light came up in the East, and Sally phoned for a minicab. She didn't think the night wasted.

She and Gené—Geneviève—had talked.

Without saying what she was, Gené had revealed a lot. She filled in, apparently from personal knowledge, a lot of the gaps. If Neil ever wrote his book, she'd be a prime source. But she wasn't scary, like Leech. She was proof that you could live with the weirdness and not be swallowed up by it. She had a real personality.

Gené had made mistakes. She said what she thought, without filtering it through a brain that framed everything as a series of crossword clues with hidden killer clauses.

In the cab, Gené was jittery.

'I'm sorry,' she said. 'I led you down the wrong path. Something happened last night. And we missed it. My fault. I thought the Seven Stars would revolve around Leech. Maybe they will, but not yet. Maybe there's too much Mimsy in the brew...'

Her mobile jarred her out of the half-sleep she had fallen into. The minicab was caught in the morning influx of commuters into Docklands.

It was Neil.

'The police have been round,' he said. 'It's to do with your client. She's been killed, Sal-love.'

She was shocked awake.

'Maureen?'

'Yes. You'll have to check in and give a statement. The pigs know you were working for her.'

Cold inside, she asked the question.

'Was it Mimsy?'

'She wasn't killed with a hammer. From what they let slip, I don't think it could have been murder. She had an allergic reaction to insect bites.'

Sally hung up and redirected the cab driver to Wimpole Street. She told Gené what had happened.

"Bitten to death?' Gené mused.

There was a policeman at the door, but Sally got through by admitting she had been asked to give a statement. Gené looked at the man over her sunglasses and was waved in without comment.

'Neat trick.'

'You wouldn't want to learn it.'

The hallway was changed. All the purple paint was gone and there was a thick, crunchy carpet. Sally realised she was standing on a layer of bloated, dead flies. The purple paint had been stripped by a million tiny mouths, which had etched into the surfaces of everything. A cloud must have filled the house. The curtains were eaten away completely, dried white smears scabbed the window-glass.

'She's trying to use it,' Gené said.

'I have to see,' Sally said.

'I know.'

They went upstairs. Policemen stood around the landing, and a couple of forensic people were expressing appalled puzzlement. Photographs were being taken.

A detective inspector issued orders that none of this was to be released to the press. He looked a hundred years old, and was too tired to shout at anyone for letting Sally and Gené into the house.

Sally explained who she was and that the dead woman had hired her to find her missing daughter. She admitted she hadn't managed to do so.

'If she's missing the way her Mum is, you might as well give the money back.'

'To whom?' she asked.

Actually, she hadn't been paid in advance. Leech would certainly cover it, but Sally didn't want to take his tainted money.

'It's not an allergic reaction,' Gené said. 'Flies don't sting.'

'No,' the inspector agreed. 'They chew.'

Sally looked into Mimsy's room. Maureen Mountmain lay on the bed. She was only recognisable by her distinctive hair, white with a red streak. Her naked bones lay in a nest of dead flies.

'It's started,' Gené said.

She had tried to call Neil but not been able to get through. Gené was silent in the cab, seeming far older after the long night and the horrors of Wimpole Street. There was a long-shot suggestion that it was all down to the new climate, hatching flies early and driving them mad.

Sally tried not to be anxious. There was no home to bring Mimsy back to. She was off the case. In Muswell Hill, Gené dropped her off.

'Don't worry, Sal. It'll take years. I'm sorry to lose you, but you can get on with your life. It comes down to those of us who live outside human time, Leech and me and the Seven Stars. Give my love to your son. I'd like to meet him one day.'

Sally watched the cab go. She wondered where Gené was headed. She had said something about needing to get in out of the sun. And getting something to drink.

If she was going to fail anyone, she was glad it was Leech—she thought now that he had wanted her to check Mimsy, somehow—though she was ripped open and bled empty about Maureen.

She went upstairs.

She had not been able to get a call through because Neil was using the modem, digging up material on the Fourth Plague of Egypt. He thought it was germane to the investigation.

'There is no investigation, dear,' she said. 'No client.'

Jerome wandered in, dressed in his too-small pajamas.

'Who was the pretty lady?' he asked.

'Were you peeking out your window?'

Her son didn't answer her.

'Okay,' she said. 'I give up. What was the Fourth Plague of Egypt?'

'You should know that,' Neil said. 'It's in *The Abominable Dr Phibes*. Flies.'

'You won't be out of pocket,' Leech said. 'I've authorised a payment. You may forward it to Shelter, if you wish.'

'I don't deserve to get paid. I did nothing. I found out nothing. Mimsy is still missing. And the Jewel of Seven Stars.'

The phone was cool in her hand.

'You *have* found something out, then.'

Leech sounded different. Tired? Maybe it was the connection?

'A little. Nothing relevant.'

'I had hoped you might influence Mimsy, by your example. I see now that was overly ambitious of me.'

Had he set Sally Rhodes, with her sword of righteousness, against Mimsy Mountmain, with her weirdstone, hoping they would cancel each other out?

'Can she hurt you, Derek?' she asked.

'This call is over. Goodbye, Sally.'

She listened to the dead line. It was now a question of living with the fear, of getting through the plague years. Derek Leech had an empire, and she had a computer-crazed kid and a boyfriend who'd never grow up. She knew, at last, that she was more suitable to survive.

Episode Six: The Dog Story

The client had fixed the meetsite, Pall Mall. Neutral ground, equidistant from his Islington monad and her Brixton piedater. He was used to getting-about. Types who needed an Information Analyst didn't want the need known. It usually meant they were in a reverse, and even a rumour could key terminal panic. Vastcorps were conservative, prone to dump at the first smokesign, trailing a plankton-field of small investors who'd unload at decreasingly sensible prices. A whisper could drag down an empire toot sweet.

Though he spoke with what he knew from old teevee to be an English accent, Jerome thought of Pall Mall, like all else, as *Paul Maul.*

The London Board of Directors had gotten so weary of Former Americans visiting the Mall and asking where the stores were that the strip had been rezoned for commercial development. Preservation-ordered buildings, no longer needed after the out-shifting of admin to Bletchley, were sub-divided into franchise premises: Leechmart, Banana Democracy, Guns 'n' Ammo, Killergrams. Some stores here were so chic they had actual goods in stock, for real-life inspection.

The client had called the place *Pal Mal*, like an elderly person would. Her face ident, however, scanned as girlish. For an inst, he'd optioned asking her whether her parents knew she was accessing their comm hook.

She had a name, not a corporate ident. Geneviève Dieudonné. He'd worked for private citizens before, though he was usually indentured to corps or gunmints. He did not come low-budget. She'd have to meet his price, either in currency or access.

She had specified an old address, between fast outlets, clothes shops and the dream parlours. A prime site neglected in the redevelopment. He was to wait outside for her.

It was a cool day at street level. The cloud-kites were over the East End, which let unfiltered sunlight pour down here, bleaching everything pastel. A few other get-abouts strolled in the chill light, toting parasols. The odd unperson nipped out, though they were supposed to stay behind the scenes, darting across the open to shade, covering their eyes against the burning glare.

He sat on a pink play-bench and turned down his earpiece, lulling the info-flow. If the client had a problem, he needed to clear his mind.

He was distracted anyway, by a barking dog. A couple of gay get-abouts were shamed by their unruly Alsatian. The hom tried to calm the dog, adjusting the collar with the handset; the fem apologised to passersby, explaining that there must be some glitch in the mood-collar.

A micro-event, but it rang a bell.

On the people-mover, there'd been another dog, a miniature of some breed yapping in an old woman's grip. Get-abouts had got about, shifting to another carriage.

Two geek dogs. Not info on which to build a case.

'Jerome Rhodes?'

She wore a thick wraparound eye-shade, a heavy sun-cloak and a wide-brimmed black straw hat with a scarlet silk band. She must have skin cancer in her genetic background, or be extra-cautious, or need the disguise. She was a pretty lady: He intuited he might have seen her before, once, long ago.

He stood and offered his hand, making a fist so the bar-code on the back was smooth. She did not produce a reader to confirm his ident. She also did not offer her hand.

'You conch that without ident exchange, no contract is legally enforceable?'

It was surprising how many of his clients were ignorant of the regs of Information Analysis.

She shrugged, cloak lifted a little by the air-flow.

'I should terminate this meet,' he said.

She took off her eyeshade and looked at him.

'But you won't,' she whispered.

It was as if she saw through his eyeshade, accessing his brain.

'I want you to locate a ghost,' she said.

That wasn't an unusual request. Ghosts were rogue idents, projected into the Info-World, often leashed to their physical persons by a monofilament of ectoplasm. Some spook-makers cultivated a swarm of ghosts. You had to mind it was a baseline form of Multiple Personality Disorder, that ghosts sprang from meat-minds.

Something about the way she had put it didn't quite scan. He was acute to precise meanings, even when words offered multiple readings.

She'd meant ghost the way he took it. But she had a B story minded, another meaning.

'A ghost, as in...?'

She smiled at his prompt.

'As in Jacob Marley? As in Henrik Ibsen? Perhaps. But, primarily, the breed of ghost you know about.'

He had a reputation as a ghost-buster. Two years ago, Walt McDisney hired him to bust a cadre of disgruntled ex-employees who assumed the idents of wholly owned cartoon characters and harassed accessors of Virtual McDisneyland. That was a big case for Rhodes Information, involving Info-World banditry, pop culture terrorism, copyright violation and several different layers of obscenity law. The culprits were under Household Arrest for the rest of their lives, shut out of the Info-World forever.

The barking Alsatian had set off another animal, a snapping terrier. They were noise-making in disharmony, not competition. Jerome heard a third canine whine, joining in from backstage. A lot of unpersons kept dogs on traditional strings.

The client was distracted, too. She slipped her eyeshade back on, but he'd caught the narrowing of her eyes. It was if she had suffered a sudden brainpain.

'What's the ghost's tag?'

'Seven Stars.'

Jerome pulled out his earpiece, shutting off info-flow, suddenly concentrating on only the A story.

'Seven Stars?'

He needed a confirm. She gave it.

'Seven Stars isn't a ghost,' he said. 'Seven Stars is a terroristcorp. Gunmints have gone after them. And vastcorps. What info do you have that puts us in a better start position than the heavy hitters?'

'Seven Stars is one person, physically. Of course, she might be considered a Legion.'

He tagged the reference.

'Mark. Chapter Five. Verses Eight and Nine. "For he said unto him, 'Come out of the man, thou unclean spirit'. And he asked him, 'What is thy name?' And he answered, saying, 'My name is Legion: for we are many'."'

'King James Version, Jerome. Very impressive. I thought Post-Christians used the Jeffrey Archer translation.'

'I'm not a P-C,' Jerome said. 'The Bible is of cultural importance beyond religious significance.'

'How are you on the Old Testament?'

He didn't want to get into a Trivial Pursuit session, so he shrugged modestly.

'Look up Exodus, Chapters Seven through Twelve.'

'The Plagues of Egypt?'

'Very good. To answer your original question, I have the ident of Seven Stars. The meat-name.'

He winced. He had not expected vulgarity from her.

'It's Mimsy Mountmain.'

She spelled it for him.

He still didn't quite believe that Seven Stars was one person. Most theorists put them down as an Info-Army, covertly funded by a consortium to disrupt the Info-World. The vastcorps all had their private security people out looking for them, not to mention various Global Information Police forces.

Over the last year, Seven Stars had been busy.

At first, the Scramble Bombs seemed random, disruptions of the info-flows. Vastcorps and gunmints set aside their info wars to post rewards for the expulsion of Seven Stars. Derek Leech himself, the visionary of the Information World, the ultimate stay-at-home, stepped out of his Pyramid for the first time in a dozen years to appear on a realwelt platform with the Managing Director of London, the CEO of McDisney-Europa and the Moderator of the Eunion.

Then came serious pranks, calculated to undermine client confidence. Jerome had been amused, with the cynicism about stay-at-homes endemic among get-abouts like him, when a hundred million people were convinced by a phreak edition of *On-Line Vogue* that the latest fashion was for rouged and exposed anuses. When a hundredth of the subscribers lipsticked their recta, it counted as a genuine fashion trend and the real *Vogue*, a Leech publication, was obliged by law to report it. The fact that the fashion-followers' registration fees went to an untraceable account in Virtual Switzerland was an extra giggle.

The pranks became murderous, and Seven Stars seemed scarier. A few high-profile ident assassinations were costly embarrassments for heads of states and CEOs, deleted from the Info-World or metamorphosed so their access signatures made all users read them as unpersons. After an ident assassination, you could always get another life, even if it meant going back twenty years and starting all over. When a random percentage of Leech-Drug prescriptions were tainted, a substantial death-toll of meat-lives—realfolk— mounted. Stay-at-homes struck dead in their monads were reclassified by their Households from home-user to waste material.

If the long-foretold Collapse were to come, Seven Stars might look good for the role of Anti-Christ. Empires were shaking, and a lot of independents were going psycho 'in the tradition of' Seven Stars.

One person. One ident. Mimsy Mountmain.

Jerome had asked the client for back-up confirmations. She just knew. That was scary in itself.

He was as good at reading people as at conning info-mass. People had read-outs and flagged items too. He believed the client. Though there was something about her that didn't scan.

Back at the monad, he jacked his earpiece into the Household and pulled in a few info-blips. He often started with a random trawl, seeing whether connections could be made.

The dog story was an epidemic. The first theory was that a sound pitched only to sensitive canine ears was causing all dogs—including the few wolves left in realwelt zoos—low-level irritation. However, no such ultra-sound could be detected by instruments other than dog-brains.

Even through his monad-block's sound-proofing, Jerome heard distinct animal noises. He was grateful that he didn't have a companion or minion dog. There were reports of minion dogs—gene-designed for guard and attack duties—savaging stay-at-home masters. It couldn't be an Info-Prank. Dogs weren't generally jacked into anything other than the Actual.

He set searchers on Mimsy Mountmain, cloaking himself for caution. For added coverage, he put a search out on Geneviève Dieudonné. It was always a smart keystroke to learn as much about the client as the quarry. Often, something the client didn't know about themselves was the breakthrough clue.

He subscribed to the usual police sites, from which he down-loaded the surface material on Seven Stars. He didn't want to chance a full-on search yet. The last thing he wanted was to flag his own name. Seven Stars could have him wiped. Or killed.

Should he make a comm link with Sister Chantal and initiate discussion on the Plagues of Egypt? Since the Fall of the Vatican, she was freelancing out of Prague but would still be up on Biblical scholarship. He skinned his thought package. He had a perfectly good reason to call Chan, but was reluctant to do so. He had an emotional case-file on her, and knew she'd interpret a call as personal rather than professional. Then they'd have to go forward or back. And he wanted to stay where they were.

He left it as it was.

The dog story was a mushrooming news-bomb, eclipsing other developing stories. Most channels offered feeble alternatives—something about an astronomical anomaly, a human interest orphan massacre, a new development in endocrinology—but the dog story was global, a stone mystery, affording a full response spectrum from farce to horror. He couldn't afford to get caught up in the mediamass of speculative coverage.

On Cloud 9, the premier Leech newsline, extreme theorists were getting the coverage: a canine groupmind, begging for a cosmic bone; a conceptual breakthrough, representing the sudden attainment of sentience in a competitor species; a literal curse of God, a rebuke for the collapse of most organised churches in the Religious Wars of '20.

Jerome forced himself to tune out on the dog story.

His search results were downloading. The first thing he learned was that Mimsy Mountmain was a real person, born 1973—which made her fifty-three now. Her mother was listed as Maureen Mountmain (d. 1998), her father was not known. There were sealed police records from the 1990s, which he'd take the trouble to gut later. Nothing much after the turn of the century. Hot links fed off to biographies of several family members, stretching back to the 1800s. They would be a distraction just now, but he made a mental flag to find out why they were supposed to be so interesting.

The real woman of mystery was Geneviève Dieudonné.

A person of that name had been born in France in 1416. She apparently died—there was some doubt about exact circumstances and date—in 1432. At sixteen.

A person of that name had been born in Canada in 1893 and died under her married name of Thompson in 1962. A life's worth of data on her scrolled past swiftly.

A person of that name was mentioned in the acknowledgements of *Some Thoughts on the Bondage of Womanhood*, by Katharine Reed. Published 1902.

And a person of that name was on the payroll of the Free French for several months in 1942. She worked in Los Angeles, presumably for the War Effort, though the nature of her service was not listed.

There was no record of the woman he had met this afternoon.

Geneviève 1893–1962 left a portfolio of photographs, from childhood through to old age. Geneviève 1902 and Geneviève 1942—definitely different from the 1893–1962 woman and probably from each other—left no pics.

It seemed likely his client had used an off-the-peg ident to contract with him—she had not offered him her hand for reading, he minded—but must also have gone to some trouble to find a name that would not yield miles of scroll on many different people down through the centuries. Over a thousand people on record were called Jerome Rhodes.

An afterthought downloaded. A search gave you public record info first, then revisited any sealed files you'd previously accessed. This blip came from his own master contacts file. A Geneviève Dieudonné was listed as a contact of the Sally Rhodes Agency in 1998. Unless on some major rejuvenative surgery kick, this could not be the same woman.

His mother had, as usual, not kept a proper record. From the notation, it was ambiguous as to whether this Geneviève was a client or an informant. She did not seem to have paid anything, which was just like Mum. Too many deadbeats rooked her out of a fee for services rendered.

He would have been five or six. He minded the times. Neil, Mum's boyfriend, was teaching him how to find things out. They had even gone to paper-and-dust libraries to look things up. It was the start of his induction into the Info-World.

Had he seen Miss Dieudonné then? At first sight, the client had seemed to ring a distant alarm. But this couldn't be the same woman.

Was his client trying to tell him something by using a name that would be in his mother's records?

Logically, he could comm-link with his Mum, retired and living in Cornwall. But he didn't like to bother her yet. He could access info on his own, and didn't need to crawl to her when problems got thorny. She had taught him to be self-reliant. Maybe neurotically so. If that was the case, he'd get it seen to eventually.

As things were, he was employed, but not contracted, to find a ghost whose name he knew on behalf of a meat-woman who was anonymous. Nice irony. He appreciated it.

He had several favoured ports into the Info-World. He usually sidestepped the dreamwelt sites that impressed the neos and plugged straight into streams of pure data, not even bothering with a customised similie. Most of the ghosts he had busted revealed too much about their meat-selves in their self-designed wish-fulfilment avatars. They all had an unhealthy preoccupation with self.

It always amazed him that the geek gunslingers were so locked into games-playing they never took in the view. It was like ignoring the stars. To him, the thrill was in the info landscape, the waves and currents and trends and collapses. He could endlessly access, anchored on a loose chain, becoming one with the world, letting it flow around and through him.

But this time, he wanted to seem like a neo.

He customised a ShadowShark and swam into dreamwelt through

a Multi-User Carnival. It was a mixture of market-place and playground, where the hustlers peddled surprise packages, containing either valuable gen or worthless tosh at the purchaser's risk, and the zap-heads conducted endless duels or orgies, getting in and out of the way.

Basically, it was a Dress-Up and Play Area.

To operate here, he not only needed to project a poseur's ident but also to intimate that there was a neo tosser at home, jacked into his parents' ports, belly bloated and limbs atrophied as he let the dreamwelt be more his home than the plush monad where he was meat-locked.

He morphed the ShadowShark from fishform to carform, and got out, wearing the distinctive cloak, mask, goggles and boots of Dr Shade, the wholly owned Leech International superhero. He had been fond of the *Dr Shade* films as a kid, despite (or maybe because of) Mum's unaccountable loathing of them (and all other Leech efforts).

The Dr Shade image was kiddie-cool enough to pass here. He had most of the heroes and heroines and gods and monsters who mingled in the carnival pegged as neo tossers. All womenshapes were Amazons with unfeasible breasts, and faces iconic of cool rebellion wandered by. Outlaws who coughed up registration fees and site subs. The Info-World welcomed phreaks and madpersons, but if you didn't pay your phone bill you were shut out, marooned forever in realwelt.

He was clever enough even to maintain a flimsy intermediate persona as 'Jonathan Chambers', Dr Shade's secret ident. If probed deeply, he'd pull out, leaving behind traces typical of a neo tosser.

As Dr Shade, he slipped through the carnival.

The dreamwelt darkened. A pack of feral kids on armoured bikes wove in and out of the crowds, blasting each other—and bystanders—to fast-reforming pixel-clouds.

Fantasy figures exposed their assets in neon-lit windows, offering eighteen varieties of non-copyright sexual access. A lot of neos bankrupted their parents by letting their bar codes be read by the info-whores and compounding the fees to infinity.

As usual, this all seemed silly. But, as usual, it was a place to start.

He passed up all the offers of sex and slid into the darker streets where the snitches lurked. Info was air and water here, but could be bought and sold like anything else.

A news-blurt cut through the scene, shaking the overhanging eaves and the artfully strewn shadows. The dog story had escalated. Gunmints issued instructions for humane disposal of soon-to-be-dangerous companions or minions. Dreamwelt denizens were warned that if they were in a realwelt monad with a dog, they should jack out immediately and disable it. Horrorshow pics flashed: users yanked out of info jaunts by ripped-open throats.

The blurt finished. The alley scene settled.

There was a scuttle of snitches. Extending his shadowcloak, he netted the one he was after. She made a fluttering attempt to break free and graciously gave in, landing delicately on his palm.

'Hello, Tink,' he said.

The cartoon fairy twinkled a greet.

Because J.M. Barrie had left the royalties on *Peter Pan* to Great Ormond Street Children's Hospital, and an Act of the Old Parliament extended that income in perpetuity, there was a copyright glitch. After the Mouse Wars, unlicensed McDisney avatars were purged from the Info-World, but the *Peter Pan* crew, with a few tiny alterations (the loss of the WMcD logo), were able to survive.

He had seen the loophole at the time and left it open. So Tinkerbelle owed him her dreamlife.

'What can you tell me about Seven Stars?'

The fairy buzzed and glowed like a tiny phosphor grenade and tried to get away.

'That tells me something,' he said, in Dr Shade's scary voice.

'It is foretold that the coming of the Seven Stars will bring about the Collapse,' Tinkerbelle shrilled.

It was the Info-World's version of Armageddon. One big plug-pulling, and global shrinkage to a dying white dot. Despite a million fail-safes, superstitions abounded, especially in the wake of the Vatican's Fall. There were always intimations of Collapse.

'Where can I find Seven Stars?'

'You can't,' the fairy shrilled. 'They find you. Then no one else does. Ever.'

Tinkerbelle turned to a blip of light and vanished.

'But I believe in fairies,' he declared.

Even here, removed from the actual, he heard the cacophony of dogs. The constant barking, breaking through all the mutes and muffles and sound-proof shields, scraped his nerves.

'Mum,' he said, 'two names. Geneviève Dieudonné. Mimsy Mountmain.'

Sally, his mother, looked distracted.

A lot of dog noise came over the comm-link. She lived in a country retirement site, where animals were a special feature.

But the names clicked.

Sally Rhodes stopped moving about the room and stood so the reader could fix her image. He adjusted the projection, so her three-dimensional bust—solid and flesh-tone, though with the tell-tale hologram sparkle—sat on his desk.

She had cut her hair and let it go grey. Her face was unlined, without the benefit of a skin-stretch.

She made a kiss-mouth and he touched his lips to the tridvid image.

They both laughed.

Then his mother nodded him to sit back.

'I tried to find Mimsy Mountmain once, for her mother. And for someone else. Her mother was killed before I could get anywhere. I was paid off. Case closed. As far as I know, the blasted girl never did show up.'

'And Geneviève?'

'She was part of it. She was also looking for Mimsy.'

'She still is. At least, someone with her name. Actually, it can't be the same woman.'

'Blonde, looks about sixteen, slightly French accent, stays out of the sun, old-fashioned girl outfits?'

'Sounds like her.'

'If it is, give her my love. It's unfinished business. I'm sorry I'm out of it.'

'So am I.'

'Nonsense. You need to be on your own.'

'How did you meet Geneviève?'

'She accosted me. In Pall Mall.'

Mum pronounced it the old way.

'Snap,' he said.

'I was looking for something called the Diogenes Club. They were out of business, but involved with whatever Mimsy Mountmain was up to. It went back years.'

'The Diogenes Club?'

'That's right. Neil dug up some stuff on them. Nothing useful, as usual.'

Jerome wondered about it. He said goodbye.

'Give yourself my love too,' said Mum.

'I will. And mine to you.'

They 'kissed' again, and cut the link.

There was shooting outside. Not a running battle, as there had been briefly three years ago in the last of the Religious Wars. This time, it was a succession of single-shots.

Jerome turned the window on and scanned Upper Street. Men in armour dealt with dogs. They used jolt-guns, one charge to the back of the skull. A clean-up krewe followed, collecting the corpses. A lot of the dogs trailed leashes, and all had collar-controls. Some unpersons harassed the pest officers. The dog story was stepping up, as if the unheard sound had become shriller, more maddening. Other species with canine levels of pitch were getting agitated.

Warnings were posted against approaching or sheltering affected animals. A raft of human interest stories offered cautionary tales of children ripped by loved family companions. Clinically blind people mind-linked to seeing-eye dogs reported that their skulls were ringing with sound, and censor blotches on the reports suggested not a few of them had become dangerous and were being treated like the street packs.

Over and over, news-streams emphasised that this was a global phenomenon. Global.

How many dogs were there in the world? Including wolves.

His teeth were on edge. He imagined he could sense the unheard sound. His eyeballs sang silently.

Did everybody feel this?

He didn't feel like comm-linking around his associates, and asking. There were thousands of mushroom sites on the dog story. Mediamass obscured any useful gen. It would take a while to purge the extremists and for a sensible centre position to coalesce. In the meantime, stay-at-homes were staying put, and get-abouts were accepting restrictions. Suggested codes of practice for travel in cities and designated country sites.

An across-bands newsblurt cut in. A major announcement was imminent on the dog story. He knew that meant a thirty-second deep-core ad probe was coming. He tore out his earpiece and hummed the *Anvil Chorus* with fingers stuck in both ears. He did not need to be infected with psycho-dependency on some new flavour of echt-burger.

Then he tuned in again. Seven Stars was claiming responsibility. The ghost's message concluded with: 'For the dogs, it will end soon.'

A scramble of experts got on-stream and began pouring opinion and speculation onto the maelstrom. He jacked out of all access and tried to think.

When one of his deep-level search engines paid off, Jerome thought somebody must be extracting the urine.

He had an address for Mimsy Mountmain. She was supposed to be a terminal stay-at-home, a shut-in on life support. She was maintained in the Mall. His client had met him outside the building in which his quarry lived.

The dog story was a constant distraction. It was hard to hack through to info that concerned him. The dog story criss-crossed and trailed over every other pathway. It had been the same during the Religious Wars.

Emergency legislation was being passed, globally. Dog ownership was now illegal. There were painless extermination programs. Some of the more liberal sub-gunmints were merely interning the animals and working on a 'cure'.

Not having a dog, Jerome didn't care. The dog story just got in the way.

He was increasingly spooked.

He tried to get back in touch with Geneviève, but there was no back-up listing for the Brixton address she had given him as her piedater. The node they had used as a comm-link was discontinued and the charges for its creation and dissolution all laid to his account.

He had let her see his bar-code. She must have some sort of hidden reader, maybe an Eyeball.

It turned out that his client was the ghost.

He had seen her in the meat. She was real, not a projection of some unknown veg like Tinkerbelle.

And now she was gone.

As Dr Shade, he was back in the carnival. The party seemed to be slowing down. Somehow, the dog story was throwing the Info-World into turmoil. It happened like that. Mammoth realwelt events made users jack out for once, depopulated the dataways. Fine. That made it easier.

Now, he was looking for Geneviève Dieudonné.

1893–1962 wasn't her. 1416–1432, though. There was something in that equation. That Geneviève didn't get to be older than his seemed to be.

What about 1902 and 1942?

He glided through archive sites, shadowcloak passing over icons and portals. Few came here but academic researchers. The neos were only interested in the now, the crashing wave of the present. And vastcorps employed balanced factions of muck-raking exposé merchants and raking-over cover-up krewes.

He moved into the past, down an almost-empty conduit. Similes of buildings lined the way, in regressing architectural styles, each with foundation stones giving away the year. The buildings housed the records.

Geneviève had yielded too few mentions. So he had to trawl wider. He had set up search engines to look for the Diogenes Club. Most of them crashed against security barriers, alerting all kinds of official warnings. He had received desist notices, but no enforcement operatives were coming at him, from inside or outside the Info-World. Regulation boards were too busy with the dog story.

During a crisis, there was a window of opportunity.

He fought against déjà vu, as he stood outside the simile of the building he had seen in realwelt yesterday morning. Then, he had just wondered why it hadn't been gutted for stores. Now, he knew it had significance.

There was even a simile of the bench where he had met his client. An information package lay on it, tied up with a big blue bow.

He looked at the gift. It could easily be a trap. He opened the package. Inside was a key-string. He ran the string through the swipe-slot, and the front door of the Diogenes Club opened.

Inside, the quality of the mimesis upgraded. As Dr Shade, he entered a gentleman's club. He heard a rustle of newspapers, the discreet footsteps of servants. He smelled various types of tobacco smoke and the old leather of the club-room chairs.

An attendant ushered him upstairs.

The Chambers of the Ruling Cabal were derelict. Cobwebs wound over everything, spun between chairs and tables and desks and map-stands. He walked through the webs without breaking strands. Everything sparkled slightly.

The darkness dispelled as someone turned up a gas lamp. It was a well-wrapped mummy, androgynous in form, adept in movement. The mummy's eyes flickered. They were tiny screens. Red figures scrolled down.

There were others. A dog-headed man, in a broad Ancient Egyptian collar. The actor, John Barrymore. A swaddled invalid in a cocoon-like wheelchair, her head supported by a leather brace. And a red entity, a gemstone which shone with the light of stars.

Seven Stars.

Of course, all these were avatars of one person. One intelligence.

He took off his goggles, and let his similie resemble himself.

'We understand you're out of pocket,' Barrymore said. 'You've been the victim of a prank.'

'I was sent to find someone who seems not to be lost.'

All the faces of Seven Stars smiled at once. Even the jewel.

'We're in a position to compensate you, and to prosecute your interests. To turn your commission around, we'd be willing to pay you well to find out the whereabouts of your former employer, the undead Mademoiselle Dieudonné.'

'Interesting,' he said.

He had a realwelt address. His mother's paper records were still in the firm's vault, and it had only taken an hour or so to find the notes Neil had deposited after the abandonment of the 1998 investigation. There, on headed notepaper, in a fine hand, was a personal thank you note, signed 'Gené'. Without accessing the Info-World, he had confirmed that the address—a suite at a private hotel in Kensington—was still occupied. It was a throwback to his mother's type of detective work. He didn't even allow himself to make comm-links, for they contrailed through the Info-World, flagging themselves. He used printed-out directories and walked across the city, avoiding dogs and euthanasia krewes, to ask questions of a human desk clerk.

The hotel was off-record. Jerome worked out it had been bought—for cash—around the turn of the century. A phantom access signature implied it to be the property of a deceased lady named Catriona Kaye, run by a permanent trust administered by a firm of lawyers, kept open in accordance with Miss Kaye's will.

Actually, it was a hidey-hole.

Invisible to the Info-World, it was a vampire's coffin.

He couldn't even claim credit for brilliant analysis. Geneviève had given him her address—the note, dated 1998, even mentioned him—and all he had done was confirm it.

'For Mam'selle Dieudonné's location, we will pay a sum equivalent to your aggregate earnings over the last five years.'

This came from the mummy.

That flagged it. He was almost but not quite annoyed enough at Geneviève to turn her over.

But the comm-link gave it away.

'I'll think about it,' he told the Seven Stars. 'It'll take time to get and confirm the info you want.'

'Very well, you have one hour.'

Jerome jacked out and cut access.

The realwelt rung with the sounds of dying dogs.

He was shocked. The sudden withdrawal from the dreamwelt was a heart-kicker, advised against by all help programs. But the realisation had been jolt enough.

He had nearly been gulled.

Now, he had to get across realwelt London. There was a severe curfew in force. All people-transport services, above and below ground, were suspended. Groups of dog-lovers had banded together to resist the extermination krewes, augmented by unpersons ready to riot for any cause, and there were outbreaks of fighting in St James's Park and Oxford Street. He would have to get round that.

He could not drive, because he'd have to log a route plan in his auto's master program, and that would register in the Info-World. In the basement, he still had the last of the bikes he had pedalled through childhood. His Dad, dead before he was born, had been a cycle messenger, and he'd felt that in pumping along tracks or out on the road he was sending out an 'I Am Here' notice to the Beyond, paying tribute in his own way to the man he had never known.

In his mind, he mapped a route, zip-zagging around trouble spots, with a few tricky double-backs to throw off anyone who might be following.

Before he stepped onto Upper Street, he took out his earpiece and left it on the table beside the door. He checked himself for any other devices with Info-World signatures.

This was like being forced to walk after learning to fly. But doing without the wings made sense.

He cycled down the street. All the surviving dogs of London were howling. He recalled an early-century saying, one Neil had been fond of: Real is real.

She was waiting for him outside the hotel, hair shining with sun, unafraid of the rays. His heart sank and he searched himself.

'Real is real,' she said, almost apologising.

She wasn't wearing the hat, cloak and eyeshade today. That had almost been a Dr Shade outfit, he realised.

'We had real people following you, not just search engines.'

'Then you knew, when you asked for the address...'

'We just wanted to see if you fit the pattern. We've met a series of people like you. Almost a family tree. We've learned to appreciate you. You've fed into us.'

'You're not Geneviève?'

She shook her head.

'No. Of course not. Though I do look like her. She wasn't my father or my mother, but she left something of herself in my mother, something that shaped me.'

'You're talking in the singular.'

'About Mimsy, yes. I am Mimsy.'

He had been right. Too late.

'But *we* are Seven Stars.'

'Is there a Geneviève?'

'Yes. She's inside. Upstairs.'

He turned to go into the hotel.

'By the way,' Mimsy said, 'beware of the dogs.'

The howling of all the dogs in London came from inside the hotel. A helmeted body lay jammed half-way out of the revolving door, protective clothing shredded.

Using a side-door, he got into the lobby and found the rest of a euthanasia krewe along with dogs alive and dead. He snatched up a jolt-gun and found it uncharged. Mimsy followed him. Indoors, she still shone. A red light, centred in her chest, radiated through transparent flesh and thin fabric. Star-points glinted, hard chips in the softer light. She was difficult to look at directly.

The dogs ignored her, but came for him.

They were too caught up in their own pain to concentrate on savaging him, but he still took too many nips and bites as he waded up the main stairs.

He threw dogs away.

On the first floor landing, a giant Rottweiler, augmented as a guard minion, snarled at him. Its teeth were steel, probably envenomed. Veins stood out on its bulbous forehead. Its eyes were maddened red jelly.

He tensed, expecting a final attack.

Something burst inside the dog's skull. Grey gruel squeezed out of its eyesockets. It fell like an unstrung puppet.

He could almost hear the killing sound. His regrown front tooth ached. The plates of his skull ground against each other. Pressure built up inside his ears, producing pain in the drums and all the spaces of his head, throbbing under his cheekbones, around his eyes, at the base of his brain.

Dogs pawed towards him and fell. Skulls detonated like bombs, spraying blood and brain matter across faded floral wallpaper.

He took hold of the banister and hauled himself up to the next landing. Mimsy skipped up beside him, unaffected. She had the mummy's red eyescreens. That avatar had been closest to her.

'This is just the first of them,' she told him. 'The new plagues. This is the curse of dogs.'

The main door of the suite was open. A man lay dead in it. He wore a black single-piece suit and had the sign of the Seven Stars on his forehead. His throat had been torn out by some animal a little daintier than a dog. Neat slices opened his veins.

'One of mine,' Mimsy admitted. 'The old girl still has some bite.'

He tried to equalise the pressure in his head, opening his mouth and forcing a desperate yawn. It helped momentarily.

'Don't worry,' Mimsy said. 'The plague will soon be over.'

She picked up a frothing Pekingese and chucked its chin. The little dog's skull pulsed like a hatching egg. She pointed it away from her, and the dog's eyes shot out on geysers of liquid brain.

'Ugh,' she said, dropping the dead thing.

He stepped over the man's body.

On a curtained four-poster bed was Mimsy's transformed twin. This was the real Geneviève, arced like a bow, clawed fingers and toes hooked into torn bedclothes. She lashed from side to side, whipping long hair. Her bloody mouth was full of swollen fang-teeth. Her eyes were red, but not with an LED light.

Veins in her temples were swelling.

'She's not human, poor love,' Mimsy said. 'She can hear things dogs can.'

Jerome wanted to go over to the bed but Geneviève snarled at him to stay away. He minded she didn't trust herself not to strike out at him.

'If she isn't human, what are you?'

'Oh, I'm completely human,' Mimsy said.

'You singular. What about you plural?'

'Seven Stars,' she said, pulling down her neckline to show the red light burning under her ribs. It grew in intensity, as the unheard noise grew.

The cries of the dogs were cutting off, one by one.

Small objects on a bedside table rattled. Vibrations throbbed through Jerome, through the hotel, the city, the world.

Mimsy's flesh parted as the jewel rose to the surface. It climbed up into the base of her throat. It seemed to be talking.

'We are come from afar,' it said. 'We are the Plague Bringer.'

For the last time, Mimsy spoke. 'Just think,' she said, 'within a minute, dogs will be an extinct species. And vampires.'

The howling had all but stopped.

The dogs were all dead. All over the world, dogs' brains burst in their heads.

Jerome ran to the bed and took Geneviève's hand. He was not surprised at the ferocity of her grip. He looked into her red eyes, hoping for an answer.

The thing that walked around in Mimsy Mountmain's body filled the room with red light.

Geneviève's eyes started from their sockets.

He *could* hear the maddening subaudible whine now.

Cracks in Geneviève's forehead spread away from her temples, leaking thin blood, snaking up into her hair. Her mouth was open in a tooth-ringed circle.

'You're Jerome,' she said, through agony. 'You are all that's left.'

Bloody tears the size of beetles crawled from her eyes, ears and nose. *1416–2025?*

She sat up in bed, a final jolt of killing current shot through her. Her head came apart with a crack. Bloody hair whipped him across the face and she was a limp doll.

The whine cut off, leaving a gaping silence.

In that silence, a world was left mad.

He turned, seeing red. Seven Stars walked out of the room.

Episode Seven: The Duel of the Seven Stars

The shock of death. Is it greater for her, after so long? Despite what the records say, she didn't quite die in her sixteenth year. She just stopped being human.

The young man holds her. She wants his blood.

The noise in her skull cuts off. A red fringe flops over her eyes. The pain ends.

Nothing.

A frozen moment. In a museum. Looking at a man looking at a mummy. His face reflected in the glass of the display case. Hers not. But he senses her, turns. Thinks about her. For a moment.

In another life...

Geneviève Sandrine Ysolde Dieudonné. Geneviève the Undying, daughter of the physician Benoit Dieudonné, daughter-in-darkness of Chandagnac, of the bloodline of Melissa d'Acques.

For her, it is over.

She is in darkness, unfeeling. She might be in woman-shape. Or something immobile, a sarsen stone, a tree. She sees nothing, but she senses.

There are others. Not waiting for her, but accepting her, recognising her.

Five others.

She knows they were once living too. And in that moment of knowing, she accepts her final death. The five are now six. They reach for her, not physically. She knows them, but their names do not come to mind.

Neither does her own.

Together, the six shine. At last, she knows perfect love.

Not yet complete, though. The Six must become Seven. Lucky Number Seven.

Then...

Red light.

Consciousness resumes, continues. She can think, remember, picture herself, imagine a world beyond. She has a sense of her body. There is still pain, and warmth.

She is not dead. Not anymore.

She is alone. Her five companions are gone. Bereft, her heart aches. A tear gathers in her eye.

Blood trickles into her mouth. Young blood, rich, peppery. It flows through her, bringing a jolt of wakefulness. Her teeth sharpen against her tongue. More blood is spilled onto her lips. She licks, red thirst alive, and feels strength growing.

Her night-senses come alive. She is acutely aware of the roughness of the cotton shift she is wearing, and of the scents that cling to it.

Hospital smells sting her.

She cannot sit. Her head is fixed in place by a contraption of steel clamps and plastic tubes. She swivels her eyes, and sees fluid flowing through the tubes, into her.

There is an alien object inside. Where the last pain was, she senses an inorganic plate, patching over the ruin of her burst skull.

She tries to raise a hand to her head. She is restrained, by a durable plastic cuff. She tries harder, and the plastic snaps.

Someone takes her hand.

'Getting your strength back, I see.'

Alarms sound.

'You're in the Pyramid,' the young man tells her. He is not a doctor. His face is familiar. 'In London Docklands, what's left of it. The Derek Leech International Building. Some of the staff call it the Last Redoubt.'

The young man is Jerome, Sally Rhodes's son.

He was there when she died.

Judging by the changes in his face, that must have been years ago.

'How long...?'

'Seven months.'

She sits up in bed.

'You've missed a ton,' he says. 'The Plagues. The Wars. The Collapse.'
She holds her head.

Her hair is close-cropped, for the first time in centuries.

'I think it's snazz,' Jerome says. 'You look like Joan of Arc.'

'Good God, I hope not.'

She remembers Jeanne d'Arc. It was during her war that Geneviève
received the Dark Kiss, became a vampire. There was blood all around.

She feels the back of her skull, fingertips pressing the skin over the
plate.

'I don't understand what Leech's doctors did,' Jerome says. 'I've still
not really scanned the info that there are such things as vampires.'

'Sorry,' she shrugs.

'Not your fault. Any rate, you're back from the dead. Leech says it's
magic and medicine. You weren't properly alive, so it was easier to bring
you back than it'd have been if you were... um?'

'A real live girl?'

'Yes, well, exactly. You were put back together months ago, but the
hardest part was what Leech calls "summoning you up". Getting you to
move back in, as it were. He's had a team of spooks—mediums, mages,
nutters—working on it. In the end, I think he did it himself, reached out into
the wherever and dragged you back. All this is new ground to me.'

'Me too,' she admits, again fingering her skull, gliding fingertips over
her fur.

'Do you want a mirror? The scars on your head are healing. And you
have none on your face.'

'A mirror would be no good to me. They don't take.'

Jerome goggles. She catches a little of his amazement, and sees herself
through his eyes, alarmingly tiny in a big bed, face small and pretty on an
egg of a head.

'I gave blood,' he confesses, shyly.

'I know,' she replies, taking his hand.

Things have changed while she was away. The boiling point of water is now
78°. That was the effect popularly known as the Plague of Fire. Around the
world, spontaneous combustion is a general hazard, and this past summer
has seen the uncontrolled burning of much surviving forested land and not a
few townships and cities.

Monsters have come out of the sea, just as in the films of the 1950s,
and devastated conurbations. That was the Plague of Dragons, though most
called it the Plague of Godzillas. There are other natural catastrophes: Insects
have predictably run rampant again. Of course, with the interconnectedness
of everything, it is hard to distinguish a genuine plague from a side-effect

like war, famine, mass psychosis and post-millennial panic.

The Plague of Babel ended electronic communications. It did not shut down the Information World, as the Collapse Theorists prophesied, but habitually scrambles three out of every four transactions, providing convincing but fabricated images as well as texts and sound effects. Many of the scrambles are just garbage, but some are malicious. Economic and military wars have been triggered by caprice.

An Empire is falling. And the Emperor has busied himself not with shoring up the barricades but with engineering her resurrection.

She wonders why Derek Leech cares so much about her.

'You are familiar with the suppressed quatrains of Nostradamus?'

'Of course.'

'In 1942, one of them led you to the Seven Stars.'

'I didn't see it. The gumshoe did.'

'Michel was sadly given to obscurity.'

'I often wondered why he never predicted anything happy. Or world-changing in a trivial sense. Elvis's appearance on the *Ed Sullivan Show*. The discovery of penicillin.'

Leech does not smile.

He is seeing her in his office at the apex of the Pyramid. Through the tinted screen-windows, the fires ravaging the city are crimson carpet patches. Black gargantuoids, lizard-tails whipping, sumo-wrestle in the burning ruins.

Banks of screens are grey and dead. This is the central node of a global net of information-flow, the heart of an electronic Yggdrasil that has bound together humanity and subjugated them to a man-shaped creature. It is just a room full of obsolete junk.

A few—Jerome's mother, for one—had protested that Leech's increasing dominion of the world reduced people to components in a global device, locked into cell-like monads, consuming garbage info, indentured spectators and consumers.

Under Derek Leech, history became soap.

When Edwin Winthrop allowed the Jewel of Seven Stars to be focused against the Axis Powers and their Ancient Masters, he smashed Empires but dipped his hands in blood. The trust handed down to him was subtly betrayed, a chink was opened in the world, and through that chink had squeezed Derek Leech.

Now, the Seven Stars rain plagues on Leech.

She should be happier.

The plagues come too late, when Leech's Pyramid is at the top of the world. They flow down the black glass sides of this building and spread out to the corners of the map.

This is the end, she thinks.

Leech takes a book from his desk. It is the only book she has seen in the Pyramid. Though access to electronic information is compromised, there is not a general falling-back to print or scribbled memos. Paper, its combustion point lowered from Bradbury's 451, is a hazard.

'During the late War, you were allowed access to only the quatrains relevant to the short term. Edwin Winthrop kept a lot from you, but a lot was kept from him. His ultimate part in all this, for instance. And yours.'

He has her attention.

At a touch, he untints the glass. The fires leap up in vividity. Even the eyes of the battling beasts now burn like unhealthy neons.

In the sky, the moon is blood-red. And Ursa Major is missing.

'This is *wrong*,' Leech says. 'Whatever you think of the world you left, this is not an acceptable alternative.'

She has to agree.

'The old world, things as they were before, can be bought back.'

'Brought back?'

'No, *bought*. Everything is economics. Things can be as they were, according to Nostradamus, with seven lives twice-lost. Seven dead will return to the Earth, and die again. You are the first, and through you the other six will be gathered. There is a death beyond death.'

'I don't fear it.'

Everyone asks her what it was like. She hasn't been able to explain.

'I envy you, Geneviève. You know things I will never access. I must content myself with everything else.'

'So, when it's over, you'll rule in Hell?'

'That, sadly, Nostradamus is silent on.'

'Ain't it just the way?'

'Indeed.'

In the heart of the Pyramid, she is ushered into an orrery, one of Leech's famous magical devices. A globe of interlocking brass and copper and steel partial spheres, gimballed like a giant gyroscope, it is a schematic of the solar system. It is an impressive bit of clockwork, but here is just a focus.

Leech has offered to dress the process up with ritual and chanting. Blood sacrifices, if necessary. But it is down to her to reach out, to travel back to the sphere from which he summoned her, to reach her companions. If they are brought to this world, they will be the Seven, who alone—according to Mad Michel—can check the unleashed plagues of the Seven Stars.

She has not told Leech that there are, by her reckoning, only Six Samurai. After all, de Nostre-Dame—whom she now regrets not visiting personally when she was a vigorous 150 and giving his throat a good wringing—is often only ball-park accurate.

One thing in the cards is that she alone will survive the coming Duel of the Seven Stars. She has already died twice—her change from human to vampire counts—and so she alone of the Merry Band has already paid her due and will live on, to see what Leech makes of the world and, unless she misses her guess, to do her best to see that it isn't as dire as it might be.

The Seventh of her Circle bothers her. Does his or her absence invalidate the whole quatrain?

Damn all cloudy prophets and smug seers. Cassandra didn't get half the kicking she deserved.

She becomes the Sun, taking her seat in the centre of the orrery.

'I shall try to shine,' she announces.

Leech isn't here, though she knows he must be watching over her from somewhere. He is a creature of the eaves, peering out of the darkness, a cosmic couch potato. Technicians of enchantment, plastic young women she thinks of as attendant demons, work the levers. And Jerome, another loose component in this clanking magical machine. If this is for anyone, it is for him. In honour of his mother.

She shuts herself down.

The orrery revolves.

Her five companions expect her. They have been incomplete. She is the pathway. Through her, they channel themselves. She senses more. Scraps of lives lost. Some familiar to her, some strange. As one, they dwindle into reality.

The orrery concludes its cycle.

She pulls herself out of the contraption, brain a-swarm with trace memories. The phenomenon is more acute than the mostly random mind-link she has with those living whose blood she has taken. It's like sharing skull-space with strangers.

'She's alone,' a woman says. 'It's over. We've failed.'

'No,' says Jerome. 'Not yet.'

Jerome helps her stand. He looks into her eyes.

Now, at last, the Circle is complete.

The red thirst comes upon her like a raging wave. Her fang-teeth sprout like bone-knives. The strangers in her skull add to her need.

'Leech said a blood sacrifice would complete the forging of the Circle,' Jerome whispers, popping his collar-seam. 'Take me.'

Her predator's lizard-like brainstem overrides all civilised restraint. In this state, she has no conscience, no personality, no qualms. She has only red thirst. She is a blood junkie, the worst sort of vampire bitch.

Her mouth fastens on Jerome's throat in urgent rape. She bites into his jugular vein, tearing through the skin and meat, and sucks in the great gouts of blood.

She feels his heartbeat under her hand.

His blood pours into her, along with much else. His mind is sucked entirely into hers, jostling with the other strangers. Chunks of stringy meat-stuff cram into her throat. She swallows and expands.

This is Geneviève, the Monster.

She sucks desperately until his heart is still and her body is bloated with blood.

She can not absorb all she has taken. Her mouth is full, her cheeks swollen.

This has happened before, three times in six hundred years. These are her most shameful secrets, the unwilling sacrifices she has taken to ensure her continuance. She tells herself the red thirst is irresistible, like a possessing spirit, but that is a rationalisation. At bottom, she is convinced that she can will herself not to kill. She does not do so, through choice. She lets the lizard-stem take over.

Whether Jerome is a willing sacrifice or not, she has sinned again. She has lost something of herself. It is too late to give him the Dark Kiss, to bring him back as a vampire. He is dead, drained meat.

The attendant demons are appalled, and stay back, afraid she will turn on them. The strangers in her skull, blooded, are growing. They speak to her, like the voices that bothered Jeanne d'Arc.

'Soon, soon, soon,' they whisper.

Four men, one woman.

No. Five men, one woman.

They are Seven. As predicted.

She is heavy, full to bursting, belly bloated, throat stretched like a snake's.

The taste of blood is ecstasy on her tongue.

At her feet lie Jerome's clothes. He is gone from them. Without his blood and his ghost, the meat has dissolved completely. His whole substance is in her.

'Now,' they cry, with one voice.

She opens her mouth, and a cloud of red matter explodes from her, pouring into the air.

Six shapes resolve in the cloud of bloody ectoplasm. The first is a thin, brown man with an open wound in his chest. He wears a classical garment and Ancient Egyptian court head-dress. This, Geneviève knows, is Pai-net'em, who kept the Jewel of Seven Stars to himself for three thousand years.

Then comes a handsome man all in black. His clothes are Elizabethan in cut, but his sharp moustache is 1920s style. He carries a plaster skull in one hand and a duelling sword in the other.

'Time is out of joint,' John Barrymore announces. 'O cursèd spite, that e'er I was born to set it right.'

Next is Edwin.

He comes together as he was long before she knew him, in a muddy officer's uniform, young and haunted, ears ringing from bombardments.

'I died,' he says. 'In the trenches. The rest was just in my mind. No. Geneviève. You were part of it. The world after the War.'

She takes his hand, feels him calm down.

'There were shadows like men,' he says.

Now, a woman joins them. Maureen Mountmain, as full of life as when Geneviève fed off her. She is less bewildered than the others.

'It's the end of it,' she says. 'Mimsy must be stopped.'

A young man Geneviève does not know has appeared. He wears cycling shorts and a baggy T-shirt. Very 1990s. His temples are shaved.

'Who are you?' she asks.

'Despatch, love.'

He opens a shoulder-bag, and looks for a parcel.

The final member of the seven is Dr Shade, the comic-strip avenger. He emerges from the last of the red mist, cloak trailing. His face is covered by a surgical mask and goggles.

A fictional character?

'That was a rush,' says Dr Shade. 'Gené, you bit me. You really bit me.'

It is Jerome. He pulls down his mask, and presses his tongue to his teeth.

'But I'm not a vampire,' he says. 'What am I?'

'You look like Dr Shade,' she says.

'That makes sense.'

'I'm glad it does to someone.'

Death has made Jerome jauntier. He isn't the serious Information Analyst she remembers. He has inwardly taken on some of the aspects of the pulp hero whose uniform he wears.

'We're the old world's last hope,' Pai-net'em says, not out loud but in their minds. 'We are to check the plagues, and destroy the jewel.'

The bike messenger, in particular, looks appalled.

Jerome's mind still races, dragging Geneviève—who is still aware of the ties of blood between them—along behind him.

'I know who you are,' Jerome says to the messenger.

'I'm Connor,' the cyclist says.

'You're my Dad,' Jerome says. 'You died.'

'We all died,' Edwin says.

'And we will all die again,' says Pai-net'em. 'Our sacrifice will heal the world. Pharaoh can rule again, justly.'

Pai-net'em had a lot to learn about Derek Leech.

'Why us?' Jerome asks. 'Why us seven?'

'Because we're all responsible for it,' Maureen says. 'We touched it and it touched us. We died so that the Seven Stars might rise, in the body of my daughter. Some of us were destroyed long before our bodies were broken.'

Barrymore nods, understanding.

'And now we're going to die again?' says Connor. 'No, thank you very much. I didn't lay down my life to redeem the world. I was knocked over by a fucking van.'

'Dad!' Jerome says, shocked. He is older than his father got to be.

'You lived on in him,' Geneviève says.

'Big deal. He's dead too, right? What a mess. I wasn't going to ride a bike all my life. I was young. I could have made it. I had projects.'

'Excuse me, Connor,' begins Edwin. 'Few of us are here by choice. We all resisted being part of this Circle. We didn't volunteer. Except for the first of us.'

He looks at Pai-net'em, the Pharaoh's minister.

'And the last,' Geneviève adds, remembering Jerome baring his throat.

'And who are you all?' Connor asked.

'We're the psychic detectives, Dad,' Jerome says, sounding more like Dr Shade than ever. 'We're the Three Musketeers and the Four Just Men, the Seven Samurai and the Seven Sinners. We are the masked avengers and the spirits of justice, protectors of the innocent and defenders of the defenceless. We are the last hope of humankind. There are mysteries to be solved, wrongs to be righted, monsters to be vanquished. Now, are you with us? To death and glory, for love and life?'

Barrymore looks as if he wished he'd made that speech.

Maureen wants to make love with this masked man, *now!*

Edwin is quietly proud. Jerome Rhodes would have been Diogenes Club material.

'If you put it like that, *son*,' Connor says, 'include me in.'

The Seven are whole.

Complete.

She feels their strength growing.

They stand together, in a circle. They link hands, and their strengths flow into each other.

'Pardon me for intruding in this inspirational moment,' Leech says, through a loud-speaker, 'but we are on a time-table.'

Leech has made available to them a customised short-hop skimmer. Jerome recognises the lines, and realises it is a Rolls Royce ShadowShark, melded with an assault helicopter and a space shuttle. It is sleek, black and radar-invisible.

Geneviève imagines that Leech must be a little sad at parting with it. It is a wonderful toy.

Jerome, of course, knows how to fly the ShadowShark.

The flight is already keyed into the vehicle's manifest. She could have guessed where it is supposed to end. It is where it all started.

Egypt.

She is the last to board.

Leech is there to see them off. She knows that he wishes he were part of it.

Some would have traded with him if they could. From her, they knew what Nostre-Dame foresaw for them. To succeed in this, they would have to die. Again.

'I will see you when this is over,' Leech says.

'If Michel wasn't playing a joke.'

She climbs into the ShadowShark.

Continental Europe is mottled with fires. Rockets streak in from the Urals. Jerome easily bests the missiles. There are flying creatures, nesting among the cloud-shields. The skimmer takes evasive action.

The Seven no longer need to talk.

Geneviève, used to touching the minds of those she feeds on, is knotted emotionally by how much more complex, more vital this is.

For the first time, she is alive and aware. Going on alone afterwards will be a tragedy. She will be haunted forever by the loss of this companionship, this clarity, this love.

She senses the bindings growing. Between Connor and Jerome is a rope of blood kinship. She is strung between Maureen and Jerome, both of whom have given life to her. Pai-net'em and Barrymore and Winthrop fit into the circle, perfectly. Their similarities are bonds. Their differences are complements.

They drink of her memories, the many lives she has sampled. She lets Pai-net'em's ancient history and Barrymore's blazing talent flow into her. She knows their loves: Edwin's life-long irritated devotion to Catriona, Maureen's hot burst of generous desire with Jeperson, Connor's calculated but real attachment to Sally.

Throughout their times, the Seven have revolved around the Jewel of Seven Stars, closing in on a tiny constellation. Between them, they understand the bauble, a lump of red malice tossed at the Earth, and know its limitations.

As they close on the Nile, they become more aware of the pulsing thing at the end of their flight path. They are hooked, and being reeled in.

If she could stop time, this is the moment she would pick.

Before the holocaust.

By the bubbling waters of the Nile squats a clear ruby pyramid, in which burn the Seven Stars.

At first, Geneviève thinks the jewel has grown to giant size, dwarfing the sphinx and the old pyramids, but it is a solid projection.

The jewel is inside.

Multitudes gather on the shores of the great river. In the past months, cults have sprung up for the worship of the Seven Stars, or emerged from historic secrecy to declare themselves the Acolytes of the Plagues. Oblations are offered up to the Red Pyramid.

Occasionally, swaths of death are cut through the crowds. That merely encourages more to gather, pressing closer, praying and starving and burning and rotting. Robed priests ritually cast themselves into the boiling river.

Having been dead, twice, and begun to form a sense of what comes after, Geneviève at last knows that the Jewel of Seven Stars is not a magical object. It offers only random cessation, cruel and needless.

It does not create anything.

Pai-net'em, who lay with the jewel in him, listening through the years to its insectile whisper, thinks it was a machine. Barrymore, who tore genius from himself as he was driven on by the jewel, feels it to be a malign imp. Maureen still believes it the catspaw of the Elder Gods for whom her uncles devoted their lives to blaspheming. To Edwin, it is a puzzle to be solved and put away. To Connor, it is unjust death, robbing him of the future. To Jerome, it is all misinformation, all garbage, all lies, all negatives, all deadtech.

And to her?

It is her enemy. And her salvation.

She knows now why the first curse—the Plague of Dogs—was aimed at her. Mimsy must have accessed the suppressed quatrains, probably when she took over the premises and archives of the Diogenes Club. Mimsy Mountmain had enough of a human mind to know that the vampire who had left traces of herself in her veins was the focus of the Circle of Seven, the only force which could break the weirdstone.

She's still my daughter, thinks Maureen.

Geneviève is infected with love for the girl in the Red Pyramid. The girl who looks so like her, as she was before the Dark Kiss, who has also been robbed of a life, of love and a world, by the Jewel of Seven Stars.

Mimsy is going to die too.

The ShadowShark settles by the Red Pyramid, on a stretch of sand blasted into glass. There are corpses set in the glass, staring up at the red sky.

They get out of the skimmer, and look at the Red Pyramid. The Seven Stars shine, trapped inside.

Geneviève feels assaulted in her mind, as when the whine that maddened dogs was killing her. The steel plate in her skull grows hot.

Pai-net'em wipes the sound from her mind.

She stands, propped up by Maureen. Her mind feels clean, invigorated. Together, they are strong.

Barrymore and Pai-net'em open a portal in the side of the Pyramid, extending their hands and willing a door to appear. On the lintel, Barrymore creates masks of Tragedy and Comedy, which Pai-net'em equips with sphinx bodies.

Barrymore gives a theatrical bow.

A whip-like tendril shoots out of the portal and lashes the actor. His flesh explodes, bursting his doublet and hose. His skull, still moustached, looks surprised. He collapses. His voice dies in their mind.

It is a needle of pain. The loss is a devastation.

Pai-net'em grasps the tendril with both hands, and yanks hard, wrenching it loose. As he pulls, a grey wrinkling runs up his arms. His face withers to mummy-shape, and he crumbles again, coming apart as dust and dirt.

Coming hard on the first loss, this knocks the Circle back. Only Jerome is strong enough in himself to support the others.

They are all going to die. She had known that. But these first deaths are still deadly blows.

Her heart is stone.

Edwin takes the lead, and steps over the still-twitching tendril. She follows, and the others come after her.

Connor, she knows, wants to turn and flee, to go far from the Pyramid, to make a life here, in this world, to have all the things he missed. Only his tie to Jerome, which he doesn't understand, keeps him on course. To him, it is possible that this is some dying fantasy, as Edwin had thought his whole post-1917 life was, and that it doesn't matter.

A tunnel leads straight to the heart of the Red Pyramid.

Statues look down at them. Faces that mean something. Voices plead and threaten.

To Edwin, it is Catriona above all. Also Declan and Bennett Mountmain, Charles Beauregard and Mycroft Holmes.

To Maureen, it is Mimsy, Richard, Leech.

To Connor, it is the agents and producers who could have opened a life for him. Contracts are offered, cheques processed, projects green-lighted.

To Jerome, it is Mum, Neil, Sister Chantal, Roger Duroc.

To her, it is the Three.

Forgotten lives, taken in red fugues. Sergei Bukharin, Annie Marriner, Davey Wales.

And Jerome. Not Three anymore, Four.

Her dead call to her, cajole, promise, abuse, fret.

There are others, a myriad bled and sampled and absorbed. They bother her like gnats. She is torn into by Chandagnac, the minstrel who had turned her and been destroyed when she might have saved him. And all those she had known and let die by not passing on the Dark Kiss, all she had let grow old and die by not succouring them with her blood.

She is a selfish parasite. She should not continue this charade of heroism.

The world is well lost, and her with it.

Jerome saves her, this time. The most recently dead, he has less time to brood, to adjust, less sense of business left unfinished. Bolstered by those aspects of Dr Shade he has taken into himself, he fights off his temptations first, and is available to help her through.

He doesn't blame her. He is grateful to her.

In this adventure, he has finally come to know his father, to understand his mother, to get out of his monad and become a part of something greater than himself. At last, he has found a realwelt as vital to him as the Info-World.

She climbs along the thread of his love. She leaves her dead behind.

The silencing of the voices comes at a cost. Connor is empty and dry and old. Edwin riddled with bullet-wounds, choking on poison gas, caked with the filth of Flanders. They are not destroyed, but they can go no further.

'Go, for us, as for yourselves,' Edwin says.

Jerome stands between Maureen and her. He takes their hands, and leads them into the centre of the Red Pyramid.

A final door opens.

The Jewel of Seven Stars is wearing Mimsy Mountmain. Geneviève feels, after six hundred years, that she is looking into a broken mirror. Mimsy's hair is still long, and her face is a perfect thing of tiny jewel facets of red fire.

This is where the plagues came from.

'Mimsy,' Maureen appeals.

The Jewel Woman turns, red-screen eyes noting their presence.

Jerome raises Dr Shade's gas-gun and fires at the Jewel Woman. His pellet shatters against the gem-shields over her face.

Once, there was a girl. Her tiny wishes and frustrations, nurtured by the jewel, powered the thing, pouring energy into it like a battery, subtly shaping the forms of the plagues it wreaks. Now, that girl is gone, a footnote. This is an alien. Geneviève isn't sure whether it is a creature or a machine, a god or a demon. If it has thoughts, they are beyond her understanding. If it has feelings, they are unearthly.

Maureen tries to love the jewel, to venerate it, to wake her daughter.

If it had fallen on another world, among other beings, would it have been different? Was it humanity that used this gift to unleash plagues? The first time, when Pharaoh gazed into its depths and wished to extend his rule beyond the known world, it was an accident, but man's character had let loose something that was somehow deserved.

Now, could Mimsy really be responsible? She had been shaped and robbed of choice as much as anyone else. Nostradamus had seen her fixed course too. The shadowmen that had taken Edwin were accumulating, in other forms, in this Red Pyramid. Mimsy was already wrapped in darkness.

Maureen touches Mimsy. The Jewel Woman thins.

'It's all right, love,' Maureen says. 'Let it end.'

Mimsy's face, soft and bewildered, is clear. The jewel carapace is gone. Jerome shoots her in the head.

Geneviève feels the pellet passing into her own brain.

Eyes alive with betrayal, Mimsy falls, the Jewel of Seven Stars rolling from her chest. The years, held back by the spell, surge like a tide as Mimsy grows old and dies within seconds. She is a corpse before the discharge from Dr Shade's gas-gun dissipates.

Maureen sobs. Geneviève hugs her, pulled close by their blood-bond. They are both ripped open by the death of the girl who had come from both of them.

The jewel is still active. It had been inside Maureen when Mimsy was conceived, when Geneviève tasted her blood. It is the dead girl's heart. The Seven Stars throb inside it, like drops of glowing blood.

The Red Pyramid is collapsing around them. Scarlet dust cascades.

Jerome picks up the Jewel of Seven Stars. Its lights reflect in his goggles. Through him, Geneviève feels its tug. It opens up possibilities. It is a source of great power. If they keep it, maybe it can be focused. For good. The world need not be left for Leech.

Jerome might *become* Dr Shade, not just dress as him.

No, says Pai-net'em. He is still part of them, freed if anything by his second death. Not yet. Perhaps never. The stone is at its weakest, emptied of plague, its host torn away, its influence overextended. It can be ended. Now.

Maureen is dead in Geneviève's embrace. She lays the woman down, brushing white hair away from her beautiful face. She has tried to do her best, to escape her family's past, to find something of worth in her inheritance. Of them all, she has loved the most.

There is night all around. The pyramid is thinned to a structure of fading light-lines. The jewel-worshippers wail at a sensed loss.

Jerome makes a fist around the jewel and squeezes. The red glow is wrapped in his black leather gauntlet.

She hears the first crack. Jerome squeezes harder.

'Get out of range, Gené,' he says. 'When this goes, I go with it. I have to die again, mind. You get to live forever. Tell Mum Connor was one of the good guys...'

The others are growing thin in her mind. Loneliness is gathering like a shadow.

Without the Seven Stars, how will humankind fare?

What is left for her?

'Go on, Gené. Run.'

'No,' she says. 'It's not fair.'

She takes the jewel from him. She is far stronger than him. Vampires have the grip of iron.

'You died for me last time,' she says, kissing him. 'Now, it's my turn. Give Sally your own message. And watch out for the world. Try not to let Derek Leech get back too much of what he had. And play outside sometimes.'

She leaves him, faster than he can register, darting with vampire swiftness through the transparent ruins. She runs out into the desert, fleet enough to skim over the soft sands. The Jewel of Seven Stars screams in her mind as she squeezes it. The faults grind against each other, the starfires boil.

It is not too late to give in.

She could *use* the weirdstone.

Other voices give her strength.

There is a loophole in Nostre-Dame, as usual. If she dies a third time, the obligation is lifted from Jerome.

She is far from the Nile, far from water, lost in unchanging sandscape. This country has not changed since she was born. Not since the settling of the continents.

She falls to her knees and looks up at the sky. Twinkling in the night, she sees Ursa Major. It is back again. The plagues are over. The world is set to rights.

And is on its own.

Sergei, Annie, Davey, Jerome.

She deserves this.

But at last she accepts forgiveness.

She crushes the jewel to red grit. Seven flames burst into fireballs, and she burns with love.

All find their moments.

Pai-net'em is honoured by Old Pharaoh, the great and wise king.

Edwin sees Catriona's smile for the first time.

John Barrymore is assaulted by applause.

Maureen Mountmain cradles Mimsy to her breast, and shares perfect love.

Connor gets the green-light on a life.

She is in the British Museum, snatching a glimpse of the reflection of a man's face, thinking of possibilities.

Jerome is free of them, journeying into the unknowable future. The thread that connects them to him stretches, and then breaks.

The sand drifts over her bones, burying them with a red scatter of jewel fragments. The Seven Stars pass from the skies, and the sun rises on the desert.

NOTES

Adrian Marcato, Hamish Corbie, Anselm Oakes, Hjalmar Poelzig and Pius Mocata. According to Ira Levin, Anthony Powell, Christopher Isherwood, Boris Karloff and Dennis Wheatley, these associates of Colonel Zenf are Jolly Bad Fellows indeed. You'll find out about Declan Mountmain in 'Seven Stars', unless you're reading the book out of order, in which case you already know what a rotter he is.

Airfix. Makers of plastic models, mostly military. In the 1960s, they developed a line in rockets.

Alder. See *Jago* and 'Cold Snap'.

Ali Bongo. Magic advisor on the TV program *Ace of Wands*.

April Treece. See also: 'Going to Series'. Notice how many redheads figure in these stories? I was specifically asked by the journalist Kat Brown to ensure that the ginger sisterhood was properly represented in fiction—then found that I'd already fulfilled that brief.

the Baltimore Gun Club. See Jules Verne's *From the Earth to the Moon*.

bathing machine. A canvas structure for the convenience of those wishing to doff their regular clothes and assume swimming costume without frightening the seagulls. These moveable changing rooms were a feature of British beaches for centuries.

the Beetle. See *The Beetle: A Mystery*, by Richard Marsh.

Benny Hill. British saucy comedian—hugely popular in the 1970s, banished to the outer darkness by feminists and alternative comedians thereafter, but lately rediscovered in a sort-of ironic manner. Though chubbily camp, he was noted for including bikini-clad pin-up girls in all his shows—and used a distinctive theme tune (last heard in *V for Vendetta*) over sped-up chases. I never really liked him, but his novelty record 'Ernie, the Fastest Milkman in the West' is some sort of classic. I once heard Doug Bradley, Pinhead from the *Hellraiser* movies, do an impromptu cover version.

Bill Owen. For more on him, see Baroness Orczy's 'Old Man in the Corner' stories.

black swine in the sewers of Hampstead. This is probably where the story of the albino alligators under New York comes from. It's the title of an excellent study of Victorian sensationalism by Thomas Boyle.

Bowdler's Hamlet. The 19th-Century version, with all the rude or exciting bits cut out. Like the TV version of *Repo Man* where the worst insult imaginable is 'melon-farmer'.

the Brownies. Cadet wing of the Girl Guides (Girl Scouts in America). They were originally called 'Rosebuds' but thought that was soppy and petitioned Lord Baden-Powell for a better name. The Brownies are called after a moralistic Victorian fairy-tale by Juliana Horatia Ewing—in which the brownies are helpful wood-elves, as opposed to the lazy boggarts.

Brown Owl. A scout-leader for the Brownies.

burked. Named for William Burke, of 'and Hare' fame, this is a method of strangulation-suffocation, originally employed by those too lazy to dig up corpses for sale to anatomy lecturers, later favoured by robbers too cowardly or ruthless to pilfer from a living, likely resisting person. You will perhaps be surprised that this mention of his favoured method of despatch presages an actual appearance—in a manner of speaking—in this narrative.

'Burlington Bertie From Bow'. A music hall song, made famous by Ella Shields, about a vagrant who poses as a toff. Burlington suggests social prominence; Bow doesn't. It was a parody of an earlier song, 'Burlington Bertie', but became much more famous than its inspiration.

bushwah. Business.

Charles Beauregard's pocket watch. In point of fact, this unusual—if not unique—chronometer is [this passage omitted from the public record under the order of Mrs Vanessa Coates, current Chair of the Ruling Cabal of the Diogenes Club.]

Charlie Peace. Victorian burglar and murderer (1832–1879).

the Comet. See 'The Original Dr Shade', *The Quorum.*

Constant Drache. See also 'Another Fish Story'.

crivens. An exclamation of astonishment.

the curse on Mitre Square. One of the early Jack the Ripper conspiracy theories—involving a ghostly monk.

a Cyberman. They tried to conquer the moon in 'The Moon Base'.

Cyrano de Bergerac. Author of *The Other World: The Comical History of the States and Empires of the Moon.*

Dan Dare. 'Pilot of the Future' in the *Eagle.*

Davey Wales. aka 'the Weymouth Strangler'. Geneviève obviously didn't count the fellow whose throat she bit out just before her own death among the victims she felt guilty about. Or the author just plain forgot until he re-read the piece for this edition.

the Demon Ace. Hans von Hellhund, terror of the skies in the First World War, and a criminal pest thereafter. Shot down by Edwin Winthrop in 1938. First mentioned in 'Coastal City'.

Dennis Rattray. Also known as Blackfist. See 'Clubland Heroes', in *Secret Files of the Diogenes Club.*

the Diogenes Club. Subsequent to the events of 'Mimsy', the institution has resumed business, though unaffiliated with the current British government. Among its current extraordinary members: Rick Coates, Christine Chambers (Lady Shade), Alexander Cash, Stacy Cotterill, Loulee Ling (Ghost Lantern Girl III), James Marion, Susan Rodway, and Karl Rattray. Sally Rhodes and Geneviève Dieudonné have been known to work with the Club, but have refused or resigned membership. The serving chair of the Ruling Cabal is Vanessa Coates.

Dr Shade. See 'The Original Dr Shade' and *The Quorum*, for Derek Leech's assumption of ownership of Dr Jonathan Chambers's night-persona. The exclusivity of Leech's rights to the name and brand are challenged by, among others, Jamie Chambers (see 'Cold Snap') and his niece Christine (aka Lady Shade).

'Donald, Where's Yer Troosers?' A 1961 novelty hit by Andy Stewart, which charted again in 1989. Rather surprisingly, sung to sinister effect by an evil robot from the future in an episode of *Terminator: The Sarah Connor Chronicles*.

the Duc de Richleau. One of the few foreigners Dennis Wheatley had any time for. See *The Devil Rides Out*.

Egdon Heath. A desolate stretch of Wessex, well known to the readers of Thomas Hardy's *Return of the Native* and Evelyn Waugh's *Vile Bodies*. Not really worth visiting unless you're a particular fan of bracken.

Eithne Orfe. Stories about her vary—did she murder her fiancé Nicholas Goodman and save the country or marry him and become one of the villainesses of the age? Or did her tale have yet another outcome?

Enoch Powell. Controversial British politician of the '60s and '70s, known for his 'views' on immigration.

the Esoteric Order of Dagon. See H.P. Lovecraft's 'Shadow Over Innsmouth'. And 'The Big Fish' and 'Another Fish Story' in *Secret Files of the Diogenes Club*.

flapper. Mode of dress, hairstyle, and behaviour adopted by teenage girls in the 1920s.

Francis Godwin. Author of *The Man in the Moone, or a Discourse of a Voyage thither, by Domingo Gonsales*.

Frank Chandler. aka Chandu the Magician.

Franz Beckert. See Fritz Lang's film *M*.

General Haig. Douglas Haig, British First World War commander. Much hated for his use of tactics which were extraordinarily wasteful of human life, and known as 'the Butcher of the Somme'.

Gene Tunney. World heavyweight boxing champion in the late 1920s.

George Bancroft. Later known for slightly stuffy pillar of society roles, but a 1920s pin-up as the romantic gangster in *Underworld*.

George Formby. Insanely popular British entertainer of the 1930s and '40s—most of his hit songs are about masturbation. 'With Me Little Ukelele in Me Hand', 'With Me Little Stick of Blackpool Rock', etc. Don't let anyone tell you the Farrelly Brothers invented this kind of humour.

Ghost Lantern Girl. A major figure in the San Francisco Tong War of 1912.

the Ghost Train you shut down in the 1950s. Long-time readers will recognise the allusion to 'The Man Who Got Off the Ghost Train' (in *The Man From the Diogenes Club*).

Giles Gallant. Later, Brigadier-General Sir Giles Gallant, and involved—none too auspiciously, sad to relate—in one of the first Diogenes Club cases declassified for general consumption, written up as 'The End of the Pier Show' and included in *The Man From the Diogenes Club.*

Granite Grant. An old pal of Sexton Blake's, later put out of the game by the Hooded Terror and the Black Quorum.

the Green Eye of the Yellow God. See the popular music hall recitative 'The Green Eye of the Yellow God', also known as 'The Ballad of Mad Carew', by J. Milton Hayes. Await the full story of Mad Carew when Mr Newman gets round to editing—i.e.: fixing the spelling and omitting the foulest swear-words ever set to paper—the section of Colonel Moran's scandalous memoirs entitled 'The Six Maledictions'.

Green Penguin. No, not some rare species or a colour-blind master criminal, but a line of paperback mysteries from the estimable British publisher.

Grimaldi. Joey Grimaldi, the 19th-Century entertainer who adapted Italian comedy style to suit British tastes and virtually invented the modern notion of the clown. If you're scared of clowns, blame him.

a Hallward portrait of Mycroft Holmes. Some said the painting got fatter when the sitter ate all the pies. They were being satirical.

Hans Pfaall. See Edgar Allan Poe's 'The Unparalleled Adventure of One Hans Pfaall'.

Harry 'Brass' Button. See 'A Drug on the Market'.

Harry D'Amour. See Clive Barker's *Lord of Illusions.*

Hawley Harvey Crippen. It's possible that history has unkindly labelled Crippen a murderer— he might simply have got his dosages mixed up while trying to calm his wife down (to put it tactfully) so as to save his own energies for Miss Ethel le Neve. Still, he's in the Chamber of Horrors as a murderer.

Hergé's Tintin. See *Destination: Moon* and *Explorers on the Moon.*

Heywood Floyd. William Sylvester in *2001: A Space Odyssey.* Roy Scheider in *2010*—though it's hard to believe he's the same character.

Hugh Drummond. Also known as 'Bulldog' Drummond, a biffer of foreigners' noses in Sapper's books.

Imogen Ames. The aunt of Susan Rodway, née Ames, who inherited some of her Talents, and developed others: for whom, see 'Cold Snap' (in *Secret Files of the Diogenes Club*) and *Jago.*

Irene Dobson. See *Jago* and 'Is There Anybody There?'

Isidore Persano and the Case of the Worm Unknown to Science. I'd reveal more about this adventure, known in the Most Secret Secret Files as 'the Worm War', but—frankly—all those unique and famous individuals did when they got together was blather at each other in lengthy paragraphs with occasional time-outs for unsatisfying sexual encounters until the Forces of Evil gave up. NB: In his indiscreet mention of the matter in 'The Problem of Thor Bridge',

John Watson calls him 'Isadora', the name under which Signor Persano was wont to frequent Dorian Gray's scandalous soirées in the skirts and mantilla of a gypsy dancer—no wonder he had to become a duellist.

I-Spy Guide. Series of educational pamphlets, compiled by 'Big Chief I-Spy'.

ITV. Independent Television. In 1971, the only one of Britain's three television channels to have advertisements.

it was Sexton Blake who pushed Sherlock Holmes off the waterfall that time. This is not true. So far as we know.

Ivor Novello. A big star in musical theatre, and a songwriter ('Keep the Home Fires Burning', 'We'll Gather Lilacs') for whom the annual Ivor Novello Awards are named. Jeremy Northam plays him in *Gosford Park.*

Jack Point. The lovelorn loon from the Gilbert & Sullivan opera *The Yeomen of the Guard.*

James Burke. Broadcaster, science journalist, television producer. Burke's magnum opus was *Connections* (1978), a ten-part, interdisciplinary documentary about conceptual breakthrough. Imagine any major TV channel these days giving prime time airspace to the equivalent of *Wired* magazine.

Janey Wilde. See 'The Big Fish' (in *Secret Files of the Diogenes Club*). Though part of 'Seven Stars', 'The Trouble With Barrymore' is also a direct sequel to that story—in which a Los Angeles Private Investigator tangles with the Esoteric Order of Dagon in the early days of America's involvement in World War II and incidentally encounters agents of the Diogenes Club.

Janice Marsh. Later a Hollywood star and a famous recluse: see 'The Big Fish' and 'Another Fish Story' (in *Secret Files of the Diogenes Club*).

Janus Stark. His adventures were in *Smash* comic when I was a lad. He cropped up again recently in Moore, Moore, & Reppion's *Albion.* Imagine a cross between Reed Richards, Oliver Twist, Houdini and Sexton Blake. A 1990s punk band was named after him.

Jenny Maple. See Patrick Hamilton's *Twenty Thousand Streets Under the Sky.* Come to that, read everything Hamilton ever wrote.

Jet Morgan. Hero of the BBC's radio science fiction series *Journey Into Space.*

John Peel. Britain's greatest disc jockey and pop savant. Many might think that the highlight of my career was doing a two-hour, two-handed radio program with the late John Peel.

John Silence. See Algernon Blackwood's *John Silence—Physician Extraordinary.*

Jonathan King. Something certainly was off about him, and he was jailed for sexual offences against minors.

Judge Keith Pursuivant, John Thunstone, Lucius Leffing, Jules de Grandin and 'Gees'. Noted psychic investigators—their cases have been written up by Manly Wade Wellman, Joseph Payne Brennan, Seabury Quinn and Jack Mann.

Julian Karswell. See 'Casting the Runes' by M.R. James.

Kafiristan. Hard to find on modern maps, but North of India. See Rudyard Kipling's 'The Man Who Would Be King'. Probably not an ideal package holiday destination, even (or especially) now.

keeping mum. Not saying anything. A WWII slogan against carelessly blabbing secrets within earshot of German spies was 'be like Dad—keep Mum!'

Keith Winton. See Fredric Brown's *What Mad Universe*. Or, in another continuum, my 'Castle in the Desert'.

Killergrams. See: 'Patricia's Profession'.

the Lake LaMetrie elasmosaur. See: 'The Monster of Lake LaMetrie' by Warden Allan Curtis.

Leo Dare. See 'A Drug on the Market'.

The Lodger. In Marie Belloc Lowndes's novel, the eponymous lodger turns out to be the serial killer known as The Avenger, and in the 1944 Laird Cregar film, he's Jack the Ripper. But in Alfred Hitchcock's 1927 silent film and Maurice Elvey's 1932 sound remake (aka *The Phantom Fiend*), in both of which Ivor Novello takes the part, the suspected lodger is innocent of the murders.

Lord Kilpartinger, the railway magnate. See 'The Man Who Got Off the Ghost Train' in *The Man From the Diogenes Club*, the first volume in the Histories of the Diogenes Club, issued in an affordable edition you either did well to acquire when it was available or are now pummelling yourself for not picking up before its resale price climbed so high as to be beyond your meagre pocket. Mr Monkey and Ms Brain could have told you at the time you'd be well-advised to make that purchase.

the Lord Mayor's parade. An annual event in London, with floats, processions, flag-waving and polite cheering. The Lord Mayor, whose office is primarily ceremonial and ancient, should not be confused with the Mayor of London, whose political position was established comparatively recently.

the Lord of Strange Deaths. Hush—speak not his name aloud, for long is the hand and swift the vengeance of Dr F- M-----. He imports exotic flora and fauna, too. If you're in the market for a deadly specimen of *vampyroteuthis infernalis* (or Hellish Vampire Squid), visit Singapore Charlie's pet shop in Limehouse, give the man behind the counter a wink, and don't tell him we sent you.

Lord Salisbury. The Prime Minister in 1897. A Victorian with a beard, and a bit of a come-down after Gladstone and Disraeli.

Loud Shit. See: *Jago*. They later sold out and changed their name to Loud Stuff so their songs could be played on Radio 1.

Louis Bauer, the Pimlico poisoner. See Patrick Hamilton's *Gaslight*.

Lucian. Lucian of Samosata, author of *A True History*, the first lunar voyage story.

Lucinda Tregellis-d'Aulney/the Aviatrix. See 'Clubland Heroes' (in *Secret Files of the Diogenes Club*).

M&S. Marks & Spencer. A chain of clothing/food stores, also popularly known as 'Marks and Sparks'.

the marriage of the sovereign to an evil consort with supernatural powers. This envelope has since been opened—it would be indiscreet, not to mention legally unwise, to specify when and what course of action was taken by the Ruling Cabal. Suffice to say, no demons live in Buckingham Palace these days.

Martin Hesselius. See J. Sheridan LeFanu's *In a Glass Darkly.* Sometimes credited as the founder of the profession of paranormal investigator, Hesselius's reputation would stand higher if fewer patients had died under his care. Catriona Kaye's monograph concludes that the good doctor was less good than had generally been supposed. Dr Harold Shipman bought a copy of the pamphlet from Iain Sinclair in the '80s.

Merneptah. Most sources—well, Cecil B. DeMille—place the Plagues of Egypt in the reign of Rameses II, mainly because he's still famous. However, Islamic tradition has it that the Biblical Pharaoh defied by Moses was Rameses's son Merneptah. Rameses was, by Egyptian accounts, a decent pharaoh, while Merneptah was a rotter, and thus far more likely to behave in a manner liable to bring curses down on his people.

Michael Bellamy. See Mr Edgar Wallace's *The Green Archer.*

Mildew Manor. See 'Mildew Manor', of course.

Milton Parsons. Among his undertaker performances are *My Favorite Blonde, Dick Tracy, Leave Her to Heaven, The Verdict, The Mighty McGurk, The Cobra Strikes, The Shanghai Chest* and *The Dead Don't Die.* If you watch 1940s movies, you'll know the face. He sometimes showed his range by playing coroners, perverts or axe-murderers.

Miss Violet Borrodale. Readers of 'Richard Riddle, Boy Detective in "The Case of the French Spy"' (in *Secret Files of the Diogenes Club*) will recognise Miss Borrodale as a stalwart of the Richard Riddle Detective Agency. It now seems that, like many a child labelled early as a discipline problem, she grew up to be a schoolmistress.

Mrs Lovat's meat pies. 'Conjure up the treat pies used to be'. Don't ask what the meat is, though.

My Nine Nights in a Harem, by 'Anonymous'. Colonel Sebastian Moran once claimed authorship. But he was a known fabulator.

the Mythwrhn. See also 'Mother Hen'.

Neil Martin. Sally acquired a boyfriend in *The Quorum,* which takes place between 'Organ Donors' and 'Mimsy'. During that case, she crossed Derek Leech again, but not without earning the grudging admiration of the Great Enchanter.

Neue Strelsau. Capital city of Ruritania.

new bug. Rookie, fresher, recent arrival.

Nicholas Goodman. See 'Mildew Manor'. Or hear it, if you can track down the full-cast audio, which has mysteriously disappeared from the internet.

Noel Edmonds. A popular British television personality who specialises in a form of torture porn passed off as light entertainment.

nosh. Food, chow, grub.

Pandora Reynolds. See Albert Lewin's film *Pandora and the Flying Dutchman*.

Patrick Moore. Broadcaster, astronomer, author of juvenile science fiction, presenter of the BBC's long-running *The Sky at Night*.

Peggy Hopkins Joyce. Much-married heiress of the 1930s.

the poll tax. This reference dates 'Organ Donors', which is now as much a period piece as the stories set in the 1970s or the 1920s. Note also the mentions of 'a portable phone', John Major, seven-channel satellite TV and an ITV franchise which is a license to print money.

the Purley Horror. A tale for which the world is not ready.

refuting the late Professor Moriarty's book about the dynamics of an asteroid. Marcus Rennes came late to this controversy. For the fate of his predecessor Neville Airey Stent, who dared bandy astro-mathematics with Moriarty, see 'The Red Planet League', a section of the memoirs of Colonel Sebastian Moran, which has been made available to the public by Mr Kim Newman.

The Return of Jason King. A never-broadcast sequel series to the ITV hit of the early 1970s, *Jason King*, itself a sequel to *Department S*. The pilot 'Wanna Revive a Television Series?' tested poorly with focus groups, and Robbie Coltrane was considered a less-than-ideal replacement for Peter Wyngarde.

Richard Jeperson. See *The Man From the Diogenes Club*.

Rob Hackwill. The monster from the *Where the Bodies Are Buried* films. Pyramid Pictures have been trying to do a deal on *Freddy vs. Jason vs. Rob* based on the Dark Horse comic miniseries.

Roderick Spode. Spode, 7th Earl of Sidcup, was the leader of a fascist group known as the Black Shorts. He could be turned into a quivering wretch by simply whispering 'I know all about Eulalie' into his ear. P.G. 'Plum' Wodehouse explained this in *The Code of the Woosters*—he got his inside gossip from Margery Device.

Rodger Baskerville. Do we really have to explain?

Roger Duroc. See: 'Where the Bodies Are Buried 2020'. Also, in another continuum, Jack Yeovil's *Demon Download*.

Rose Farrar. The circumstances of her itemisation in the Mausoleum Collection are revealed in 'Angel Down, Sussex'; those of her eventual departure in 'Cold Snap'. The 'something similar' was dealt with by Charles Beauregard in 'The Gypsies in the Wood'. All these stirring accounts of derring-do and desperation can be found in *Secret Files of the Diogenes Club*, a previous publication from the esteemed house of Mr Monkey and Ms Brain.

rounders. Baseball. A game for *girls*.

the Secret History plays. You don't want to know about *Richard IV, Boudicea* and *Henry VII, Part Two*. Actually, you probably do—but if we told you, they wouldn't be secret, would they? The few scholars allowed access to the forbidden folios rate Shakespeare's *Caligula, Tyrant of Rome* as better than *Hamlet, Prince of Denmark*—and it has a higher body-count.

the shadowmen. It might be worth mentioning that I wrote 'The Biafran Bank Manager' some years before Steven Moffat scripted the *Doctor Who* episodes 'Blink', in which monsters move when no one is looking at them, and 'Silence in the Library', which has killer shadows.

shamming. Faking, dissembling.

The Simon Dee Show. A talk show on the BBC. Host Dee, a star on a level with Johnny Carson in the US, fell from grace in 1970—with a suddenness and lack of explanation usually reserved for heads of the Politburo.

Sir Francis Varney. He threw himself into a live volcano, so we'll never know if he was truly among Geneviève's party. See *Varney the Vampire, or: The Feast of Blood*, by James Malcolm Rymer or Thomas Preskett Prest. It takes 868 close-printed pages to get to Vesuvius.

Sir Henry Merrivale. His exploits as a sleuth were chronicled by John Dickson Carr in books from *The Plague Court Murders* to *The Cavalier's Cup*.

Sir Michael Calme. Chairman of the Royal Society for Psychical Research at the turn of the century, and a rival of Mr Thomas Carnacki. To their mutual embarrassment, he became the celebrated ghost-finder's stepfather.

Sister Chantal Juillerat. See 'Where the Bodies Are Buried 2020'. Also, in another continuum, Jack Yeovil's *Demon Download*.

Skaro. Home planet of the Daleks.

Sky Ray lollies. Space-themed iced treat.

Sooty. Puppet bear, conjurer—perhaps a soul-sucking mass murderer (see: Byrne, Eugene; Gaiman, Neil; and Newman, Kim, 'Who Was Jack the Ripper?' (in *Prince of Stories: The Many Worlds of Neil Gaiman*).

The Splendid Six. See 'Clubland Heroes' (in *Secret Files of the Diogenes Club*).

Sweet/afters/pudding. Dessert.

the Swinging Blue Jeans. A popular beat combo, m'lud.

tana leaves. Useful for bringing mummies back to life, according to Universal pictures.

Temptations, Ltd. Prop: R. Chetwynd-Hayes and P. Cushing. Shoplifting is not advised. See: *From Beyond the Grave* (1974).

Thomas Carnacki. See William Hope Hodgson's *Carnacki, the Ghost Finder*. Mycroft Holmes's secret file on Carnacki has recently come to light, and contains surprising revelations about the personal life of the pioneering psychic investigator and his involvement with the Diogenes Club.

Ticia Frump. Later married into a distinguished New England family. At Drearcliff, she came top in French.

Tiny Chiselhurst. See also 'Going to Series'.

Titch and Quackers. A television show with a ventriloquist (Ray Alan) whose wooden friends were a schoolboy and a duck. I remember being *very annoyed* when the BBC replaced it with something as trivial as the Prime Minister talking about the budget.

Tizer. A uniquely British soft drink. Slightly less horrible than Vimto.

Tommy Atkins. The archetypal British soldier. The name comes from a First World War-era brochure about how to fill in the application form for the army.

The Two Ronnies. Ronnie Corbett and Ronnie Barker, a comedy team who starred in a long-running BBC show. Madeline Smith, Cyd Hayman, Sue Lloyd and Kate O'Mara were among the pretty girls who appeared—and were allowed to be funnier than the comparable crumpet in *Benny Hill* on the other side.

the Unnameables. See: 'The Big Fish' (in *Secret Files of the Diogenes Club*).

Varno Zhoule. See 'Tomorrow Town' (in *The Man From the Diogenes Club*).

Wednesday Play. A BBC1 drama slot. Among the most significant works broadcast under this rubric were *Cathy Come Home, Up the Junction* and Dennis Potter's *Nigel Barton* plays and *Son of Man.* Too many of these dramas were wiped.

Where the Bodies Are Buried. See *Where the Bodies Are Buried* (Alchemy Press), which collects 'Where the Bodies Are Buried', 'Where the Bodies Are Buried II: Sequel Hook', 'Where the Bodies Are Buried 3: Black and White and Red All Over', and 'Where the Bodies Are Buried 2020'.

Who was the skeleton in the closet?/The Biafran Bank Manager. This sick joke, current in playgrounds circa 1971, refers to a TV ad campaign for Barclays which stressed the friendliness and availability of their staff by showing a middle-class couple in need of financial advice opening their wardrobe to find a smiling bank manager there. Even at the time, it struck me as a more sinister than reassuring image. Shortly before this, press photos of starving, painfully thin Biafrans—victims of a Nigerian blockade—had an impact comparable to the news footage of similarly suffering Ethiopians that led to Band Aid in the 1980s.

Wiv 'er 'ead tucked underneaf 'er arm, she waa-aa-alked the Bloody Tower! From a music hall song. Sometimes you wonder why Marilyn Manson and Ice-T get such a hard time—considering the things our grandparents and great-grandparents took for family entertainment.

the Wurzels. Somerset's greatest band. In 1969, they still retained the authenticity of 'Blackbird, I'll 'Ave 'Ee' and had not yet succumbed to the sell-out commercialism of 'I've Got a Brand New Combine Harvester'.

Yeomen Warders. You know, beefeaters.

ABOUT THE AUTHOR

Kim Newman is a novelist, critic and broadcaster. His fiction includes *The Night Mayor*, *Bad Dreams*, *Jago*, the *Anno Dracula* novels and stories, *The Quorum*, *The Original Dr Shade and Other Stories*, *Famous Monsters*, *Seven Stars*, *Unforgivable Stories*, *Dead Travel Fast*, *Life's Lottery*, *Back in the USSA* (with Eugene Byrne), *Where the Bodies Are Buried*, *Doctor Who: Time and Relative* and *The Man From the Diogenes Club* under his own name and *The Vampire Genevieve* and *Orgy of the Blood Parasites* as Jack Yeovil. His non-fiction books include *Nightmare Movies*, *Ghastly Beyond Belief* (with Neil Gaiman), *Horror: 100 Best Books* (with Stephen Jones), *Wild West Movies*, *The BFI Companion to Horror*, *Millennium Movies* and BFI Classics studies of *Cat People* and *Doctor Who*. He is a contributing editor to *Sight & Sound* and *Empire* magazines and has written and broadcast widely on a range of topics, scripting radio documentaries about Val Lewton and role-playing games and TV programs about movie heroes and Sherlock Holmes. His short story "Week Woman" was adapted for the TV series *The Hunger,* and he has directed and written a tiny short film *Missing Girl* (http://www.johnnyalucard.com/missinggirl.html). He has won the Bram Stoker Award, the International Horror Critics Award, the British Science Fiction Award and the British Fantasy Award but doesn't like to boast about them. He was born in Brixton (London), grew up in the West Country, went to University near Brighton and now lives in Islington (London). His official web-site, "Dr. Shade's Laboratory", can be found at www.johnnyalucard.com.